ADVENTURES OF HUCKLEBERRY FINN

MARK TWAIN

ADVENTURES OF HUCKLEBERRY FINN

With an Introduction
and Contemporary Criticism

Edited by MARY R. REICHARDT

Ignatius Critical Editions Editor
JOSEPH PEARCE

IGNATIUS PRESS   SAN FRANCISCO

Cover art:
Hippolyte Sebron, *The Mississippi*.
Musee de la cooperation franco-americaine, Blerancourt, France

Photo Credit: Réunion des Musées Nationaux / Art Resource, N.Y.

Cover design by John Herreid

© 2009 Ignatius Press, San Francisco
All rights reserved
ISBN 978-1-58617-296-1
Library of Congress Control Number 2008933486
Printed in the United States of America ∞

Tradition is the extension of Democracy through time; it is the proxy of the dead and the enfranchisement of the unborn.

Tradition may be defined as the extension of the franchise. Tradition means giving votes to the most obscure of all classes, our ancestors. It is the democracy of the dead. Tradition refuses to submit to the small and arrogant oligarchy of those who merely happen to be walking about. All democrats object to men being disqualified by the accident of birth; tradition objects to their being disqualified by the accident of death. Democracy tells us not to neglect a good man's opinion, even if he is our groom; tradition asks us not to neglect a good man's opinion, even if he is our father. I, at any rate, cannot separate the two ideas of democracy and tradition.

—G. K. Chesterton

Ignatius Critical Editions—Tradition-Oriented Criticism for a new generation

CONTENTS

ADVENTURES OF HUCKLEBERRY FINN:
AN INTRODUCTION

Mary R. Reichardt
University of St. Thomas

One of the world's great books, *Adventures of Huckleberry Finn* was written at the peak of Mark Twain's career and, perhaps more visibly than other literary masterpieces, clearly resulted from a combination of his unique life experiences and talents. Samuel Langhorne Clemens was born in 1835 in the tiny hamlet of Florida, Missouri, and moved with his family as a child to the growing frontier town of Hannibal, Missouri, on the Mississippi River. His father died when he was twelve and, like his older brother Orion, he went to work as a printer, a skill that was to serve him well for many years and that also helped foster his love of reading and language. Soon he began to contribute sketches and letters to the various newspapers he worked for in Missouri and Iowa. Restless at the age of twenty-two, Clemens set out by steamboat for South America but decided midtrip to fulfill a childhood dream of becoming a river pilot. Thus began two years of apprenticeship under the tutelage of the famed pilot Horace Bixby as Clemens developed an intimate knowledge of the lower Mississippi River from Saint Louis to New Orleans. It was difficult work, but "in that brief, sharp schooling, I got personally and familiarly acquainted with about all the different types of human nature that are to be found in fiction, biography, or history", he later wrote.[1] He received his pilot's license in 1859, but only a few years later his riverboat career was cut short due to the outbreak of the

---

[1] Mark Twain, *Life on the Mississippi* (New York: Harper and Brothers, 1917), p. 163.

Civil War. A brief stint with a loosely organized Confederate volunteer brigade, the Marion Rangers, quickly dashed any thoughts of enlisting. Rather, Sam Clemens then did what many young men were doing or longing to do in the mid-nineteenth century—he "lit out for the Territory".

It was in the West that Samuel Clemens forged the persona of Mark Twain. His plan to make a fortune prospecting for silver in Nevada and California soon turned into the more realistic journalist's trade, for which he was now well trained. As a reporter and freelance writer for the *Territorial Enterprise* in Virginia City, Nevada, Clemens began contributing humorous sketches and hoaxes as "filler" to the paper—sometimes getting himself in trouble for their coarse content—and he first signed one of these "Mark Twain" in 1863, the pseudonym for a riverboat term meaning "two fathoms deep", or safe water. The first story to make his name known nationally, "Jim Smiley and His Jumping Frog", was based on a tall tale he heard while sitting around a campfire in a California mining camp and was published in the New York *Saturday Press* in 1865 as well as in the Western literary journal the *Californian*. In a time when travel was difficult and media limited to telegraphs and newspapers, Twain found that Eastern readers were eager to hear about the West with its unique characters, lore, and language. The influential editor of the *Atlantic Monthly*, William Dean Howells, whom Twain met in 1869 and who became his lifelong friend and supporter, was an advocate for the so-called local-color realistic fiction that was then growing in popularity. With his keen eye for character and ear for dialect, Twain began to capitalize on this interest.

At the same time that he was honing his writing skills, Twain was developing what would become his trademark style of humor. His delight in the comedic aspects of the tall tale and the hoax was augmented by his admiration of the day's most famous comic writer and lecturer, Artemus Ward (Charles Farrar Browne), whom the newspaperman Twain proudly escorted around town when Ward arrived on tour in Virginia City. Ward's deadpan delivery of often illogical material punctuated by a look of innocent surprise when becoming "aware" of his auditors made audiences roar with laughter. The emphasis was on the manner of telling rather than the matter, and Twain, deeply impressed, was soon exploiting the possibilities of the technique for his own budding lecture style. He delivered his first public lecture, on his travels to the Sandwich (now Hawaiian) Islands, in San Francisco in 1866. Petrified, he arranged beforehand for friends to sit in the audience and laugh on cue, but his fears proved unfounded: he was a smashing success. For the rest of his life, especially during the periods when he needed to pay off debt, Twain performed his stand-up routine across the United States and in Europe, usually to wildly enthusiastic crowds. He was rapidly turning into, as one recent commentator has put it without exaggeration, the "nation's first rock star".[2]

Twain also incorporated some of Artemus Ward's techniques as well as those of the Southwestern humorists in his writing. His first major book, *The Innocents Abroad*, uses the comic narrative stance of, as the title indicates, the "innocent" encountering experience. The book evolved from a worldwide cruise Twain took as a newspaper correspondent in 1867: his assignment was to write sketches back to the paper that were then issued in installment form. Twain and his fellow passengers, most of whom had signed on to the cruise as religious pilgrims, departed from New York on the *Quaker City* and toured ports in Europe and the Holy Land before returning five and a half months later. Twain's observations of Europe in particular continually pit the rough and naïve but goodhearted and down-to-earth American "New World" character against the corrupt and cynical "Old World". Pointed social criticism is tempered by comedy that ranges from broad slapstick to biting satire. Romance encounters realism, and fiction blends with fact. Published in 1869 to wide acclaim, *The Innocents Abroad* established Twain as a writer of humorous travel literature, a vein he continued most notably in *Roughing It* (1872), an account of his stagecoach journey out West.

[2] Ron Powers, *Mark Twain: A Life* (New York: Free Press, 2005), p. 164.

On the *Quaker City*, Twain met a young man named Charles Langdon, who later introduced the author to his sister, Olivia "Livy" Langdon. From Elmira, New York, the Langdons were a wealthy and cultured family. Although she turned his proposal down several times, Livy finally agreed to marry Sam Clemens; when they wed in 1870, she was twenty-five and he ten years her senior. Now well established as a successful author and lecturer, and having married into an upper-crust Eastern family, Twain, the frontier boy from Missouri, at this point epitomized the American rags-to-riches success story. Although tragedy always seemed to be intermingled with joy—over the coming years, Twain would experience the death of three of his four children and his beloved wife as well as spectacular financial failures—he was now approaching the pinnacle of his writing years. The Clemens family built an expensive and elaborate mansion in Hartford, Connecticut, now kept as a shrine to Twain's memory and visited by throngs of literary pilgrims each year. The Clemens family also spent considerable time at Quarry Farm in upstate New York, the home of Livy's sister and brother-in-law.

It was his close friend, the Congregational minister Joseph Twichell, who suggested to Twain that his own memories might be a rich vein of material for his writing. As Twain wrote to Howells, "Twichell & I have had a long walk in the woods & I got to telling him about old Mississippi days of steamboating glory & grandeur.... He said, 'What a virgin subject to hurl into a magazine!' I hadn't thought of that before."[3] Howells was enthusiastic about the project, and Twain produced seven installment pieces for the 1875 *Atlantic Monthly* based on recollections of his cub piloting days entitled "Old Times on the Mississippi". His memories were soon roaming back even farther in time, and *The Adventures of Tom Sawyer* appeared the following year. *Tom Sawyer* is a work of nostalgia. The fictional town of Saint Petersburg was based on

[3] *Mark Twain–Howells Letters*, ed. Henry Nash Smith and William M. Gibson (Cambridge, Mass.: Belknap Press of Harvard University Press, 1960), 1:34.

Twain's memories of Hannibal, and characters such as Tom and Sid Sawyer, Cousin Mary, Aunt Polly, and Becky Thatcher were all modeled on, or composite creations of, people Twain had known while growing up in that town. The story follows the episodic antics of Tom as he artfully enlists others to help him whitewash a fence, feeds painkiller to a cat, flirts with his schoolmate Becky Thatcher, and then, in a more serious vein, becomes involved with a dangerous group of murderers and thieves. Together with his friend Huckleberry Finn, Tom finds a pile of gold—$12,000—which the boys receive when Injun Joe is found dead in a cave. *Tom Sawyer* has delighted generations of children, not the least because Twain here purposely reversed the typical nineteenth-century moralistic "good boy" story for a "bad boy" story—and the "bad boy", Tom, is rewarded in the end.

Tom Sawyer may be a "bad boy", but he remains a largely conventional boy in the book. Although an orphan (his lack of parentage is never explained) who is prone to lies and disobedience, his pranks are, for the most part, harmless. Twain aborted his plan to extend Tom's story into adulthood, for, he concluded, readers would soon "conceive a hearty contempt for him".[4] In fact, by the time he finished writing *Tom Sawyer*, he had already become far more interested in the character of Huckleberry Finn, described in *Tom Sawyer* as "the juvenile pariah of the village", the kind of low-class boy parents warn their children away from.[5] The abused son of a bigoted drunk, an outcast, and barely educated, Huck seems an unlikely hero, but Twain understood how not only focusing on him but allowing him to tell his own tale might provide the depth and innovation that *Tom Sawyer* lacks. As the title page and opening lines make clear, *Adventures of Huckleberry Finn* began as a sequel of sorts, capitalizing on *Tom Sawyer's* success. Twain was finding a ready market for such writing. As

---

[4] Ibid., 1:91.

[5] Mark Twain, *The Adventures of Tom Sawyer* (New York: Penguin Books, 1986), p. 45.

the frontier as he had known it in the Missouri of the 1830s and 1840s was rapidly receding farther and farther west, and as antebellum industrialization changed the pace of American life, a certain nostalgia for the past as well as a desire to read about the expanding country's local-color folkways and characters resulted. In addition, as the period of Reconstruction with its continued unrest and threat of mobs and lynchings kept racial tensions at the forefront of the nation's concerns, Twain also began to show himself interested in capturing black characters and speech patterns, as he did for the first time in the 1874 piece "A True Story", in which an ex-slave, Aunt Rachel, tells her poignant tale.

As with *Tom Sawyer*, Twain based *Huckleberry Finn* in large part on his memories of growing up in Hannibal. In his autobiography, he recalled that he modeled the character of Huck on a boy whose father was one of several well-known town drunks: "I have drawn Tom Blankenship exactly as he was", Twain wrote. "He was ignorant, unwashed, insufficiently fed; but he had as good a heart as ever any boy had. His liberties were totally unrestricted. He was the only really independent person—boy or man—in the community . . . and was envied by all the rest of us."[6] Huck's colorful character is indeed captivating in its own right, but the crowning achievement of *Huckleberry Finn* is Huck's language. Unlike the conventional third-person narrator of *Tom Sawyer*, Huck's vernacular, full of homey idiom and appalling grammar, strikes the reader as fresh, vivid, and charming. Twain, indeed, was forging something new in American literature, a departure from the "bookish" English of the day, and he was accordingly accused by some critics of lowering the standards of proper speech. In the "Explanatory" he attached to the opening pages of the novel, he stated that he used seven shades of dialect in its narration, and scholars have shown this to be true. Evidence also confirms that, although seemingly spontaneous, Twain labored over

---

[6] Mark Twain, *Mark Twain's Autobiography*, edited and with an introduction by Albert Bigelow Paine (New York: Harper and Brothers, 1924), 2:174–75.

reproducing the book's vernacular, revising it many times until it suited him as authentic speech from that time and place. As he once wrote to Howells, "I amend dialect stuff by talking & talking & *talking* it till it sounds right."[7]

Huck's deadpan delivery, too, was the perfect vehicle for Twain's social satire. Although shrewd and practical, a result of his rough upbringing, Huck still maintains a youthful innocence that makes his laconic impressions of what he sees and experiences all the more poignant. As the whole "quality of the world" passes before his eyes—gentlemen and humbugs, black slaves and white "trash", "rapscallions" and country jakes—he records the situation matter-of-factly with little power of analysis, self-reflection, or moralizing. Huck's grave narration—he rarely laughs and does not get the point of riddles—and the irony that often results from the disparity between how he relates an event and the event itself lend a certain wistfulness to his character. As John Gerber states, "The result is that there is little raucous humor in *Huckleberry Finn* and much that is tinged with melancholy."[8] While many readers of the novel fondly recall the beauty, peace, and freedom of Huck and Jim's river trip, this is no Romantic idyll in the benign and nurturing arms of Nature. Wild and unpredictable as it is, the Mississippi River is but the lesser of two evils as shore life increasingly proves more treacherous. Generally unsurprised by the depravity of human nature—although he does express amazement at the unrelenting greed of the King and Duke—Huck can tell "stretchers" and assume false identities as easily as any experienced con artist if it suits his pleasure or helps him survive. In his heavy-handed satire of the pre–Civil War South, Twain's overall point seems clear: a slaveholding society is, *by its very nature*, deeply corrupt, resulting in manifold layers of greed, deception, and hypocrisy. It is a system of lies built on lies and the elaborate contortions used to cover them up. Increasingly, Huck flees back

[7] *Mark Twain–Howells Letters*, 1:26.
[8] John C. Gerber, *Mark Twain* (Boston: G.K. Hall, 1988), p. 107.

to the raft for a moment of respite and companionship with Jim (who, we can safely assume, is always tense and fearful), but in this chance world anything can happen, and the entire raft trip is underscored by a consistently ominous tone.

With his newfound interest in Huck, Twain composed the first sixteen chapters of what would become *Huckleberry Finn* in 1876. But he put the manuscript down at the point where, as Huck and Jim float down the Mississippi, they miss the crucial confluence of rivers at Cairo, Illinois, in a dense fog and the raft is smashed by a steamboat. The story is now confusing—while attempting to free Jim from slavery, the two are actually headed deeper into slaveholding territory—and Twain may not have known how to proceed. He set the manuscript aside and turned to new projects that intrigued him more or were more immediately lucrative. When he returned to the work in the winter of 1879–1880, he penned several hundred more pages, most likely through what is now chapter 21. As most readers note, the tone in these central chapters changes from the relatively lighthearted escapades of Tom and his gang in Saint Petersburg to an exposé of the degradation, moral squalor, and violence of the small towns lining the Mississippi. The Grangerford-Shepherdson feud, the bawdy Royal Nonesuch, the Sherburn-Boggs murder, the slovenly and cruel loafers on the streets of muddy Bricksville—each of these scenes reveals a dark side of human nature. The raft has been all but hijacked by the ruthless King and Duke, who serve the plot by providing a plausible reason for the continued voyage downriver.

Meanwhile, Twain was working on another project: gathering material to turn his *Atlantic Monthly* cub piloting sketches into a full-length work (resulting in *Life on the Mississippi* [1883]). In order to refresh his memories, he embarked on a nostalgic tour of the Mississippi River in 1882, spending three days in Hannibal. The trip may have renewed his interest in *Huckleberry Finn*—as did his acute need of money at the time—and he returned to the manuscript once again, completing it in 1883. Readers often express dismay at the last ten chapters of the book, the so-called "evasion" chapters, where through preposterous coincidences Tom Sawyer reappears and is back to his high jinks, this time insisting on doing things "in style" in freeing the imprisoned Jim. Huck defers to Tom, and in doing so, his role as both protagonist and moral agent seems compromised. Some critics, however, see a certain formal or thematic correctness to these last chapters: for example, they help further the novel's anti-Romantic themes by making readers disgusted here with Tom's unrelenting "playing" at life. However one views these chapters, it is important to note that the book so often considered *the* greatest American novel is actually a work of extraordinary unevenness in tone and content. For many readers, this roughness adds to rather than detracts from *Huckleberry Finn*'s fascination. As one critic has remarked about Twain's oeuvre in general, his "very shortcomings as a writer present a stimulating challenge." [9]

Always a religious skeptic, Twain became increasingly cynical in his old age. Like other satirists who devote a lifetime to exposing the foibles and failings of humankind, he grew deeply pessimistic about the possibility of human virtue or reform. A series of disastrous financial losses in the 1890s, most notably a huge investment in the Paige typesetting machine, forced the Clemens family to abandon their Hartford home and live more cheaply in Europe, where Twain undertook a grueling lecture series to pay off his debts. He blamed himself for his beloved daughter Susy's death from meningitis in 1896, just as he had years earlier when his only son Langdon died as an infant, and he suffered from severe bouts of rheumatism. After *Huckleberry Finn*, his writings, such as *A Connecticut Yankee in King Arthur's Court* (1889), *The Tragedy of Pudd'nhead Wilson* (1894), "The Man That Corrupted Hadleyburg" (1899), and "The Mysterious Stranger" fragments left at his death, exhibit a pronounced and bleak determinism.

Twain died in 1910. A complex and temperamental man, he has proven endlessly appealing to psychoanalytic critics,

---

[9] Henry Nash Smith, introduction to *Mark Twain: A Collection of Critical Essays* (Englewood Cliffs, N.J.: Prentice-Hall, 1963), p. 12.

who often tend too readily to conflate Mark Twain, the persona, with Sam Clemens, the man. A larger-than-life personality, Mark Twain remains a national figure today. At Twain's death, Howells wrote about his longtime friend, "Emerson, Longfellow, Lowell, Holmes—I knew them all and all the rest of our sages, poets, seers, critics, humorists; they were like one another and like other literary men; but Clemens was sole, incomparable, the Lincoln of our literature." [10]

Note on the Text

Adventures of Huckleberry Finn was first published in England (by Chatto and Windus) and Canada (by Dawson Brothers) on December 10, 1884. The American edition was released by Twain's publishing firm, Charles Webster and Company, on February 18, 1885. This edition of the text is that of the first edition by Chatto and Windus. As such, it follows the British style of the original first edition and not the American style of the later American edition.

[10] William Dean Howells, *My Mark Twain: Reminiscences and Criticisms* (New York, 1910), p. 101.

The Text of

ADVENTURES OF
HUCKLEBERRY FINN

ADVENTURES
OF
HUCKLEBERRY FINN

(*TOM SAWYERS COMRADE*)

SCENE: THE MISSISSIPPI VALLEY
TIME: FORTY TO FIFTY YEARS AGO[1]

BY
MARK TWAIN
(SAMUEL L. CLEMENS)

WITH 174 ILLUSTRATIONS

CHATTO & WINDUS, PICCADILLY 1884

INTRODUCTION

---

[1] *Forty to Fifty Years Ago*: The first edition of *Adventures of Huckleberry Finn* was published in 1884; hence, the novel is set between about 1834 and 1844.

NOTICE

PERSONS attempting to find a motive in this narrative will be prosecuted; persons attempting to find a moral in it will be banished; persons attempting to find a plot in it will be shot.

BY ORDER OF THE AUTHOR

Per G. G., CHIEF OF ORDNANCE.

EXPLANATORY

IN this book a number of dialects are used, to wit: the Missouri Negro dialect; the extremest form of the backwoods Southwestern dialect; the ordinary 'Pike-County' dialect; and four modified varieties of this last.[2] The shadings have not been done in a hap-hazard fashion, or by guess-work; but painstakingly, and with the trustworthy guidance and support of personal familiarity with these several forms of speech.

I make this explanation for the reason that without it many readers would suppose that all these characters were trying to talk alike and not succeeding.

THE AUTHOR.

---

[2] Despite the comic tone of this "Explanatory", Twain was known for his interest and skill in accurately rendering regional dialects in his works. *Pike-County*: county in northeast Missouri between St. Louis and Hannibal.

CHAPTER 1

You don't know about me, without you have read a book by the name of *The Adventures of Tom Sawyer*,[1] but that ain't no matter. That book was made by Mr Mark Twain, and he told the truth, mainly. There was things which he stretched, but mainly he told the truth. That is nothing. I never seen anybody but lied, one time or another, without it was Aunt Polly, or the widow, or maybe Mary. Aunt Polly—Tom's Aunt Polly, she is—and Mary, and the Widow Douglas, is all told about in that book—which is mostly a true book; with some stretchers, as I said before.

Now the way that the book winds up, is this: Tom and me found the money that the robbers hid in the cave, and it made us rich. We got six thousand dollars apiece—all gold. It was an awful sight of money when it was piled up. Well, Judge Thatcher, he took it and put it out at interest, and it fetched us a dollar a day apiece, all the year round—more than a body could tell what to do with. The Widow Douglas, she took me for her son, and allowed she would sivilize me; but it was rough living in the house all the time, considering how dismal regular and decent the widow was in all her ways; and so when I couldn't stand it no longer, I lit out. I got into my old rags, and my sugar-hogshead[2] again, and was free and satisfied. But Tom Sawyer, he hunted me up and said he was going to start a band of robbers, and I might join if I would go back to the widow and be respectable. So I went back.

[1] *The Adventures of Tom Sawyer*: Twain was planning a sequel to *Tom Sawyer* soon after it was published in 1876, but it took him eight years, writing in fits and starts, to complete one. Huck Finn appears as a relatively minor character in *Tom Sawyer*, where he is described as "the juvenile pariah of the village ... son of the town drunkard". Twain relied largely on his childhood memories of Hannibal, Missouri, in his portrayal of characters in both books.

[2] *hogshead*: large barrel used for storage.

The widow she cried over me, and called me a poor lost lamb, and she called me a lot of other names, too, but she never meant no harm by it. She put me in them new clothes again, and I couldn't do nothing but sweat and sweat, and feel all cramped up. Well, then, the old thing commenced again. The widow rung a bell for supper, and you had to come to time. When you got to the table you couldn't go right to eating, but you had to wait for the widow to tuck down her head and grumble a little over the victuals,[3] though there warn't really anything the matter with them. That is, nothing only everything was cooked by itself. In a barrel of odds and ends it is different; things get mixed up, and the juice kind of swaps around, and the things go better.

After supper she got out her book and learned me about Moses and the Bulrushers;[4] and I was in a sweat to find out all about him; but by-and-by she let it out that Moses had been dead a considerable long time; so then I didn't care no more about him; because I don't take no stock in dead people.

Pretty soon I wanted to smoke, and asked the widow to let me. But she wouldn't. She said it was a mean practice and wasn't clean, and I must try to not do it any more. That is just the way with some people. They get down on a thing when they don't know nothing about it. Here she was a bothering about Moses, which was no kin to her, and no use to anybody, being gone, you see, yet finding a power of fault with me for doing a thing that had some good in it. And she took snuff too; of course that was all right, because she done it herself.

Her sister, Miss Watson, a tolerable slim old maid, with goggles on, had just come to live with her, and took a set at me now, with a spelling-book. She worked me middling hard for

---

[3] *victuals*: food; sometimes modified to "vittles".
[4] *Moses and the Bulrushers*: In Exodus 2:1–10, the Hebrew baby Moses was floated down a river in a basket and found by Pharaoh's daughter. Moses later delivered the Israelites from their bondage in Egypt to the Promised Land and thus became in Negro lore a figure of freedom from slavery. Although the religious skeptic Huck dismisses the lesson here, the story of Moses will form a thematic backdrop for Huck's quest to help his slave friend Jim to freedom.

about an hour, and then the widow made her ease up. I couldn't stood it much longer. Then for an hour it was deadly dull, and I was fidgety. Miss Watson would say, 'Don't put your feet up there, Huckleberry'; and 'don't scrunch up like that, Huckleberry—set up straight'; and pretty soon she would say, 'Don't gap[5] and stretch like that, Huckleberry—why don't you try to behave?' Then she told me all about the bad place,[6] and I said I wished I was there. She got mad, then, but I didn't mean no harm. All I wanted was to go somewheres; all I wanted was a change, I warn't particular. She said it was wicked to say what I said; said she wouldn't say it for the whole world; *she* was going to live so as to go to the good place. Well, I couldn't see no advantage in going where she was going, so I made up my mind I wouldn't try for it. But I never said so, because it would only make trouble, and wouldn't do no good.

Now she had got a start, and she went on and told me all about the good place. She said all a body would have to do there was to go around all day long with a harp and sing, forever and ever. So I didn't think much of it. But I never said so. I asked her if she reckoned Tom Sawyer would go there, and, she said, not by a considerable sight. I was glad about that, because I wanted him and me to be together.

Miss Watson she kept pecking at me, and it got tiresome and lonesome. By-and-by they fetched the niggers[7] in and had prayers, and then everybody was off to bed. I went up to my room with a piece of candle and put it on the table. Then I set down in a chair by the window and tried to think of something cheerful, but it warn't no use. I felt so lonesome I most wished I was dead. The stars was shining, and the leaves rustled in the woods ever so mournful; and I heard an owl, away off, who-whooing about somebody that was dead, and a whippowill and a dog crying about somebody that was going

---

[5] *gap*: yawn.

[6] *the bad place*: i.e., Hell.

[7] *niggers*: Missouri was a slaveholding state at the time, and Miss Watson owns slaves. From *negro*, meaning "black" in Spanish, "nigger" was a conventional term for a black person at the time.

to die;[8] and the wind was trying to whisper something to me and I couldn't make out what it was, and so it made the cold shivers run over me. Then away out in the woods I heard that kind of a sound that a ghost makes when it wants to tell about something that's on its mind and can't make itself understood, and so can't rest easy in its grave and has to go about that way every night grieving. I got so down-hearted and scared, I did wish I had some company. Pretty soon a spider went crawling up my shoulder, and I flipped it off and it lit in the candle; and before I could budge it was all shriveled up. I didn't need anybody to tell me that that was an awful bad sign and would fetch me some bad luck, so I was scared and most shook the clothes off of me. I got up and turned around in my tracks three times and crossed my breast every time; and then I tied up a little lock of my hair with a thread to keep witches away. But I hadn't no confidence. You do that when you've lost a horse-shoe that you've found, instead of nailing it up over the door, but I hadn't ever heard anybody say it was any way to keep off bad luck when you'd killed a spider.

I set down again, a shaking all over, and got out my pipe for a smoke; for the house was all as still as death, now, and so the widow wouldn't know. Well, after a long time I heard the clock away off in the town go boom—boom—boom—twelve licks—and all still again—stiller than ever. Pretty soon I heard a twig snap, down in the dark amongst the trees—something was a stirring. I set still and listened. Directly I could just barely hear a '*me-yow! me-yow!*' down there. That was good! Says I, '*me-yow! me-yow!*' as soft as I could, and then I put out the light and scrambled out of the window onto the shed. Then I slipped down to the ground and crawled in amongst the trees, and sure enough there was Tom Sawyer waiting for me.

[8] *owl . . . whippowill . . . dog crying about somebody that was going to die:* Intent on capturing folkways in this time and place, Twain details here and in the following pages many regional superstitions and traditions. Most have European origins. The cry of the owl, whippoorwill, and dog were said to portend impending death.

CHAPTER 2

We went tip-toeing along a path amongst the trees back towards the end of the widow's garden, stooping down so as the branches wouldn't scrape our heads. When we was passing by the kitchen I fell over a root and made a noise. We scrouched down and laid still. Miss Watson's big nigger, named Jim, was setting in the kitchen door; we could see him pretty clear, because there was a light behind him. He got up and stretched his neck out about a minute, listening. Then he says:

'Who dah?'

He listened some more; then he come tip-toeing down and stood right between us; we could a touched him, nearly. Well, likely it was minutes and minutes that there warn't a sound, and we all there so close together. There was a place on my ankle that got to itching; but I dasn't scratch it; and then my ear begun to itch; and next my back, right between my shoulders. Seemed like I'd die if I couldn't scratch. Well, I've noticed that thing plenty of times since. If you are with the quality,[1] or at a funeral, or trying to go to sleep when you ain't sleepy—if you are anywheres where it won't do for you to scratch, why you will itch all over in upwards of a thousand places. Pretty soon Jim says:

'Say—who is you? Whar is you? Dog my cats ef I didn' hear sumf'n. Well, I knows what I's gwyne to do. I's gwyne to set down here and listen tell I hears it agin.'

So he set down on the ground betwixt me and Tom. He leaned his back up against a tree, and stretched his legs out till one of them most touched one of mine. My nose begun to itch. It itched till the tears come into my eyes. But I dasn't scratch. Then it begun to itch on the inside. Next I got to itching underneath. I didn't know how I was going to set still.

[1] *the quality*: respectable or high-class members of society.

9

This miserableness went on as much as six or seven minutes; but it seemed a sight longer than that. I was itching in eleven different places now. I reckoned I couldn't stand it more'n a minute longer, but I set my teeth hard and got ready to try. Just then Jim begun to breathe heavy; next he begun to snore—and then I was pretty soon comfortable again.

Tom he made a sign to me—kind of a little noise with his mouth—and we went creeping away on our hands and knees. When we was ten foot off, Tom whispered to me and wanted to tie Jim to the tree for fun; but I said no; he might wake and make a disturbance, and then they'd find out I warn't in. Then Tom said he hadn't got candles enough, and he would slip in the kitchen and get some more. I didn't want him to try. I said Jim might wake up and come. But Tom wanted to resk it; so we slid in there and got three candles, and Tom laid five cents on the table for pay. Then we got out, and I was in a sweat to get away; but nothing would do Tom but he must crawl to where Jim was, on his hands and knees, and play something on him. I waited, and it seemed a good while, everything was so still and lonesome.

As soon as Tom was back, we cut along the path, around the garden fence, and by-and-by fetched up on the steep top of the hill on the other side of the house. Tom said he slipped Jim's hat off his head and hung it on a limb right over him, and Jim stirred a little, but he didn't wake. Afterwards Jim said the witches bewitched him and put him in a trance, and rode him all over the State, and then set him under the trees again and hung his hat on a limb to show who done it. And next time Jim told it he said they rode him down to New Orleans: and after that, every time he told it he spread it more and more, till by-and-by he said they rode him all over the world, and tired him most to death, and his back was all over saddle-boils. Jim was monstrous proud about it, and he got so he wouldn't hardly notice the other niggers. Niggers would come miles to hear Jim tell about it, and he was more looked up to than any nigger in that country. Strange niggers would stand with their mouths open and look him all over, same as if he was a wonder. Niggers is always talking about witches in the dark by the kitchen fire; but whenever one was talking and letting on to know all about such things, Jim would happen in and say, 'Hm! What you know 'bout witches?' and that nigger was corked up[2] and had to take a back seat. Jim always kept that five-center piece around his neck with a string and said it was a charm the devil give to him with his own hands and told him he could cure anybody with it and fetch witches whenever he wanted to, just by saying something to it; but he never told what it was he said to it. Niggers would come from all around there and give Jim anything they had, just for a sight of that five-center piece; but they wouldn't touch it, because the devil had had his hands on it. Jim was most ruined, for a servant, because he got so stuck up on account of having seen the devil and been rode by witches.

Well, when Tom and me got to the edge of the hill-top, we looked away down into the village[3] and could see three or four lights twinkling, where there was sick folks, may be; and the stars over us was sparkling ever so fine; and down by the village was the river, a whole mile broad, and awful still and grand. We went down the hill and found Jo Harper, and Ben Rogers, and two or three more of the boys, hid in the old tanyard.[4] So we unhitched a skiff[5] and pulled down the river two mile and a half, to the big scar on the hillside, and went ashore.

We went to a clump of bushes, and Tom made everybody swear to keep the secret, and then showed them a hole in the hill, right in the thickest part of the bushes. Then we lit the candles and crawled in on our hands and knees. We went about two hundred yards, and then the cave opened up. Tom poked

---

[2] *corked up*: stopped or defeated.

[3] *the village*: The town of St. Petersburg is modeled on Hannibal, Missouri, a bustling port on the Mississippi where Twain lived from age three to seventeen. Hannibal's population grew from about one thousand to three thousand persons during Twain's residence there.

[4] *tanyard*: the part of a tannery (a place where animal skin is processed into goods) that holds the vats employed in this work.

[5] *skiff*: light rowboat.

about amongst the passages and pretty soon ducked under a wall where you wouldn't a noticed that there was a hole. We went along a narrow place and got into a kind of room, all damp and sweaty and cold, and there we stopped. Tom says:

'Now we'll start this band of robbers and call it Tom Sawyer's Gang. Everybody that wants to join has got to take an oath, and write his name in blood.'

Everybody was willing. So Tom got out a sheet of paper that he had wrote the oath on, and read it. It swore every boy to stick to the band, and never tell any of the secrets; and if anybody done anything to any boy in the band, whichever boy was ordered to kill that person and his family must do it, and he mustn't eat and he mustn't sleep till he had killed them and hacked a cross in their breasts, which was the sign of the band. And nobody that didn't belong to the band could use that mark, and if he did he must be sued; and if he done it again he must be killed. And if anybody that belonged to the band told the secrets, he must have his throat cut, and then have his carcass burnt up and the ashes scattered all around, and his name blotted off of the list with blood and never mentioned again by the gang, but have a curse put on it and be forgot, forever.

Everybody said it was a real beautiful oath, and asked Tom if he got it out of his own head. He said, some of it, but the rest was out of pirate books, and robber books, and every gang that was high-toned had it.

Some thought it would be good to kill *the families* of boys that told the secrets. Tom said it was a good idea, so he took a pencil and wrote it in. Then Ben Rogers says:

'Here's Huck Finn, he hain't got no family—what you going to do 'bout him?'

'Well, hain't he got a father?' says Tom Sawyer.

'Yes, he's got a father, but you can't never find him, these days. He used to lay drunk with the hogs in the tanyard, but he hain't been seen in these parts for a year or more.'

They talked it over, and they was going to rule me out, because they said every boy must have a family or somebody to kill, or else it wouldn't be fair and square for the others. Well, nobody could think of anything to do—everybody was stumped, and set still. I was most ready to cry; but all at once I thought of a way, and so I offered them Miss Watson—they could kill her. Everybody said:

'Oh, she'll do, she'll do. That's all right. Huck can come in.'

Then they all stuck a pin in their fingers to get blood to sign with, and I made my mark on the paper.

'Now,' says Ben Rogers, 'what's the line of business of this Gang?'

'Nothing only robbery and murder,' Tom said.

'But who are we going to rob? houses—or cattle—or—'

'Stuff! stealing cattle and such things ain't robbery, it's burglary,' says Tom Sawyer. 'We ain't burglars. That ain't no sort of style. We are highwaymen. We stop stages and carriages on the road, with masks on, and kill the people and take their watches and money.'

'Must we always kill the people?'

'Oh, certainly. It's best. Some authorities think different, but mostly it's considered best to kill them. Except some that you bring to the cave here and keep them till they're ransomed.'

'Ransomed? What's that?'

'I don't know. But that's what they do. I've seen it in books; and so of course that's what we've got to do.'

'But how can we do it if we don't know what it is?'

'Why blame it all, we've *got* to do it. Don't I tell you it's in the books? Do you want to go to doing different from what's in the books, and get things all muddled up?'

'Oh, that's all very fine to *say*, Tom Sawyer, but how in the nation[6] are these fellows going to be ransomed if we don't know how to do it to them? that's the thing *I* want to get at. Now what do you *reckon* it is?'

'Well I don't know. But per'aps if we keep them till they're ransomed, it means that we keep them till they're dead.'

---

[6] *how in the nation*: euphemism for "how in damnation".

'Now, that's something *like*. That'll answer. Why couldn't you said that before? We'll keep them till they're ransomed to death—and a bothersome lot they'll be, too, eating up everything and always trying to get loose.'

'How you talk, Ben Rogers. How can they get loose when there's a guard over them, ready to shoot them down if they move a peg?'

'A guard. Well, that *is* good. So somebody's got to set up all night and never get any sleep, just so as to watch them. I think that's foolishness. Why can't a body take a club and ransom them as soon as they get here?'

'Because it ain't in the books so—that's why. Now Ben Rogers, do you want to do things regular, or don't you?—that's the idea. Don't you reckon that the people that made the books knows what's the correct thing to do? Do you reckon *you* can learn 'em anything? Not by a good deal. No, sir, we'll just go on and ransom them in the regular way.'

'All right. I don't mind; but I say it's a fool way, anyhow. Say—do we kill the women, too?'

'Well, Ben Rogers, if I was as ignorant as you I wouldn't let on. Kill the women? No—nobody ever saw anything in the books like that. You fetch them to the cave, and you're always as polite as pie to them; and by-and-by they fall in love with you and never want to go home any more.'

'Well, if that's the way, I'm agreed, but I don't take no stock in it. Mighty soon we'll have the cave so cluttered up with women, and fellows waiting to be ransomed, that there won't be no place for the robbers. But go ahead, I ain't got nothing to say.'

Little Tommy Barnes was asleep, now, and when they waked him up he was scared, and cried, and said he wanted to go home to his ma, and didn't want to be a robber any more.

So they all made fun of him, and called him cry-baby, and that made him mad, and he said he would go straight and tell all the secrets. But Tom give him five cents to keep quiet, and said we would all go home and meet next week and rob somebody and kill some people.

Ben Rogers said he couldn't get out much, only Sundays, and so he wanted to begin next Sunday; but all the boys said it would be wicked to do it on Sunday, and that settled the thing. They agreed to get together and fix a day as soon as they could, and then we elected Tom Sawyer first captain and Jo Harper second captain of the Gang, and so started home.

I clumb up the shed and crept into my window just before day was breaking. My new clothes was all greased up and clayey, and I was dog-tired.

CHAPTER 3

Well, I got a good going-over in the morning, from old Miss Watson, on account of my clothes; but the widow she didn't scold, but only cleaned off the grease and clay and looked so sorry that I thought I would behave a while if I could. Then Miss Watson she took me in the closet and prayed,[1] but nothing come of it. She told me to pray every day, and whatever I asked for I would get it. But it warn't so. I tried it. Once I got a fish-line, but no hooks. It warn't any good to me without hooks. I tried for the hooks three or four times, but somehow I couldn't make it work. By-and-by, one day, I asked Miss Watson to try for me, but she said I was a fool. She never told me why, and I couldn't make it out no way.

I set down, one time, back in the woods, and had a long think about it. I says to myself, if a body can get anything they pray for, why don't Deacon Winn get back the money he lost on pork? Why can't the widow get back her silver snuff-box that was stole? Why can't Miss Watson fat up? No, says I to myself, there ain't nothing in it. I went and told the widow about it, and she said the thing a body could get by praying for it was 'spiritual gifts'. This was too many for me, but she told me what she meant—I must help other people, and do everything I could for other people, and look out for them all the time, and never think about myself. This was including Miss Watson, as I took it. I went out in the woods and turned it over in my mind a long time, but I couldn't see no advantage about it—except for the other people—so at last I reckoned I wouldn't worry about it any more, but just let it go. Sometimes the widow would take me one side and talk about

---

[1] *took me in the closet and prayed*: Miss Watson takes Jesus' words in Matthew 6:6 (AV) literally: "But when you pray, go into your closet, close the door, and pray to your Father in secret."

Providence in a way to make a body's mouth water; but maybe next day Miss Watson would take hold and knock it all down again. I judged I could see that there was two Providences, and a poor chap would stand considerable show with the widow's Providence, but if Miss Watson's got him there warn't no help for him any more. I thought it all out, and reckoned I would belong to the widow's, if he wanted me, though I couldn't make out how he was a-going to be any better off then than what he was before, seeing I was so ignorant and so kind of low-down and ornery.

Pap he hadn't been seen for more than a year, and that was comfortable for me; I didn't want to see him no more. He used to always whale[2] me when he was sober and could get his hands on me; though I used to take to the woods most of the time when he was around. Well, about this time he was found in the river drowned, about twelve mile above town, so people said. They judged it was him, anyway; said this drowned man was just his size, and was ragged, and had uncommon long hair—which was all like pap—but they couldn't make nothing out of the face, because it had been in the water so long it warn't much like a face at all. They said he was floating on his back in the water. They took him and buried him on the bank. But I warn't comfortable long, because I happened to think of something. I knowed mighty well that a drownded man don't float on his back, but on his face. So I knowed, then, that this warn't pap, but a woman dressed up in man's clothes. So I was uncomfortable again. I judged the old man would turn up again by-and-by, though I wished he wouldn't.

We played robber now and then about a month, and then I resigned. All the boys did. We hadn't robbed nobody, we hadn't killed any people, but only just pretended. We used to hop out of the woods and go charging down on hog-drovers and women in carts taking garden stuff to market, but we never hived[3] any of them. Tom Sawyer called the hogs 'ingots',

---

[2] *whale*: beat or thrash vigorously.
[3] *hived*: got.

and he called the turnips and stuff 'julery' and we would go to the cave and pow-wow over what we had done and how many people we had killed and marked. But I couldn't see no profit in it. One time Tom sent a boy to run about town with a blazing stick, which he called a slogan (which was the sign for the Gang to get together), and then he said he had got secret news by his spies that next day a whole parcel of Spanish merchants and rich A-rabs was going to camp in Cave Hollow with two hundred elephants, and six hundred camels, and over a thousand 'sumter' mules,[4] all loaded down with di'monds, and they didn't have only a guard of four hundred soldiers, and so we would lay in ambuscade, as he called it, and kill the lot and scoop the things. He said we must slick up our swords and guns, and get ready. He never could go after even a turnip-cart but he must have the swords and guns all scoured up for it; though they was only lath and broomsticks, and you might scour at them till you rotted and then they warn't worth a mouthful of ashes more than what they was before. I didn't believe we could lick such a crowd of Spaniards and A-rabs, but I wanted to see the camels and elephants, so I was on hand next day, Saturday, in the ambuscade; and when we got the word, we rushed out of the woods and down the hill. But there warn't no Spaniards and A-rabs, and there warn't no camels nor no elephants. It warn't anything but a Sunday-school picnic, and only a primer-class at that. We busted it up, and chased the children up the hollow; but we never got anything but some doughnuts and jam, though Ben Rogers got a rag doll, and Jo Harper got a hymn-book and a tract;[5] and then the teacher charged in and made us drop everything and cut. I didn't see no di'monds, and I told Tom Sawyer so. He said there was loads of them there, anyway; and he said there was A-rabs there, too, and elephants and things. I said, why couldn't we see them, then? He said if I warn't so ignorant, but had read a book called

---

[4] '*sumter*' *mules*: sumpter mules or pack mules.
[5] *tract*: religious pamphlet or leaflet.

'Don Quixote'[6] I would know without asking. He said it was all done by enchantment. He said there was hundreds of soldiers there, and elephants and treasure, and so on, but we had enemies which he called magicians, and they had turned the whole thing into an infant Sunday school, just out of spite. I said, all right, then the thing for us to do was to go for the magicians. Tom Sawyer said I was a numskull.

'Why,' says he, 'a magician could call up a lot of genies, and they would hash you up like nothing before you could say Jack Robinson. They are as tall as a tree and as big around as a church.'

'Well,' I says, 's'pose we got some genies to help *us*—can't we lick the other crowd then?'

'How you going to get them?'

'I don't know. How do *they* get them?'

'Why they rub an old tin lamp[7] or an iron ring, and then the genies come tearing in, with the thunder and lightning a-ripping around and the smoke a-rolling, and everything they're told to do they up and do it. They don't think nothing of pulling a shot tower[8] up by the roots, and belting a Sunday-school superintendent over the head with it—or any other man.'

'Who makes them tear around so?'

'Why, whoever rubs the lamp or the ring. They belong to whoever rubs the lamp or the ring, and they've got to do whatever he says. If he tells them to build a palace forty miles long, out of di'monds, and fill it full of chewing gum, or whatever you want, and fetch an emperor's daughter from China for you to marry, they've got to do it—and they've got to do it before

---

[6] *'Don Quixote'*: In one of the chapters of this 1605 work by Spanish author Miguel de Cervantes, Don Quixote mistakes a herd of sheep for an army of "Arabs, Spaniards, Christians and pagans", and he is convinced that it is a magician's work.

[7] *they rub an old tin lamp*: In The Arabian Nights' Entertainments, first released in English in 1838–1841, Aladdin conjures up a genie by rubbing a lamp.

[8] *shot tower*: tall structure where gunshot is manufactured by dropping molten lead into water.

sun-up next morning, too. And more—they've got to waltz that palace around over the country wherever you want it, you understand.'

'Well,' says I, 'I think they are a pack of flatheads for not keeping the palace themselves 'stead of fooling them away like that. And what's more—if I was one of them I would see a man in Jericho before I would drop my business and come to him for the rubbing of an old tin lamp.'

'How you talk, Huck Finn. Why, you'd *have* to come when he rubbed it, whether you wanted to or not.'

'What, and I as high as a tree and as big as a church? All right, then; I *would* come; but I lay I'd make that man climb the highest tree there was in the country.'

'Shucks, it ain't no use to talk to you, Huck Finn. You don't seem to know anything, somehow—perfect sap-head.'

I thought all this over for two or three days, and then I reckoned I would see if there was anything in it. I got an old tin lamp and an iron ring and went out in the woods and rubbed and rubbed till I sweat like an Injun, calculating to build a palace and sell it; but it warn't no use, none of the genies come. So then I judged that all that stuff was only just one of Tom Sawyer's lies. I reckoned he believed in the A-rabs and the elephants, but as for me I think different. It had all the marks of a Sunday school.

CHAPTER 4

Well, three or four months run along, and it was well into the winter, now. I had been to school most all the time, and could spell, and read, and write just a little, and could say the multiplication table up to six times seven is thirty-five, and I don't reckon I could ever get any further than that if I was to live forever. I don't take no stock in mathematics, anyway.

At first I hated the school, but by-and-by I got so I could stand it. Whenever I got uncommon tired I played hookey, and the hiding I got next day done me good and cheered me up. So the longer I went to school the easier it got to be. I was getting sort of used to the widow's ways, too, and they warn't so raspy on me. Living in a house, and sleeping in a bed, pulled on me pretty tight, mostly, but before the cold weather I used to slide out and sleep in the woods, sometimes, and so that was a rest to me. I liked the old ways best, but I was getting so I liked the new ones, too, a little bit. The widow said I was coming along slow but sure, and doing very satisfactory. She said she warn't ashamed of me.

One morning I happened to turn over the salt-cellar[1] at breakfast. I reached for some of it as quick as I could, to throw over my left shoulder and keep off the bad luck, but Miss Watson was in ahead of me, and crossed me off. She says, 'Take your hands away, Huckleberry—what a mess you are always making.' The widow put in a good word for me, but that warn't going to keep off the bad luck, I knowed that well enough. I started out, after breakfast, feeling worried and shaky, and wondering where it was going to fall on me, and what it was going to be. There is ways to keep off some kinds of bad luck, but this wasn't one of them kind; so I never tried to do anything, but just poked along low-spirited and on the watch-out.

[1] *salt-cellar*: small vessel for holding salt.

I went down the front garden and clumb over the stile, where you go through the high board fence. There was an inch of new snow on the ground, and I seen somebody's tracks. They had come up from the quarry and stood around the stile a while, and then went on around the garden fence. It was funny they hadn't come in, after standing around so. I couldn't make it out. It was very curious, somehow. I was going to follow around, but I stooped down to look at the tracks first. I didn't notice anything at first, but next I did. There was a cross in the left boot-heel made with big nails, to keep off the devil.

I was up in a second and shinning down the hill. I looked over my shoulder every now and then, but I didn't see nobody. I was at Judge Thatcher's as quick as I could get there. He said:

'Why, my boy, you are all out of breath. Did you come for your interest?'

'No, sir,' I says; 'is there some for me?'

'Oh, yes, a half-yearly is in, last night. Over a hundred and fifty dollars. Quite a fortune for you. You better let me invest it along with your six thousand, because if you take it you'll spend it.'

'No, sir,' I says, 'I don't want to spend it. I don't want it at all—nor the six thousand, nuther. I want you to take it; I want to give it to you—the six thousand and all.'

He looked surprised. He couldn't seem to make it out. He says:

'Why, what can you mean, my boy?'

I says, 'Don't you ask me no questions about it, please. You'll take it—won't you?'

He says:

'Well, I'm puzzled. Is something the matter?'

'Please take it,' says I, 'and don't ask me nothing—then I won't have to tell no lies.'

He studied a while, and then he says:

'Oho-o. I think I see. You want to *sell* all your property to me—not give it. That's the correct idea.'

Then he wrote something on a paper and read it over, and
says:

'There—you see it says "for a consideration". That means I
have bought it of you and paid you for it. Here's a dollar for
you. Now, you sign it.'

So I signed it, and left.

Miss Watson's nigger, Jim, had a hair-ball[2] as big as your
fist, which had been took out of the fourth stomach of an ox,
and he used to do magic with it. He said there was a spirit
inside of it, and it knowed everything. So I went to him that
night and told him pap was here again, for I found his tracks
in the snow. What I wanted to know was, what he was going
to do, and was he going to stay? Jim got out his hair-ball, and
said something over it, and then he held it up and dropped it
on the floor. It fell pretty solid, and only rolled about an inch.
Jim tried it again, and then another time, and it acted just the
same. Jim got down on his knees and put his ear against it and
listened. But it warn't no use; he said it wouldn't talk. He said
sometimes it wouldn't talk without money. I told him I had
an old slick counterfeit quarter that warn't no good because
the brass showed through the silver a little, and it wouldn't
pass nohow, even if the brass didn't show, because it was so
slick it felt greasy, and so that would tell on it every time. (I
reckoned I wouldn't say nothing about the dollar I got from
the judge.) I said it was pretty bad money, but maybe the hair-
ball would take it, because maybe it wouldn't know the difference. Jim smelt it, and bit it, and rubbed it, and said he
would manage so the hair-ball would think it was good. He
said he would split open a raw Irish potato and stick the quarter in between and keep it there all night, and next morning
you couldn't see no brass, and it wouldn't feel greasy no more,
and so anybody in town would take it in a minute, let alone a
hair-ball. Well, I knowed a potato would do that before, but I
had forgot it.

---

[2] *hair-ball*: densely round mass of hair from an animal's stomach. Jim's hairball
superstitions have their origins in African voodoo.

Jim put the quarter under the hair-ball and got down and listened again. This time he said the hair-ball was all right. He said it would tell my whole fortune if I wanted it to. I says, go on. So the hair-ball talked to Jim, and Jim told it to me. He says:

'Yo' ole father doan' know, yit, what he's a-gwyne to do. Sometimes he spec he'll go 'way, en den agin he spec he'll stay. De bes' way is to res' easy en let de ole man take his own way. Dey's two angels hoverin' roun' 'bout him. One uv 'em is white en shiny, en 'tother one is black. De white one gits him to go right, a little while, den de black one sail in en bust it all up. A body can't tell, yit, which one gwyne to fetch him at de las'. But you is all right. You gwyne to have considable trouble in yo' life, en considable joy. Sometimes you gwyne to git hirt, en sometimes you gwyne to git sick; but every time you's gwyne to git well agin. Dey's two gals flyin' 'bout you in yo' life. One uv 'em's light en 'tother one is dark. One is rich en 'tother is po'. You's gwyne to marry de po' one fust en de rich one by-en-by. You wants to keep 'way fum de water as much as you kin, en don't run no resk, 'kase it's down in de bills[3] dat you's gwyne to git hung.'

When I lit my candle and went up to my room that night, there set pap, his own self!

[3] *down in de bills*: foreordained.

CHAPTER 5

I had shut the door to. Then I turned around, and there he was. I used to be scared of him all the time, he tanned[1] me so much. I reckoned I was scared now, too; but in a minute I see I was mistaken. That is, after the first jolt, as you may say, when my breath sort of hitched—he being so unexpected; but right away after, I see I warn't scared of him worth bothering about.

He was most fifty, and he looked it. His hair was long and tangled and greasy, and hung down, and you could see his eyes shining through like he was behind vines. It was all black, no gray; so was his long, mixed-up whiskers. There warn't no color in his face, where his face showed; it was white; not like another man's white, but a white to make a body sick, a white to make a body's flesh crawl—a tree-toad white, a fish-belly white. As for his clothes—just rags, that was all. He had one ankle resting on 'tother knee; the boot on that foot was busted, and two of his toes stuck through, and he worked them now and then. His hat was laying on the floor; an old black slouch with the top caved in, like a lid.

I stood a-looking at him; he set there a-looking at me, with his chair tilted back a little. I set the candle down. I noticed the window was up; so he had clumb in by the shed. He kept a-looking me all over. By-and-by he says:

'Starchy clothes—very. You think you're a good deal of a big-bug, *don't* you?'

'Maybe I am, maybe I ain't,' I says.

'Don't you give me none o' your lip,' says he. 'You've put on considerble many frills since I been away. I'll take you down a peg before I get done with you. You're educated, too, they say; can read and write. You think you're better'n your father, now, don't you, because he can't? *I'll* take it out of you. Who told

---

[1] *tanned*: beat.

25

you you might meddle with such hifalut'n foolishness, hey?—
who told you you could?'

'The widow. She told me.'

'The widow, hey?—and who told the widow she could put
in her shovel about a thing that ain't none of her business?'

'Nobody never told her.'

'Well, I'll learn her how to meddle. And looky here—you
drop that school, you hear? I'll learn people to bring up a boy
to put on airs over his own father and let on to be better'n
what *he* is. You lemme catch you fooling around that school
again, you hear? Your mother couldn't read, and she couldn't
write, nuther, before she died. None of the family couldn't,
before *they* died. *I* can't; and here you're a-swelling yourself up
like this. I ain't the man to stand it—you hear? Say—lemme
hear you read.'

I took up a book and begun something about General Washington and the wars. When I'd read about a half a minute, he
fetched the book a whack with his hand and knocked it across
the house. He says:

'It's so. You can do it. I had my doubts when you told me.
Now looky here; you stop that putting on frills. I won't have
it. I'll lay for you, my smarty; and if I catch you about that
school I'll tan you good. First you know you'll get religion,
too. I never see such a son.'

He took up a little blue and yaller picture of some cows and
a boy, and says:

'What's this?'

'It's something they give me for learning my lessons good.'

He tore it up, and says—

'I'll give you something better—I'll give you a cowhide.'[2]

He set there a-mumbling and a-growling a minute, and then
he says—

'*Ain't* you a sweet-scented dandy, though? A bed; and bed-
clothes; and a look'n-glass; and a piece of carpet on the floor—

---

[2] *I'll give you a cowhide*: Pap threatens to flog Huck with a whip of rawhide or
braided leather.

and your own father got to sleep with the hogs in the tanyard. I never see such a son. I bet I'll take some o' these frills out o' you before I'm done with you. Why there ain't no end to your airs—they say you're rich. Hey?—how's that?'

'They lie—that's how.'

'Looky here—mind how you talk to me; I'm a-standing about all I can stand, now—so don't gimme no sass. I've been in town two days, and I hain't heard nothing but about you bein' rich. I heard about it away down the river, too. That's why I come. You git me that money to-morrow—I want it.'

'I hain't got no money.'

'It's a lie. Judge Thatcher's got it. You git it. I want it.'

'I hain't got no money, I tell you. You ask Judge Thatcher; he'll tell you the same.'

'All right. I'll ask him; and I'll make him pungle,[3] too, or I'll know the reason why. Say—how much you got in your pocket? I want it.'

'I hain't got only a dollar, and I want that to—'

'It don't make no difference what you want it for—you just shell it out.'

He took it and bit it to see if it was good, and then he said he was going down town to get some whisky; said he hadn't had a drink all day. When he had got out on the shed, he put his head in again, and cussed me for putting on frills and try-ing to be better than him; and when I reckoned he was gone, he come back and put his head in again, and told me to mind about that school, because he was going to lay for me and lick me if I didn't drop that.

Next day he was drunk, and he went to Judge Thatcher's and bullyragged him and tried to make him give up the money, but he couldn't, and then he swore he'd make the law force him.

The judge and the widow went to law to get the court to take me away from him and let one of them be my guardian; but it was a new judge that had just come, and he didn't know

---

[3] *pungle:* pay up.

the old man: so he said courts mustn't interfere and separate families if they could help it; said he'd druther not take a child away from its father. So Judge Thatcher and the widow had to quit on the business.

That pleased the old man till he couldn't rest. He said he'd cowhide me till I was black and blue if I didn't raise some money for him. I borrowed three dollars from Judge Thatcher, and pap took it and got drunk and went a-blowing around and cussing and whooping and carrying on; and he kept it up all over town, with a tin pan, till most midnight; then they jailed him, and next day they had him before court, and jailed him again for a week. But he said *he* was satisfied; said he was boss of his son, and he'd make it warm for *him*.

When he got out the new judge said he was agoing to make a man of him. So he took him to his own house, and dressed him up clean and nice, and had him to breakfast and dinner and supper with the family, and was just old pie to him, so to speak. And after supper he talked to him about temperance and such things till the old man cried, and said he'd been a fool, and fooled away his life; but now he was agoing to turn over a new leaf and be a man nobody wouldn't be ashamed of, and he hoped the judge would help him and not look down on him. The judge said he could hug him for them words; so *he* cried, and his wife she cried again; pap said he'd been a man that had always been misunderstood before, and the judge said he believed it. The old man said that what a man wanted that was down, was sympathy; and the judge said it was so; so they cried again. And when it was bedtime, the old man rose up and held out his hand, and says:

'Look at it gentlemen, and ladies all; take ahold of it; shake it. There's a hand that was the hand of a hog; but it ain't so no more; it's the hand of a man that's started in on a new life, and 'll die before he'll go back. You mark them words—don't forget I said them. It's a clean hand now; shake it—don't be afeard.'

So they shook it, one after the other, all around, and cried. The judge's wife she kissed it. Then the old man he signed a pledge—made his mark. The judge said it was the holiest time on record, or something like that. Then they tucked the old man into a beautiful room, which was the spare room, and in the night sometime he got powerful thirsty and dumb out onto the porch-roof and slid down a stanchion[4] and traded his new coat for a jug of forty-rod,[5] and clumb back again and had a good old time; and towards daylight he crawled out again, drunk as a fiddler, and rolled off the porch and broke his left arm in two places and was most froze to death when somebody found him after sun-up. And when they come to look at that spare room, they had to take soundings[6] before they could navigate it.

The judge he felt kind of sore. He said he reckoned a body could reform the ole man with a shot-gun, maybe, but he didn't know no other way.

---

[4] *stanchion*: roof post.

[5] *forty-rod*: whiskey so strong it could knock a man a distance of forty rods. A rod is 5.50 yards; hence, forty rods is 220 yards.

[6] *to take soundings*: to probe to ascertain the depth of a body of water. Huck uses nautical language here to describe the deplorable condition of Pap's room—soaking, evidently, with whiskey.

CHAPTER 6

Well, pretty soon the old man was up and around again, and then he went for Judge Thatcher in the courts to make him give up that money, and he went for me, too, for not stopping school. He catched me a couple of times and thrashed me, but I went to school just the same, and dodged him or outrun him most of the time. I didn't want to go to school much, before, but I reckoned I'd go now to spite pap. That law trial was a slow business; appeared like they warn't ever going to get started on it; so every now and then I'd borrow two or three dollars off of the judge for him, to keep from getting a cowhiding. Every time he got money he got drunk; and every time he got drunk he raised Cain[1] around town; and every time he raised Cain he got jailed. He was just suited—this kind of thing was right in his line.

He got to hanging around the widow's too much, and so she told him at last, that if he didn't quit using around there she would make trouble for him. Well, *wasn't* he mad? He said he would show who was Huck Finn's boss. So he watched out for me one day in the spring, and catched me, and took me up the river about three mile, in a skiff, and crossed over to the Illinois shore where it was woody and there warn't no houses but an old log hut in a place where the timber was so thick you couldn't find it if you didn't know where it was.

He kept me with him all the time, and I never got a chance to run off. We lived in that old cabin, and he always locked the door and put the key under his head, nights. He had a gun which he had stole, I reckon, and we fished and hunted, and that was what we lived on. Every little while he locked me in and went down to the store, three miles, to the ferry, and traded fish and game for whisky and fetched it home and got drunk

[1] *raised Cain:* created a disturbance.

and had a good time, and licked me. The widow she found out where I was, by-and-by, and she sent a man over to try to get hold of me, but pap drove him off with the gun, and it warn't long after that till I was used to being where I was, and liked it, all but the cowhide part.

It was kind of lazy and jolly, laying off comfortable all day, smoking and fishing, and no books nor study. Two months or more run along, and my clothes got to be all rags and dirt, and I didn't see how I'd ever got to like it so well at the widow's, where you had to wash, and eat on a plate, and comb up, and go to bed and get up regular, and be forever bothering over a book and have old Miss Watson pecking at you all the time. I didn't want to go back no more. I had stopped cussing, because the widow didn't like it; but now I took to it again because pap hadn't no objections. It was pretty good times up in the woods there, take it all around.

But by-and-by pap got too handy with his hick'ry,[2] and I couldn't stand it. I was all over welts. He got to going away so much, too, and locking me in. Once he locked me in and was gone three days. It was dreadful lonesome. I judged he had got drowned and I wasn't ever going to get out any more. I was scared. I made up my mind I would fix up some way to leave there. I had tried to get out of that cabin many a time, but I couldn't find no way. There warn't a window to it big enought for a dog to get through. I couldn't get up the chimbly, it was too narrow. The door was thick solid oak slabs. Pap was pretty careful not to leave a knife or anything in the cabin when he was away; I reckon I had hunted the place over as much as a hundred times; well, I was 'most all the time at it, because it was about the only way to put in the time. But this time I found something at last; I found an old rusty wood-saw without any handle; it was laid in between a rafter and the clapboards of the roof. I greased it up and went to work. There was an old horse-blanket nailed against the logs at the far end of the cabin behind the table, to keep the wind from blowing

---

[2] *too handy with his hick'ry*: too vigorous in beating with a hickory stick.

through the chinks and putting the candle out. I got under the table and raised the blanket and went to work to saw a section of the big bottom log out, big enough to let me through. Well, it was a good long job, but I was getting towards the end of it when I heard pap's gun in the woods. I got rid of the signs of my work, and dropped the blanket and hid my saw, and pretty soon pap come in.

Pap warn't in a good humor—so he was his natural self. He said he was down to town, and everything was going wrong. His lawyer said he reckoned he would win his lawsuit and get the money, if they ever got started on the trial; but then there was ways to put it off a long time, and Judge Thatcher knowed how to do it. And he said people allowed there'd be another trial to get me away from him and give me to the widow for my guardian, and they guessed it would win, this time. This shook me up considerable, because I didn't want to go back to the widow's any more and be so cramped up and sivilized, as they called it. Then the old man got to cussing, and cussed everything and everybody he could think of, and then cussed them all over again to make sure he hadn't skipped any, and after that he polished off with a kind of a general cuss all round, including a considerable parcel of people which he didn't know the names of, and so called them what's-his-name, when he got to them, and went right along with his cussing.

He said he would like to see the widow get me. He said he would watch out, and if they tried to come any such game on him he knowed of a place six or seven mile off, to stow me in, where they might hunt till they dropped and they couldn't find me. That made me pretty uneasy again, but only for a minute; I reckoned I wouldn't stay on hand till he got that chance.

The old man made me go to the skiff and fetch the things he had got. There was a fifty-pound sack of corn meal, and a side of bacon, ammunition, and a four-gallon jug of whisky, and an old book and two newspapers for wadding,[3] besides

---

[3] *wadding*: material used to hold powder in a gun.

some tow.[4] I toted up a load, and went back and set down on the bow of the skiff to rest. I thought it all over, and I reckoned I would walk off with the gun and some lines, and take to the woods when I run away. I guessed I wouldn't stay in one place, but just tramp right across the country, mostly night times, and hunt and fish to keep alive, and so get so far away that the old man nor the widow couldn't ever find me any more. I judged I would saw out and leave that night if pap got drunk enough, and I reckoned he would. I got so full of it I didn't notice how long I was staying, till the old man hollered and asked me whether I was asleep or drownded.

I got the things all up to the cabin, and then it was about dark. While I was cooking supper the old man took a swig or two and got sort of warmed up, and went to ripping again. He had been drunk over in town, and laid in the gutter all night, and he was a sight to look at. A body would a thought he was Adam, he was just all mud.[5] Whenever his liquor begun to work, he most always went for the govment. This time he says:

'Call this a govment! why, just look at it and see what it's like. Here's the law a-standing ready to take a man's son away from him—a man's own son, which he has had all the trouble and all the anxiety and all the expense of raising. Yes, just as that man has got that son raised at last, and ready to go to work and begin to do suthin' for *him* and give him a rest, the law up and goes for him. And they call *that* govment! That ain't all, nuther. The law backs that old Judge Thatcher up and helps him to keep me out o' my property. Here's what the law does. The law takes a man worth six thousand dollars and upards, and jams him into an old trap of a cabin like this, and lets him go round in clothes that ain't fitten for a hog. They call that govment! A man can't get his rights in a govment like this. Sometimes I've a mighty notion to just leave the

[4] *tow*: hemp or jute fibers used for rope.
[5] *Adam, he was just all mud*: In Genesis 2:7 (NAB), God created Adam "out of the clay of the ground".

country for good and all. Yes, and I *told* 'em so; I told old
Thatcher so to his face. Lots of 'em heard me, and can tell
what I said. Says I, for two cents I'd leave the blamed country
and never come anear it agin. Them's the very words. I says,
look at my hat—if you call it a hat—but the lid raised up and
the rest of it goes down till its below my chin, and then it
ain't rightly a hat at all, but more like my head was shoved up
through a jint o' stovepipe. Look at it, says I—such a hat for
me to wear—one of the wealthiest men in this town, if I could
git my rights.

'Oh, yes, this is a wonderful govment, wonderful. Why, looky
here. There was a free nigger there, from Ohio;[6] a mulatter,
most as white as a white man. He had the whitest shirt on
you ever see, too, and the shinest hat; and there ain't a man
in that town that's got as fine clothes as what he had; and
he had a gold watch and chain, and a silver-headed cane—
the awfulest old gray-headed nabob[7] in the State. And what
do you think? they said he was a p'fessor in a college, and
could talk all kinds of languages, and knowed everything.
And that ain't the wust. They said he could *vote*, when he
was at home. Well, that let me out. Thinks I, what is the
country a-coming to? It was 'lection day, and I was just about
to go and vote, myself, if I warn't too drunk to get there;
but when they told me there was a State in this country
where they'd let that nigger vote, I drawed out. I says I'll
never vote agin. Them's the very words I said; they all
heard me; and the country may rot for all me—I'll never
vote agin as long as I live. And to see the cool way
of that nigger—why, he wouldn't a give me the road if
I hadn't shoved him out o' the way. I says to the people,
why ain't this nigger put up at auction and sold?—that's
what I want to know. And what do you reckon they said?
Why, they said he couldn't be sold till he'd been in the

---

[6] *free nigger there, from Ohio:* Slavery had been abolished in Ohio by the 1787
Northwest Ordinance. However, Pap is wrong later in this paragraph: free blacks
were not allowed to vote in that state.

[7] *nabob:* wealthy or prominent man.

State six months,[8] and he hadn't been there that long yet. There, now—that's a specimen. They call that a govment that can't sell a free nigger till he's been in the State six months. Here's a govment that calls itself a govment, and lets on to be a govment, and thinks it is a govment, and yet's got to set stock-still for six whole months before it can take ahold of a prowling, thieving, infernal, white-shirted free nigger, and—'

Pap was agoing on so, he never noticed where his old limber legs was taking him to, so he went head over heels over the tub of salt pork,[9] and barked[10] both shins, and the rest of his speech was all the hottest kind of language—mostly hove[11] at the nigger and the govment, though he give the tub some, too, all along, here and there. He hopped around the cabin considerable, first on one leg and then on the other, holding first one shin and then the other one, and at last he let out with his left foot all of a sudden and fetched the tub a rattling kick. But it warn't good judgment, because that was the boot that had a couple of his toes leaking out of the front end of it; so now he raised a howl that fairly made a body's hair raise, and down he went in the dirt, and rolled there, and held his toes; and the cussing he done then laid over anything he had ever done previous. He said so his own self, afterwards. He had heard old Sowberry Hagan in his best days, and he said it laid over him, too; but I reckon that was sort of piling it on, maybe.

After supper pap took the jug, and said he had enough whisky there for two drunks and one delirium tremens. That was always his word. I judged he would be blind drunk in about an hour, and then I would steal the key, or saw myself out, one or 'tother.

---

[8] *he couldn't be sold till he'd been in the State six months*: Many slaveholding states, including Missouri, prohibited free blacks from entering, with some exceptions. Those who did enter were required to register, be licensed, and adhere to other strict regulations or they could be deemed runaways.

[9] *tub of salt pork*: Fat pork meat was preserved and flavored in vats of salt or brine.

[10] *barked*: skinned.

[11] *hove*: past tense of "heave", to throw or push. Here it means to "go after" or "rail against".

He drank, and drank, and tumbled down on his blankets, by-and-by; but luck didn't run my way. He didn't go sound asleep, but was uneasy. He groaned, and moaned, and thrashed around this way and that, for a long time. At last I got so sleepy I couldn't keep my eyes open, all I could do, and so before I knowed what I was about I was sound asleep, and the candle burning.

I don't know how long I was asleep, but all of a sudden there was an awful scream and I was up. There was pap, looking wild and skipping around every which way and yelling about snakes.[12] He said they was crawling up his legs; and then he would give a jump and scream, and say one had bit him on the cheek—but I couldn't see no snakes. He started and run round and round the cabin, hollering 'take him off! take him off! he's biting me on the neck!' I never see a man look so wild in the eyes. Pretty soon he was all fagged out, and fell down panting; then he rolled over and over, wonderful fast, kicking things every which way, and striking and grabbing at the air with his hands, and screaming, and saying there was devils ahold of him. He wore out, by-and-by, and laid still a while, moaning. Then he laid stiller, and didn't make a sound. I could hear the owls and the wolves, away off in the woods, and it seemed terrible still. He was laying over by the corner. By-and-by he raised up, part way, and listened, with his head to one side. He says very low:

'Tramp—tramp—tramp; that's the dead; tramp—tramp—tramp; they're coming after me; but I won't go—Oh, they're here! don't touch me—don't! hands off—they're cold; let go—Oh, let a poor devil alone!'

Then he went down on all fours and crawled off begging them to let him alone, and he rolled himself up in his blanket and wallowed in under the old pine table, still a-begging; and then he went to crying. I could hear him through the blanket.

[12] *There was pap . . . snakes:* Pap was correct when he stated, above, that he had enough whiskey left for the delirium tremens. What follows is a terrifyingly accurate representation of such an alcoholic fit.

By-and-by he rolled out and jumped up on his feet looking wild and he see me and went for me. He chased me round and round the place, with a clasp-knife, calling me the Angel of Death and saying he would kill me and then I couldn't come for him no more. I begged, and told him I was only Huck, but he laughed *such* a screechy laugh, and roared and cussed, and kept on chasing me up. Once when I turned short and dodged under his arm he made a grab and got me by the jacket between my shoulders, and I thought I was gone; but I slid out of the jacket quick as lightning, and saved myself. Pretty soon he was all tired out, and dropped down with his back against the door, and said he would rest a minute and then kill me. He put his knife under him, and said he would sleep and get strong, and then he would see who was who.

So he dozed off, pretty soon. By-and-by I got the old split-bottom[13] chair and clumb up, as easy as I could, not to make any noise, and got down the gun. I slipped the ramrod down it to make sure it was loaded, and then I laid it across the turnip barrel, pointing towards pap, and set down behind it to wait for him to stir. And how slow and still the time did drag along.

[13] *split-bottom*: splint-bottomed; that is, a chair the seat of which is constructed of woven thin strips of wood.

CHAPTER 7

'Git up! what you 'bout!'

I opened my eyes and looked around, trying to make out where I was. It was after sun-up, and I had been sound asleep. Pap was standing over me, looking sour—and sick, too. He says—

'What you doin' with this gun?'

I judged he didn't know nothing about what he had been doing, so I says:

'Somebody tried to get in, so I was laying for him.'

'Why didn't you roust me out?'

'Well I tried to, but I couldn't; I couldn't budge you.'

'Well, all right. Don't stand there palavering[1] all day, but out with you and see if there's a fish on the lines for breakfast. I'll be along in a minute.'

He unlocked the door and I cleared out, up the river bank. I noticed some pieces of limbs and such things floating down, and a sprinkling of bark; so I knowed the river had begun to rise. I reckoned I would have great times, now, if I was over at the town. The June rise used to be always luck for me; because as soon as that rise begins, here comes cord-wood floating down, and pieces of log rafts—sometimes a dozen logs together; so all you have to do is to catch them and sell them to the wood yards and the sawmill.

I went along up the bank with one eye out for pap and 'tother one out for what the rise might fetch along. Well, all at once, here comes a canoe; just a beauty, too, about thirteen or fourteen foot long, riding high like a duck. I shot head first off of the bank, like a frog, clothes and all on, and struck out for the canoe. I just expected there'd be somebody laying down in it, because people often done that to fool folks, and when a chap

[1] *palavering*: chatting idly.

had pulled a skiff out most to it they'd raise up and laugh at him. But it warn't so this time. It was a drift-canoe, sure enough, and I clumb in and paddled her ashore. Thinks I, the old man will be glad when he sees this—she's worth ten dollars. But when I got to shore pap wasn't in sight yet, and as I was running her into a little creek like a gully, all hung over with vines and willows, I struck another idea; I judged I'd hide her good, and then, stead of taking to the woods when I run off, I'd go down the river about fifty mile and camp in one place for good, and not have such a rough time tramping on foot.

It was pretty close to the shanty, and I thought I heard the old man coming, all the time; but I got her hid; and then I out and looked around a bunch of willows, and there was the old man down the path apiece just drawing a bead on a bird with his gun. So he hadn't seen anything.

When he got along, I was hard at it taking up a 'trot' line.[2] He abused me a little for being so slow, but I told him I fell in the river and that was what made me so long. I knowed he would see I was wet, and then he would be asking questions. We got five cat-fish off the lines and went home.

While we laid off, after breakfast, to sleep up, both of us being about wore out, I got to thinking that if I could fix up some way to keep pap and the widow from trying to follow me, it would be a certainer thing than trusting to luck to get far enough off before they missed me; you see, all kinds of things might happen. Well, I didn't see no way for a while, but by-and-by pap raised up a minute, to drink another barrel of water, and he says:

'Another time a man comes a-prowling round here, you roust me out, you hear? That man warn't here for no good. I'd a shot him. Next time, you roust me out, you hear?'

Then he dropped down and went to sleep again—but what he had been saying give me the very idea I wanted. I says to myself, I can fix it now so nobody won't think of following me.

---

[2] *'trot' line*: fishing line holding several baited hooks and suspended over a stream.

About twelve o'clock we turned out and went along up the bank. The river was coming up pretty fast, and lots of driftwood going by on the rise. By-and-by, along comes part of a log raft— nine logs fast together. We went out with the skiff and towed it ashore. Then we had dinner. Anybody but pap would a waited and seen the day through, so as to catch more stuff; but that warn't pap's style. Nine logs was enough for one time; he must shove right over to town and sell. So he locked me in and took the skiff and started off towing the raft about half-past three. I judged he wouldn't come back that night. I waited till I reckoned he had got a good start, then I out with my saw and went to work on that log again. Before he was 'tother side of the river I was out of the hole; him and his raft was just a speck on the water away off yonder.

I took the sack of corn meal and took it to where the canoe was hid, and shoved the vines and branches apart and put it in; then I done the same with the side of bacon; then the whisky jug; I took all the coffee and sugar there was, and all the ammunition; I took the wadding; I took the bucket and gourd, I took a dipper and a tin cup, and my old saw and two blankets, and the skillet and the coffee-pot. I took fish-lines and matches and other things—everything that was worth a cent. I cleaned out the place. I wanted an axe, but there wasn't any, only the one out at the wood pile, and I knowed why I was going to leave that. I fetched out the gun, and now I was done.

I had wore the ground a good deal, crawling out of the hole and dragging out so many things. So I fixed that as good as I could from the outside by scattering dust on the place, which covered up the smoothness and the sawdust. Then I fixed the piece of log back into its place, and put two rocks under it and one against it to hold it there,—for it was bent up at that place, and didn't quite touch ground. If you stood four or five foot away and didn't know it was sawed, you wouldn't ever notice it; and besides, this was the back of the cabin and it warn't likely anybody would go fooling around there.

It was all grass clear to the canoe; so I hadn't left a track. I followed around to see. I stood on the bank and looked out over the river. All safe. So I took the gun and went up a piece into the woods and was hunting around for some birds, when I see a wild pig; hogs soon went wild in them bottoms after they had got away from the prairie farms. I shot this fellow and took him into camp.

I took the axe and smashed in the door—I beat it and hacked it considerable, a-doing it. I fetched the pig in and took him back nearly to the table and hacked into his throat with the axe, and laid him down on the ground to bleed—I say ground, because it *was* ground—hard packed, and no boards. Well, next I took an old sack and put a lot of big rocks in it,—all I could drag—and I started it from the pig and dragged it to the door and through the woods down to the river and dumped it in, and down it sunk, out of sight. You could easy see that something had been dragged over the ground. I did wish Tom Sawyer was there, I knowed he would take an interest in this kind of business, and throw in the fancy touches. Nobody could spread himself like Tom Sawyer in such a thing as that.

Well, last I pulled out some of my hair, and bloodied the axe good, and stuck it on the back side, and slung the axe in the corner. Then I took up the pig and held him to my breast with my jacket (so he couldn't drip) till I got a good piece below the house and then dumped him into the river. Now I thought of something else. So I went and got the bag of meal and my old saw out of the canoe and fetched them to the house. I took the bag to where it used to stand, and ripped a hole in the bottom of it with the saw, for there warn't no knives and forks on the place—pap done everything with his clasp-knife, about the cooking. Then I carried the sack about a hundred yards across the grass and through the willows east of the house, to a shallow lake that was five mile wide and full of rushes—and ducks too, you might say, in the season. There was a slough or a creek leading out of it on the other side, that went miles away, I don't know where, but it didn't go to the river. The meal sifted out and made a little track all the way to the lake. I dropped pap's whetstone[3] there too, so as to look like it had been done by accident. Then I tied up the rip in the meal sack with a string, so it wouldn't leak no more, and took it and my saw to the canoe again.

It was about dark, now; so I dropped the canoe down the river under some willows that hung over the bank, and waited for the moon to rise. I made fast to a willow; then I took a bite to eat, and by-and-by laid down in the canoe to smoke a pipe and lay out a plan. I says to myself, they'll follow the track of that sackful of rocks to the shore and then drag the river for me. And they'll follow that meal track to the lake and go browsing down the creek that leads out of it to find the robbers that killed me and took the things. They won't ever hunt the river for anything but my dead carcass. They'll soon get tired of that, and won't bother no more about me. All right; I can stop anywhere I want to. Jackson's Island[4] is good enough for me; I know that island pretty well, and nobody ever comes there. And then I can paddle over to town, nights, and slink around and pick up things I want. Jackson's Island's the place.

I was pretty tired, and the first thing I knowed, I was asleep. When I woke up I didn't know where I was, for a minute. I set up and looked around, a little scared. Then I remembered. The river looked miles and miles across. The moon was so bright I could a counted the drift logs that went a slipping along, black and still, hundreds of yards out from shore. Everything was dead quiet, and it looked late, and *smelt* late. You know what I mean—I don't know the words to put it in.

I took a good gap and a stretch, and was just going to unhitch and start, when I heard a sound away over the water. I listened. Pretty soon I made it out. It was that dull kind of a regular sound that comes from oars working in rowlocks when it's a still night. I peeped out through the willow branches,

---

[3] *whetstone*: stone used for sharpening knives or other tools.

[4] *Jackson's Island*: In depicting this island, Twain was probably recalling Glasscock's Island, now eroded, downstream from Hannibal and near the Illinois shore. Several major scenes from *Tom Sawyer* also take place on Jackson's Island.

and there it was—a skiff, away across the water. I couldn't tell how many was in it. It kept a-coming, and when it was abreast of me I see there warn't but one man in it. Thinks I, maybe it's pap, though I warn't expecting him. He dropped below me, with the current, and by-and-by he come a-swinging up shore in the easy water, and he went by so close I could a reached out the gun and touched him. Well, it *was* pap, sure enough— and sober, too, by the way he laid to his oars.

I didn't lose no time. The next minute I was a-spinning down stream soft but quick in the shade of the bank. I made two mile and a half, and then struck out a quarter of a mile or more towards the middle of the river, because pretty soon I would be passing the ferry landing and people might see me and hail me. I got out amongst the drift-wood and then laid down in the bottom of the canoe and let her float. I laid there and had a good rest and a smoke out of my pipe, looking away into the sky, not a cloud in it. The sky looks ever so deep when you lay down on your back in the moonshine; I never knowed it before. And how far a body can hear on the water such nights! I heard people talking at the ferry landing. I heard what they said, too, every word of it. One man said it was getting towards the long days and the short nights, now. 'Tother one said *this* warn't one of the short ones, he reckoned—and then they laughed, and he said it over again and they laughed again; then they waked up another fellow and told him, and laughed, but he didn't laugh; he ripped out something brisk and said let him alone. The first fellow said he 'lowed to tell it to his old woman—she would think it was pretty good; but he said that warn't nothing to some things he had said in his time. I heard one man say it was nearly three o'clock, and he hoped daylight wouldn't wait more than about week longer. After that, the talk got further and further away, and I couldn't make out the words any more, but I could hear the mumble; and now and then a laugh, too, but it seemed a long ways off.

I was away below the ferry now. I rose up and there was Jackson's Island, about two mile and a half down stream, heavy-timbered and standing up out of the middle of the river, big and dark and solid, like a steamboat without any lights. There warn't any signs of the bar at the head—it was all under water, now.

It didn't take me long to get there. I shot past the head at a ripping rate, the current was so swift, and then I got into the dead water and landed on the side towards the Illinois shore. I run the canoe into a deep dent in the bank that I knowed about; I had to part the willow branches to get in; and when I made fast nobody could a seen the canoe from the outside.

I went up and set down on a log at the head of the island and looked out on to the big river and the black driftwood, and away over to the town, three mile away, where there was three or four lights twinkling. A monstrous big lumber raft was about a mile up stream, coming along down, with a lantern in the middle of it. I watched it come creeping down, and when it was most abreast of where I stood I heard a man say, 'Stern oars, there! heave her head to stabboard!' I heard that just as plain as if the man was by my side.

There was a little gray in the sky, now; so I stepped into the woods and laid down for a nap before breakfast.

CHAPTER 8

The sun was up so high when I waked, that I judged it was after eight o'clock. I laid there in the grass and the cool shade, thinking about things and feeling rested and ruther comfortable and satisfied. I could see the sun out at one or two holes, but mostly it was big trees all about, and gloomy in there amongst them. There was freckled places on the ground where the light sifted down through the leaves, and the freckled places swapped about a little, showing there was a little breeze up there. A couple of squirrels set on a limb and jabbered at me very friendly.

I was powerful lazy and comfortable—didn't want to get up and cook breakfast. Well, I was dozing off again, when I thinks I hears a deep sound of 'boom!' away up the river. I rouses up and rests on my elbow and listens; pretty soon I hears it again. I hopped up and went and looked out at a hole in the leaves, and I see a bunch of smoke laying on the water a long ways up—about abreast the ferry. And there was the ferryboat full of people, floating along down. I knowed what was the matter, now. 'Boom!' I see the white smoke squirt out of the ferryboat's side. You see, they was firing cannon over the water, trying to make my carcass come to the top.[1]

I was pretty hungry, but it warn't going to do for me to start a fire, because they might see the smoke. So I set there and watched the cannon-smoke and listened to the boom. The river was a mile wide, there, and it always looks pretty on a summer morning—so I was having a good enough time seeing them hunt for my remainders, if I only had a bite to eat. Well, then I happened to think how they always put quicksilver in loaves of bread and float them off because they always

[1] *they was firing cannon over the water* ... : A common belief in both England and the United States at the time was that gunfire would raise a dead body from the bottom of a lake or river.

go right to the drownded carcass and stop there.[2] So says I, I'll keep a lookout, and if any of them's floating around after me, I'll give them a show. I changed to the Illinois edge of the island to see what luck I could have, and I warn't disappointed. A big double loaf come along, and I most got it, with a long stick, but my foot slipped and she floated out further. Of course I was where the current set in the closest to the shore—I knowed enough for that. But by-and-by along comes another one, and this time I won. I took out the plug and shook out the little dab of quicksilver, and set my teeth in. It was 'baker's bread'—what the quality eat—none of your low-down corn-pone.

I got a good place amongst the leaves, and set there on a log, munching the bread and watching the ferry-boat, and very well satisfied. And then something struck me. I says, now I reckon the widow or the parson or somebody prayed that this bread would find me, and here it has gone and done it. So there ain't no doubt but there is something in that thing. That is, there's something in it when a body like the widow or the parson prays, but it don't work for me, and I reckon it don't work for only just the right kind.

I lit a pipe and had a good long smoke and went on watching. The ferry-boat was floating with the current, and I allowed[3] I'd have a chance to see who was aboard when she come along, because she would come in close, where the bread did. When she'd got pretty well along down towards me, I put out my pipe and went to where I fished out the bread, and laid down behind a log on the bank in a little open place. Where the log forked I could peep through.

By-and-by she come along, and she drifted in so close that they could a run out a plank and walked ashore. Most everybody was on the boat. Pap, and Judge Thatcher, and Bessie Thatcher, and Jo Harper, and Tom Sawyer, and his old Aunt

---

[2] *they always put quicksilver in loaves of bread . . .* : another widely held belief of the time. Quicksilver is mercury.
[3] *allowed*: reckoned or deduced.

Polly, and Sid and Mary, and plenty more. Everybody was talk-ing about the murder, but the captain broke in and says:

'Look sharp, now; the current sets in the closest here, and maybe he's washed ashore and got tangled amongst the brush at the water's edge. I hope so, anyway.'

I didn't hope so. They all crowded up and leaned over the rails, nearly in my face, and kept still, watching with all their might. I could see them first-rate, but they couldn't see me. Then the captain sung out:

'Stand away!' and the cannon let off such a blast right before me that it made me deef with the noise and pretty near blind with the smoke, and I judged I was gone. If they'd a had some bullets in, I reckon they'd a got the corpse they was after. Well, I see I warn't hurt, thanks to goodness. The boat floated on and went out of sight around the shoulder of the island. I could hear the booming, now and then, further and further off, and by-and-by after an hour, I didn't hear it no more. The island was three mile long. I judged they had got to the foot, and was giving it up. But they didn't yet a while. They turned around the foot of the island and started up the channel on the Missouri side, under steam, and booming once in a while as they went. I crossed over to that side and watched them. When they got abreast the head of the island they quit shoot-ing and dropped over to the Missouri shore and went home to the town.

I knowed I was all right now. Nobody else would come a-hunting after me. I got my traps out of the canoe and made me a nice camp in the thick woods. I made a kind of a tent out of my blankets to put things under so the rain couldn't get at them. I catched a cat-fish and haggled him open with my saw, and towards sundown I started my camp fire and had sup-per. Then I set out a line to catch some fish for breakfast.

When it was dark I set by my camp fire smoking, and feel-ing pretty satisfied; but by-and-by it got sort of lonesome, and so I went and set on the bank and listened to the currents washing along, and counted the stars and drift-logs and rafts that come down, and then went to bed; there ain't no better way to put in time when you are lonesome; you can't stay so, you soon get over it.

And so for three days and nights. No difference—just the same thing. But the next day I went exploring around down through the island. I was boss of it; it all belonged to me, so to say, and I wanted to know all about it; but mainly I wanted to put in the time.[4] I found plenty strawberries, ripe and prime; and green summer-grapes, and green razberries; and the green blackberries was just beginning to show. They would all come handy by-and-by, I judged.

Well, I went fooling along in the deep woods till I judged I warn't far from the foot of the island. I had my gun along, but I hadn't shot nothing; it was for protection; thought I would kill some game nigh[5] home. About this time I mighty near stepped on a good sized snake, and it went sliding off through the grass and flowers, and I after it, trying to get a shot at it. I clipped along, and all of a sudden I bounded right on to the ashes of a camp fire that was still smoking.

My heart jumped up amongst my lungs. I never waited for to look further, but uncocked my gun and went sneaking back on my tip-toes as fast as ever I could. Every now and then I stopped a second, amongst the thick leaves, and listened; but my breath come so hard I couldn't hear nothing else. I slunk along another piece further, then listened again; and so on, and so on; if I see a stump, I took it for a man; if I trod on a stick and broke it, it made me feel like a person had cut one of my breaths in two and I only got half, and the short half, too.

When I got to camp I warn't feeling very brash, there warn't much sand in my craw;[6] but I says, this ain't no time to be fooling around. So I got all my traps into my canoe again so as

---

[4] *to put in the time*: to pass the time.

[5] *nigh*: near.

[6] *sand in my craw*: i.e., courage in my gut. A bird uses sand particles to help it digest hard seeds. A "craw" is a stomach. Hence, to have "sand in one's craw" means to face something hard or difficult. Later Huck shortens the phrase to just the word "sand".

to have them out of sight, and I put out the fire and scattered the ashes around to look like an old last year's camp, and then clumb a tree.

I reckon I was up in the tree two hours; but I didn't see nothing, I didn't hear nothing—I only *thought* I heard and seen as much as a thousand things. Well, I couldn't stay up there forever; so at last I got down, but I kept in the thick woods and on the lookout all the time. All I could get to eat was berries and what was left over from breakfast.

By the time it was night I was pretty hungry. So when it was good and dark, I slid out from shore before moonrise and paddled over to the Illinois bank—about a quarter of a mile. I went out in the woods and cooked a supper, and I had about made up my mind I would stay there all night, when I hear a *plunkety-plunk, plunkety-plunk*, and says to myself, horses coming; and next I hear people's voices. I got everything into the canoe as quick as I could, and then went creeping through the woods to see what I could find out. I hadn't got far when I hear a man say:

'We better camp here, if we can find a good place; the horses is about beat out. Let's look around.'

I didn't wait, but shoved out and paddled away easy. I tied up in the old place, and reckoned I would sleep in the canoe.

I didn't sleep much. I couldn't, somehow, for thinking. And every time I waked up I thought somebody had me by the neck. So the sleep didn't do me no good. By-and-by I says to myself, I can't live this way; I'm agoing to find out who it is that's here on the island with me; I'll find it out or bust. Well, I felt better, right off.

So I took my paddle and slid out from shore just a step or two, and then let the canoe drop along down amongst the shadows. The moon was shining, and outside of the shadows it made it most as light as day. I poked along well onto a hour, everything still as rocks and sound asleep. Well by this time I was most down to the foot of the island. A little ripply, cool breeze begun to blow, and that was as good as saying the night was about done. I give her a turn with the paddle and brung her nose to shore; then I got my gun and slipped out and into the edge of the woods. I set down there on a log and looked out through the leaves. I see the moon go off watch and the darkness begin to blanket the river. But in a little while I see a pale streak over the tree-tops, and knowed the day was coming. So I took my gun and slipped off towards where I had run across that camp fire, stopping every minute or two to listen. But I hadn't no luck, somehow; I couldn't seem to find the place. But by-and-by, sure enough, I catched a glimpse of fire, away through the trees. I went for it, cautious and slow. By-and-by I was close enough to have a look, and there laid a man on the ground. It most give me the fan-tods.[7] He had a blanket around his head, and his head was nearly in the fire. I set there behind a clump of bushes, in about six foot of him, and kept my eyes on him steady. It was getting gray daylight, now. Pretty soon he gapped, and stretched himself, and hove off the blanket, and it was Miss Watson's Jim! I bet I was glad to see him. I says:

'Hello, Jim!' and skipped out.

He bounced up and stared at me wild. Then he drops down on his knees, and puts his hands together and says:

'Doan' hurt me—don't! I hain't ever done no harm to a ghos'. I awluz liked dead people, en done all I could for 'em. You go en git in de river agin, whah you b'longs, en doan' do nuffn to Ole Jim, 'at 'uz awluz yo' fren'.'

Well, I warn't long making him understand I warn't dead. I was ever so glad to see Jim. I warn't lonesome, now. I told him I warn't afraid of *him* telling the people where I was. I talked along, but he only set there and looked at me; never said nothing. Then I says:

'It's good daylight. Le's get breakfast. Make up your camp fire good.'

'What's de use er making' up de camp fire to cook strawbries en sich truck? But you got a gun, hain't you? Den we kin git sumfn better den strawbries.'

---

[7] *fan-tods*: willies or creeps.

'Strawberries and such truck,' I says. 'Is that what you live on?'

'I couldn' git nuffn else,' he says.

'Why, how long you been on the island, Jim?'

'I come heah de night arter you's killed.'

'What, all that time?'

'Yes-indeedy.'

'And ain't you had nothing but that kind of rubbage to eat?'

'No, sah—nuffin else.'

'Well, you must be most starved, ain't you?'

'I reck'n I could eat a hoss. I think I could. How long you ben on de island'?'

'Since the night I got killed.'

'No! W'y, what has you lived on? But you got a gun. Oh, yes, you got a gun. Dat's good. Now you kill sumfn en I'll make up de fire.'

So we went over to where the canoe was, and while he built a fire in a grassy open place amongst the trees, I fetched meal and bacon and coffee, and coffee-pot and frying-pan, and sugar and tin cups, and the nigger was set back considerable, because he reckoned it was all done with witchcraft. I catched a good big cat-fish, too, and Jim cleaned him with his knife, and fried him.

When breakfast was ready, we lolled on the grass and eat it smoking hot. Jim laid it in with all his might, for he was most about starved. Then when we had got pretty well stuffed, we laid off and lazied.

By-and-by Jim says:

'But looky here, Huck, who wuz it dat 'uz killed in dat shanty, ef it warn't you?'

Then I told him the whole thing, and he said it was smart. He said Tom Sawyer couldn't get up no better plan than what I had. Then I says:

'How do you come to be here, Jim, and how'd you get here?' He looked pretty uneasy, and didn't say nothing for a minute. Then he says:

'Maybe I better not tell.'

'Why, Jim?'

'Well, dey's reasons. But you wouldn' tell on me ef I 'uz to tell you, would you, Huck?'

'Blamed if I would, Jim.'

'Well, I b'lieve you, Huck. I—I *run off.*'

'Jim!'

'But mind, you said you wouldn't tell—you know you said you wouldn't tell, Huck.'

'Well, I did. I said I wouldn't, and I'll stick to it. Honest *injun* I will. People would call me a low down Ablitionist[8] and despise me for keeping mum—but that don't make no difference. I ain't agoing to tell, and I ain't agoing back there anyways. So now, le's know all about it.'

'Well, you see, it 'uz dis way. Ole Missus—dat's Miss Watson—she pecks on me all de time, en treats me pooty rough, but she awluz said she wouldn' sell me down to Orleans.[9] But I noticed dey wuz a nigger trader roun' de place considable, lately, en I begin to git oneasy. Well, one night I creeps to de do', pooty late, en de do' warn't quite shet, en I hear ole missus tell de widder she gwyne to sell me down to Orleans, but she didn' want to, but she could git eight hund'd dollars for me, en it 'uz sich a big stack o' money she couldn' resis'. De widder she try to git her to say she wouldn' do it, but I never waited to hear de res'. I lit out mighty quick, I tell you.

'I tuck out en shin down de hill en 'spec to steal a skift 'long de sho' som'ers 'bove de town, but dey wuz people a-stirrin' yit, so I hid in de ole tumble-down cooper shop[10] on de bank to wait for everybody to go 'way. Well, I wuz dah all night.

---

[8] *Ablitionist*: abolitionist, or a person who works to abolish slavery. The abolitionist movement in the United States grew rapidly during the 1830s and 1840s.

[9] *sell me down to Orleans*: Being "sold down the river" to New Orleans, Louisiana, into the Deep South, was a fearful prospect for a slave because it often meant hard labor on a sugar or cotton plantation, separation from family, and little to no chance of possible escape.

[10] *cooper shop*: barrel-making shop.

De wuz somebody roun' all de time. 'Long 'bout six in de mawnin', skifts begin to go by, en 'bout eight er nine every skift
dat went 'long wuz talkin' 'bout how yo' pap come over to de
town en say you's killed. Dese las' skifts wuz full o' ladies en
genlmen agoin' over for to see de place. Sometimes dey'd pull
up at de sho' en take a res' b'fo' dey started acrost, so by de
talk I got to know all 'bout de killin'. I 'uz powerful sorry you's
killed, Huck, but I ain't no mo', now.

'I laid dah under de shavins all day. I 'uz hungry, but I warn't
afeard; bekase I knowed ole missus en de widder wuz goin' to
start to de camp-meetn'[11] right arter breakfas' en be gone all
day, en dey knows I goes off wid de cattle 'bout daylight, so
dey wouldn' 'spec to see me roun' de place, en so dey wouldn'
miss me tell arter dark in de evenin'. De yuther servants wouldn'
miss me, kase dey'd shin out en take holiday, soon as de ole
folks 'uz out'n de way.

'Well, when it come dark I tuck out up de river road, en
went 'bout two mile er more to whah dey warn't no houses.
I'd made up my mine 'bout what I's agwyne to do. You see ef
I kep' on tryin' to git away afoot, de dogs 'ud track me; ef I
stole a skift to cross over, dey'd miss dat skift, you see, en dey'd
know 'bout whah I'd lan' on de yuther side en whah to pick
up my track. So I says, a raff is what I's arter; it doan' *make* no
track.

'I see a light a-comin' roun' de p'int, bymeby, so I wade' in
en shove' a log ahead o' me, en swum more'n half-way acrost
de river, en got in 'mongst de drift-wood, en kep' my head
down low, en kinder swum agin de current tell de raff come
along. Den I swum to de stern uv it, en tuck aholt. It clouded
up on 'uz pooty dark for a little while. So I clumb up en laid
down on de planks. De men 'uz all 'way yonder in de middle,
whah de lantern wuz. De river wuz arisin' en dey wuz a good

---

[11] *camp-meetn'*: Outdoor religious revival services were frequent on the American frontier, especially in the South among Methodist, Baptist, and Presbyterian denominations. Families often came from long distances and camped out in
tents or wagons in order to worship together, sing hymns, hear preaching, and
socialize.

current; so I reck'n'd 'at by fo' in de mawnin' I'd be twenty-five mile down de river, en den I'd slip in, jis' b'fo' daylight, en swim asho' en take to de woods on de Illinoi side.[12]

'But I didn' have no luck. When we 'uz mos' down to de head er de islan', a man begin to come aft wid de lantern. I see it warn't no use fer to wait, so I slid overboard, en struck out fer de islan'. Well, I had a notion I could lan' mos' any-whers, but I couldn't—bank too bluff. I 'uz mos' to de foot er de islan' b'fo' I foun' a good place. I went into de woods en jedged I wouldn' fool wid raffs no mo', long as dey move de lantern roun' so. I had my pipe en a plug er dog-leg,[13] en some matches in my cap, en dey warn't wet, so I 'uz all right.'

'And so you ain't had no meat nor bread to eat all this time? Why didn't you get mud-turkles?'[14]

'How you gwyne to git'm? You can't slip up on um en grab um; en how's a body gwyne to hit um wid a rock? How could a body do it in de night? en I warn't gwyne to show myself on de bank in de daytime.'

'Well, that's so. You've had to keep in the woods all the time, of course. Did you hear 'em shooting the cannon?'

'Oh, yes. I knowed dey was arter you. I see um go by heah; watched um thoo de bushes.'

Some young birds come along, flying a yard or two at a time and lighting. Jim said it was a sign it was going to rain. He said it was a sign when young chickens flew that way, and so he reckoned it was the same way when young birds done it. I

---

[12] *en swim asho' . . . on de Illinoi side*: Since Illinois was not a slaveholding state at the time, readers often question why Jim didn't merely swim or row there from Jackson's Island, which he could have easily done. Jim would have been aware that, while a nominally free state, Illinois authorities arrested blacks who had no freedom papers, and substantial rewards were offered to citizens for the capture and return of runaway slaves under the Fugitive Slave Act of 1793. Thus, southern Illinois was a highly dangerous place for a runaway slave. It is quite plausible, therefore, that the safest route to freedom was what Jim and Huck attempt to do as the novel continues: head down the Mississippi River to Cairo, Illinois, then go northeast up the Ohio River past Illinois and Indiana and to the free state of Ohio.

[13] *dog-leg*: cheap tobacco.

[14] *mud-turkles*: mud turtles.

was going to catch some of them, but Jim wouldn't let me. He said it was death. He said his father laid mighty sick once, and some of them catched a bird, and his old granny said his father would die, and he did.

And Jim said you mustn't count the things you are going to cook for dinner, because that would bring bad luck. The same if you shook the table-cloth after sundown. And he said if a man owned a bee-hive, and that man died, the bees must be told about it before sun-up next morning, or else the bees would all weaken down and quit work and die. Jim said bees wouldn't sting idiots; but I didn't believe that, because I had tried them lots of times myself, and they wouldn't sting me.

I had heard about some of these things before, but not all of them. Jim knowed all kinds of signs. He said he knowed most everything. I said it looked to me like all the signs was about bad luck, and so I asked him if there warn't any good-luck signs. He says:

'Mighty few—an' *dey* ain' no use to a body. What you want to know when good luck's a-comin' for? want to keep it off?' And he said: 'Ef you's got hairy arms en a hairy breas', it's a sign dat you's agwyne to be rich. Well, dey's some use in a sign like dat, 'kase it's so fur ahead. You see, maybe you's got to be po' a long time fust, en so you might git discourage' en kill yo'sef 'f you didn' know by de sign dat you gwyne to be rich bymeby.'

'Have you got hairy arms and a hairy breast, Jim?'

'What's de use to ax dat question? don' you see I has?'

'Well, are you rich?'

'No, but I ben rich wunst, and gwyne to be rich agin. Wunst I had foteen dollars, but I tuck to specalat'n', en got busted out.'

'What did you speculate in, Jim?'

'Well, fust I tackled stock.'

'What kind of stock?'

'Why, live stock. Cattle, you know. I put ten dollars in a cow. But I ain' gwyne to resk no mo' money in stock. De cow up 'n' died on my han's.'

'So you lost the ten dollars.'

'No, I didn' lose it all. I on'y los' 'bout nine of it. I sole de hide en taller[15] for a dollar en ten cents.'

'You had five dollars and ten cents left. Did you speculate any more?'

'Yes. You know dat one-laigged nigger dat b'longs to old Misto Bradish? well, he sot up a bank, en say anybody dat put in a dollar would git fo' dollars mo' at de en' er de year. Well, all de niggers went in, but dey didn' have much. I wuz de on'y one dat had much. So I stuck out for mo' dan fo' dollars, en I said 'f I didn't git it I'd start a bank myself. Well o' course dat nigger want' to keep me out er de business, bekase he say dey warn't business 'nough for two banks, so he say I could put in my five dollars en he pay me thirty-five at de en' er de year.

'So I done it. Den I reck'n'd I'd inves' de thirty-five dollars right off en keep things a-movin'. Dey wuz a nigger name' Bob, dat had ketched a wood-flat,[16] en his marster didn' know it; en I bought it off'n him en told him to take de thirty-five dollars when de en' er de year come; but somebody stole de wood-flat dat night, en nex' day de one-laigged nigger say de bank is busted. So dey didn' none uv us git no money.'

'What did you do with the ten cents, Jim?'

'Well, I 'uz gwyne to spen' it, but I had a dream, en de dream tole me to give it to a nigger name' Balum—Balum's Ass[17] dey call him for short, he's one er dem chuckle-heads, you know. But he's lucky, dey say, en I see I warn't lucky. De dream say let Balum inves' de ten cents en he'd make a raise for me. Well, Balum he tuck de money, en when he wuz in church he hear de preacher say dat whoever give to de po' len' to de Lord, en boun' to git his money back a hund'd times. So Balum he tuck en give de ten cents to de po,' en laid low to see what wuz gwyne to come of it.'

---

[15] *taller*: tallow, or animal fat.

[16] *wood-flat*: flat-bottomed boat used to haul wood.

[17] *Balum's Ass*: In Numbers 22:21–35, the prophet Balaam's ass sees the Lord's angel before Balaam himself does, so the ass stops and refuses to move. She later reproves Balaam for beating her for her supposed stubbornness.

'Well, what did come of it, Jim?'

'Nuffn' never come of it. I couldn' manage to k'leck dat money no way; en Balum he couldn'. I ain' gwyne to len' no mo' money 'dout I see de security. Boun' to git yo' money back a hund'd times, de preacher says! Ef I could git de ten *cents* back, I'd call it squah, en be glad er de chanst.'

'Well, it's all right, anyway, Jim, long as you're going to be rich again some time or other.'

'Yes—en I's rich now, come to look at it. I owns mysef, en I's wuth eight hund'd dollars. I wisht I had de money, I wouldn' want no mo'.'

CHAPTER 9

I wanted to go and look at a place right about the middle of the island, that I'd found when I was exploring; so we started, and soon got to it, because the island was only three miles long and a quarter of a mile wide.

This place was a tolerable long steep hill or ridge, about forty foot high. We had a rough time getting to the top, the sides was so steep and the bushes so thick. We tramped and clumb around all over it, and by-and-by found a good big cavern in the rock, most up to the top on the side towards Illinois. The cavern was as big as two or three rooms bunched together, and Jim could stand up straight in it. It was cool in there. Jim was for putting our traps in there, right away, but I said we didn't want to be climbing up and down there all the time.

Jim said if we had the canoe hid in a good place, and had all the traps in the cavern, we could rush there if anybody was to come to the island, and they would never find us without dogs. And besides, he said them little birds had said it was going to rain, and did I want the things to get wet?

So we went back and got the canoe and paddled up abreast the cavern, and lugged all the traps up there. Then we hunted up a place close by to hide the canoe in, amongst the thick willows. We took some fish off of the lines and set them again, and begun to get ready for dinner.

The door of the cavern was big enough to roll a hogshead in, and on one side of the door the floor stuck out a little bit and was flat and a good place to build a fire on. So we built it there and cooked dinner.

We spread the blankets inside for a carpet, and eat our dinner in there. We put all the other things handy at the back of the cavern. Pretty soon it darkened up and begun to thunder and lighten; so the birds was right about it. Directly it begun

to rain, and it rained like all fury, too, and I never see the
wind blow so. It was one of these regular summer storms. It
would get so dark that it looked all blue-black outside, and
lovely; and the rain would thrash along by so thick that the
trees off a little ways looked dim and spider-webby; and here
would come a blast of wind that would bend the trees down
and turn up the pale underside of the leaves; and then a perfect ripper of a gust would follow along and set the branches
to tossing their arms as if they was just wild; and next, when
it was just about the bluest and blackest—*fst!* it was as bright
as glory and you'd have a little glimpse of tree-tops a-plunging
about, away off yonder in the storm, hundreds of yards further
than you could see before; dark as sin again in a second, and
now you'd hear the thunder let go with an awful crash and
then go rumbling, grumbling, tumbling down the sky towards
the under side of the world, like rolling empty barrels down
stairs, where it's long stairs and they bounce a good deal, you
know.

'Jim, this is nice,' I says. 'I wouldn't want to be nowhere
else but here. Pass me along another hunk of fish and some
hot cornbread'.

'Well, you wouldn't a ben here, 'f it hadn't a ben for Jim.
You'd a ben down dah in de woods widout any dinner, en git-
tin' mos' drownded, too, dat you would, honey. Chickens knows
when its gwyne to rain, en so do de birds, chile.'

The river went on raising and raising for ten or twelve days,
till at last it was over the banks. The water was three or four
foot deep on the island in the low places and on the Illinois
bottom. On that side it was a good many miles wide; but on
the Missouri side it was the same old distance across—a half a
mile—because the Missouri shore was just a wall of high bluffs.

Daytimes we paddled all over the island in the canoe. It
was mighty cool and shady in the deep woods even if the sun
was blazing outside. We went winding in and out amongst the
trees; and sometimes the vines hung so thick we had to back
away and go some other way. Well, on every old broken-down
tree, you could see rabbits, and snakes, and such things; and

when the island had been overflowed a day or two, they got so tame, on account of being hungry, that you could paddle right up and put your hand on them if you wanted to; but not the snakes and turtles—they would slide off in the water. The ridge our cavern was in, was full of them. We could a had pets enough if we'd wanted them.

One night we catched a little section of a lumber raft— nice pine planks. It was twelve foot wide and about fifteen or sixteen foot long, and the top stood above water six or seven inches, a solid level floor. We could see saw-logs[1] go by in the daylight, sometimes, but we let them go; we didn't show our- selves in daylight.

Another night, when we was up at the head of the island, just before daylight, here comes a frame house down, on the west side. She was a two-story, and tilted over, considerable. We paddled out and got aboard—clumb in at an up-stairs win- dow. But it was too dark to see yet, so we made the canoe fast and set in her to wait for daylight.

The light begun to come before we got to the foot of the island. Then we looked in at the window. We could make out a bed, and a table, and two old chairs, and lots of things around about on the floor; and there was clothes hanging against the wall. There was something laying on the floor in the far cor- ner that looked like a man. So Jim says:

'Hello, you!'

But it didn't budge. So I hollered again, and then Jim says:

'De man ain't asleep—he's dead. You hold still—I'll go en see.'

He went and bent down and looked, and says:

'It's a dead man. Yes, indeedy; naked, too. He's ben shot in de back. I reck'n he's ben dead two er three days. Come in, Huck, but doan' look at his face—it's too gashly.'

I didn't look at him at all. Jim throwed some old rags over him, but he needn't done it; I didn't want to see him. There was heaps of old greasy cards scattered around over the floor,

---

[1] *saw-logs*: logs suitable for sawing into lumber.

and old whisky bottles, and a couple of masks made out of black cloth; and all over the walls was the ignorantest kind of words and pictures, made with charcoal. There was two old dirty calico dresses, and a sun-bonnet, and some women's underclothes, hanging against the wall, and some men's clothing, too. We put the lot into the canoe; it might come good. There was a boy's old speckled straw hat on the floor; I took that too. And there was a bottle that had had milk in it; and it had a rag stopper for a baby to suck. We would a took the bottle, but it was broke. There was a seedy old chest, and an old hair trunk[2] with the hinges broke. They stood open, but there warn't nothing left in them that was any account. The way things was scattered about, we reckoned the people left in a hurry and warn't fixed so as to carry off most of their stuff.

We got an old tin lantern, and a butcher knife without any handle, and a bran-new Barlow knife[3] worth two bits[4] in any store, and a lot of tallow candles, and a tin candlestick, and a gourd, and a tin cup, and a ratty old bed-quilt off the bed, and a reticule[5] with needles and pins and beeswax and buttons and thread and all such truck in it, and a hatchet and some nails, and a fish-line as thick as my little finger, with some monstrous hooks on it, and a roll of buckskin, and a leather dog-collar, and a horse-shoe, and some vials of medicine that didn't have no label on them; and just as we was leaving I found a tolerable good curry-comb, and Jim he found a ratty old fiddle-bow, and a wooden leg. The straps was broke off of it, but barring that, it was a good enough leg, though it was too long for me and not long enough for Jim, and we couldn't find the other one, though we hunted all around.

And so, take it all around, we made a good haul. When we was ready to shove off, we was a quarter of a mile below the

---

[2] *hair trunk*: typical nineteenth-century trunk with a covering of animal hair on rawhide.
[3] *Barlow knife*: type of single-bladed jack knife, named for its inventor.
[4] *two bits*: a quarter dollar, or twenty-five cents.
[5] *reticule*: woman's drawstring bag.

island, and it was pretty broad day; so I made Jim lay down in the canoe and cover up with the quilt, because if he set up, people could tell he was a nigger a good ways off. I paddled over to the Illinois shore, and drifted down most a half a mile doing it. I crept up the dead water under the bank, and hadn't no accidents and didn't see nobody. We got home all safe.

CHAPTER 10

After breakfast I wanted to talk about the dead man and guess out how he come to be killed, but Jim didn't want to. He said it would fetch bad luck; and besides, he said, he might come and ha'nt us; he said a man that warn't buried was more likely to go a-ha'nting around than one that was planted[1] and comfortable. That sounded pretty reasonable, so I didn't say no more; but I couldn't keep from studying over it and wishing I knowed who shot the man, and what they done it for.

We rummaged the clothes we'd got, and found eight dollars in silver sewed up in the lining of an old blanket overcoat. Jim said he reckoned the people in that house stole the coat, because if they'd a knowed the money was there they wouldn't a left it. I said I reckoned they killed him, too; but Jim didn't want to talk about that. I says:

'Now you think it's bad luck; but what did you say when I fetched in the snake-skin that I found on the top of the ridge day before yesterday? You said it was the worst bad luck in the world to touch a snake-skin with my hands. Well, here's your bad luck! We've raked in all this truck and eight dollars besides. I wish we could have some bad luck like this every day, Jim.'

'Never you mind, honey, never you mind. Don't you git too peart.[2] It's a-comin'. Mind I tell you, it's a-comin'.'

It did come, too. It was a Tuesday that we had that talk. Well, after dinner Friday, we was laying around in the grass at the upper end of the ridge, and got out of tobacco. I went to the cavern to get some, and found a rattlesnake in there. I killed him, and curled him up on the foot of Jim's blanket, ever so natural, thinking there'd be some fun when Jim found him there. Well, by night I forgot all about the snake, and

[1] *planted*: i.e., buried.
[2] *Don't you git too peart*: don't get too "pert", i.e., self-assured or cocky.

when Jim flung himself down on the blanket while I struck a light, the snake's mate was there, and bit him.

He jumped up yelling, and the first thing the light showed was the varmint curled up and ready for another spring. I laid him out in a second with a stick, and Jim grabbed pap's whisky jug and begun to pour it down.[3]

He was barefooted, and the snake bit him right on the heel. That all comes of my being such a fool as to not remember that wherever you leave a dead snake its mate always comes there and curls around it. Jim told me to chop off the snake's head and throw it away, and then skin the body and roast a piece of it. I done it, and he eat it and said it would help cure him. He made me take off the rattles and tie them around his wrist, too. He said that that would help. Then I slid out quiet and throwed the snakes clear away among the bushes; for I warn't going to let Jim find out it was all my fault, not if I could help it.

Jim sucked and sucked at the jug, and now and then he got out of his head and pitched around and yelled; but every time he come to himself he went to sucking at the jug again. His foot swelled up pretty big, and so did his leg; but by-and-by the drunk begun to come, and so I judged he was all right; but I'd druther been bit with a snake than pap's whisky.

Jim was laid up for four days and nights. Then the swelling was all gone and he was around again. I made up my mind I wouldn't ever take aholt of a snake-skin again with my hands, now that I see what had come of it. Jim said he reckoned I would believe him next time. And he said that handling a snake-skin was such awful bad luck that maybe we hadn't got to the end of it yet. He said he druther see the new moon over his left shoulder as much as a thousand times than take up a snake-skin in his hand. Well, I was getting to feel that way myself, though I've always reckoned that looking at the

---

[3] *Jim grabbed pap's whiskey jug . . .* : The conventional cure for snakebite at the time was all the whiskey one could drink, presumably to "flush" the poison out of the system.

new moon over your left shoulder is one of the carelessest and foolishest things a body can do. Old Hank Bunker done it once, and bragged about it; and in less than two years he got drunk and fell off of the shot tower and spread himself out so that he was just a kind of a layer, as you may say; and they slid him edgeways between two barn doors for a coffin, and buried him so, so they say, but I didn't see it. Pap told me. But anyway, it all come of looking at the moon that way, like a fool.

Well, the days went along, and the river went down between its banks again; and about the first thing we done was to bait one of the big hooks with a skinned rabbit and set it and catch a cat-fish that was as big as a man, being six foot two inches long, and weighed over two hundred pounds. We couldn't handle him, of course; he would a flung us into Illinois. We just set there and watched him rip and tear around till he drownded. We found a brass button in his stomach, and a round ball, and lots of rubbage. We split the ball open with the hatchet, and there was a spool in it. Jim said he'd had it there a long time, to coat it over so and make a ball of it. It was as big a fish as was ever catched in the Mississippi, I reckon. Jim said he hadn't ever seen a bigger one. He would a been worth a good deal over at the village. They peddle out such a fish as that by the pound in the market house there; everybody buys some of him; his meat's as white as snow and makes a good fry.

Next morning I said it was getting slow and dull, and I wanted to get a stirring up, some way. I said I reckoned I would slip over the river and find out what was going on. Jim liked that notion; but he said I must go in the dark and look sharp. Then he studied it over and said, couldn't I put on some of them old things and dress up like a girl? That was a good notion, too. So we shortened up one of the calico gowns and I turned up my trowser-legs to my knees and got into it. Jim hitched it behind with the hooks, and it was a fair fit. I put on the sun-bonnet and tied in under my chin, and then for a body to look in and see my face was like looking down a joint of stove-pipe. Jim said nobody would know me, even in the daytime, hardly. I practiced around all day to get the hang of things, and by-and-by I could do pretty well in them, only Jim said I didn't walk like a girl; and he said I must quit pulling up my gown to get at my britches pocket. I took notice, and done better.

I started up the Illinois shore in the canoe just after dark.

I started across to the town from a little below the ferry landing, and the drift of the current fetched me in at the bottom of the town. I tied up and started along the bank. There was a light burning in a little shanty that hadn't been lived in for a long time, and I wondered who had took up quarters there. I slipped up and peeped in at the window. There was a woman about forty year old in there, knitting by a candle that was on a pine table. I didn't know her face; she was a stranger, for you couldn't start a face[4] in that town that I didn't know. Now this was lucky, because I was weakening; I was getting afraid I had come; people might know my voice and find me out. But if this woman had been in such a little town two days she could tell me all I wanted to know; so I knocked at the door, and made up my mind I wouldn't forget I was a girl.

[4] *start a face*: raise a face.

CHAPTER 11

'Come in,' says the woman, and I did. She says:

'Take a cheer.'

I done it. She looked me all over with her little shiny eyes, and says:

'What might your name be?'

'Sarah Williams.'

'Where 'bouts do you live? In this neighborhood?'

'No'm. In Hookerville,[1] seven mile below. I've walked all the way and I'm all tired out.'

'Hungry, too, I reckon. I'll find you something.'

'No'm, I ain't hungry. I was so hungry I had to stop two mile below here at a farm; so I ain't hungry no more. It's what makes me so late. My mother's down sick, and out of money and everything, and I come to tell my uncle Abner Moore. He lives at the upper end of the town, she says. I hain't ever been here before. Do you know him?'

'No; but I don't know everybody yet. I haven't lived here quite two weeks. It's a considerable ways to the upper end of the town. You better stay here all night. Take off your bonnet.'

'No,' I says, 'I'll rest a while, I reckon, and go on. I ain't afeared of the dark.'

She said she wouldn't let me go by myself, but her husband would be in by-and-by, maybe in a hour and a half, and she'd send him along with me. Then she got to talking about her husband, and about her relations up the river, and her relations down the river, and about how much better off they used to was, and how they didn't know but they'd made a mistake coming to our town, instead of letting well alone—and so on and so on, till I was afeared *I* had made a mistake coming to

---

[1] *Hookerville*: Elsewhere in his writings Twain identified "Hookerville" as Saverton, Missouri, about six miles south of Hannibal.

her to find out what was going on in the town; but by-and-by she dropped onto pap and the murder, and then I was pretty willing to let her clatter right along. She told about me and Tom Sawyer finding the six thousand dollars (only she got it ten) and all about pap and what a hard lot he was, and what a hard lot I was, and at last she got down to where I was murdered. I says:

'Who done it? We've heard considerable about these goings on, down in Hookerville, but we don't know who 'twas that killed Huck Finn.'

'Well, I reckon there's a right smart chance of people *here* that'd like to know who killed him. Some thinks old Finn done it himself.'

'No—is that so?'

'Most everybody thought it at first. He'll never know how nigh he come to getting lynched. But before night they changed around and judged it was done by a runaway nigger named Jim.'

'Why *he*—'

I stopped. I reckoned I better keep still. She run on, and never noticed I had put in at all.

'The nigger run off the very night Huck Finn was killed. So there's a reward out for him—three hundred dollars. And there's a reward out for old Finn too—two hundred dollars. You see, he come to town the morning after the murder, and told about it, and was out with 'em on the ferry-boat hunt, and right away after he up and left. Before night they wanted to lynch him, but he was gone, you see. Well, next day they found out the nigger was gone; they found out he hadn't ben seen since ten o'clock the night the murder was done. So then they put it on him, you see, and while they was full of it, next day back comes old Finn and went boo-hooing to Judge Thatcher to get money to hunt for the nigger all over Illinois with. The judge give him some, and that evening he got drunk and was around till after midnight with a couple of mighty hard looking strangers, and then went off with them. Well, he hain't come back sence, and they ain't looking for him back till this thing blows over a little, for people thinks now that he killed his boy and fixed things so folks would think robbers done it, and then he'd get Huck's money without having to bother a long time with a lawsuit. People do say he warn't any too good to do it. Oh, he's sly, I reckon. If he don't come back for a year, he'll be all right. You can't prove anything on him, you know; everything will be quieted down then, and he'll walk into Huck's money as easy as nothing.'

'Yes, I reckon so, 'm. I don't see nothing in the way of it. Has everybody quit thinking the nigger done it?'

'Oh, no, not everybody. A good many thinks he done it. But they'll get the nigger pretty soon, now, and maybe they can scare it out of him.'

'Why, are they after him yet?'

'Well, you're innocent, ain't you! Does three hundred dollars lay round every day for people to pick up? Some folks thinks the nigger ain't far from here. I'm one of them—but I hain't talked it around. A few days ago I was talking with an old couple that lives next door in the log shanty, and they happened to say hardly anybody ever goes to that island over yonder that they call Jackson's Island. Don't anybody live there? says I. No, nobody, says they. I didn't say any more, but I done some thinking. I was pretty near certain I'd seen smoke over there, about the head of the island, a day or two before that, so I says to myself, like as not that nigger's hiding over there; anyway, says I, it's worth the trouble to get the place a hunt. I hain't seen any smoke sence, so I reckon maybe he's gone, if it was him: but husband's going over to see—him and another man. He was gone up the river; but he got back today and I told him as soon as he got here two hours ago.'

I had got so uneasy I couldn't set still. I had to do something with my hands; so I took up a needle off of the table and went to threading it. My hands shook, and I was making a bad job of it. When the woman stopped talking, I looked up, and she was looking at me pretty curious, and smiling a little. I put down the needle and thread and let on to be interested—and I was, too—and says:

'Three hundred dollars is a power of money. I wish my mother could get it. Is your husband going over there tonight?'

'Oh, yes. He went up town with the man I was telling you of, to get a boat and see if they could borrow another gun. They'll go over after midnight.'

'Couldn't they see better if they was to wait till daytime?'

'Yes. And couldn't the nigger see better, too? After midnight he'll likely be asleep, and they can slip around through the woods and hunt up his camp fire all the better for the dark, if he's got one.'

'I didn't think of that.'

The woman kept looking at me pretty curious, and I didn't feel a bit comfortable. Pretty soon she says:

'What did you say your name was, honey?'

'M—Mary Williams.'

Somehow it didn't seem to me that I said it was Mary before, so I didn't look up; seemed to me I said it was Sarah; so I felt sort of cornered, and was afeared maybe I was looking it, too. I wished the woman would say something more; the longer she set still, the uneasier I was. But now she says:

'Honey, I thought you said it was Sarah when you first come in?'

'Oh, yes'm, I did. Sarah Mary Williams. Sarah's my first name. Some calls me Sarah, some calls me Mary.'

'Oh, that's the way of it?'

'Yes'm.'

I was feeling better, then, but I wished I was out of there, anyway. I couldn't look up yet.

Well, the woman fell to talking about how hard times was, and how poor they had to live, and how the rats was as free as if they owned the place, and so forth, and so on, and then I got easy again. She was right about the rats. You'd see one stick his nose out of a hole in the corner every little while. She said she had to have things handy to throw at them when she was alone, or they wouldn't give her no peace. She showed me a bar of lead, twisted up into a knot, and said she was a good shot with it generly, but she'd wrenched her arm a day or two ago, and didn't know whether she could throw true, now. But she watched for a chance, and directly she banged away at a rat, but she missed him wide, and said 'Ouch!' it hurt her arm so. Then she told me to try for the next one. I wanted to be getting away before the old man got back, but of course I didn't let on. I got the thing, and the first rat that showed his nose I let drive, and if he'd a stayed where he was he'd a been a tolerable sick rat. She said that that was first-rate, and she reckoned I would hive the next one. She went and got the lump of lead and fetched it back and brought along a hank of yarn,[2] which she wanted me to help her with. I held up my two hands and she put the hank over them and went on talking about her and her husband's matters. But she broke off to say:

'Keep your eye on the rats. You better have the lead in your lap, handy.'

So she dropped the lump into my lap, just at that moment, and I clapped my legs together on it and she went on talking. But only about a minute. Then she took off the hank and looked me straight in the face, but very pleasant, and says:

'Come, now—what's your real name?'

'Wh-what, mum?'

'What's your real name? Is it Bill, or Tom, or Bob?—or what is it?'

I reckon I shook like a leaf, and I didn't know hardly what to do. But I says:

'Please to don't poke fun at a poor girl like me, mum. If I'm in the way, here, I'll—'

'No, you won't. Set down and stay where you are. I ain't going to hurt you, and I ain't going to tell on you, nuther. You just tell me your secret, and trust me. I'll keep it; and what's more, I'll help you. So'll my old man, if you want him to. You

---

[2] *hank of yarn*: coiled bundle of yarn. The woman engages Huck's help in winding the coiled yarn into a ball.

see, you're a runaway 'prentice[3]—that's all. It ain't anything. There ain't any harm in it. You've been treated bad, and you made up your mind to cut. Bless you, child, I wouldn't tell on you. Tell me all about it, now—that's a good boy.'

So I said it wouldn't be no use to try to play it any longer, and I would just make a clean breast and tell her everything, but she mustn't go back on her promise. Then I told her my father and mother was dead, and the law had bound me out to a mean old farmer in the country thirty mile back from the river, and he treated me so bad I couldn't stand it no longer; he went away to be gone a couple of days, and so I took my chance and stole some of his daughter's old clothes, and cleared out, and I had been three nights coming the thirty miles; I traveled nights, and hid day-times and slept, and the bag of bread and meat I carried from home lasted me all the way and I had a plenty. I said I believed my uncle Abner Moore would take care of me, and so that was why I struck out for this town of Goshen.

'Goshen, child? This ain't Goshen. This is St. Petersburg. Goshen's ten mile further up the river. Who told you this was Goshen?'

'Why, a man I met at day-break this morning, just as I was going to turn into the woods for my regular sleep. He told me when the roads forked I must take the right hand, and five mile would fetch me to Goshen.'

'He was drunk I reckon. He told you just exactly wrong.'

'Well, he did act like he was drunk, but it ain't no matter now. I got to be moving along. I'll fetch Goshen before day-light.'

'Hold on a minute. I'll put you up[4] a snack to eat. You might want it.'

---

[3] *runaway 'prentice*: An indentured apprentice system was active in the country from its earliest days. An apprentice served a master without pay for a set number of years with the promise of being freed and, often, set up in a trade after the period of servitude. Because it was a legal agreement, a runaway apprentice was breaking the law.

[4] *put you up*: prepare or fix for you.

So she put me up a snack, and says:

'Say—when a cow's laying down, which end of her gets up first? Answer up prompt, now—don't stop to study over it. Which end gets up first?'

'The hind end, mum.'

'Well, then, a horse?'

'The for'rard end, mum.'

'Which side of a tree does the most moss grow on?'

'North side.'

'If fifteen cows is browsing on a hillside, how many of them eats with their heads pointed the same direction?'

'The whole fifteen, mum.'

'Well, I reckon you *have* lived in the country. I thought maybe you was trying to hocus⁵ me again. What's your real name, now?'

'George Peters, mum.'

'Well, try to remember it, George. Don't forget and tell me it's Elexander before you go, and then get out by saying it's George-Elexander when I catch you. And don't go about women in that old calico. You do a girl tolerable poor, but you might fool men, maybe. Bless you, child, when you set out to thread a needle, don't hold the thread still and fetch the needle up to it; hold the needle still and poke the thread at it—that's the way a woman most always does; but a man always does 'tother way. And when you throw at a rat or anything hitch yourself up a tip-toe, and fetch your hand up over your head as awkard as you can, and miss your rat about six or seven foot. Throw stiff-armed from the shoulder, like there was a pivot there for it to turn on—like a girl; not from the wrist and elbow, with your arm out to one side, like a boy. And mind you, when a girl tries to catch anything in her lap, she throws her knees apart: she don't clap them together, the way you did when you catched the lump of lead. Why, I spotted you for a boy when you was threading the needle; and I contrived the other things just to make certain. Now trot along

---

⁵ *hocus*: trick or deceive.

to your uncle, Sarah Mary Williams George Elexander Peters, and if you get into trouble you send word to Mrs Judith Loftus, which is me, and I'll do what I can to get you out of it. Keep the river road, all the way, and next time you tramp, take shoes and socks with you. The river road's a rocky one, and your feet 'll be in a condition when you get to Goshen, I reckon.'

I went up the bank about fifty yards, and then I doubled on my tracks and slipped back to where my canoe was, a good piece below the house. I jumped in and was off in a hurry. I went up stream far enough to make the head of the island, and then started across. I took off the sun-bonnet, for I didn't want no blinders on, then. When I was about the middle, I hear the clock begin to strike; so I stops and listens; the sound come faint over the water, but clear—eleven. When I struck the head of the island I never waited to blow, though I was most winded, but I shoved right into the timber where my old camp used to be, and started a good fire there on a high-and-dry spot.

Then I jumped in the canoe and dug out for our place a mile and a half below, as hard as I could go. I landed, and slopped through the timber and up the ridge and into the cavern. There Jim laid, sound asleep on the ground. I roused him out and says:

'Git up and hump yourself, Jim! There ain't a minute to lose. They're after us!'

Jim never asked no questions, he never said a word; but the way he worked for the next half an hour showed about how he was scared. By that time everything we had in the world was on our raft and she was ready to be shoved out from the willow cover where she was hid. We put out the camp fire at the cavern the first thing, and didn't show a candle outside after that.

I took the canoe out from shore a little piece and took a look, but if there was a boat around I couldn't see it, for stars and shadows ain't good to see by. Then we got out the raft and slipped along down in the shade, past the foot of the island dead still, never saying a word.

CHAPTER 12

It must a been close onto one o'clock when we got below the island at last, and the raft did seem to go mighty slow. If a boat was to come along, we was going to take to the canoe and break for the Illinois shore; and it was well a boat didn't come, for we hadn't ever thought to put the gun into the canoe, or a fishing-line or anything to eat. We was in ruther too much of a sweat to think of so many things. It warn't good judgment to put *everything* on the raft.

If the men went to the island, I just expect they found the camp fire I built, and watched it all night for Jim to come. Anyways, they stayed away from us, and if my building the fire never fooled them it warn't no fault of mine. I played it as low-down on them as I could.

When the first streak of day begun to show, we tied up to a tow-head in a big bend on the Illinois side, and hacked off cotton-wood branches with the hatchet and covered up the raft with them so she looked like there had been a cave-in in the bank there. A tow-head is a sand-bar that has cotton-woods on it as thick as harrow-teeth.[1]

We had mountains on the Missouri shore and heavy timber on the Illinois side, and the channel was down the Missouri shore at that place, so we warn't afraid of anybody running across us. We laid there all day and watched the rafts and steamboats spin down the Missouri shore, and up-bound steamboats fight the big river in the middle. I told Jim all about the time I had jabbering with that woman; and Jim said she was a smart one, and if she was to start after us herself *she* wouldn't set down and watch a camp fire—no, sir, she'd fetch a dog. Well, then, I said, why couldn't she tell her husband to

[1] A *tow-head is a sand-bar* ... : Such small islands or sandbars are probably called "tow-heads" because of their sandy color, tow being flax or hemp fibers. A harrow is a farm implement used to prepare earth for planting.

fetch a dog? Jim said he bet she did think of it by the time the men was ready to start, and he believed they must a gone up town to get a dog and so they lost all that time, or else we wouldn't be here on a tow-head sixteen or seventeen mile below the village—no, indeedy, we would be in that same old town again. So I said I didn't care what was the reason they didn't get us, as long as they didn't.

When it was beginning to come on dark, we poked our head out of the cottonwood thicket and looked up, and down, and across; nothing in sight; so Jim took up some of the top planks of the raft and built a snug wigwam to get under in blazing weather and rainy, and to keep the things dry. Jim made a floor for the wigwam, and raised it a foot or more above the level of the raft, so now the blankets and all the traps was out of the reach of steamboat waves. Right in the middle of the wigwam we made a layer of dirt about five or six inches deep with a frame around it for to hold it to its place; this was to build a fire on in sloppy weather or chilly; the wigwam would keep it from being seen. We made an extra steering oar, too, because one of the others might get broke, on a snag or something. We fixed up a short forked stick to hang the old lantern on; because we must always light the lantern whenever we see a steamboat coming down stream, to keep from getting run over; but we wouldn't have to light it for upstream boats unless we see we was in what they call a 'crossing'; for the river was pretty high yet, very low banks being still a little under water; so up-bound boats didn't always run the channel, but hunted easy water.

This second night we run between seven and eight hours, with a current that was making over four mile an hour. We catched fish, and talked, and we took a swim now and then to keep off sleepiness. It was kind of solemn, drifting down the big still river, laying on our backs looking up at the stars, and we didn't ever feel like talking loud, and it warn't often that we laughed, only a little kind of a low chuckle. We had mighty good weather, as a general thing, and nothing ever happened to us at all, that night, nor the next, nor the next.

Every night we passed towns, some of them away up on black hillsides, nothing but just a shiny bed of lights, not a house could you see. The fifth night we passed St. Louis,[2] and it was like the whole world lit up. In St. Petersburg they used to say there was twenty or thirty thousand people in St. Louis, but I never believed it till I see that wonderful spread of lights at two o'clock that still night. There warn't a sound there; everybody was asleep.

Every night, now, I used to slip ashore, towards ten o'clock, at some little village, and buy ten or fifteen cents' worth of meal or bacon or other stuff to eat; and sometimes I lifted a chicken that warn't roosting comfortable, and took him along. Pap always said, take a chicken when you get a chance, because if you don't want him yourself you can easy find somebody that does, and a good deed ain't ever forgot. I never see pap when he didn't want the chicken himself, but that is what he used to say, anyway.

Mornings, before daylight, I slipped into corn fields and borrowed a watermelon, or a mushmelon,[3] or a punkin, or some new corn, or things of that kind. Pap always said it warn't no harm to borrow things, if you was meaning to pay them back, sometime; but the widow said it warn't anything but a soft name for stealing, and no decent body would do it. Jim said he reckoned the widow was partly right and pap was partly right; so the best way would be for us to pick out two or three things from the list and say we wouldn't borrow them any more—then he reckoned it wouldn't be no harm to borrow the others. So we talked it over all one night, drifting along down the river, trying to make up our minds whether to drop the watermelons, or the cantelopes, or the mushmelons, or what. But towards daylight we got it all settled satisfactory, and concluded to drop crabapples and p'simmons.[4] We warn't

---

[2] *St. Louis*: Near the confluence of the Mississippi and Missouri rivers, St. Louis began as a fur trading post in 1764, was incorporated as a city in 1823, and was greatly expanding in population during this time period.

[3] *mushmelon*: muskmelon.

[4] *p'simmons*: persimmons, fruit of several species of trees of the genus *Diospyros*.

feeling just right, before that, but it was all comfortable now. I was glad the way it come out, too, because crabapples ain't ever good, and the p'simmons wouldn't be ripe for two or three months yet.

We shot a water-fowl, now and then, that got up too early in the morning or didn't go to bed early enough in the evening. Take it all around, we lived pretty high.

The fifth night below St. Louis we had a big storm after midnight, with a power of thunder and lightning, and the rain poured down in a solid sheet. We stayed in the wigwam and let the raft take care of itself. When the lightning glared out we could see a big straight river ahead, and high rocky bluffs on both sides. By-and-by says I, 'Hel-*lo*, Jim, looky yonder!' It was a steamboat that had killed herself on a rock. We was drifting straight down on her. The lightning showed her very distinct. She was leaning over, with part of her upper deck above water, and you could see every little chimbly-guy[5] clean and clear, and a chair by the big bell, with an old slouch hat hanging on the back of it when the flashes come.

Well, it being away in the night, and stormy, and all so mysterious-like, I felt just the way any other boy would a felt when I see that wreck laying there so mournful and lonesome in the middle of the river. I wanted to get aboard of her and slink around a little, and see what there was there. So I says:

'Le's land on her, Jim.'

But Jim was dead against it, at first. He says:

'I doan' want to go fool'n 'long er no wrack. We's doin' blame' well, en we better let blame' well alone, as de good book says. Like as not dey's a watchman on dat wrack.'

'Watchman your grandmother,' I says; 'there ain't nothing to watch but the texas[6] and the pilothouse; and do you reckon anybody's going to resk his life for a texas and a pilothouse

---

[5] *chimbly-guy*: cable used to wire together the chimneys, or smokestacks, on a steamboat. A "guy" is any type of a rope, chain, or wire used to brace something.

[6] *texas*: officer's cabin, so named because it is the largest cabin on the ship (as Texas is the largest state in the Union).

such a night as this, when it's likely to break up and wash off down the river any minute?' Jim couldn't say nothing to that, so he didn't try. 'And besides,' I says, 'we might borrow something worth having, out of the captain's stateroom. Seegars, *I* bet you—and cost five cents apiece, solid cash. Steamboat captains is always rich, and get sixty dollars a month, and *they* don't care a cent what a thing costs, you know, long as they want it. Stick a candle in your pocket; I can't rest, Jim, till we give her a rummaging. Do you reckon Tom Sawyer would ever go by this thing? Not for pie, he wouldn't. He'd call it an adventure—that's what he'd call it; and he'd land on that wreck if it was his last act. And wouldn't he throw style into it?—wouldn't he spread himself, nor nothing? Why, you'd think it was Christopher C'lumbus discovering Kingdom-Come. I wish Tom Sawyer *was* here.'

Jim he grumbled a little, but give in. He said we mustn't talk any more than we could help, and then talk mighty low. The lightning showed us the wreck again, just in time, and we fetched the starboard derrick,[7] and made fast there.

The deck was high out, here. We went sneaking down the slope of it to labboard,[8] in the dark, towards the texas, feeling our way slow with our feet, and spreading our hands out to fend off the guys, for it was so dark we couldn't see no sign of them. Pretty soon we struck the forward end of the skylight, and clumb onto it; and the next step fetched us in front of the captain's door, which was open, and by Jimminy, away down through the texas-hall we see a light! and all in the same second we seem to hear low voices in yonder!

Jim whispered and said he was feeling powerful sick, and told me to come along. I says, all right; and was going to start for the raft; but just then I heard a voice wail out and say:

'Oh, please don't, boys; I swear I won't ever tell!'

Another voice said, pretty loud:

[7] *starboard derrick*: Similar to a crane, a derrick is a hoisting device with a hook mounted on a mast or pole that can move in all directions. "Starboard" is the right-hand side of a ship looking forward; Huck sometimes says "stabboard".

[8] *labboard*: larboard, or left-hand side of a ship looking forward.

'It's a lie, Jim Turner. You've acted this way before. You always want more'n your share of the truck, and you've always got it, too, because you've swore 't if you didn't you'd tell. But this time you've said it jest one time too many. You're the mean-est, treacherousest hound in this country.'

By this time Jim was gone for the raft. I was just a-biling with curiosity; and I says to myself, Tom Sawyer wouldn't back out now, and so I won't either; I'm agoing to see what's going on here. So I dropped on my hands and knees, in the little passage, and crept aft in the dark, till there warn't but about one stateroom betwixt me and the cross-hall of the texas. Then, in there I see a man stretched on the floor and tied hand and foot, and two men standing over him, and one of them had a dim lantern in his hand, and the other one had a pistol. This one kept pointing the pistol at the man's head on the floor and saying—

'I'd *like* to! And I orter, too, a mean skunk!'

The man on the floor would shrivel up, and say: 'Oh, please don't, Bill—I hain't ever goin' to tell.'

And every time he said that, the man with the lantern would laugh, and say:

"Deed you *ain't*! You never said no truer thing 'n that, you bet you.' And once he said: 'Hear him beg! and yit if we hadn't got the best of him and tied him, he'd a killed us both. And what *for*? Jist for noth'n. Jist because we stood on our *rights*— that's what for. But I lay you ain't agoin' to threaten nobody any more, Jim Turner. Put *up* that pistol, Bill.'

Bill says:

'I don't want to, Jake Packard. I'm for killin' him—and didn't he kill old Hatfield jist the same way—and don't he deserve it?'

'But I don't *want* him killed, and I've got my reasons for it.'

'Bless yo' heart for them words, Jake Packard! I'll never for-git you, long's I live!' says the man on the floor, sort of blubbering.

Packard didn't take no notice of that, but hung up his lan-tern on a nail, and started towards where I was, there in the dark, and motioned Bill to come. I crawfished[9] as fast as I could, about two yards, but the boat slanted so that I couldn't make very good time; so to keep from getting run over and catched I crawled into a stateroom on the upper side. The man come a-pawing along in the dark, and when Packard got to my stateroom, he says:

'Here—come in here.'

And in he come, and Bill after him. But before they got in, I was up in the upper berth, cornered, and sorry I come. Then they stood there, with their hands on the ledge of the berth, and talked. I couldn't see them, but I could tell where they was, by the whisky they'd been having. I was glad I didn't drink whisky; but it wouldn't made much difference, anyway, because most of the time they couldn't a treed[10] me because I didn't breathe. I was too scared. And besides, a body *couldn't* breathe, and hear such talk. They talked low and earnest. Bill wanted to kill Turner. He says:

'He's said he'll tell, and he will. If we was to give both our shares to him *now*, it wouldn't make no difference after the row, and the way we've served him. Shore's you're born, he'll turn State's evidence; now you hear *me*. I'm for putting him out of his troubles.'

'So'm I,' says Packard, very quiet.

'Blame it, I'd sorter begun to think you wasn't. Well, then, that's all right. Les' go and do it.'

'Hold on a minute; I hain't had my say yit. You listen to me. Shooting's good, but there's quieter ways if the thing's *got* to be done. But what *I* say, is this; it ain't good sense to go court'n around after a halter,[11] if you can git at what you're up to in some way that's jist as good and at the same time don't bring you into no resks. Ain't that so?'

'You bet it is. But how you goin' to manage it this time?'

[9] *crawfished*: crawled backward.

[10] *treed*: cornered, as someone who is caught up a tree.

[11] *to go court'n around after a halter*: i.e., to perpetrate a crime that brings one dangerously close to being arrested and executed. A halter is a noose or rope used to hang criminals.

'Well, my idea is this: we'll rustle around and gether up whatever pickins we've overlooked in the staterooms, and shove for shore and hide the truck. Then we'll wait. Now I say it ain't agoin' to be more 'n two hours befo' this wrack breaks up and washes off down the river. See? He'll be drownded, and won't have nobody to blame for it but his own self. I reckon that's a considerable sight better 'n killin' of him. I'm unfavorable to killin' a man as long as you can git around it; it ain't good sense, it ain't good morals. Ain't I right?'

'Yes—I reck'n you are. But s'pose she *don't* break up and wash off?'

'Well, we can wait the two hours anyway, and see, can't we?'

'All right, then; come along.'

So they started, and I lit out, all in a cold sweat, and scrambled forward. It was dark as pitch there; but I said in a kind of a coarse whisper, 'Jim!' and he answered up, right at my elbow, with a sort of a moan, and I says:

'Quick, Jim, it ain't no time for fooling around and moaning; there's a gang of murderers in yonder, and if we don't hunt up their boat and set her drifting down the river so these fellows can't get away from the wreck, there's one of 'em going to be in a bad fix. But if we find their boat we can put *all* of 'em in a bad fix—for the Sheriff 'll get 'em. Quick—hurry! I'll hunt the labboard side, you hunt the stabboard. You start at the raft, and—'

'Oh, my lordy, lordy! *Raf*'? Dey ain' no raf no mo', she done broke loose en gone!—'en here we is!'

CHAPTER 13

Well, I catched my breath and most fainted. Shut up on a wreck with such a gang as that! But it warn't no time to be sentimentering. We'd *got* to find that boat, now—had to have it for ourselves. So we went a-quaking and shaking down the stabboard side, and slow work it was too—seemed a week before we got to the stern. No sign of a boat. Jim said he didn't believe he could go any further—so scared he hadn't hardly any strength left, he said. But I said come on, if we get left on this wreck, we are in a fix, sure. So on we prowled, again. We struck for the stern of the texas, and found it, and then scrabbled along forwards on the skylight, hanging on from shutter to shutter, for the edge of the skylight was in the water. When we got pretty close to the cross-hall door, there was the skiff, sure enough! I could just barely see her. I felt ever so thankful. In another second I would a been aboard of her; but just then the door opened. One of the men stuck his head out, only about a couple of foot from me, and I thought I was gone; but he jerked it in again, and says:

'Heave that blame lantern out o' sight, Bill!'

He flung a bag of something into the boat, and then got in himself, and set down. It was Packard. Then Bill *he* come out and got in. Packard says, in a low voice:

'All ready—shove off!'

I couldn't hardly hang onto the shutters, I was so weak. But Bill says:

'Hold on—'d you go through him?'

'No. Didn't you?'

'No. So he's got his share o' the cash, yet.'

'Well, then, come along—no use to take truck and leave money.'

'Say—won't he suspicion what we're up to?'

'Maybe he won't. But we got to have it anyway. Come along.'

83

So they got out and went in.

The door slammed to, because it was on the careened side;[1] and in a half second I was in the boat, and Jim come a tumbling after me. I out with my knife and cut the rope, and away we went!

We didn't touch an oar, and we didn' speak nor whisper, nor hardly even breathe. We went gliding swift along, dead silent, past the tip of the paddle-box, and past the stern; then in a second or two more we was a hundred yards below the wreck, and the darkness soaked her up, every last sign of her, and we was safe, and knowed it.

When we was three or four hundred yards down stream, we see the lantern show like a little spark at the texas door, for a second, and we knowed by that that the rascals had missed their boat, and was beginning to understand that they was in just as much trouble, now, as Jim Turner was.

Then Jim manned the oars, and we took out after our raft. Now was the first time that I begun to worry about the men—I reckon I hadn't had time to before. I begun to think how dreadful it was, even for murderers, to be in such a fix. I says to myself, there ain't no telling but I might come to be a murderer myself, yet, and then how would *I* like it? So says I to Jim:

'The first light we see, we'll land a hundred yards below it or above it, in a place where it's a good hiding-place for you and the skiff, and then I'll go and fix up some kind of a yarn, and get somebody to go for that gang and get them out of their scrape, so they can be hung when their time comes.'

But that idea was a failure; for pretty soon it begun to storm again, and this time worse than ever. The rain poured down, and never a light showed; everybody in bed, I reckon. We boomed along down the river, watching for lights and watching for our raft. After a long time the rain let up, but the clouds staid, and the lightning kept whimpering, and by-and-by a flash showed us a black thing ahead, floating, and we made for it.

---

[1] *careened side*: side of the boat turned out of the water.

It was the raft, and mighty glad was we to get aboard of it again. We seen a light, now, away down to the right, on shore. So I said I would go for it. The skiff was half full of plunder which that gang had stole, there on the wreck. We hustled it onto the raft in a pile, and I told Jim to float along down, and show a light when he judged he had gone about two mile, and keep it burning till I come; then I manned my oars and shoved for the light. As I got down towards it, three or four more showed—up on a hillside. It was a village. I closed in above the shore-light, and laid on my oars and floated. As I went by, I see it was a lantern hanging on the jackstaff of a double-hull ferry-boat. I skimmed around for the watchman, a-wondering whereabouts he slept; and by-and-by I found him roosting on the bitts,[2] forward, with his head down between his knees. I give his shoulder two or three little shoves, and begun to cry.

He stirred up, in a kind of a startlish way; when he see it was only me, he took a good gap and stretch, and then he says:

'Hello, what's up? Don't cry, bub. What's the trouble?'

I says:

'Pap, and mam, and sis, and—'

Then I broke down. He says:

'Oh, dang it, now, *don't* take on so, we all has to have our troubles and this'n 'll come out all right. What's the matter with 'em?'

'They're—they're—are you the watchman of the boat?'

'Yes,' he says, kind of pretty-well-satisfied like. 'I'm the captain and the owner, and the mate, and the pilot, and watchman, and head deck-hand; and sometimes I'm the freight and passengers. I ain't as rich as old Jim Hornback, and I can't be so blame' generous and good to Tom, Dick and Harry as what he is, and slam around money the way he does; but I've told him a many a time 't I wouldn't trade places with him; for,

[2] *bitts*: vertical posts strung together with ropes or cables on the deck of a steamboat.

says I, a sailor's life's the life for me, and I'm denied[3] if I'd live two mile out o' town, where there ain't nothing ever goin' on, not for all his spondulicks[4] and as much more on top of it. Says I—'

I broke in and says:

'They're in an awful peck of trouble, and—'

'*Who* is?'

'Why, pap, and mam, and sis, and Miss Hooker; and if you'd take your ferry-boat and go up there—'

'Up where? Where are they?'

'On the wreck.'

'What wreck?'

'Why, there ain't but one.'

'What, you don't mean the *Walter Scott*?'[5]

'Yes.'

'Good land! what are they doin' *there*, for gracious sakes?'

'Well, they didn't go there a-purpose.'

'I bet they didn't! Why, great goodness, there ain't no chance for 'em if they don't git off mighty quick! Why, how in the nation did they ever git into such a scrape?'

'Easy enough. Miss Hooker was a-visiting, up there to the town—'

'Yes, Booth's Landing—go on.'

'She was a-visiting, there at Booth's Landing, and just in the edge of the evening she started over with her nigger woman in the horse-ferry, to stay all night at her friend's house, Miss What-you-may-call-her, I disremember her name, and they lost their steering-oar, and swung around and went a-floating down, stern-first, about two mile, and saddle-baggsed[6] on the wreck,

---

[3] *denied*: euphemism for "damned".

[4] *spondulicks*: money.

[5] Walter Scott: In *Life on the Mississippi* (1883), Twain took aim at the Romantic "disease" and "sham chivalries" of Sir Walter Scott's novels, such as *Ivanhoe* (1819), then enormously popular. Twain's symbolic sinking of the *Walter Scott* and the considerable terrors that Huck and Jim experience aboard the doomed steamship signal the demise of a false Romantic view of life.

[6] *saddle-baggsed*: pulled up against or partly on top of, as saddlebags straddle a horse.

and the ferry man and the nigger woman and the horses was all lost, but Miss Hooker she made a grab and got aboard the wreck. Well about an hour after dark, we come along down in our trading-scow,[7] and it was so dark we didn't notice the wreck till we was right on it; and so *we* saddle-baggsed; but all of us was saved but Bill Whipple—and oh, he *was* the best cretur!—I most wish't it had been me, I do.'

'My George! It's the beatenest thing I ever struck. And *then* what did you all do?'

'Well, we hollered and took on, but it's so wide there, we couldn't make nobody hear. So pap said somebody got to get ashore and get help somehow. I was the only one that could swim, so I made a dash for it, and Miss Hooker she said if I didn't strike help sooner, come here and hunt up her uncle, and he'd fix the thing. I made the land about a mile below, and been fooling along ever since, trying to get people to do something, but they said, 'What, in such a night and such a current? there ain't no sense in it; go for the steam-ferry.' Now if you'll go, and—'

'By Jackson, I'd *like* to, and blame it I don't know but I will; but who in the dingnation's agoin' to *pay* for it? Do you reckon your pap—'

'Why *that's* all right. Miss Hooker she told *me, particular,* that her uncle Hornback—'

'Great guns! is *he* her uncle? Looky here, you break for that light over yonder-way, and turn out west when you git there, and about a quarter of a mile out you'll come to the tavern; tell 'em to dart you out to Jim Hornback's and he'll foot the bill. And don't you fool around any, because he'll want to know the news. Tell him I'll have his niece all safe before he can get to town. Hump yourself, now;[8] I'm agoing up around the corner here, to roust out my engineer.'

I struck for the light, but as soon as he turned the corner I went back and got into my skiff and bailed her out and then

---

[7] *trading-scow:* boat for carrying goods or supplies.
[8] *Hump yourself:* hustle or hurry.

pulled up shore in the easy water about six hundred yards, and tucked myself in among some woodboats; for I couldn't rest easy till I could see the ferry-boat start. But take it all around, I was feeling rather comfortable on accounts of taking all this trouble for that gang, for not many would a done it. I wished the widow knowed about it. I judged she would be proud of me for helping these rapscallions,[9] because rapscallions and dead beats is the kind the widow and good people takes the most interest in.

Well, before long, here comes the wreck, dim and dusky, sliding along down! A kind of cold shiver went through me, and then I struck out for her. She was very deep, and I see in a minute there warn't much chance for anybody being alive in her. I pulled all around her and hollered a little, but there wasn't any answer; all dead still. I felt a little bit heavy-hearted about the gang, but not much, for I reckoned if they could stand it, I could.

Then here comes the ferry-boat; so I shoved for the middle of the river on a long down-stream slant; and when I judged I was out of eye-reach, I laid on my oars, and looked back and see her go and smell around the wreck for Miss Hooker's remainders, because the captain would know her uncle Hornback would want them; and then pretty soon the ferry-boat give it up and went for shore, and I laid into my work and went a-booming down the river.

It did seem a powerful long time before Jim's light showed up; and when it did show, it looked like it was a thousand mile off. By the time I got there the sky was beginning to get a little gray in the east; so we struck for an island, and hid the raft, and sunk the skiff, and turned in and slept like dead people.

---

[9] *rapscallions*: rascals.

CHAPTER 14

By-and-by, when we got up, we turned over the truck the gang had stole off of the wreck, and found boots, and blankets, and clothes, and all sorts of other things, and a lot of books, and a spyglass, and three boxes of seegars. We hadn't ever been this rich before, in neither of our lives. The seegars was prime. We laid off all the afternoon in the woods talking, and me reading the books, and having a general good time. I told Jim all about what happened inside the wreck, and at the ferry-boat; and I said these kinds of things was adventures; but he said he didn't want no more adventures. He said that when I went in the texas and he crawled back to get on the raft and found her gone, he nearly died; because he judged it was all up with *him*, anyway it could be fixed; for if he didn't get saved he would get drownded; and if he did get saved, whoever saved him would send him back home so as to get the reward, and then Miss Watson would sell him South, sure. Well, he was right; he was most always right; he had an uncommon level head, for a nigger.

I read considerable to Jim about kings, and dukes, and earls, and such, and how gaudy they dressed, and how much style they put on, and called each other your majesty, and your grace, and your lordship, and so on, 'stead of mister; and Jim's eyes bugged out, and he was interested. He says:

'I didn' know dey was so many un um. I hain't hearn 'bout none un um, skasely, but ole King Sollermun,[1] onless you counts dem kings dat's in a pack er k'yards. How much do a king git?'

'Get?' I says; 'why, they get a thousand dollars a month if they want it; they can have just as much as they want; everything belongs to them.'

---

[1] *King Sollermun*: In 1 Kings 3:16–27, the wise man King Solomon was asked to settle a quarrel between two women over the rightful parentage of a child. His threat to cut the child in two and distribute half to each woman quickly brought to light the true mother.

'*Ain'* dat gay? En what dey got to do, Huck?'

'*They* don't do nothing! Why how you talk. They just set around.'

'No—is dat so?'

'Of course it is. They just set around. Except maybe when there 's a war; then they go to the war. But other times they just lazy around; or go hawking—just hawking and sp—Sh!—d' you hear a noise?'

We skipped out and looked; but it warn't nothing but the flutter of a steamboat's wheel, away down coming around the point; so we come back.

'Yes,' says I, 'and other times, when things is dull, they fuss with the parlyment; and if everybody don't go just so he whacks their heads off. But mostly they hang round the harem.'

'Roun' de which?'

'Harem.'

'What's de harem?'

'The place where he keep his wives. Don't you know about the harem? Solomon had one; he had about a million wives.'

'Why, yes, dat's so; I—I'd done forgot it. A harem's a bo'd'n-house,[2] I reck'n. Mos' likely dey had rackety times in de nussery. En I reck'n de wives quarrels considable; en dat 'crease de racket. Yit dey say Sollermun de wises' man dat ever live'. I doan' take no stock in dat. Bekase why: would a wise man want to live in de mids' er sich a blimblammin' all de time? No—'deed he wouldn't. A wise man 'ud take en buil' a biler-factry; en den he could shet *down* de biler-factry when he want to res'.'

'Well, but he *was* the wisest man, anyway; because the widow she told me so, her own self.'

'I doan k'yer what de widder say, he *warn't* no wise man, nuther. He had some er de dad-fetchedes'[3] ways I ever see. Does you know 'bout dat chile dat he 'uz gwyne to chop in two?'

---

[2] *bo'd'n-house*: boarding house.
[3] *dad-fetchedes'*: euphemism for "goddamned".

'Yes, the widow told me all about it.'

'*Well*, den! Warn' dat de beatenes' notion in de worl'? You jes' take en look at it a minute. Dah's de stump, dah—dat's one er de women; heah's you—dat's de yuther one; I's Sollermun; en dish-yer dollar bill's de chile. Bofe un you claims it. What does I do? Does I shin aroun' mongs' de neighbors en fine out which un you de bill *do* b'long to, en han' it over to de right one, all safe en soun', de way dat anybody dat had any gumption would? No—I take en whack de bill in *two*, en give half un it to you, en de yuther half to de yuther woman. Dat's de way Sollermun was gwyne to do wid de chile. Now I want to ast you: what's de use er dat half a bill?—can't buy noth'n wid it. En what use is a half a chile? I would'n give a dern for a million un um.'

'But hang it, Jim, you've clean missed the point—blame it, you've missed it a thousand mile.'

'Who? Me? Go 'long. Doan' talk to *me* 'bout yo' pints. I reck'n I knows sense when I sees it; en dey ain' no sense in sich doin's as dat. De 'spute warn't 'bout a half a chile, de 'spute was 'bout a whole chile; en de man dat think he kin settle a 'spute 'bout a whole child wid a half a chile, doan' know enough to come in out'n de rain. Doan' talk to me 'bout Sollermun, Huck, I knows him by de back.'

'But I tell you you don't get the point.'

'Blame de pint! I reck'n I knows what I knows. En mine you, de *real* pint is down furder—it's down deeper. It lays in de way Sollermun was raised. You take a man dat's got on'y one er two chillen; is dat man gwyne to be waseful o' chillen? No, he ain't; he can't 'ford it. *He* know how to value 'em. But you take a man dat's got 'bout five million chillen runnin' roun' de house, en it's diffunt. *He* as soon chop a chile in two as a cat. Dey's plenty mo'. A chile er two, mo' er less, warn't no consekens to Sollermun, dad fetch him!'

I never see such a nigger. If he got a notion in his head once, there warn't no getting it out again. He was the most down on Solomon of any nigger I ever see. So I went to talking about other kings, and let Solomon slide. I told about Louis

Sixteenth that got his head cut off in France long time ago; and about his little boy the dolphin,[4] that would a been a king, but they took and shut him up in jail, and some say he died there.

'Po' little chap.'

'But some says he got out and got away, and come to America.'

'Dat's good! But he'll be pooty lonesome—dey ain' no kings here, is dey, Huck?'

'No.'

'Den he cain't get no situation. What he gwyne to do?'

'Well, I don't know. Some of them gets on the police, and some of them learns people how to talk French.'

'Why, Huck, doan' de French people talk de same way we does?'

'*No*, Jim; you couldn't understand a word they said—not a single word.'

'Well, now, I be ding-busted! How do dat come?'

'*I* don't know; but it's so. I got some of their jabber out of a book. Spose a man was to come to you and say *Polly-voo-franzy*—what would you think?'

'I wouldn't think nuff'n; I'd take en bust him over de head. Dat is, if he warn't white. I wouldn't 'low no nigger to call me dat.'

'Shucks, it ain't calling you anything. It's only saying do you know how to talk French.'

'Well, den, why couldn't he *say* it?'

'Why, he *is* a-saying it. That's a Frenchman's *way* of saying it.'

'Well, it's a blame' ridicklous way, en I doan' want to hear no mo' 'bout it. Dey ain' no sense in it.'

---

[4] *Louis Sixteenth . . . the dolphin*: The last king of France, Louis XVI, was executed in 1793 at the height of the French Revolution. His little son, Louis Charles (1785–1795?), the dauphin or heir to the French throne, was put in prison and probably died there, although rumors persisted that he had escaped and come to the United States. Over the years several people claimed to be the surviving dauphin.

'Looky here, Jim; does a cat talk like we do?'

'No, a cat don't.'

'Well, does a cow?'

'No, a cow don't, nuther.'

'Does a cat talk like a cow, or a cow talk like a cat?'

'No, dey don't.'

'It's natural and right for 'em to talk different from each other, ain't it?'

' 'Course.'

'And ain't it natural and right for a cat and a cow to talk different from *us*?'

'Why, mos' sholy it is.'

'Well, then, why ain't it natural and right for a *Frenchman* to talk different from us? You answer me that.'

'Is a cat a man, Huck?'

'No.'

'Well, den, dey ain't no sense in a cat talkin' like a man. Is a cow a man?—er is a cow a cat?'

'No, she ain't either of them.'

'Well, den, she ain' got no business to talk like either one er the yuther of 'em. Is a Frenchman a man?'

'Yes.'

'*Well*, den! Dad blame it, why doan' he *talk* like a man? You answer me *dat*!'

I see it warn't no use wasting words—you can't learn a nigger to argue. So I quit.

CHAPTER 15

We judged that three nights more would fetch us to Cairo, at the bottom of Illinois, where the Ohio River comes in, and that was what we was after.[1] We would sell the raft and get on a steamboat and go way up the Ohio among the free States, and then be out of trouble.

Well, the second night a fog begun to come on, and we made for a tow-head to tie to, for it wouldn't do to try to run in fog; but when I paddled ahead in the canoe, with the line, to make fast, there warn't anything but little saplings to tie to. I passed the line around one of them right on the edge of the cut bank, but there was a stiff current, and the raft come booming down so lively she tore it out by the roots and away she went. I see the fog closing down, and it made me so sick and scared I couldn't budge for most a half a minute it seemed to me—and then there warn't no raft in sight; you couldn't see twenty yards. I jumped into the canoe and run back to the stern and grabbed the paddle and set her back a stroke. But she didn't come. I was in such a hurry I hadn't untied her. I got up and tried to untie her, but I was so excited my hands shook so I couldn't hardly do anything with them.

As soon as I got started I took out after the raft, hot and heavy, right down the tow-head. That was all right as far as it went, but the tow-head warn't sixty yards long, and the minute I flew by the foot of it I shot out into the solid white fog, and hadn't no more idea which way I was going than a dead man.

Thinks I, it won't do to paddle; first I know I'll run into the bank or a tow-head or something; I got to set still and float,

[1] *Cairo . . . that was what we was after*: The town of Cairo (pronounced *kay-row*), at the southernmost tip of Illinois, is where the Ohio River flows into the Mississippi River. The plan is to turn at Cairo up the Ohio River to the free state of Ohio, which had the most extensive network of Underground Railroads and thus would offer Jim the best chance of freedom.

and yet it's mighty fidgety business to have to hold your hands still at such a time. I whooped[2] and listened. Away down there, somewheres, I hears a small whoop, and up comes my spirits. I went tearing after it, listening sharp to hear it again. The next time it come, I see I warn't heading for it but heading away to the right of it. And the next time, I was heading away to the left of it—and not gaining on it much, either, for I was flying around, this way and that and 'tother, but it was going straight ahead all the time.

I did wish the fool would think to beat a tin pan, and beat it all the time, but he never did, and it was the still places between the whoops that was making the trouble for me. Well, I fought along, and directly I hears the whoop *behind* me. I was tangled good, now. That was somebody else's whoop, or else I was turned around.

I throwed the paddle down. I heard the whoop again; it was behind me yet, but in a different place; it kept coming, and kept changing its place, and I kept answering, till by-and-by it was in front of me again and I knowed the current had swung the canoe's head down stream and I was all right, if that was Jim and not some other raftsman hollering. I couldn't tell nothing about voices in a fog, for nothing don't look natural nor sound natural in a fog.

The whooping went on, and in about a minute I come a booming down on a cut bank with smoky ghosts of big trees on it, and the current threw me off to the left and shot by, amongst a lot of snags that fairly roared, the current was tearing by them so swift.

In another second or two it was solid white and still again. I set perfectly still, then, listening to my heart thump, and I reckon I didn't draw a breath while it thumped a hundred.

I just give up, then. I knowed what the matter was. That cut bank was an island, and Jim had gone down 'tother side of it. It warn't no tow-head, that you could float by in ten

[2] *whooped*: shouted.

minutes. It had the big timber of a regular island; it might be five or six mile long and more than a half a mile wide.

I kept quiet, with my ears cocked, about fifteen minutes, I reckon. I was floating along, of course, four or five mile an hour; but you don't ever think of that. No, you *feel* like you are laying dead still on the water; and if a little glimpse of a snag slips by, you don't think to yourself how fast *you're* going, but you catch your breath and think, my! how that snag's tearing along. If you think it ain't dismal and lonesome out in a fog that way, by yourself, in the night, you try it once—you'll see.

Next, for about a half an hour, I whoops now and then; at last I hears the answer a long ways off, and tries to follow it, but I couldn't do it, and directly I judged I'd got into a nest of tow-heads, for I had little dim glimpses of them on both sides of me, sometimes just a narrow channel between; and some that I couldn't see, I knowed was there, because I'd hear the wash of the current against the old dead brush and trash that hung over the banks. Well, I warn't long losing the whoops, down amongst the tow-heads; and I only tried to chase them a little while, anyway, because it was worse than chasing a Jack-o-lantern. You never knowed a sound dodge around so, and swap places so quick and so much.

I had to claw away from the bank pretty lively, four or five times, to keep from knocking the islands out of the river; and so I judged the raft must be butting into the bank every now and then, or else it would get further ahead and clear out of hearing—it was floating a little faster than what I was.

Well, I seemed to be in the open river again, by-and-by, but I couldn't hear no sign of a whoop nowheres. I reckoned Jim had fetched up on a snag, maybe, and it was all up with him. I was good and tired, so I laid down in the canoe and said I wouldn't bother no more. I didn't want to go to sleep, of course; but I was so sleepy I couldn't help it; so I thought I would take just one little cat-nap.

But I reckon it was more than a cat-nap, for when I waked up the stars was shining bright, the fog was all gone, and I was spinning down a big bend stern first. First I didn't know where

I was; I thought I was dreaming; and when things begun to come back to me, they seemed to come up dim out of last week.

It was a monstrous big river here, with the tallest and the thickest kind of timber on both banks; just a solid wall, as well as I could see, by the stars. I looked away down stream, and seen a black speck on the water. I took out after it; but when I got to it it warn't nothing but a couple of saw-logs made fast together. Then I see another speck, and chased that; then another, and this time I was right. It was the raft.

When I got to it Jim was setting there with his head down between his knees, asleep, with his right arm hanging over the steering oar. The other oar was smashed off, and the raft was littered up with leaves and branches and dirt. So she'd had a rough time.

I made fast and laid down under Jim's nose on the raft, and begun to gap, and stretch my fists out against Jim, and says:

'Hello, Jim, have I been asleep? Why didn't you stir me up?'

'Goodness gracious, is dat you, Huck? En you ain' dead— you ain' drownded—you's back again? It's too good for true, honey, it's too good for true. Lemme look at you, chile, lemme feel o' you. No, you ain' dead! you's back agin, 'live en soun', jis de same ole Huck—de same ole Huck, thanks to goodness!'

'What's the matter with you, Jim? You been a drinking?'

'Drinkin'? Has I ben a drinkin'? Has I had a chance to be a drinkin'?'

'Well, then, what makes you talk so wild?'

'How does I talk wild?'

'*How*? why, hain't you been talking about my coming back, and all that stuff, as if I'd been gone away?'

'Huck—Huck Finn, you look me in de eye; look me in de eye. *Hain't* you ben gone away?'

'Gone away? Why, what in the nation do you mean? *I* hain't been gone anywheres. Where would I go to?'

'Well, looky here, boss, dey's sumf'n wrong, dey is. Is I *me*, or who *is* I? Is I heah, or whah *is* I? Now dat's what I wants to know.'

'Well, I think you're here, plain enough, but I think you're a tangle-headed old fool, Jim.'

'I is, is I? Well you answer me dis. Didn't you tote out de line in de canoe, fer to make fas' to de tow-head?'

'No, I didn't. What tow-head? I hain't seen no tow-head.'

'You hain't seen no tow-head? Looky here—didn't de line pull loose en de raf' go a hummin' down de river, en leave you en de canoe behine in de fog?'

'What fog?'

'Why *de* fog. De fog dat's ben aroun' all night. En didn't you whoop, en didn't I whoop, tell we got mix' up in de islands en one un us got los' en 'tother one was jis' as good as los', 'kase he didn't know whah he wuz? En didn't I bust up agin a lot er dem islands en have a turrible time en mos' git drownded? Now ain' dat so, boss—ain't it so? You answer me dat.'

'Well, this is too many for me, Jim. I hain't seen no fog, nor no islands, nor no troubles, nor nothing. I been setting here talking with you all night till you went to sleep about ten minutes ago, and I reckon I done the same. You couldn't a got drunk in that time, so of course you've been dreaming.'

'Dad fetch it, how is gwyne to dream all dat in ten minutes?'

'Well, hang it all, you did dream it, because there didn't any of it happen.'

'But Huck, it's all jis' as plain to me as—'

'It don't make no difference how plain it is, there ain't nothing in it. I know, because I've been here all the time.'

Jim didn't say nothing for about five minutes, but set there studying over it. Then he says:

'Well, den, I reck'n I did dream it, Huck; but dog my cats ef it ain't de powerfullest dream I ever see. En I hain't ever had no dream b'fo' dat's tired me like dis one.'

'Oh, well, that's all right, because a dream does tire a body like everything, sometimes. But this one was a staving[3] dream—tell me all about it, Jim.'

---

[3] *staving*: smashing, or really wonderful.

So Jim went to work and told me the whole thing right through, just as it happened, only he painted it up considerable. Then he said he must start in and ' 'terpret' it, because it was sent for a warning. He said the first tow-head stood for a man that would try to do us some good, but the current was another man that would get us away from him. The whoops was warnings that would come to us every now and then, and if we didn't try hard to make out to understand them they'd just take us into bad luck, 'stead of keeping us out of it. The lot of tow-heads was troubles we was going to get into with quarrelsome people and all kinds of mean folks, but if we minded our business and didn't talk back and aggravate them, we would pull through and get out of the fog and into the big clear river, which was the free States, and wouldn't have no more trouble.

It had clouded up pretty dark just after I got onto the raft, but it was clearing up again, now.

'Oh, well, that's all interpreted well enough, as far as it goes, Jim,' I says; 'but what does *these* things stand for?'

It was the leaves and rubbish on the raft, and the smashed oar. You could see them first rate, now.

Jim looked at the trash, and then looked at me, and back at the trash again. He had got the dream fixed so strong in his head that he couldn't seem to shake it loose and get the facts back into its place again, right away. But when he did get the thing straightened around, he looked at me steady, without ever smiling, and says:

'What do dey stan' for? I's gwyne to tell you. When I got all wore out wid work, en wid de callin' for you, en went to sleep, my heart wuz mos' broke bekase you wuz los', en I didn' k'yer no mo' what become er me en de raf'. En when I wake up en fine you back again', all safe en soun', de tears come en I could a got down on my knees en kiss' yo' foot I's so thankful. En all you wuz thinkin 'bout wuz how you could make a fool uv ole Jim wid a lie. Dat truck dah is *trash*; en trash is what people is dat puts dirt on de head er dey fren's en makes 'em ashamed.'

Then he got up slow, and walked to the wigwam, and went in there, without saying anything but that. But that was enough. It made me feel so mean[4] I could almost kissed *his* foot to get him to take it back.

It was fifteen minutes before I could work myself up to go and humble myself to a nigger—but I done it, and I warn't ever sorry for it afterwards, neither. I didn't do him no more mean tricks, and I wouldn't done that one if I'd a knowed it would make him feel that way.

[4] *mean:* ashamed or low-down.

CHAPTER 16

We slept most all day, and started out at night, a little ways behind a monstrous long raft that was as long going by as a procession. She had four long sweeps[1] at each end, so we judged she carried as many as thirty men, likely. She had five big wigwams aboard, wide apart, and an open camp fire in the middle, and a tall flag-pole at each end. There was a power of style about her. It *amounted* to something being a raftsman on such a craft as that.

We went drifting down into a big bend, and the night clouded up and got hot. The river was very wide, and was walled with solid timber on both sides; you couldn't see a break in it hardly ever, or a light. We talked about Cairo, and wondered whether we would know it when we got to it. I said likely we wouldn't, because I had heard say there warn't but about a dozen houses there, and if they didn't happen to have them lit up, how was we going to know we was passing a town? Jim said if the two big rivers joined together there, that would show. But I said maybe we might think we was passing the foot of an island and coming into the same old river again. That disturbed Jim—and me too. So the question was, what to do? I said, paddle ashore the first time a light showed, and tell them pap was behind, coming along with a trading-scow, and was a green hand at the business, and wanted to know how far it was to Cairo. Jim thought it was a good idea, so we took a smoke on it and waited.

There warn't nothing to do, now, but to look out sharp for the town, and not pass it without seeing it. He said he'd be mighty sure to see it, because he'd be a free man the minute he seen it, but if he missed it he'd be in the slave country

---

[1] *sweeps*: oars.

again and no more show for freedom. Every little while he jumps up and says:

'Dah she is!'

But it warn't. It was Jack-o-lanterns, or lightning-bugs; so he set down again, and went to watching, same as before. Jim said it made him all over trembly and feverish to be so close to freedom. Well, I can tell you it made me all over trembly and feverish, too, to hear him, because I begun to get it through my head that he *was* most free—and who was to blame for it? Why, *me*. I couldn't get that out of my conscience, no how nor no way. It got to troubling me so I couldn't rest; I couldn't stay still in one place. It hadn't ever come home to me before, what this thing was that I was doing. But now it did; and it staid with me, and scorched me more and more. I tried to make out to myself that *I* warn't to blame, because *I* didn't run Jim off from his rightful owner; but it warn't no use, conscience up and says, every time, 'But you knowed he was running for his freedom, and you could a paddled ashore and told somebody.' That was so—I couldn't get around that, noway. That was where it pinched. Conscience says to me, 'What had poor Miss Watson done to you, that you could see her nigger go off right under your eyes and never say one single word? What did that poor old woman do to you, that you could treat her so mean? Why, she tried to learn you your book, she tried to learn you your manners, she tried to be good to you every way she knowed how. *That's* what she done.'

I got to feeling so mean and so miserable I most wished I was dead. I fidgeted up and down the raft, abusing myself to myself, and Jim was fidgeting up and down past me. We neither of us could keep still. Every time he danced around and says, 'Dah's Cairo!' it went through me like a shot, and I thought if it *was* Cairo I reckoned I would die of miserableness.

Jim talked out loud all the time while I was talking to myself. He was saying how the first thing he would do when he got to a free State he would go to saving up money and never spend a single cent, and when he got enough he would buy his wife,[2] which was owned on a farm close to where Miss Watson lived; and then they would both work to buy the two children, and if their master wouldn't sell them, they'd get an Ab'litionist to go and steal them.

It most froze me to hear such talk. He wouldn't ever dared to talk such talk in his life before. Just see what a difference it made in him the minute he judged he was about free. It was according to the old saying, 'give a nigger an inch and he'll take an ell.'[3] Thinks I, this is what comes of my not thinking. Here was this nigger which I had as good as helped to run away, coming right out flat-footed and saying he would steal his children—children that belonged to a man I didn't even know; a man that hadn't ever done me no harm.

I was sorry to hear Jim say that, it was such a lowering of him. My conscience got to stirring me up hotter than ever, until at last I says to it, 'Let up on me—it ain't too late, yet— I'll paddle ashore at the first light, and tell.' I felt easy, and happy, and light as a feather, right off. All my troubles was gone. I went to looking out sharp for a light, and sort of singing to myself. By-and-by one showed. Jim sings out:

'We's safe, Huck, we's safe! Jump up and crack yo' heels, dat's de good ole Cairo at las', I jis knows it!'

I says:

'I'll take the canoe and go see, Jim. It mightn't be, you know.'

He jumped and got the canoe ready, and put his old coat in the bottom for me to set on, and give me the paddle; and as I shoved off, he says:

'Pooty soon I'll be a-shout'n for joy, en I'll say, it's all on accounts o' Huck; I's a free man, en I couldn't ever ben free ef it hadn' ben for Huck; Huck done it. Jim won't ever forgit

---

[2] *he would buy his wife*: Under some circumstances, it was possible for an ex-slave to do just this: purchase freedom for his wife and his children.

[3] *give a nigger an inch and he'll take an ell*: a familiar phrase of the time period meaning "give way to a slave in a small way, and he'll attempt to take even more" (an ell is a unit of measurement equal to forty-five inches). The famous American figure Frederick Douglass makes ironic use of this demeaning saying in his account of his escape from slavery, *Narrative of Frederick Douglass* (1845).

you, Huck; you's de bes' fren' Jim's ever had; en you's de *only* fren' ole Jim's got now.'

I was paddling off, all in a sweat to tell on him; but when he says this, it seemed to kind of take the tuck[4] all out of me. I went along slow then, and I warn't right down certain whether I was glad I started or whether I warn't. When I was fifty yards off, Jim says:

'Dah you goes, de ole true Huck; de on'y white genlman dat ever kep' his promise to ole Jim.'

Well, I just felt sick. But I says, I *got* to do it—I can't get *out* of it. Right then, along comes a skiff with two men in it, with guns, and they stopped and I stopped. One of them says:

'What's that, yonder?'

'A piece of a raft,' I says.

'Do you belong on it?'

'Yes, sir.'

'Any men on it?'

'Only one, sir.'

'Well, there's five niggers run off tonight, up yonder above the head of the bend. Is your man white or black?'

I didn't answer up prompt. I tried to, but the words wouldn't come. I tried, for a second or two, to brace up and out with it, but I warn't man enough—hadn't the spunk of a rabbit. I see I was weakening; so I just give up trying, and up and says—

'He's white.'

'I reckon we'll go and see for ourselves.'

'I wish you would,' says I, 'because it's pap that's there, and maybe you'd help me tow the raft ashore where the light is. He's sick—and so is mam and Mary Ann.'

'Oh, the devil! we're in a hurry, boy. But I s'pose we've got to. Come—buckle to your paddle, and let's get along.'

I buckled to my paddle and they laid to their oars. When we had made a stroke or two, I says:

---

[4] *tuck*: vigor or energy.

'Pap'll be mighty much obleeged to you, I can tell you. Every-body goes away when I want them to help me tow the raft ashore, and I can't do it by myself.'

'Well, that's infernal mean. Odd, too. Say, boy, what's the matter with your father?'

'It's the—a—the—well, it ain't anything, much.'

They stopped pulling. It warn't but a mighty little ways to the raft, now. One says:

'Boy, that's a lie. What *is* the matter with your pap? Answer up square, now, and it'll be the better for you.'

'I will, sir, I will, honest—but don't leave us, please. It's the—the—gentlemen, if you'll only pull ahead, and let me heave you the head-line, you won't have to come a-near the raft—please do.'

'Set her back, John, set her back!' says one. They backed water. 'Keep away, boy—keep to looard. Confound it, I just expect the wind has blowed it to us. Your pap's got the small-pox,[5] and you know it precious well. Why didn't you come out and say so? Do you want to spread it all over?'

'Well,' says I, a-blubbering, 'I've told everybody before, and then they just went away and left us.'

'Poor devil, there's something in that. We are right down sorry for you, but we—well, hang it, we don't want the small-pox, you see. Look here, I'll tell you what to do. Don't you try to land by yourself, or you'll smash everything to pieces. You float along down about twenty miles and you'll come to a town on the left-hand side of the river. It will be long after sun-up, then, and when you ask for help, you tell them your folks are all down with chills and fever. Don't be a fool again, and let people guess what is the matter. Now we're trying to do you a kindness; so you just put twenty miles between us, that's a good boy. It wouldn't do any good to land yonder where the light is—it's only a wood-yard. Say—I reckon your father's poor, and I'm bound to say he's in pretty hard luck.

---

[5] *small-pox*: an acute and contagious viral disease, greatly feared at the time partly because it often left its survivors scarred with pockmarks.

Here—I'll put a twenty dollar gold piece on this board, and you get it when it floats by. I feel mighty mean to leave you, but my kingdom! it won't do to fool with small-pox, don't you see?'

'Hold on, Parker,' says the other man, 'here's a twenty to put on the board for me. Good-bye, boy, you do as Mr Parker told you, and you'll be all right.'

'That's so, my boy—good-bye, good-bye. If you see any run-away niggers, you get help and nab them, and you can make some money by it.'

'Good-bye, sir,' says I, 'I won't let no runaway niggers get by me if I can help it.'

They went off, and I got aboard the raft, feeling bad and low, because I knowed very well I had done wrong, and I see it warn't no use for me to try to learn to do right; a body that don't get *started* right when he's little, ain't got no show— when the pinch comes there ain't nothing to back him up and keep him to his work, and so he gets beat. Then I thought a minute, and says to myself, hold on,—s'pose you'd a done right and give Jim up; would you felt better than what you do now? No, says I, I'd feel bad—I'd feel just the same way I do now. Well, then, says I, what's the use you learning to do right, when it's troublesome to do right and ain't no trouble to do wrong, and the wages is just the same? I was stuck. I couldn't answer that. So I reckoned I wouldn't bother no more about it, but after this always do whichever come handiest at the time.

I went into the wigwam; Jim warn't there. I looked all around; he warn't anywhere. I says:

'Jim!'

'Here I is, Huck. Is dey out o' sight yit? Don't talk loud.'

He was in the river, under the stern oar, with just his nose out. I told him they was out of sight, so he come aboard. He says:

'I was a-listenin' to all de talk, en I slips into de river en was gwyne to shove for sho' if dey come aboard. Den I was gwyne to swim to de raf' again when dey was gone. But lawsy,[6] how you did fool 'em, Huck! Dat *wuz* de smartes' dodge! I tell you, chile, I 'speck it save' ole Jim—ole Jim ain't gwyne to forgit you for dat, honey.'

Then we talked about the money. It was a pretty good raise, twenty dollars apiece. Jim said we could take deck passage on a steamboat now, and the money would last us as far as we wanted to go in the free States. He said twenty mile more warn't far for the raft to go, but he wished we was already there.

Towards daybreak we tied up, and Jim was mighty particular about hiding the raft good. Then he worked all day fixing things in bundles, and getting all ready to quit rafting.

That night about ten we hove in sight of the lights of a town away down in a left-hand bend.

I went off in the canoe, to ask about it. Pretty soon I found a man out in the river with a skiff, setting a trot-line. I ranged up and says:

'Mister, is that town Cairo?'

'Cairo? no. You must be a blame' fool.'

'What town is it, mister?'

'If you want to know, go and find out. If you stay here bothering' around me for about a half a minute longer, you'll get something you won't want.'

I paddled to the raft. Jim was awful disappointed, but I said never mind, Cairo would be the next place, I reckoned.

We passed another town before daylight, and I was going out again; but it was high ground, so I didn't go. No high ground about Cairo, Jim said. I had forgot it. We laid up for the day, on a tow-head tolerable close to the left-hand bank. I begun to suspicion something. So did Jim. I says:

'Maybe we went by Cairo in the fog that night.'

He says:

'Doan' less' talk about it, Huck. Po' niggers can't have no luck. I awluz 'spected dat rattle-snake skin warn't done wid its work.'

---

[6] *lawsy*: also sometimes "'laws", a euphemism for "Lord".

'I wish I'd never seen that snake-skin, Jim—I do wish I'd never laid eyes on it.'

'It ain't yo' fault, Huck; you didn' know. Don't you blame yo'self 'bout it.'

When it was daylight, here was the clear Ohio water in shore, sure enough, and outside was the old regular Muddy![7] So it was all up with Cairo.

We talked it all over. It wouldn't do to take to the shore; we couldn't take the raft up the stream, of course. There warn't no way but to wait for dark, and start back in the canoe and take the chances. So we slept all day amongst the cotton-wood thicket, so as to be fresh for the work, and when we went back to the raft about dark the canoe was gone!

We didn't say a word for a good while. There warn't anything to say. We both knowed well enough it was some more work of the rattle-snake skin; so what was the use to talk about it? It would only look like we was finding fault, and that would be bound to fetch more bad luck—and keep on fetching it, too, till we knowed enough to keep still.

By-and-by we talked about what we better do, and found there warn't no way but just to go along down with the raft till we got a chance to buy a canoe to go back in. We warn't going to borrow it when there warn't anybody around, the way pap would do, for that might set people after us.

So we shoved out, after dark, on the raft.

Anybody that don't believe yet, that it's foolishness to handle a snake-skin, after all that that snake-skin done for us, will believe it now, if they read on and see what more it done for us.

The place to buy canoes is off of rafts laying up at shore. But we didn't see no rafts laying up; so we went along during three hours and more. Well, the night got gray, and ruther thick, which is the next meanest thing to fog. You can't tell

---

[7] *here was the clear Ohio water* . . . : Huck realizes they have missed Cairo when he sees the relatively clear water of the Ohio River flowing alongside the muddy water of the Mississippi River.

the shape of the river, and you can't see no distance. It got to be very late and still, and then along comes a steamboat up the river. We lit the lantern, and judged she would see it. Upstream boats didn't generly come close to us; they go out and follow the bars and hunt for easy water under the reefs; but nights like this they bull[8] right up the channel against the whole river.

We could hear her pounding along, but we didn't see her good till she was close. She aimed right for us. Often they do that and try to see how close they can come without touching; sometimes the wheel bites off a sweep, and then the pilot sticks his head out and laughs, and thinks he's mighty smart. Well, here she comes, and we said she was going to try to shave us; but she didn't seem to be sheering off a bit. She was a big one, and she was coming in a hurry, too, looking like a black cloud with rows of glow-worms around it; but all of a sudden she bulged out, big and scary, with a long row of wide-open furnace doors shining like red-hot teeth, and her monstrous bows and guards hanging right over us. There was a yell at us, and a jingling of bells to stop the engines, a powwow of cussing, and whistling of steam—and as Jim went overboard on one side and I on the other, she come smashing straight through the raft.

I dived—and I aimed to find the bottom, too, for a thirty-foot wheel had got to go over me, and I wanted it to have plenty of room. I could always stay under water a minute; this time I reckon I staid under water a minute and a half. Then I bounced for the top in a hurry, for I was nearly busting. I popped out to my arm-pits and blowed the water out of my nose, and puffed a bit. Of course there was a booming current; and of course that boat started her engines again ten seconds after she stopped them, for they never cared much for raftsmen; so now she was churning along up the river, out of sight in the thick weather, though I could hear her.

[8] *bull*: i.e., charge or advance like an angry bull.

I sung out for Jim about a dozen times, but I didn't get any answer; so I grabbed a plank that touched me while I was 'treading water,' and struck out for shore, shoving it ahead of me. But I made out to see that the drift of the current was towards the left-hand shore,[9] which meant that I was in a crossing; so I changed off and went that way.

It was one of these long, slanting, two-mile crossings; so I was a good long time in getting over. I made a safe landing, and clum up the bank. I couldn't see but a little ways, but I went poking along over rough ground for a quarter of a mile or more, and then I run across a big old-fashioned double log house before I noticed it. I was going to rush by and get away, but a lot of dogs jumped out and went to howling and barking at me, and I knowed better than to move another peg.

[9] *left-hand shore*: Huck heads with the current to the left bank, an area close to the border of Kentucky and Tennessee, where the Grangerford-Shepherdson feud now takes place.

CHAPTER 17

In about half a minute somebody spoke out of a window, without putting his head out, and says:

'Be done, boys! Who's there?'

I says:

'It's me.'

'Who's me?'

'George Jackson, sir.'

'What do you want?'

'I don't want nothing, sir. I only want to go along by, but
the dogs won't let me.'

'What are you prowling around here this time of night,
for—hey?'

'I warn't prowling around, sir; I fell overboard off of the
steamboat.'

'Oh, you did, did you? Strike a light there, somebody. What
did you say your name was?'

'George Jackson, sir. I'm only a boy.'

'Look here; if you're telling the truth, you needn't be afraid—
nobody 'll hurt you. But don't try to budge; stand right where
you are. Rouse out Bob and Tom, some of you, and fetch the
guns. George Jackson, is there anybody with you?'

'No, sir, nobody.'

I heard the people stirring around in the house, now, and
see a light. The man sung out:

'Snatch that light away, Betsy, you old fool—ain't you got
any sense? Put it on the floor behind the front door. Bob, if
you and Tom are ready, take your places.'

'All ready.'

'Now, George Jackson, do you know the Shepherdsons?'

'No, sir—I never heard of them.'

'Well, that may be so, and it mayn't. Now, all ready. Step
forward, George Jackson. And mind, don't you hurry—come

111

mighty slow. If there's anybody with you, let him keep back—if he shows himself he'll be shot. Come along, now. Come slow; push the door open, yourself—just enough to squeeze in, d' you hear?'

I didn't hurry, I couldn't if I'd a wanted to. I took one slow step at a time, and there warn't a sound, only I thought I could hear my heart. The dogs were as still as the humans, but they followed a little behind me. When I got to the three log door-steps, I heard them unlocking and unbarring and unbolting. I put my hand on the door and pushed it a little and a little more, till somebody said, 'There, that's enough—put your head in.' I done it, but I judged they would take it off.

The candle was on the floor, and there they all was, look-ing at me, and me at them, for about a quarter of a minute. Three big men with guns pointed at me, which made me wince, I tell you; the oldest, gray and about sixty, the other two thirty or more—all of them fine and handsome—and the sweetest old gray-headed lady, and back of her two young women which I couldn't see right well. The old gentleman says:

'There—I reckon it's all right. Come in.'

As soon as I was in, the old gentleman he locked the door and barred it and bolted it, and told the young men to come in with their guns, and they all went in a big parlor that had a new rag carpet on the floor, and got together in a corner that was out of range of the front windows—there warn't none on the side. They held the candle, and took a good look at me, and all said, 'Why *he* ain't a Shepherdson—no, there ain't any Shepherdson about him.' Then the old man said he hoped I wouldn't mind being searched for arms, because he didn't mean no harm by it—it was only to make sure. So he didn't pry into my pockets, but only felt outside with his hands, and said it was all right. He told me to make myself easy and at home, and tell all about myself; but the old lady says:

'Why bless you, Saul, the poor thing's as wet as he can be; and don't you reckon it may be he's hungry?'

'True for you, Rachel—I forgot.'

So the old lady says:

'Betsy' (this was a nigger woman), 'you fly around and get him something to eat, as quick as you can, poor thing; and one of you girls go and wake up Buck and tell him—Oh, here he is himself. Buck, take this little stranger and get the wet clothes off from him and dress him up in some of yours that's dry.'

Buck looked about as old as me—thirteen or fourteen or along there, though he was a little bigger than me. He hadn't on anything but a shirt, and he was very frowsy-headed. He come in gaping and digging one fist into his eyes, and he was dragging a gun along with the other one. He says:

'Ain't they no Shepherdsons around?'

They said, no, 'twas a false alarm.

'Well,' he says, 'if they'd a ben some, I reckon I'd a got one.'

They all laughed, and Bob says:

'Why, Buck, they might have scalped us all, you've been so slow in coming.'

'Well, nobody come after me, and it ain't right. I'm always kep' down; I don't get no show.'

'Never mind, Buck, my boy,' says the old man, 'you'll have show enough, all in good time, don't you fret about that. Go 'long with you now, and do as your mother told you.'

When we got up stairs to his room, he got me a coarse shirt and a roundabout[1] and pants of his, and I put them on. While I was at it he asked me what my name was, but before I could tell him, he started to telling me about a blue jay and a young rabbit he had catched in the woods day before yesterday, and he asked me where Moses was when the candle went out. I said I didn't know; I hadn't heard about it before, no way.

'Well, guess,' he says.

'How'm I going to guess,' says I, 'when I never heard tell about it before?'

'But you can guess, can't you? It's just as easy.'

'*Which* candle?' I says.

---

[1] *roundabout*: tight-fitting short jacket.

'Why, any candle,' he says.

'I don't know where he was,' says I; 'where was he?'

'Why he was in the *dark*! That's where he was!'

'Well, if you knowed where he was, what did you ask me for?'

'Why, blame it, it's a riddle, don't you see? Say, how long are you going to stay here? You got to stay always. We can just have booming times—they don't have no school now. Do you own a dog? I've got a dog—and he'll go in the river and bring out chips that you throw in. Do you like to comb up, Sundays, and all that kind of foolishness? You bet I don't, but ma she makes me. Confound these ole britches, I reckon I'd better put 'em on, but I'd ruther not, it's so warm. Are you all ready? All right—come along, old hoss.'

Cold corn-pone, cold corn-beef, butter and butter-milk—that is what they had for me down there, and there ain't nothing better that ever I've come across yet. Buck and his ma and all of them smoked cob pipes, except the nigger woman, which was gone, and the two young women. They all smoked and talked, and I eat and talked. The young women had quilts around them, and their hair down their backs. They all asked me questions, and I told them how pap and me and all the family was living on a little farm down at the bottom of Arkansaw, and my sister Mary Ann run off and got married and never was heard of no more, and Bill went to hunt them and he warn't heard of no more, and Tom and Mort died, and then there warn't nobody but just me and pap left, and he was just trimmed down to nothing, on account of his troubles; so when he died I took what there was left, because the farm didn't belong to us, and started up the river, deck passage, and fell overboard; and that was how I come to be here. So they said I could have a home there as long as I wanted it. Then it was most daylight, and everybody went to bed, and I went to bed with Buck, and when I waked up in the morning, drat it all, I had forgot what my name was. So I laid there about an hour trying to think, and when Buck waked up, I says:

'Can you spell, Buck?'

'Yes,' he says.

'I bet you can't spell my name,' says I.

'I bet you what you dare I can,' says he.

'All right,' says I, 'go ahead.'

'G-o-r-g-e J-a-x-o-n—there now,' he says.

'Well,' says I, 'you done it, but I didn't think you could. It ain't no slouch of a name to spell[2]—right off without studying.'

I set it down,[3] private, because somebody might want *me* to spell it, next, and so I wanted to be handy with it and rattle it off like I was used to it.

It was a mighty nice family, and a mighty nice house, too. I hadn't seen no house out in the country before that was so nice and had so much style. It didn't have an iron latch on the front door, nor a wooden one with a buckskin string, but a brass knob to turn, the same as houses in a town. There warn't no bed in the parlor, not a sign of a bed; but heaps of parlors in towns had beds in them. There was a big fireplace that was bricked on the bottom, and the bricks was kept clean and red by pouring water on them and scrubbing them with another brick; sometimes they washed them over with red water-paint that they call Spanish-brown, same as they do in town. They had big brass dog-irons[4] that could hold up a saw-log. There was a clock on the middle of the mantel-piece, with a picture of a town painted on the bottom half of the glass front, and a round place in the middle of it for the sun, and you could see the pendulum swing behind it. It was beautiful to hear that clock tick; and sometimes when one of these peddlers had been along and scoured her up and got her in good shape, she would start in and strike a hundred and fifty, before she got tuckered out. They wouldn't took any money for her.

Well, there was a big outlandish parrot on each side of the clock, made out of something like chalk, and painted up gaudy.

---

[2] *It ain't no slouch of a name to spell*: i.e., it is not an easy name to spell.

[3] *set it down*: wrote it down.

[4] *dog-irons*: andirons.

By one of the parrots was a cat made of crockery, and a crockery dog by the other; and when you pressed down on them they squeaked, but didn't open their mouths nor look different nor interested. They squeaked through underneath. There was a couple of big wild-turkey-wing fans spread out behind those things. On a table in the middle of the room was a kind of a lovely crockery basket that had apples and oranges and peaches and grapes piled up in it which was much redder and yellower and prettier than real ones is, but they warn't real because you could see where pieces had got chipped off and showed the white chalk or whatever it was, underneath.

This table had a cover made out of beautiful oil-cloth,[5] with a red and blue spread-eagle painted on it, and a painted border all around. It come all the way from Philadelphia, they said. There was some books too, piled up perfectly exact, on each corner of the table. One was a big family Bible, full of pictures. One was 'Pilgrim's Progress,'[6] about a man that left his family it didn't say why. I read considerable in it now and then. The statements was interesting, but tough. Another was 'Friendship's Offering,'[7] full of beautiful stuff and poetry; but I didn't read the poetry. Another was Henry Clay's Speeches,[8] and another was Dr Gunn's Family Medicine,[9] which told you all about what to do if a body was sick or dead. There was a Hymn Book, and a lot of other books. And there was nice split-bottom chairs, and perfectly sound, too—not bagged down in the middle and busted, like an old basket.

[5] *oil-cloth*: cloth with a resin coating to make it durable.

[6] *'Pilgrim's Progress'*: John Bunyon's *The Pilgrim's Progress* (1678) is a religious allegory about the travels of a character named Christian through many trials to the Celestial City. Next to the Bible, it was a familiar book in a nineteenth-century Protestant household.

[7] *'Friendship's Offering'*: first published in 1841, a popular mid-nineteenth-century annual gift book containing sentimental verse, stories, and illustrations.

[8] *Henry Clay's Speeches*: Henry Clay (1777–1852) was a Kentucky senator, secretary of state, and congressman known for his eloquence.

[9] *Dr Gunn's Family Medicine*: First published in 1832, John C. Gunn's encyclopedia of medicine was highly popular and went through many editions.

They had pictures hung on the walls—mainly Washingtons and Lafayettes,[10] and battles, and Highland Marys,[11] and one called 'Signing the Declaration'.[12] There was some that they called crayons,[13] which one of the daughters which was dead made her own self when she was only fifteen years old. They was different from any pictures I ever see before; blacker, mostly, than is common. One was a woman in a slim black dress, belted small under the arm-pits, with bulges like a cabbage in the middle of the sleeves, and a large black scoop-shovel bonnet with a black veil, and white slim ankles crossed about with black tape, and very wee black slippers, like a chisel, and she was leaning pensive on a tombstone on her right elbow, under a weeping willow, and her other hand hanging down her side holding a white handkerchief and a reticule, and underneath the picture it said 'Shall I Never See Thee More Alas'.[14] Another one was a young lady with her hair all combed up straight to the top of her head, and knotted there in front of a comb[15] like a chair-back, and she was crying into a hand-kerchief and had a dead bird laying on its back in her other hand with its heels up, and underneath the picture it said 'I Shall Never Hear Thy Sweet Chirrup More Alas'. There was one where a young lady was at a window looking up at the moon, and tears running down her cheeks; and she had an

[10] *Lafayettes*: French aristocrat the Marquis de Lafayette (1757–1834) fought on the American side in the Revolutionary War.

[11] *Highland Marys*: Mary Campbell, the sweetheart of Scottish poet Robert Burns, died young in 1786 and became the subject of sentimental songs, poems, and paintings.

[12] *'Signing the Declaration'*: most likely a copy of John Trumball's famous 1820 painting, *The Declaration of Independence, July 4, 1776*.

[13] *crayons*: drawings in paste or pastel.

[14] In the artist's obsession with death, Twain ridicules this nineteenth-century Romantic tendency. Funereal or mourning pictures with tombstones, willows, and mourners, and elaborately sentimental obituary verses, such as the daughter's "Ode to Stephen Dowling Bots, Dec'd" (see below), were typical of the period. This sensibility later found affirmation in Queen Victoria's lifelong mourning of her husband, Prince Albert, after his death in 1861. Like the Grang-erfords do for their daughter, Queen Victoria preserved Albert's bedroom exactly as it appeared when he died.

[15] *comb*: ornamental device used to keep the hair in place.

open letter in one hand with black sealing-wax[16] showing on one edge of it, and she was mashing a locket with a chain to it against her mouth, and underneath the picture it said 'And Art Thou Gone Yes Thou Art Gone Alas'. These was all nice pictures, I reckon, but I didn't somehow seem to take to them, because if ever I was down a little, they always give me the fan-tods. Everybody was sorry she died, because she had laid out a lot more of these pictures to do, and a body could see by what she had done what they had lost. But I reckoned, that with her disposition, she was having a better time in the graveyard. She was at work on what they said was her greatest picture when she took sick, and every day and every night it was her prayer to be allowed to live till she got it done, but she never got the chance. It was a picture of a young woman in a long white gown, standing on the rail of a bridge all ready to jump off, with her hair all down her back, and looking up to the moon, with the tears running down her face, and she had two arms folded across her breast, and two arms stretched out in front, and two more reaching up towards the moon—and the idea was, to see which pair would look best and then scratch out all the other arms; but, as I was saying, she died before she got her mind made up, and now they kept this picture over the head of the bed in her room, and every time her birthday come they hung flowers on it. Other times it was hid with a little curtain. The young woman in the picture had a kind of a nice sweet face, but there was so many arms it made her look too spidery, seemed to me.

This young girl kept a scrap-book when she was alive, and used to paste obituaries and accidents and cases of patient suffering in it out of the *Presbyterian Observer*,[17] and write poetry after them out of her own head. It was very good poetry. This

---

[16] *sealing-wax*: wax used to seal letters.

[17] *Presbyterian Observer*: A newspaper of this name did not begin publication until 1872. Twain may have had in mind popular papers such as the *Christian Observer* and the *Presbyterian Sentinel*, both in circulation during the time period of the novel.

is what she wrote about a boy by the name of Stephen Dowling Bots that fell down a well and was drownded:

ODE TO STEPHEN DOWLING BOTS, DEC'D. [18]

> And did young Stephen sicken,
>   And did young Stephen die?
> And did the sad hearts thicken,
>   And did the mourners cry?
>
> No; such was the fate of
>   Young Stephen Dowling Bots;
> Though sad hearts round him thickened,
>   'Twas not from sickness' shots.
>
> No whooping-cough did rack his frame,
>   Nor measles drear, with spots;
> Not these impaired the sacred name
>   Of Stephen Dowling Bots.
>
> Despised love struck not with woe
>   That head of curly knots,
> Nor stomach troubles laid him low,
>   Young Stephen Dowling Bots.
>
> O no. Then list with tearful eye,
>   Whilst I his fate do tell.
> His soul did from this cold world fly,
>   By falling down a well.
>
> They got him out and emptied him;
>   Alas it was too late;
> His spirit was gone for to sport aloft
>   In the realms of the good and great.

If Emmeline Grangerford could make poetry like that before
she was fourteen, there ain't no telling what she could a done
by-and-by. Buck said she could rattle off poetry like nothing.
She didn't ever have to stop to think. He said she would slap

[18] *Dec'd*: deceased.

down a line, and if she couldn't find anything to rhyme with it she would just scratch it out and slap down another one, and go ahead. She warn't particular, she could write about any-thing you choose to give her to write about, just so it was sad-ful. Every time a man died, or a woman died, or a child died, she would be on hand with her 'tribute' before he was cold. She called them tributes. The neighbors said it was the doctor first, then Emmeline, then the undertaker—the undertaker never got in ahead of Emmeline but once, and then she hung fire on a rhyme for the dead person's name, which was Whistler. She warn't ever the same, after that; she never complained, but she kind of pined away and did not live long. Poor thing, many's the time I made myself go up to the little room that used to be hers and get out her poor old scrapbook and read in it when her pictures had been aggravating me and I had soured on her a little. I liked all that family, dead ones and all, and warn't going to let anything come between us. Poor Emmeline made poetry about all the dead people when she was alive, and it didn't seem right that there warn't nobody to make some about her, now she was gone; so I tried to sweat out a verse or two myself, but I couldn't seem to make it go, somehow. They kept Emmeline's room trim and nice and all the things fixed in it just the way she liked to have them when she was alive, and nobody ever slept there. The old lady took care of the room herself, though there was plenty of niggers, and she sewed there a good deal and read her Bible there, mostly.

Well, as I was saying about the parlor, there was beautiful curtains on the windows: white, with pictures painted on them, of castles with vines all down the walls, and cattle coming down to drink. There was a little old piano, too, that had tin pans in it, I reckon, and nothing was ever so lovely as to hear the young ladies sing, 'The Last Link is Broken' and play 'The Battle of Prague' on it.[19] The walls of all the rooms

---

[19] *'The Last Link is Broken'* ... *'The Battle of Prague'*: The first is a song by William Clifton, written around 1840; the second is a piano piece by Franz Kotzwara, composed in 1788.

was plastered, and most had carpets on the floors, and the whole house was whitewashed on the outside.

It was a double house, and the big open place betwixt them was roofed and floored, and sometimes the table was set there in the middle of the day, and it was a cool, comfortable place. Nothing couldn't be better. And warn't the cooking good, and just bushels of it too!

CHAPTER 18

Col. Grangerford was a gentleman, you see. He was a gentleman all over; and so was his family. He was well born, as the saying is, and that's worth as much in a man as it is in a horse, so the Widow Douglas said, and nobody ever denied that she was of the first aristocracy in our town; and pap he always said it, too, though he warn't no more quality than a mud-cat,[1] himself. Col. Grangerford was very tall and very slim, and had a darkish-paly complexion, not a sign of red in it anywheres; he was clean-shaved every morning, all over his thin face, and he had the thinnest kind of lips, and the thinnest kind of nostrils, and a high nose, and heavy eyebrows, and the blackest kind of eyes, sunk so deep back that they seemed like they was looking out of caverns at you, as you may say. His forehead was high, and his hair was black and straight, and hung to his shoulders. His hands was long and thin, and every day of his life he put on a clean shirt and a full suit from head to foot made out of linen so white it hurt your eyes to look at it; and on Sundays he wore a blue tail-coat with brass buttons on it. He carried a mahogany cane with a silver head to it.[2] There warn't no frivolishness about him, not a bit, and he warn't ever loud. He was as kind as he could be—you could feel that, you know, and so you had confidence. Sometimes he smiled, and it was good to see; but when he straightened himself up like a liberty-pole,[3] and the lightning begun to flicker out from under his eyebrows you wanted to climb a tree first, and find out what the matter was afterwards. He didn't ever have to tell anybody to mind their manners—everybody was always good mannered where he was. Everybody loved to have him

[1] *mud-cat:* catfish.
[2] The description of Colonel Grangerford is a familiar nineteenth-century type of the Southern aristocratic gentleman or plantation owner.
[3] *liberty-pole:* flagstaff.

around, too; he was sunshine most always—I mean he made it seem like good weather. When he turned into a cloud-bank it was awful dark for a half a minute and that was enough; there wouldn't nothing go wrong again for a week.

When him and the old lady come down in the morning, all the family got up out of their chairs and give them good-day, and didn't set down again till they had set down. Then Tom and Bob went to the sideboard where the decanters was, and mixed a glass of bitters and handed it to him, and he held it in his hand and waited till Tom's and Bob's was mixed, and then they bowed and said 'Our duty to you, sir, and madam'; and *they* bowed the least bit in the world and said thank you, and so they drank, all three, and Bob and Tom poured a spoonful of water on the sugar and the mite of whisky or apple brandy in the bottom of their tumblers, and give it to me and Buck, and we drank to the old people too.

Bob was the oldest, and Tom next. Tall, beautiful men with very broad shoulders and brown faces, and long black hair and black eyes. They dressed in white linen from head to foot, like the old gentleman, and wore broad Panama hats.[4]

Then there was Miss Charlotte, she was twenty-five, and tall and proud and grand, but as good as she could be, when she warn't stirred up; but when she was, she had a look that would make you wilt in your tracks, like her father. She was beautiful.

So was her sister, Miss Sophia, but it was a different kind. She was gentle and sweet, like a dove, and she was only twenty.

Each person had their own nigger to wait on them—Buck, too. My nigger had a monstrous easy time, because I warn't used to having anybody do anything for me, but Buck's was on the jump most of the time.

This was all there was of the family, now; but there used to be more—three sons; they got killed; and Emmeline that died.

The old gentleman owned a lot of farms, and over a hundred niggers. Sometimes a stack of people would come there,

---

[4] *Panama hats:* lightweight straw hats.

horse-back, from ten or fifteen mile around, and stay five or six days, and have such junketings[5] round about and on the river, and dances and picnics in the woods, day-times, and balls at the house, nights. These people was mostly kin-folks of the family. The men brought their guns with them. It was a handsome lot of quality, I tell you.

There was another clan of aristocracy around there—five or six families—mostly of the name of Shepherdson. They was as high-toned, and well born, and rich and grand, as the tribe of Grangerfords. The Shepherdsons and the Grangerfords used the same steamboat landing, which was about two mile above our house; so sometimes when I went up there with a lot of our folks I used to see a lot of the Shepherdsons there, on their fine horses.

One day Buck and me was away out in the woods, hunting, and heard a horse coming. We was crossing the road. Buck says:

'Quick! Jump for the woods!'

We done it, and then peeped down the woods through the leaves. Pretty soon a splendid young man come galloping down the road, setting his horse easy and looking like a soldier. He had his gun across his pommel. I had seen him before. It was young Harney Shepherdson. I heard Buck's gun go off at my ear, and Harney's hat tumbled off from his head. He grabbed his gun and rode straight to the place where we was hid. But we didn't wait. We started through the woods on a run. The woods warn't thick, so I looked over my shoulder, to dodge the bullet, and twice I seen Harney cover Buck with his gun; and then he rode away the way he come—to get his hat, I reckon, but I couldn't see. We never stopped running till we got home. The old gentleman's eyes blazed a minute—'twas pleasure, mainly, I judged—then his face sort of smoothed down, and he says, kind of gentle:

'I don't like that shooting from behind a bush. Why didn't you step into the road, my boy?'

---

[5] *junketings*: festivities.

'The Shepherdsons don't, father. They always take advantage.'

Miss Charlotte she held her head up like a queen while Buck was telling his tale, and her nostrils spread and her eyes snapped. The two young men looked dark, but never said nothing. Miss Sophia she turned pale, but the color come back when she found the man warn't hurt.

Soon as I could get Buck down by the corn-cribs under the trees by ourselves, I says:

'Did you want to kill him, Buck?'

'Well, I bet I did.'

'What did he do to you?'

'Him? He never done nothing to me.'

'Well, then, what did you want to kill him for?'

'Why nothing—only it's on account of the feud.'

'What's a feud?'

'Why, where was you raised? Don't you know what a feud is?'

'Never heard of it before—tell me about it.'

'Well,' says Buck, 'a feud is this way. A man has a quarrel with another man, and kills him; then that other man's brother kills *him*; then the other brothers, on both sides, goes for one another; then the *cousins* chip in—and by-and-by everybody's killed off, and there ain't no more feud. But it's kind of slow, and takes a long time.'

'Has this one been going on long, Buck?'

'Well I should *reckon!* it started thirty year ago, or som'ers along there. There was trouble 'bout something and then a lawsuit to settle it; and the suit went agin one of the men, and so he up and shot the man that won the suit—which he would naturally do, of course. Anybody would.'

'What was the trouble about, Buck?—land?'

'I reckon maybe—I don't know.'

'Well, who done the shooting?—was it a Grangerford or a Shepherdson?'

'Laws, how do *I* know? it was so long ago.'

'Don't anybody know?'

'Oh, yes, pa knows, I reckon, and some of the other old folks; but they don't know, now, what the row was about in the first place.'

'Has there been many killed, Buck?'

'Yes—right smart chance of funerals. But they don't always kill. Pa's got a few buck-shot in him; but he don't mind it 'cuz he don't weigh much anyway. Bob's been carved up some with a bowie,[6] and Tom's been hurt once or twice.'

'Has anybody been killed this year, Buck?'

'Yes, we got one and they got one. 'Bout three months ago my cousin Bud, fourteen year old, was riding through the woods on t'other side of the river, and didn't have no weapon with him, which was blame' foolishness, and in a lonesome place he hears a horse a-coming behind him, and sees old Baldy Shepherdson a-linkin' after him with his gun in his hand and his white hair a-flying in the wind; and 'stead of jumping off and taking to the brush, Bud 'lowed he could outrun him; so they had it, nip and tuck, for five mile or more, the old man a-gaining all the time; so at last Bud seen it warn't any use, so he stopped and faced around so as to have the bullet holes in front, you know, and the old man he rode up and shot him down. But he didn't git much chance to enjoy his luck, for inside of a week our folks laid *him* out.'

'I reckon that old man was a coward, Buck.'

'I reckon he *warn't* a coward. Not by a blame' sight. There ain't a coward amongst them Shepherdsons—not a one. And there ain't no cowards amongst the Grangerfords, either. Why, that old man kep' up his end in a fight one day, for a half an hour, against three Grangerfords, and come out winner. They was all a-horseback; he lit off of his horse and got behind a little wood-pile, and kep' his horse before him to stop the bullets; but the Grangerfords staid on their horses and capered around the old man, and peppered away at him, and he peppered away at them. Him and his horse both went home pretty

---

[6] *bowie:* bowie knife, a hunting knife named for the American pioneer and soldier Jim Bowie (1796–1836).

leaky and crippled, but the Grangerfords had to be *fetched* home—and one of 'em was dead, and another died the next day. No, sir, if a body's out hunting for cowards, he don't want to fool away any time amongst them Shepherdsons, becuz they don't breed any of that *kind*.'

Next Sunday we all went to church, about three mile, everybody a-horseback. The men took their guns along, so did Buck, and kept them between their knees or stood them handy against the wall. The Shepherdsons done the same. It was pretty ornery preaching—all about brotherly love, and such-like tiresomeness; but everybody said it was a good sermon, and they all talked it over going home, and had such a powerful lot to say about faith, and good works, and free grace, and preforeordestination,[7] and I don't know what all, that it did seem to me to be one of the roughest Sundays I had run across yet.

About an hour after dinner everybody was dozing around, some in their chairs and some in their rooms, and it got to be pretty dull. Buck and a dog was stretched out on the grass in the sun, sound asleep. I went up to our room, and judged I would take a nap myself. I found that sweet Miss Sophia standing in her door, which was next to ours, and she took me in her room and shut the door very soft, and asked me if I liked her, and I said I did; and she asked me if I would do something for her and not tell anybody, and I said I would. Then she said she'd forgot her Testament, and left it in the seat at church, between two other books and would I slip out quiet and go there and fetch it to her, and not say nothing to nobody. I said I would. So I slid out and slipped off up the road, and there warn't anybody at the church, except maybe a hog or two, for there warn't any lock on the door, and hogs likes a puncheon floor[8] in summer-time because it's cool. If you notice, most folks don't go to church only when they've got to; but a hog is different.

---

[7] *preforeordestination*: Huck combines here two Presbyterian tenets, "predestination" and "foreordination".

[8] *puncheon floor*: log floor.

Says I to myself something's up—it ain't natural for a girl to be in such a sweat about a Testament; so I give it a shake, and out drops a little piece of paper with '*Half-past two*' wrote on it with a pencil. I ransacked it, but couldn't find anything else. I couldn't make anything out of that, so I put the paper in the book again, and when I got home and up stairs, there was Miss Sophia in her door waiting for me. She pulled me in and shut the door; then she looked in the Testament till she found the paper, and as soon as she read it she looked glad; and before a body could think, she grabbed me and give me a squeeze, and said I was the best boy in the world, and not to tell anybody. She was mighty red in the face, for a minute, and her eyes lighted up and it made her powerful pretty. I was a good deal aston-ished, but when I got my breath I asked her what the paper was about, and she asked me if I had read it, and I said no, and she asked me if I could read writing, and I told her 'no, only coarse-hand,'[9] and then she said the paper warn't anything but a book-mark to keep her place, and I might go and play now.

I went off down to the river, studying over this thing, and pretty soon I noticed that my nigger was following along behind. When we was out of sight of the house, he looked back and around a second, and then comes a-running, and says:

'Mars[10] Jawge, if you'll come down into de swamp, I'll show you a whole stack o' water-moccasins.'[11]

Thinks I, that's mighty curious; he said that yesterday. He oughter know a body don't love water-moccasins enough to go around hunting for them. What is he up to anyway? So I says—

'All right, trot ahead.'

I followed a half a mile, then he struck out over the swamp and waded ankle deep as much as another half mile. We come to a little flat piece of land which was dry and very thick with trees and bushes and vines, and he says—

[9] *coarse-hand*: printing rather than cursive script.
[10] *Mars*: Master.
[11] *water-moccasins*: type of poisonous snake.

'You shove right in dah, jist a few steps, Mars Jawge, dah's whah dey is. I's seed 'm befo', I don't k'yer to see 'em no mo'.'

Then he slopped right along and went away, and pretty soon the trees hid him. I poked into the place a-ways, and come to a little open patch as big as a bedroom, all hung around with vines, and found a man lying there asleep—and by jings it was my old Jim!

I waked him up, and I reckoned it was going to be a grand surprise to him to see me again, but it warn't. He nearly cried, he was so glad, but he warn't surprised. He said he swum along behind me, that night, and heard me yell every time, but dasn't answer, because he didn't want nobody to pick *him* up, and take him into slavery again. Says he—

'I got hurt a little, en couldn't swim fas', so I wuz a considable way behine you, towards de las'; when you landed I reck'ned I could ketch up wid you on de lan' 'dout havin' to shout at you, but when I see dat house I begin to go slow. I 'uz off too fur to hear what dey say to you—I wuz 'fraid o' de dogs—but when it 'uz all quiet agin, I knowed you's in de house, so I struck out for de woods to wait for day. Early in de mawnin' some er de niggers come along, gwyne to de fields, en dey tuck me en showed me dis place, whah de dogs can't track me on accounts o' de water, en dey brings me truck to eat every night, en tells me how you's a gitt'n along.'

'Why didn't you tell my Jack to fetch me here sooner, Jim?'

'Well, 'twarn't no use to 'sturb you, Huck, tell we could do sumfn—but we's all right now. I ben a-buyin' pots en pans en vittles, as I got a chanst, en a patchin' up de raf', nights, when—'

'*What* raft, Jim?'

'Our ole raf'.'

'You mean to say our old raft warn't smashed all to flinders?' [12]

'No, she warn't. She was tore up a good deal—one en' of her was—but dey warn't no great harm done, on'y our traps was mos' all los'. Ef we hadn' dive' so deep en swum so fur

---

[12] *flinders*: splinters.

under water, en de night hadn' ben so dark, en we warn't so sk'yerd, en ben sich punkin-heads, as de sayin' is, we'd a seed de raf'. But it's jis' as well we didn't, 'kase now she's all fixed up agin mos' as good as new, en we's got a new lot o' stuff, too, in de place o' what 'uz los'.'

'Why, how did you get hold of the raft again, Jim—did you catch her?'

'How I gwyne to ketch her, en I out in de woods? No, some er de niggers foun' her ketched on a snag, along heah in de ben', en dy hid her in a crick, 'mongst de willows, en dey wuz so much jawin' 'bout which un 'um she b'long to de mos', dat I come to heah 'bout it pooty soon, so I ups en settles de trouble by tellin' 'um she don't b'long to none uv um, but to you en me; en I ast 'm if dey gwyne to grab a young white genl-man's propaty, en git a hid'n for it? Den I gin 'm ten cents apiece, en dey 'uz mighty well satisfied, en wisht some mo' raf's 'ud come along en make 'm rich agin. Dey's mighty good to me, dese niggers is, en whatever I wants 'm to do fur me, I doan' have to ast 'm twice, honey. Dat Jack's a good nigger, en pooty smart.'

'Yes, he is. He ain't ever told me you was here; told me to come, and he'd show me a lot of water-moccasins. If anything happens, *he* ain't mixed up in it. He can say he never seen us together, and it'll be the truth.'

I don't want to talk much about the next day. I reckon I'll cut it pretty short. I waked up about dawn, and was agoing to turn over and go to sleep again, when I noticed how still it was—didn't seem to be anybody stirring. That warn't usual. Next I noticed that Buck was up and gone. Well, I gets up, a-wondering, and goes down stairs—nobody around; every-thing as still as a mouse. Just the same outside; thinks I, what does it mean? Down by the wood-pile I comes across my Jack, and says:

'What's it all about?'

Says he:

'Don't you know, Mars Jawge?'

'No,' says I, 'I don't.'

'Well, den, Miss Sophia's run off! 'deed she has. She run off in de night, sometime—nobody don't know jis' when—run off to git married to dat young Harney Shepherdson, you know—leastways, so dey 'spec. De fambly foun' it out, 'bout half an hour ago—maybe a little mo'—en' I *tell* you dey warn't no time los'. Sich another hurryin' up guns en hosses *you* never see! De women folks has gone for to stir up de relations, en ole Mars Saul en de boys tuck dey guns en rode up de river road for to try to ketch dat young man en kill him 'fo' he kin git acrost de river wid Miss Sophia. I reck'n dey's gwyne to be mighty rough times.'

'Buck went off 'thout waking me up.'

'Well I reck'n he *did*! Dey warn't gwyne to mix you up in it. Mars Buck he loaded up his gun en 'lowed he's gwyne to fetch home a Shepherdson or bust. Well, dey'll be plenty un 'm dah, I reck'n, en you bet you he'll fetch one ef he gits a chanst.'

I took up the river road as hard as I could put. By-and-by I begin to hear guns a good ways off. When I come in sight of the log store and the wood-pile where the steamboats lands, I worked along under the trees and brush till I got to a good place, and then I clumb up into the forks of a cotton-wood that was out of reach, and watched. There was a wood-rank[13] four foot high, a little ways in front of the tree, and first I was going to hide behind that; but maybe it was luckier I didn't.

There was four or five men cavorting around on their horses in the open place before the log store, cussing and yelling, and trying to get at a couple of young chaps that was behind the wood-rank alongside of the steamboat landing—but they couldn't come it. Every time one of them showed himself on the river side of the wood-pile he got shot at. The two boys was squatting back to back behind the pile, so they could watch both ways.

By-and-by the men stopped cavorting around and yelling. They started riding towards the store; then up gets one of the boys, draws a steady bead over the wood-rank, and drops one

[13] *wood-rank*: woodpile.

of them out of his saddle. All the men jumped off of their horses and grabbed the hurt one and started to carry him to the store; and that minute the two boys started on the run. They got half-way to the tree I was in before the men noticed. Then the men see them, and jumped on their horses and took out after them. They gained on the boys, but it didn't do no good, the boys had too good a start; they got to the wood-pile that was in front of my tree, and slipped in behind it and so they had the bulge on[14] the men again. One of the boys was Buck, and the other was a slim young chap about nineteen years old.

The men ripped around awhile, and then rode away. As soon as they was out of sight, I sung out to Buck and told him. He didn't know what to make of my voice coming out of the tree, at first. He was awful surprised. He told me to watch out sharp and let him know when the men come in sight again; said they was up to some devilment or other—wouldn't be gone long. I wished I was out of that tree, but I dasn't come down. Buck begun to cry and rip, and 'lowed that him and his cousin Joe (that was the other young chap) would make up for this day, yet. He said his father and his two brothers was killed, and two or three of the enemy. Said the Shepherdsons laid for them, in ambush. Buck said his father and brothers ought to waited for their relations—the Shepherdsons was too strong for them. I asked him what was become of young Harney and Miss Sophia. He said they'd got across the river and was safe. I was glad of that; but the way Buck did take on because he didn't manage to kill Harney that day he shot at him—I hain't ever heard anything like it.

All of a sudden, bang! bang! bang! goes three or four guns—the men had slipped around through the woods and come in from behind without their horses! The boys jumped for the river—both of them hurt—and as they swum down the current the men run along the bank shooting at them and singing out, 'Kill them, kill them!' It made me so sick I most fell

---

[14] *had the bulge on*: had the upper hand of.

out of the tree. I ain't agoing to tell *all* that happened—it would make me sick again if I was to do that. I wished I hadn't ever come ashore that night, to see such things. I ain't ever going to get shut of them—lots of times I dream about them.

I staid in the tree till it begun to get dark, afraid to come down. Sometimes I heard guns away off in the woods; and twice I seen little gangs of men gallop past the log store with guns; so I reckoned the trouble was still agoing on. I was mighty down-hearted; so I made up my mind I wouldn't ever go anear that house again, because I reckoned I was to blame, some-how. I judged that that piece of paper meant that Miss Sophia was to meet Harney somewheres at half-past two and run off; and I judged I ought to told her father about that paper and the curious way she acted, and then maybe he would a locked her up and this awful mess wouldn't ever happened.

When I got down out of the tree, I crept along down the river bank a piece, and found the two bodies laying in the edge of the water, and tugged at them till I got them ashore; then I covered up their faces, and got away as quick as I could. I cried a little when I was covering up Buck's face, for he was mighty good to me.

It was just dark, now. I never went near the house, but struck through the woods and made for the swamp. Jim warn't on his island, so I tramped off in a hurry for the crick, and crowded through the willows, red-hot to jump aboard and get out of that awful country—the raft was gone! My souls, but I was scared! I couldn't get my breath for most a minute. Then I raised a yell. A voice not twenty-five foot from me, says—

'Good lan'! is dat you, honey? Doan' make no noise.'

It was Jim's voice—nothing ever sounded so good before. I run along the bank a piece and got aboard, and Jim he grabbed me and hugged me, he was so glad to see me. He says—

'Laws bless you, chile, I 'uz right down sho' you's dead agin. Jack's been heah, he says he reck'n you's ben shot, kase you didn' come home no mo'; so I's jes' dis minute a startin' de raf' down towards de mouf er de crick, so's to be all ready for to shove out en leave soon as Jack comes agin en tells me for certain you *is* dead. Lawsy, I's mighty glad to get you back agin, honey.'

I says—

'All right—that's mighty good; they won't find me, and they'll think I've been killed, and floated down the river— there's something up there that'll help them to think so—so don't you lose no time, Jim, but just shove off for the big water as fast as ever you can.'

I never felt easy till the raft was two mile below there and out in the middle of the Mississippi. Then we hung up our signal lantern, and judged that we was free and safe once more. I hadn't had a bite to eat since yesterday; so Jim he got out some corn-dodgers and buttermilk, and pork and cabbage, and greens—there ain't nothing in the world so good, when it's cooked right—and whilst I eat my supper we talked, and had a good time. I was powerful glad to get away from the feuds, and so was Jim to get away from the swamp. We said there warn't no home like a raft, after all. Other places do seem so cramped up and smothery, but a raft don't. You feel mighty free and easy and comfortable on a raft.

CHAPTER 19

Two or three days and nights went by; I reckon I might say they swum by, they slid along so quiet and smooth and lovely. Here is the way we put in the time. It was a monstrous big river down there—sometimes a mile and a half wide; we run nights, and laid up and hid day-times; soon as night was most gone, we stopped navigating and tied up—nearly always in the dead water under a tow-head; and then cut young cotton-woods and willows and hid the raft with them. Then we set out the lines. Next we slid into the river and had a swim, so as to freshen up and cool off; then we set down on the sandy bottom where the water was about knee deep, and watched the daylight come. Not a sound, anywheres—perfectly still—just like the whole world was asleep, only sometimes the bullfrogs a-cluttering, maybe. The first thing to see, looking away over the water, was a kind of dull line—that was the woods on t'other side—you couldn't make nothing else out; then a pale place in the sky; then more paleness, spreading around; then the river softened up, away off, and warn't black any more, but gray; you could see little dark spots drifting along, ever so far away—trading scows, and such things; and long black streaks—rafts; sometimes you could hear a sweep screaking; or jumbled up voices, it was so still, and sounds come so far; and by-and-by you could see a streak on the water which you know by the look of the streak that there's a snag there in a swift current which breaks on it and makes the streak look that way; and you see the mist curl up off of the water, and the east reddens up, and the river, and you make out a log cabin in the edge of the woods, away on the bank on t'other side of the river, being a wood-yard, likely, and piled by them cheats so you can throw a dog through it anywheres;[1] then the nice breeze springs up, and comes fanning you from over there, so cool and fresh, and sweet to smell, on account of the woods and the flowers; but sometimes not that way, because they've left dead fish laying around, gars,[2] and such, and they do get pretty rank; and next you've got the full day, and every-thing smiling in the sun, and the song-birds just going it!

A little smoke couldn't be noticed, now, so we would take some fish off of the lines, and cook up a hot breakfast. And afterwards we would watch the lonesomeness of the river, and kind of lazy along, and by-and-by lazy off to sleep. Wake up, by-and-by, and look to see what done it, and maybe see a steamboat, coughing along up stream, so far off towards the other side you couldn't tell nothing about her only whether she was stern-wheel or side-wheel; then for about an hour there wouldn't be nothing to hear nor nothing to see—just solid lonesomeness. Next you'd see a raft sliding by, away off yonder, and maybe a galoot[3] on it chopping, because they're most always doing it on a raft; you'd see the axe flash, and come down—you don't hear nothing; you see that axe go up again, and by the time it's above the man's head, then you hear the *k'chunk!*—it had took all that time to come over the water. So we would put in the day, lazying around, listening to the stillness. Once there was a thick fog, and the rafts and things that went by was beating tin pans so the steamboats wouldn't run over them. A scow or a raft went by so close we could hear them talking and cussing and laughing—heard them plain; but we couldn't see no sign of them; it made you feel crawly, it was like spirits carrying on that way in the air. Jim said he believed it was spirits; but I says:

'No, spirits wouldn't say, "dern the dern fog".'

Soon as it was night, out we shoved; when we got her out to about the middle, we let her alone, and let her float

---

[1] *piled by them cheats* . . . : Stacked wood was customarily sold by volume, which included gaps large enough to "throw a dog through".

[2] *gars*: A gar is a type of fish, usually deemed inedible.

[3] *galoot*: neophyte or untried young sailor.

where-ever the current wanted her to; then we lit the pipes, and dangled our legs in the water and talked about all kinds of things—we was always naked, day and night, whenever the mosquitoes would let us—the new clothes Buck's folks made for me was too good to be comfortable, and besides I didn't go much on clothes, nohow.

Sometimes we'd have that whole river all to ourselves for the longest time. Yonder was the banks and the islands, across the water; and maybe a spark—which was a candle in a cabin window—and sometimes on the water you could see a spark or two—on a raft or a scow, you know; and maybe you could hear a fiddle or a song coming over from one of them crafts. It's lovely to live on a raft. We had the sky, up there, all speckled with stars, and we used to lay on our backs and look up at them, and discuss about whether they was made, or only just happened—Jim he allowed they was made, but I allowed they happened; I judged it would have took too long to *make* so many. Jim said the moon could a *laid* them; well, that looked kind of reasonable, so I didn't say nothing against it, because I've seen a frog lay most as many, so of course it could be done. We used to watch the stars that fell, too, and see them streak down. Jim allowed they'd got spoiled and was hove out of the nest.

Once or twice of a night we would see a steamboat slipping along in the dark, and now and then she would belch a whole world of sparks up out of her chimbleys, and they would rain down in the river and look awful pretty; then she would turn a corner and her lights would wink out and her pow-wow[4] shut off and leave the river still again; and by-and-by her waves would get to us, a long time after she was gone, and joggle the raft a bit, and after that you wouldn't hear nothing for you couldn't tell how long, except maybe frogs or something.

After midnight the people on shore went to bed, and then for two or three hours the shores was black—no more sparks

---

[4] *pow-wow*: usually, a meeting or conference to discuss a matter of importance, but Huck uses the word here and elsewhere to mean a loud noise or racket.

in the cabin windows. These sparks was our clock—the first one that showed again meant morning was coming, so we hunted a place to hide and tie up, right away.

One morning about day-break, I found a canoe and crossed over a chute[5] to the main shore—it was only two hundred yards—and paddled about a mile up a crick amongst the cypress woods, to see if I couldn't get some berries. Just as I was passing a place where a kind of a cow-path crossed the crick, here comes a couple of men tearing up the path as tight as they could foot it. I thought I was a goner, for whenever anybody was after anybody I judged it was *me*—or maybe Jim. I was about to dig out from there in a hurry, but they was pretty close to me then, and sung out and begged me to save their lives—said they hadn't been doing nothing, and was being chased for it—said there was men and dogs a-coming. They wanted to jump right in, but I says—

'Don't you do it. I don't hear the dogs and horses yet; you've got time to crowd through the brush and get up the crick a little ways; then you take to the water and wade down to me and get in—that'll throw the dogs off the scent.'

They done it, and soon as they was aboard I lit out for our tow-head, and in about five or ten minutes we heard the dogs and the men away off, shouting. We heard them come along towards the crick, but couldn't see them; they seemed to stop and fool around a while; then, as we got further and further away all the time, we couldn't hardly hear them at all; by the time we had left a mile of woods behind us and struck the river, everything was quiet, and we paddled over to the tow-head and hid in the cotton-woods and was safe.

One of these fellows was about seventy, or upwards, and had a bald head and very gray whiskers. He had an old battered-up slouch hat on, and greasy blue woolen shirt, and ragged old blue jeans britches stuffed into his boot tops, and home-knit galluses[6]—no, he only had one. He had an old long-tailed blue

---

[5] *chute*: narrow river channel.
[6] *galluses*: suspenders.

jeans coat with slick brass buttons, flung over his arm, and both of them had big fat ratty-looking carpetbags.[7]

The other fellow was about thirty and dressed about as ornery. After breakfast we all laid off and talked, and the first thing that come out was that these chaps didn't know one another.

'What got you into trouble?' says the baldhead to t'other chap.

'Well, I'd been selling an article to take the tartar off the teeth—and it does take it off, too, and generly the enamel along with it—but I staid about one night longer than I ought to, and was just in the act of sliding out when I ran across you on the trail this side of town, and you told me they were coming, and begged me to help you to get off. So I told you I was expecting trouble myself and would scatter out *with* you. That's the whole yarn—what's yourn?'

'Well, I'd ben a-runnin' a little temperance revival[8] thar, 'bout a week, and was the pet of the women-folks, big and little, for I was makin' it mighty warm for the rummies,[9] I *tell* you, and takin' as much as five or six dollars a night—ten cents a head, children and niggers free—and business a growin' all the time; when somehow or another a little report got around, last night, that I had a way of puttin' in my time with a private jug, on the sly. A nigger rousted me out this mornin', and told me the people was getherin' on the quiet, with their dogs and horses, and they'd be along pretty soon and give me 'bout half an hour's start, and then run me down, if they could; and if they got me they'd tar and feather me and ride me on a rail,[10] sure. I didn't wait for no breakfast—I warn't hungry.'

'Old man,' says the young one, 'I reckon we might double-team it together; what do you think?'

---

[7] *carpetbags*: typical nineteenth-century traveling bags made of carpet.

[8] *temperance revival*: public gathering to promote abstinence from alcohol, called a "revival" because of its tie to frontier evangelical religion.

[9] *rummies*: drunkards.

[10] *tar and feather me and ride me on a rail*: both cruel punishments inflicted on offenders by Southern mobs. The first involved pouring hot tar over the victim and then shaking feathers on him; the second involved carrying the victim sitting straddle on a sharp split log.

'I ain't undisposed. What's your line—mainly?'

'Jour printer,[11] by trade; do a little in patent medicines; theatre-actor—tragedy, you know; take a turn at mesmerism and phrenology[12] when there's a chance; teach singing-geography school[13] for a change; sling a lecture, sometimes—oh, I do lots of things—most anything that comes handy, so it ain't work. What's your lay?'

'I've done considerable in the doctoring way in my time. Layin' on o' hands is my best holt[14]—for cancer, and paralysis, and sich things; and I k'n tell a fortune pretty good, when I've got somebody along to find out the facts for me. Preachin's my line, too; and workin' camp-meetin's; and missionaryin' around.'

Nobody never said anything for a while; then the young man hove a sigh and says—

'Alas!'

'What're you alassin' about?' says the baldhead.

'To think I should have lived to be leading such a life, and be degraded down into such company.' And he begun to wipe the corner of his eye with a rag.

'Dern your skin, ain't the company good enough for you?' says the baldhead, pretty pert and uppish.

'Yes, it *is* good enough for me; it's as good as I deserve; for who fetched me so low, when I was so high? *I* did myself. I don't blame *you*, gentlemen—far from it; I don't blame anybody. I deserve it all. Let the cold world do its worst; one thing I know—there's a grave somewhere for me. The world may go on just as its always done, and take everything from me—loved

---

[11] *Jour printer*: journeyman, or wandering printer who worked for daily wages. He was often a rascal figure in nineteenth-century lore.

[12] *mesmerism and phrenology*: Sessions in mesmerism (hypnotism) and phrenology (a pseudoscience that claimed to read a person's character by the bumps on his head) were popular forms of entertainment in the nineteenth century.

[13] *singing-geography school*: lessons where geographical facts are chanted or sung so as to commit them to memory.

[14] *Layin' on o' hands is my best holt*: The man's money-making schemes mostly involve religion. "Laying on of hands" is a practice some evangelical congregations use to pray for afflicted members. "Best holt" means "specialty".

ones, property, everything—but it can't take that. Some day I'll lie down in it and forget it all, and my poor broken heart will be at rest.' He went on a-wiping.

'Drot[15] your pore broken heart,' says the baldhead; 'what are you heaving your pore broken heart at *us* f'r? *We* hain't done nothing.'

'No, I know you haven't. I ain't blaming you, gentlemen. I brought myself down—yes, I did it myself. It's right I should suffer—perfectly right—I don't make any moan.'[16]

'Brought you down from whar? Whar was you brought down from?'

'Ah, you would not believe me; the world never believes— let it pass—'tis no matter. The secret of my birth—'

'The secret of your birth? Do you mean to say—'

'Gentlemen,' says the young man, very solemn, 'I will reveal it to you, for I feel I may have confidence in you. By rights I am a duke!'

Jim's eyes bugged out when he heard that; and I reckon mine did, too. Then the baldhead says: 'No! you can't mean it?'

'Yes. My great-grandfather, eldest son of the Duke of Bridge-water, fled to this country about the end of the last century, to breathe the pure air of freedom; married here, and died, leaving a son, his own father dying about the same time. The second son of the late duke seized the title and estates—the infant real duke was ignored. I am the lineal descendant of that infant—I am the rightful Duke of Bridgewater; and here am I, forlorn, torn from my high estate, hunted of men, despised by the cold world, ragged, worn, heart-broken, and degraded to the companionship of felons on a raft!'

Jim pitied him ever so much, and so did I. We tried to comfort him, but he said it warn't much use, he couldn't be much comforted; said if we was a mind to acknowledge him, that would do him more good than most anything else; so we said we would, if he would tell us how. He said we ought to bow,

---

[15] *Drot:* like "dern" above, a euphemism for "damn".

[16] *make any moan:* complain.

when we spoke to him, and say 'Your Grace,' or 'My Lord,' or 'Your Lordship'—and he wouldn't mind it if we called him plain 'Bridgewater,' which he said was a title, anyway, and not a name; and one of us ought to wait on him at dinner, and do any little thing for him he wanted done.

Well, that was all easy, so we done it. All through dinner Jim stood around and waited on him, and says, 'Will yo' Grace have some o' dis, or some o' dat?' and so on, and a body could see it was mighty pleasing to him.

But the old man got pretty silent, by-and-by—didn't have much to say, and didn't look pretty comfortable over all that petting that was going on around that duke. He seemed to have something on his mind. So, along in the afternoon, he says:

'Looky here, Bilgewater,' he says, 'I'm nation sorry for you, but you ain't the only person that's had troubles like that.'

'No?'

'No, you ain't. You ain't the only person that's ben snaked down wrongfully out'n a high place.'

'Alas!'

'No, you ain't the only person that's had a secret of his birth.' And by jing, *he* begins to cry.

'Hold! What do you mean?'

'Bilgewater, kin I trust you?' says the old man, still sort of sobbing.

'To the bitter death!' He took the old man by the hand and squeezed it, and says, 'The secret of your being: speak!'

'Bilgewater, I am the late Dauphin!'

You bet you Jim and me stared, this time. Then the duke says:

'You are what?'

'Yes, my friend, it is too true—your eyes is lookin' at this very moment on the pore disappeared Dauphin, Looy the Seventeen, son of Looy the Sixteen and Marry Antonette.'[17]

---

[17] *the pore disappeared Dauphin . . .* : The dauphin's mother, the French queen Marie Antoinette, was executed in 1793 during the French Revolution.

'You! At your age! No! You mean you're the late Charlemagne; you must be six or seven hundred years old, at the very least.'[18]

'Trouble has done it, Bilgewater, trouble has done it; trouble has brung these gray hairs and this premature balditude. Yes, gentlemen, you see before you, in blue jeans and misery, the wanderin', exiled, trampled-on and sufferin' rightful King of France.'

Well, he cried and took on so, that me and Jim didn't know hardly what to do, we was so sorry—and so glad and proud we'd got him with us, too. So we set in, like we done before with the duke, and tried to comfort *him*. But he said it warn't no use, nothing but to be dead and done with it all could do him any good; though he said it often made him feel easier and better for a while if people treated him according to his rights, and got down on one knee to speak to him, and always called him 'Your Majesty', and waited on him first at meals, and didn't set down in his presence till he asked them. So Jim and me set to majestying him, and doing this and that and t'other for him, and standing up till he told us we might set down. This done him heaps of good, and so he got cheerful and comfortable. But the duke kind of soured on him, and didn't look a bit satisfied with the way things was going; still, the king acted real friendly towards him, and said the duke's great-grandfather and all the other Dukes of Bilgewater was a good deal thought of by *his* father and was allowed to come to the palace considerable; but the duke staid huffy a good while, till by-and-by the king says:

'Like as not we got to be together a blamed long time, on this h-yer raft, Bilgewater, and so what's the use o' your bein' sour? It'll only make things oncomfortable. It ain't my fault I warn't born a duke, it ain't your fault you warn't born a king—so what's the use to worry? Make the best o'things the way you

[18] *You mean you're the late Charlemagne* ... : Had the dauphin escaped and survived, he would have been about fifty-five years old at the time the novel is set. Huck earlier described the man as "about seventy, or upwards". Charlemagne, king of the Franks, died in 814.

find 'em, says I—that's my motto. This ain't no bad thing that we've struck here—plenty grub and an easy life—come, give us your hand, Duke, and less all be friends.'

The duke done it, and Jim and me was pretty glad to see it. It took away all the uncomfortableness, and we felt mighty good over it, because it would a been a miserable business to have any unfriendliness on the raft; for what you want, above all things, on a raft, is for everybody to be satisfied, and feel right and kind towards the others.

It didn't take me long to make up my mind that these liars warn't no kings nor dukes, at all, but just low-down humbugs and frauds. But I never said nothing, never let on; kept it to myself; it's the best way; then you don't have no quarrels, and don't get into no trouble. If they wanted us to call them kings and dukes, I hadn't no objections, 'long as it would keep peace in the family; and it wan't no use to tell Jim, so I didn't tell him. If I never learnt nothing else out of pap, I learnt that the best way to get along with his kind of people is to let them have their own way.

CHAPTER 20

They asked us considerable many questions; wanted to know what we covered up the raft that way for, and laid by in the day-time instead of running—was Jim a runaway nigger? Says I—

'Goodness sakes, would a runaway nigger run *south?*'

No, they allowed he wouldn't. I had to account for things some way, so I says:

'My folks was living in Pike County, in Missouri, where I was born, and they all died off but me and pa and my brother Ike. Pa, he 'lowed he'd break up and go down and live with Uncle Ben, who's got a little one-horse place on the river, forty-four mile below Orleans. Pa was pretty poor, and had some debts; so when he'd squared up there warn't nothing left but sixteen dollars and our nigger, Jim. That warn't enough to take us fourteen hundred mile, deck passage[1] nor no other way. Well, when the river rose, pa had a streak of luck one day; he ketched this piece of a raft; so we reckoned we'd go down to Orleans on it. Pa's luck didn't hold out; a steamboat run over the forrard corner of the raft, one night, and we all went overboard and dove under the wheel; Jim and me come up, all right, but pa was drunk, and Ike was only four years old, so they never come up no more. Well, for the next day or two we had considerable trouble, because people was always coming out in skiffs and trying to take Jim away from me, saying they believed he was a runaway nigger. We don't run daytimes no more, now; nights they don't bother us.'

The duke says—

'Leave me alone to cipher out a way so we can run in the day-time if we want to. I'll think the thing over—I'll invent a

---

[1] *deck passage*: steerage, or the lowest and most inexpensive class aboard a steamship.

plan that'll fix it. We'll let it along for today, because of course
we don't want to go by that town yonder in daylight—it
mightn't be healthy.'

Towards night it began to darken up and look like rain; the
heat lightning was squirting around, low down in the sky, and
the leaves was beginning to shiver—it was going to be pretty
ugly, it was easy to see that. So the duke and the king went to
overhauling our wigwam, to see what the beds was like. My
bed was a straw tick—better than Jim's which was a corn-
shuck tick;[2] there's always cobs around about in a shuck tick,
and they poke into you and hurt; and when you roll over, the
dry shucks sound like you was rolling over in a pile of dead
leaves; it makes such a rustling that you wake up. Well, the
duke allowed he would take my bed; but the king allowed he
wouldn't. He says—

'I should a reckoned the difference in rank would a sejested
to you that a corn-shuck bed warn't just fitten for me to sleep
on. Your Grace'll take the shuck bed yourself.'

Jim and me was in a sweat again, for a minute, being afraid
there was going to be some more trouble amongst them; so we
was pretty glad when the duke says—

' 'Tis my fate to be always ground into the mire under the
iron heel of oppression. Misfortune has broken my once haughty
spirit; I yield, I submit; 'tis my fate. I am alone in the world—
let me suffer; I can bear it.'

We got away as soon as it was good and dark. The king told
us to stand well out towards the middle of the river, and not
show a light till we got a long ways below the town. We come
in sight of the little bunch of lights by-and-by—that was the
town, you know—and slid by, about a half a mile out, all right.
When we was three-quarters of a mile below, we hoisted up
our signal lantern; and about ten o'clock it come on to rain
and blow and thunder and lighten like everything; so the king

---

[2] *straw tick . . . corn-shuck tick*: two typical fillers for a "tick", or mattress, at
the time. The latter was filled with corn husks and thus less comfortable than a
straw-filled tick.

told us to both stay on watch till the weather got better; then him and the duke crawled into the wigwam and turned in for the night. It was my watch below, till twelve, but I wouldn't a turned in, anyway, if I'd had a bed; because a body don't see such a storm as that every day in the week, not by a long sight. My souls, how the wind did scream along! And every second or two there'd come a glare that lit up the white-caps for a half a mile around, and you'd see the islands looking dusty through the rain, and the trees thrashing around in the wind; then comes a *h-wack!*—bum! bum! bumble-umble-um-bum-bum-bum-bum—and the thunder would go rumbling and grumbling away, and quit—and then *rip* comes another flash and another sockdolager.[3] The waves most washed me off the raft, sometimes, but I hadn't any clothes on, and didn't mind. We didn't have no trouble about snags; the lightning was glaring and flittering around so constant that we could see them plenty soon enough to throw her head this way or that and miss them.

I had the middle watch,[4] you know, but I was pretty sleepy by that time, so Jim he said he would stand the first half of it for me; he was always mighty good, that way, Jim was. I crawled into the wigwam, but the king and the duke had their legs sprawled around so there warn't no show for me; so I laid outside—I didn't mind the rain, because it was warm, and the waves warn't running so high, now. About two they come up again, though, and Jim was going to call me, but he changed his mind because he reckoned they warn't high enough yet to do any harm; but he was mistaken about that, for pretty soon all of a sudden along comes a regular ripper, and washed me overboard. It most killed Jim a-laughing. He was the easiest nigger to laugh that ever was, anyway.

I took the watch, and Jim he laid down and snored away; and by-and-by the storm let up for good and all; and the first cabin-light that showed, I rousted him out and we slid the raft into hiding-quarters for the day.

---

[3] *sockdolager*: knock-out punch; here, a huge rumble of thunder.
[4] *middle watch*: typically midnight to four in the morning.

The king got out an old ratty deck of cards, after breakfast, and him and the duke played seven-up[5] a while, five cents a game. Then they got tired of it, and allowed they would 'lay out a campaign,' as they called it. The duke went down into his carpet-bag and fetched up a lot of little printed bills, and read them out loud. One bill said 'The celebrated Dr Armand de Montalban of Paris,' would 'lecture on the Science of Phrenology' at such and such a place, on the blank day of blank, at ten cents admission, and 'furnish charts of character at twenty-five cents apiece.' The duke said that was *him*. In another bill he was the 'world renowned Shaks-perean tragedian, Garrick the Younger, of Drury Lane, Lon-don.'[6] In other bills he had a lot of other names and done other wonderful things, like finding water and gold with a 'divining rod',[7] 'dissipating witch-spells', and so on. By-and-by he says—

'But the histrionic muse is the darling. Have you ever trod the boards,[8] Royalty?'

'No,' says the king.

'You shall, then, before you're three days older, Fallen Gran-deur,' says the duke. 'The first good town we come to, we'll hire a hall and do the sword-fight in Richard III and the bal-cony scene in Romeo and Juliet.[9] How does that strike you?'

'I'm in, up to the hub, for anything that will pay, Bilgewa-ter, but you see I don't know nothing about play-actn', and hain't ever seen much of it. I was too small when pap used to have 'em at the palace. Do you reckon you can learn me?'

'Easy!'

---

[5] *seven-up*: also known as all fours, a trumping card game won by the player who first scores seven points.

[6] *Garrick the Younger, of Drury Lane, London*: The famous Shakespearian actor David Garrick (1717–1779) managed the Drury Lane Theatre in London. There was no Garrick the Younger.

[7] *divining rod*: rod believed to aid in locating underground water or minerals.

[8] *trod the boards*: walked the stage, i.e., performed in a theater.

[9] *sword-fight in Richard III and the balcony scene in Romeo and Juliet*: along with Hamlet's "To be or not to be" soliloquy, all Shakespearian scenes often enacted by traveling performers.

'All right. I'm jist a-freezn'[10] for something fresh, anyway. Less commence, right away.'

So the duke he told him all about who Romeo was, and who Juliet was, and said he was used to being Romeo, so the king could be Juliet.

'But if Juliet's such a young gal, Duke, my peeled head and my white whiskers is goin' to look oncommon odd on her, maybe.'

'No, don't you worry—these country jakes[11] won't ever think of that. Besides, you know, you'll be in costume, and that makes all the difference in the world; Juliet's in a balcony, enjoying the moonlight before she goes to bed, and she's got on her nightgown and her ruffled night-cap. Here are the costumes for the parts.'

He got out two or three curtain-calico suits, which he said was meedyevil armor for Richard III, and t'other chap, and a long white cotton night-shirt and a ruffled night-cap to match. The king was satisfied; so the duke got out his book and read the parts over in the most splendid spread-eagle[12] way, prancing around and acting at the same time, to show how it had got to be done; then he give the book to the king and told him to get his part by heart.

There was a little one-horse town[13] about three mile down the bend, and after dinner the duke said he had ciphered out his idea about how to run in daylight without it being dangersome for Jim; so he allowed he would go down to the town and fix that thing. The king allowed he would go too, and see if he couldn't strike something. We was out of coffee, so Jim said I better go along with them in the canoe and get some.

When we go there, there warn't nobody stirring; streets empty, and perfectly dead and still, like Sunday. We found a

---

[10] *a-freezn'*: longing.

[11] *jakes*: "Jake" is a slang word for someone boorish and unsophisticated.

[12] *spread-eagle*: extravagant.

[13] *little one-horse town*: Later called "Pokeville", the location of this town is not identified but is possibly on the Arkansas side south of Tennessee.

sick nigger sunning himself in a back yard, and he said everybody that warn't too young or too sick or too old, was gone to
camp-meeting, about two mile back in the woods. The king
got the directions, and allowed he'd go and work that camp-
meeting for all it was worth, and I might go, too.

The duke said what he was after was a printing office. We
found it; a little bit of a concern, up over a carpenter shop—
carpenters and printers all gone to the meeting, and no doors
locked. It was a dirty, littered-up place, and had ink marks, and
handbills with pictures of horses and runaway niggers on them,
all over the walls. The duke shed his coat and said he was all
right, now. So me and the king lit out for the camp-meeting.

We got there in about a half an hour, fairly dripping, for it
was a most awful hot day. There was as much as a thousand
people there, from twenty miles around. The woods was full
of teams and wagons, hitched everywheres, feeding out of the
wagon troughs and stomping to keep off the flies. There was
sheds made out of poles and roofed over with branches, where
they had lemonade and gingerbread to sell, and piles of watermelons and green corn and such-like truck.

The preaching was going on under the same kinds of sheds,
only they was bigger and held crowds of people. The benches
was made out of outside slabs of logs, with holes bored in the
round side to drive sticks into for legs. They didn't have no
backs. The preachers had high platforms to stand on, at one
end of the sheds. The women had on sun-bonnets; and some
had linsey-woolsey frocks,[14] some gingham ones, and a few of
the young ones had on calico. Some of the young men was
bare-footed, and some of the children didn't have on any clothes
but just a tow-linen[15] shirt. Some of the old women was knitting, and some of the young folks was courting on the sly.

The first shed we come to, the preacher was lining out a
hymn. He lined out two lines, everybody sung it, and it was
kind of grand to hear it, there was so many of them and they

---

[14] *linsey-woolsey frocks*: dresses made out of a mixture of wool and linen cloth.
[15] *tow-linen*: cloth made out of hemp or flax.

done it in such a rousing way; then he lined out two more for them to sing—and so on. The people woke up more and more, and sung louder and louder; and towards the end, some begun to groan, and some begun to shout. Then the preacher begun to preach; and begun in earnest, too; and went weaving first to one side of the platform and then the other, and then a leaning down over the front of it, with his arms and his body going all the time, and shouting his words out with all his might; and every now and then he would hold up his Bible and spread it open, and kind of pass it around this way and that, shouting, 'It's the brazen serpent in the wilderness! Look upon it and live!'[16] And people would shout out, 'Glory!— A-*a-men!*' And so he went on, and the people groaning and crying and saying amen:

'Oh, come to the mourners' bench! come, black with sin! (*amen!*) come, sick and sore! (*amen!*) come, lame and halt, and blind! (*amen!*) come, pore and needy, sunk in shame! (*a-a- men!*) come all that's worn, and soiled, and suffering!—come with a broken spirit! come with a contrite heart! come in your rags and sin and dirt! the waters that cleanse is free, the door of heaven stands open—oh, enter in and be at rest!' (*a-a- men! glory, glory hallelujah!*)[17]

And so on. You couldn't make out what the preacher said, any more, on account of the shouting and crying. Folks got up, everywheres in the crowd, and worked their way, just by main strength, to the mourners' bench, with the tears running down their faces; and when all the mourners had got up there to the front benches in a crowd, they sung, and shouted, and flung themselves down on the straw, just crazy and wild.

[16] *It's the brazen serpent in the wilderness! Look upon it and live!* In Numbers 21:6–9, God allows the Israelites to be bitten by snakes as punishment but then commands Moses to mount a bronze serpent on a pole so that those who look at it can be healed.

[17] *Oh, come to the mourners' bench! . . . :* The preacher uses typical language of the "altar call", or call to pentitence, in certain Protestant evangelical services, including revivals. Pentitents come forward and take their place at the "mourners' bench" to grieve over their sins.

Well, the first I knowed, the king got agoing; and you could hear him over everybody; and next he went a-charging up on to the platform and the preacher he begged him to speak to the people, and he done it. He told them he was a pirate— been a pirate for thirty years, out in the Indian Ocean, and his crew was thinned out considerable, last spring, in a fight, and he was home now, to take out some fresh men, and thanks to goodness he'd been robbed last night, and put ashore off of a steam-boat without a cent, and he was glad of it, it was the blessedest thing that ever happened to him, because he was a changed man now, and happy for the first time in his life; and poor as he was, he was going to start right off and work his way back to the Indian Ocean and put in the rest of his life trying to turn the pirates into the true path; for he could do it better than anybody else, being acquainted with all the pirate crews in that ocean; and though it would take him a long time to get there, without money, he would get there anyway, and every time he convinced a pirate he would say to him, 'Don't you thank me, don't you give me no credit, it all belongs to them dear people in Pokeville camp-meeting, natural broth- ers and benefactors of the race—and that dear preacher there, the truest friend a pirate ever had!'

And then he busted into tears, and so did everybody. Then somebody sings out, 'Take up a collection for him, take up a collection!' Well, a half a dozen made a jump to do it, but somebody sings out, 'Let *him* pass the hat around!' Then every- body said it, the preacher too.

So the king went all through the crowd with his hat, swab- bing his eyes, and blessing the people and praising them and thanking them for being so good to the poor pirates away off there; and every little while the prettiest kind of girls, with the tears running down their cheeks, would up and ask him would he let them kiss him, for to remember him by; and he always done it; and some of them he hugged and kissed as many as five or six times—and he was invited to stay a week; and everybody wanted him to live in their houses, and said they'd think it was an honor; but he said as this was the last day of the camp-meeting he couldn't do no good, and besides he was in a sweat to get to the Indian Ocean right off and go to work on the pirates.

When we got back to the raft and he come to count up, he found he had collected eighty-seven dollars and seventy-five cents. And then he had fetched away a three-gallon jug of whisky, too, that he found under a wagon when we was starting home through the woods. The king said, take it all around, it laid over any day he'd ever put in in the missionarying line. He said it warn't no use talking, heathens don't amount to shucks, alongside of pirates, to work a camp-meeting with.

The duke was thinking *he'd* been doing pretty well, till the king come to show up, but after that he didn't think so so much. He had set up and printed off two little jobs for farmers, in that printing office—horse bills—and took the money, four dollars. And he had got in ten dollars' worth of advertisements for the paper, which he said he would put in for four dollars if they would pay in advance—so they done it. The price of the paper was two dollars a year, but he took in three subscriptions for half a dollar apiece on condition of them paying him in advance; they were going to pay in cord-wood[18] and onions, as usual, but he said he had just bought the concern and knocked down the price as low as he could afford it, and was going to run it for cash. He set up a little piece of poetry, which he made, himself, out of his own head—three verses—kind of sweet and saddish—the name of it was, 'Yes, crush, cold world, this breaking heart'—and he left that all set up and ready to print in the paper and didn't charge nothing for it. Well, he took in nine dollars and a half, and said he'd done a pretty square day's work for it.

Then he showed us another little job he'd printed and hadn't charged for, because it was for us. It had a picture of a runaway nigger, with a bundle on a stick, over his shoulder, and '$200 reward' under it. The reading was all about Jim, and just described him to a dot. It said he run away from St. Jacques'

---

[18] *cord-wood*: wood cut for fuel.

plantation, forty miles below New Orleans, last winter, and likely went north, and whoever would catch him and send him back, he could have the reward and expenses.

'Now,' says the duke, 'after tonight we can run in the day-time if we want to. Whenever we see anybody coming, we can tie Jim hand and foot with a rope, and lay him in the wigwam and show this handbill and say we captured him up the river, and were too poor to travel on a steamboat, so we got this little raft on credit from our friends and are going down to get the reward. Handcuffs and chains would look still bet-ter on Jim, but it wouldn't go well with the story of us being so poor. Too much like jewelry. Ropes are the correct thing—we must preserve the unities, as we say on the boards.'

We all said the duke was pretty smart, and there couldn't be no trouble about running daytimes. We judged we could make miles enough that night to get out of the reach of the pow-wow we reckoned the duke's work in the printing office was going to make in that little town—then we could boom right along, if we wanted to.

We laid low and kept still, and never shoved out till nearly ten o'clock; then we slid by, pretty wide away from the town, and didn't hoist our lantern till we was clear out of sight of it.

When Jim called me to take the watch at four in the morn-ing, he says—

'Huck, does you reck'n we gwyne to run acrost any mo' kings on dis trip?'

'No,' I says, 'I reckon not.'

'Well,' says he, 'dat's all right, den. I doan' mine one er two kings, but dat's enough. Dis one's powerful drunk, en de duke ain' much better.'

I found Jim had been trying to get him to talk French, so he could hear what it was like; but he said he had been in this country so long, and had so much trouble, he'd forgot it.

CHAPTER 21

It was after sun-up, now, but we went right on, and didn't tie up. The king and the duke turned out, by-and-by, looking pretty rusty; but after they'd jumped overboard and took a swim, it chippered them up a good deal. After breakfast the king he took a seat on a corner of the raft, and pulled off his boots and rolled up his britches, and let his legs dangle in the water, so as to be comfortable, and lit his pipe, and went to getting his Romeo and Juliet by heart. When he had got it pretty good, him and the duke begun to practice it together. The duke had to learn him over and over again, how to say every speech; and he made him sigh, and put his hand on his heart, and after while he said he done it pretty well; 'only,' he says, 'you mustn't bellow out *Romeo!* that way, like a bull—you must say it soft, and sick, languishy, so—R-o-o-meo! that is the idea; for Juliet's a dear sweet mere child of a girl, you know, and she don't bray like a jackass.'

Well, next they got out a couple of long swords that the duke made out of oak laths, and begun to practice the sword-fight—the duke called himself Richard III; and the way they laid on, and pranced around the raft was grand to see. But by-and-by the king tripped and fell overboard, and after that they took a rest, and had a talk about all kinds of adventures they'd had in other times along the river.

After dinner, the duke says:

'Well, Capet,[1] we'll want to make this a first-class show, you know, so I guess we'll add a little more to it. We want a little something to answer encores with, anyway.'

'What's onkores, Bilgewater?'

The duke told him, and then says:

---

[1] *Capet*: the surname by which Louis XVI of France was called after he was dethroned.

'I'll answer by doing the Highland fling or the sailor's horn-pipe;[2] and you—well, let me see—oh, I've got it—you can do Hamlet's soliloquy.'

'Hamlet's which?'

'Hamlet's soliloquy, you know; the most celebrated thing in Shakespeare. Ah, it's sublime, sublime! Always fetches the house. I haven't got it in the book—I've only got one volume—but I reckon I can piece it out from memory. I'll just walk up and down a minute, and see if I can call it back from recollection's vaults.'

So he went to marching up and down, thinking, and frowning horrible every now and then; then he would hoist up his eyebrows; next he would squeeze his hand on his forehead and stagger back and kind of moan; next he would sigh, and next he'd let on to drop a tear. It was beautiful to see him. By-and-by he got it. He told us to give attention. Then he strikes a most noble attitude, with one leg shoved forwards, and his arms stretched away up, and his head tilted back, looking up at the sky; and then he begins to rip and rave and grit his teeth; and after that, all through his speech he howled, and spread around, and swelled up his chest, and just knocked the spots out of any acting ever *I* see before. This is the speech—I learned it, easy enough, while he was learning it to the king:[3]

To be, or not to be; that is the bare bodkin
That makes calamity of so long life;
For who would fardels bear, till Birnam Wood do come
    to Dunsinane,
But that the fear of something after death

---

[2] *Highland fling or the sailor's horn-pipe*: two vigorous dances performed in place without a partner. The former is a traditional Scottish victory dance; the latter was originally performed by British sailors on ships for the purpose of exercise.

[3] The "soliloquy" that follows is a highly mutilated version of Hamlet's. It incorporates lines from several other Shakespearean plays, including *Macbeth* and *Richard III*.

Murders the innocent sleep,
Great nature's second course,
And makes us rather sling the arrows of outrageous fortune
Than fly to others that we know not of.
There's the respect must give us pause:
Wake Duncan with thy knocking! I would thou couldst;
For who would bear the whips and scorns of time,
The oppressor's wrong, the proud man's contumely,
The law's delay, and the quietus which his pangs might take,
In the dead waste and middle of the night, when churchyards
     yawn
In customary suits of solemn black,
But that the undiscovered country from whose bourne no trav-
eler returns,
Breathes forth contagion on the world,
And thus the native hue of resolution, like the poor cat i' the
     adage,
Is sicklied o'er with care,
And all the clouds that lowered o'er our housetops,
With this regard their currents turn awry,
And lose the name of action.
'Tis a consummation devoutly to be wished. But soft you, the
     fair Ophelia:
Ope not thy ponderous and marble jaws,
But get thee to a nunnery—go!

Well, the old man he liked that speech, and he mighty soon
got it so he could do it first rate. It seemed like he was just
born for it; and when he had his hand in and was excited, it
was perfectly lovely the way he would rip and tear and rair up
behind when he was getting it off.

The first chance we got, the duke he had some show bills
printed; and after that, for two or three days as we floated along,
the raft was a most uncommon lively place, for there warn't
nothing but sword-fighting and rehearsing—as the duke called
it—going on all the time. One morning, when we was pretty
well down the State of Arkansaw, we come in sight of a little

one-horse town[4] in a big bend, so we tied up about three-
quarters of a mile above it, in the mouth of a crick which was
shut in like a tunnel by the cypress trees, and all of us but Jim
took the canoe and went down there to see if there was any
chance in that place for our show.

We struck it mighty lucky; there was going to be a circus
there that afternoon, and the country people was already beginning to come in, in all kinds of old shackly wagons, and on
horses. The circus would leave before night, so our show would
have a pretty good chance. The duke he hired the court house,
and we went around and stuck up our bills. They read like
this:

Shaksperean Revival! ! !
Wonderful Attraction
For One Night Only!
The world renowned tragedians,
David Garrick the younger, of Drury Lane Theatre, London,
and
Edmund Kean the elder,[5] of the Royal Haymarket Theatre,
White-
chapel, Pudding Lane, Piccadilly, London, and the
Royal Continental Theatres, in their sublime
Shaksperean Spectacle entitled
The Balcony Scene
in Romeo and Juliet! ! !
Romeo .... Mr Garrick.
Juliet .... Mr Kean.
Assisted by the whole strength of the company!
New costumes, new scenery, new appointments!
Also:
The thrilling, masterly, and blood-curdling
Broad-sword conflict

---

[4] *little one-horse town*: Later named "Bricksville", this town may have been
modeled on that of Napoleon, Arkansas.

[5] *Edmund Kean the elder*: Kean (1789–1833) was a famous English actor who
performed at such London theaters as the Haymarket.

In Richard III! ! !

Richard III ....Mr Garrick.

Richmond..........................Mr Kean.

also:

(by special request,)

Hamlet's Immortal Soliloquy! !

By the Illustrious Kean!

Done by him 300 consecutive nights in Paris!

For One Night Only,

On account of imperative European engagements!

Admission 25 cents; children and servants, 10 cents.

Then we went loafing around the town. The stores and houses was most all old shackly dried-up frame concerns that hadn't ever been painted; they was set up three or four foot above ground on stilts, so as to be out of reach of the water when the river was overflowed. The houses had little gardens around them, but they didn't seem to raise hardly anything in them but jimpson weeds,[6] and sunflowers, and ash-piles, and old curled-up boots and shoes, and pieces of bottles, and rags, and played-out tin-ware. The fences was made of different kinds of boards, nailed on at different times; and they leaned every which-way, and had gates that didn't generly have but one hinge—a leather one. Some of the fences had been white-washed, some time or another, but the duke said it was in Clumbus's time, like enough. There was generly hogs in the garden, and people driving them out.

All the stores was along one street. They had white-domestic awnings in front, and the country people hitched their horses to the awning-posts. There was empty dry-goods boxes under the awnings, and loafers roosting on them all day long, whittling them with their Barlow knives; and chawing tobacco, and gaping and yawning and stretching—a mighty ornery lot. They generly had on yellow straw hats most as wide as an umbrella, but didn't wear no coats nor waistcoats; they called

---

[6] *jimpson weeds:* poisonous and foul-smelling weeds of the nightshade family.

one another Bill, and Buck, and Hank, and Joe, and Andy, and talked lazy and drawly, and used considerable many cuss-words. There was as many as one loafer leaning up against every awning-post, and he most always had his hands in his britches pockets, except when he fetched them out to lend a chaw of tobacco or scratch. What a body was hearing amongst them, all the time was—

'Gimme a chaw 'v tobacker, Hank.'

'Cain't—I hain't got but one chaw left. Ask Bill.'

Maybe Bill he gives him a chaw; maybe he lies and says he ain't got none. Some of them kinds of loafers never has a cent in the world, nor a chaw of tobacco of their own. They get all their chawing by borrowing—they say to a fellow, 'I wisht you'd len' me a chaw, Jack, I jist this minute give Ben Thompson the last chaw I had'—which is a lie, pretty much every time; it don't fool nobody but a stranger; but Jack ain't no stranger, so he says—

'*You* give him a chaw, did you? so did your sister's cat's grand-mother. You pay me back the chaws you've aweady borry'd off'n me, Lafe Buckner, then I'll loan you one or two ton of it, and won't charge you no back intrust, nuther.'

'Well, I *did* pay you back some of it wunst.'

'Yes, you did—'bout six chaws. You borry'd store tobacker and paid back nigger-head.' [7]

Store tobacco is flat black plug, but these fellows mostly chaws the natural leaf twisted. When they borrow a chaw, they don't generly cut it off with a knife, but they set the plug in between their teeth, and gnaw with their teeth and tug at the plug with their hands till they get it in two—then sometimes the one that owns the tobacco looks mournful at it when it's handed back, and says, sarcastic—

'Here, gimme the *chaw*, and you take the *plug*.'

All the streets and lanes was just mud, they warn't nothing else *but* mud—mud as black as tar, and nigh about a foot deep in some places; and two or three inches deep in *all* the places.

---

[7] *nigger-head*: strong black chewing tobacco.

The hogs loafed and grunted around, everywheres. You'd see a muddy sow and a litter of pigs come lazying along the street and whollop herself right down in the way, where folks had to walk around her, and she'd stretch out, and shut her eyes, and wave her ears, whilst the pigs was milking her, and look as happy as if she was on salary. And pretty soon you'd hear a loafer sing out, 'Hi! *so* boy! sick him, Tige!' and away the sow would go, squealing most horrible, with a dog or two swinging to each ear, and three or four dozen more a-coming; and then you would see all the loafers get up and watch the thing out of sight, and laugh at the fun and look grateful for the noise. Then they'd settle back again till there was a dog-fight. There couldn't anything wake them up all over, and make them happy all over, like a dog-fight—unless it might be putting turpentine on a stray dog and setting fire to him, or tying a tin pan to his tail and see him run himself to death.

On the river front some of the houses was sticking out over the bank, and they was bowed and bent, and about ready to tumble in. The people had moved out of them. The bank was caved away under one corner of some others, and that corner was hanging over. People lived in them yet, but it was dangersome, because sometimes a strip of land as wide as a house caves in at a time. Sometimes a belt of land a quarter of a mile deep will start in and cave along and cave along till it all caves into the river in one summer. Such a town as that has to be always moving back, and back, and back, because the river's always gnawing at it.

The nearer it got to noon that day, the thicker and thicker was the wagons and horses in the streets, and more coming all the time. Families fetched their dinners with them, from the country, and eat them in the wagons. There was considerable whiskey drinking going on, and I seen three fights. By-and-by somebody sings out—

'Here comes old Boggs!—in from the country for his little old monthly drunk—here he comes, boys!'

All the loafers looked glad—I reckoned they was used to having fun out of Boggs. One of them says—

'Wonder who he's a gwyne to chaw up this time. If he'd a chawed up all the men he's ben a gwyne to chaw up in the last twenty year, he'd have a considerable reputation, now.'

Another one says, 'I wisht old Boggs 'd threaten me, 'cuz then I'd know I warn't gwyne to die for a thousan' year.'

Boggs comes a-tearing along on his horse, whooping and yelling like an Injun, and singing out—

'Cler the track, thar. I'm on the waw-path, and the price uv coffins is a gwyne to raise.'

He was drunk, and weaving about in his saddle; he was over fifty year old, and had a very red face. Everybody yelled at him, and laughed at him, and sassed him, and he sassed back and said he'd attend to them and lay them out in their regular turns, but he couldn't wait now, because he'd come to town to kill old Colonel Sherburn, and his motto was 'meat first, and spoon vittles to top off on.'

He see me, and rode up and says—

'Whar'd you come f'm, boy? You prepared to die?'

Then he rode on. I was scared; but a man says—

'He don't mean nothing; he's always a carryin' on like that when he's drunk. He's the best-naturedest old fool in Arkansaw—never hurt nobody, drunk nor sober.'

Boggs rode up before the biggest store in town and bent his head down so he could see under the curtain of the awning, and yells—

'Come out here, Sherburn! Come out and meet the man you've swindled. You're the houn' I'm after, and I'm a gwyne to have you, too!'

And so he went on, calling Sherburn everything he could lay his tongue to, and the whole street packed with people listening and laughing and going on. By-and-by a proud-looking man about fifty-five—and he was a heap the best dressed man in that town, too—steps out of the store, and the crowd drops back on each side to let him come. He says to Boggs, mighty ca'm and slow—he says:

'I'm tired of this; but I'll endure it till one o'clock. Till one o'clock, mind—no longer. If you open your mouth against me only once, after that time, you can't travel so far but I will find you.'

Then he turns and goes in. The crowd looked mighty sober; nobody stirred, and there warn't no more laughing. Boggs rode off blackguarding Sherburn as loud as he could yell, all down the street; and pretty soon back he comes and stops before the store, still keeping it up. Some men crowded around him and tried to get him to shut up, but he wouldn't; they told him it would be one o'clock in about fifteen minutes, and so he *must* go home—he must go right away. But it didn't do no good. He cussed away, with all his might, and throwed his hat down in the mud and rode over it, and pretty soon away he went a-raging down the street again, with his gray hair a-flying. Everybody that could get a chance at him tried their best to coax him off his horse so they could lock him up and get him sober; but it warn't no use—up the street he would tear again, and give Sherburn another cussing. By-and-by somebody says—

'Go for his daughter!—quick, go for his daughter; sometimes he'll listen to her. If anybody can persuade him, she can.'

So somebody started on a run. I walked down street a ways, and stopped. In about five or ten minutes, here comes Boggs again—but not on his horse. He was a-reeling across the street towards me, bareheaded, with a friend on both sides of him aholt of his arms and hurrying him along. He was quiet, and looked uneasy; and he warn't handing back any, but was doing some of the hurrying himself. Somebody sings out—

'Boggs!'

I looked over there to see who said it, and it was that Colonel Sherburn. He was standing perfectly still, in the street, and had a pistol raised in his right hand—not aiming it, but holding it out with the barrel tilted up towards the sky. The same second I see a young girl coming on the run, and two men with her. Boggs and the men turned round, to see who called him, and when they see the pistol the men jumped to one side, and the pistol barrel come down slow and steady to a level—both barrels cocked. Boggs throws up both of his hands, and says, 'O Lord, don't shoot!' Bang! goes the first shot, and he staggers back clawing at the air—bang! goes the second one, and he tumbles backwards onto the ground, heavy and solid, with his arms spread out. That young girl screamed out, and comes rushing, and down she throws herself on her father, crying, and saying, 'Oh, he's killed him, he's killed him!' The crowd closed up around them, and shouldered and jammed one another, with their necks stretched, trying to see, and people on the inside trying to shove them back, and shouting, 'Back, back! give him air, give him air!'

Colonel Sherburn he tossed his pistol onto the ground, and turned around on his heels and walked off.[8]

They took Boggs to a little drug store, the crowd pressing around, just the same, and the whole town following, and I rushed and got a good place at the window, where I was close to him and could see in. They laid him on the floor, and put one large Bible under his head, and opened another one and spread it on his breast—but they tore open his shirt first, and I seen where one of the bullets went in. He made about a dozen long gasps, his breast lifting the Bible up when he drawed in his breath, and letting it down again when he breathed it out—and after that he laid still; he was dead. Then they pulled his daughter away from him, screaming and crying, and took her off. She was about sixteen, and very sweet and gentle-looking, but awful pale and scared.

Well, pretty soon the whole town was there, squirming and scrouging and pushing and shoving to get at the window and have a look, but people that had the places wouldn't give them up, and folks behind them was saying all the time, 'Say, now, you've looked enough, you fellows; 'taint right and 'taint fair, for you to stay thar all the time, and never give nobody a chance; other folks has their rights as well as you.'

There was considerable jawing back, so I slid out, thinking maybe there was going to be trouble. The streets was full, and

[8] This incident was based on an actual murder that Twain witnessed in Hannibal as a boy in 1845 and later said he never forgot. Twain's father, Justice John M. Clemens, was involved in the subsequent trial of the man on whom Sherburn is modeled.

everybody was excited. Everybody that seen the shooting was telling how it happened, and there was a big crowd packed around each one of these fellows, stretching their necks and listening. One long lanky man, with long hair and a big white fur stove-pipe hat on the back of his head, and a crooked-handled cane, marked out the places on the ground where Boggs stood, and where Sherburn stood, and the people following him around from one place to t'other and watching every-thing he done, and bobbing their heads to show they under-stood, and stooping a little and resting their hands on their thighs to watch him mark the places on the ground with his cane; and then he stood up straight and stiff where Sherburn had stood, frowning and having his hat-brim down over his eyes, and sung out, 'Boggs!' and then fetched his cane down slow to a level, and says 'Bang!' staggered backwards, says 'Bang!' again, and fell down flat on his back. The people that had seen the thing said he done it perfect; said it was just exactly the way it all happened. Then as much as a dozen people got out their bottles and treated him.

Well, by-and-by somebody said Sherburn ought to be lynched. In about a minute everybody was saying it; so away they went, mad and yelling, and snatching down every clothes-line they come to, to do the hanging with.

CHAPTER 22

They swarmed up the street towards Sherburn's house, a-whooping and yelling and raging like Injuns, and everything had to clear the way or get run over and tromped to mush, and it was awful to see. Children was heeling it ahead of the mob, screaming and trying to get out of the way; and every window along the road was full of women's heads, and there was nigger boys in every tree, and bucks and wenches looking over every fence; and as soon as the mob would get nearly to them they would break and skaddle back out of reach. Lots of the women and girls was crying and taking on, scared most to death.

They swarmed up in front of Sherburn's palings[1] as thick as they could jam together, and you couldn't hear yourself think for the noise. It was a little twenty-foot yard. Some sung out 'Tear down the fence! tear down the fence!' Then there was a racket of ripping and tearing and smashing, and down she goes, and the front wall of the crowd begins to roll in like a wave.

Just then Sherburn steps out on to the roof of his little front porch, with a double-barrel gun in his hand, and takes his stand, perfectly ca'm and deliberate, not saying a word. The racket stopped, and the wave sucked back.

Sherburn never said a word—just stood there, looking down. The stillness was awful creepy and uncomfortable. Sherburn run his eye slow along the crowd; and wherever it struck, the people tried a little to outgaze him, but they couldn't; they dropped their eyes and looked sneaky. Then pretty soon Sherburn sort of laughed; not the pleasant kind, but the kind that makes you feel like when you are eating bread that's got sand in it.

Then he says, slow and scornful:

[1] *palings*: picket fence.

'The idea of *you* lynching anybody! It's amusing. The idea of you thinking you had pluck enough to lynch a *man*! Because you're brave enough to tar and feather poor friendless cast-out women that come along here, did that make you think you had grit enough to lay your hands on a *man*? Why, a *man's* safe in the hands of ten thousand of your kind—as long as it's day-time and you're not behind him.

'Do I know you? I know you clear through. I was born and raised in the South, and I've lived in the North; so I know the average all around. The average man's a coward. In the North he lets anybody walk over him that wants to, and goes home and prays for a humble spirit to bear it. In the South one man, all by himself, has stopped a stage full of men, in the day-time, and robbed the lot. Your newspapers call you a brave people so much that you think you *are* braver than any other people—whereas you're just *as* brave, and no braver. Why don't your juries hang murderers? Because they're afraid the man's friends will shoot them in the back, in the dark—and it's just what they *would* do.

'So they always acquit; and then a *man* goes in the night, with a hundred masked cowards at his back, and lynches the rascal. Your mistake is, that you didn't bring a man with you; that's one mistake, and the other is that you didn't come in the dark, and fetch your masks. You brought *part* of a man— Buck Harkness, there—and if you hadn't had him to start you, you'd a taken it out in blowing.[2]

'You didn't want to come. The average man don't like trouble and danger. *You* don't like trouble and danger. But if only *half* a man—like Buck Harkness, there—shouts "Lynch him, lynch him!" you're afraid to back down—afraid you'll be found out to be what you are—*cowards*—and so you raise a yell, and hang yourselves onto that half-a-man's coat tail, and come raging up here, swearing what big things you're going to do. The pitifulest thing out is a mob; that's what an army is—a mob;

---

[2] *if you hadn't had him to start you* . . . : i.e., if you didn't have Buck Harkness to take the lead, you would have taken revenge by mere boasting or windy talk.

they don't fight with courage that's born in them, but with courage that's borrowed from their mass, and from their officers. But a mob without any *man* at the head of it, is *beneath* pitifulness. Now the thing for *you* to do, is to droop your tails and go home and crawl in a hole. If any real lynching's going to be done, it will be done in the dark, Southern fashion; and when they come they'll bring their masks, and fetch a *man* along. Now *leave*—and take your half-a-man with you'— tossing his gun up across his left arm and cocking it, when he says this.

The crowd washed back sudden, and then broke all apart and went tearing off every which way, and Buck Harkness he heeled it after them, looking tolerable cheap. I could a staid, if I'd a wanted to, but I didn't want to.

I went to the circus, and loafed around the back side till the watchmen went by, and then dived in under the tent. I had my twenty-dollar gold piece and some other money, but I reckoned I better save it, because there ain't no telling how soon you are going to need it, away from home and amongst strangers, that way. You can't be too careful. I ain't opposed to spending money on circuses, when there ain't no other way, but there ain't no use in *wasting* it on them.

It was a real bully[3] circus. It was the splendidest sight that ever was, when they all come riding in, two and two, a gentleman and lady, side by side, the men just in their drawers and undershirts, and no shoes nor stirrups, and resting their hands on their thighs, easy and comfortable—there must a' been twenty of them—and every lady with a lovely complexion, and perfectly beautiful, and looking just like a gang of real sure-enough queens, and dressed in clothes that cost millions of dollars, and just littered with diamonds. It was a powerful fine sight; I never see anything so lovely. And then one by one they got up and stood, and went a-weaving around the ring so gentle and wavy and graceful, the men looking ever so tall and airy and straight, with their heads bobbing

[3] *bully:* excellent; first-rate.

and skimming along, away up there under the tent-roof, and
every lady's rose-leafy dress flapping soft and silky around her
hips, and she looking like the most loveliest parasol.

And then faster and faster they went, all of them dancing,
first one foot stuck out in the air and then the other, the horses
leaning more and more, and the ring-master going round and
round the centre-pole, cracking his whip and shouting 'hi!—
hi!' and the clown cracking jokes behind him; and by-and-by
all hands dropped the reins, and every lady put her knuckles
on her hips and every gentleman folded his arms, and then
how the horses did lean over and hump themselves! And so,
one after the other they all skipped off into the ring, and made
the sweetest bow I ever see, and then scampered out, and everybody clapped their hands and went just about wild.

Well, all through the circus they done the most astonishing things; and all the time that clown carried on so it most
killed the people. The ring-master couldn't ever say a word
to him but he was back at him quick as a wink with the
funniest things a body ever said; and how he ever *could* think
of so many of them, and so sudden and so pat, was what I
couldn't noway understand. Why, I couldn't a thought of them
in a year. And by-and-by a drunk man tried to get into the
ring—said he wanted to ride; said he could ride as well as
anybody that ever was. They argued and tried to keep him
out, but he wouldn't listen, and the whole show come to a
standstill. Then the people begun to holler at him and make
fun of him, and that made him mad, and he begun to rip and
tear; so that stirred up the people, and a lot of men begun to
pile down off of the benches and swarm towards the ring,
saying, 'Knock him down! throw him out!' and one or two
women begun to scream. So, then, the ring-master he made
a little speech, and said he hoped there wouldn't be no disturbance, and if the man would promise he wouldn't make
no more trouble, he would let him ride, if he thought he could
stay on the horse. So everybody laughed and said all right,
and the man got on. The minute he was on, the horse begun
to rip and tear and jump and cavort around, with two circus

men hanging onto his bridle trying to hold him, and the drunk man hanging onto his neck, and his heels flying in the air every jump, and the whole crowd of people standing up shouting and laughing till the tears rolled down. And at last, sure enough, all the circus men could do, the horse broke loose, and away he went like the very nation, round and round the ring, with that sot[4] laying down on him and hanging to his neck, with first one leg hanging most to the ground on one side, and then t'other one on t'other side, and the people just crazy. It warn't funny to me, though; I was all of a tremble to see his danger. But pretty soon he struggled up astraddle and grabbed the bridle, a-reeling this way and that; and the next minute he sprung up and dropped the bridle and stood! and the horse agoing like a house afire too. He just stood up there, a-sailing around as easy and comfortable as if he warn't ever drunk in his life—and then he begun to pull off his clothes and sling them. He shed them so thick they kind of clogged up the air, and altogether he shed seventeen suits. And then, there he was, slim and handsome, and dressed the gaudiest and prettiest you ever saw, and he lit onto that horse with his whip and made him fairly hum—and finally skipped off, and made his bow and danced off to the dressing-room, and everybody just a-howling with pleasure and astonishment.

Then the ring-master he see how he had been fooled, and he *was* the sickest ring-master you ever see, I reckon. Why, it was one of his own men! He had got up that joke all out of his own head, and never let on to nobody. Well, I felt sheepish enough, to be took in so, but I wouldn't a been in that ring-master's place, not for a thousand dollars. I don't know; there may be bullier circuses than what that one was, but I never struck them yet. Anyways it was plenty good enough for *me*; and wherever I run across it, it can have all of *my* custom, every time.[5]

---

[4] *sot*: drunk.

[5] *it can have all of* my *custom, every time*: i.e., I will patronize, or attend, this circus every time I can.

Well, that night we had *our* show; but there warn't only about twelve people there; just enough to pay expenses. And they laughed all the time, and that made the duke mad; and everybody left, anyway, before the show was over, but one boy which was asleep. So the duke said these Arkansaw lunkheads couldn't come up to Shakspeare; what they wanted was low comedy—and may be something ruther worse than low comedy, he reckoned. He said he could size their style. So next morning he got some big sheets of wrapping-paper and some black paint, and drawed off some handbills and stuck them up all over the village. The bills said:

AT THE COURT HOUSE!

FOR 3 NIGHTS ONLY !

The World-Renowned Tragedians

DAVID GARRICK THE YOUNGER!

AND

EDMUND KEAN THE ELDER!

Of the London and Continental
Theatres,

In their Thrilling Tragedy of

THE KING'S CAMELOPARD

OR

THE ROYAL NONESUCH! ! !

Admission 50 cents.

Then at the bottom was the biggest line of all—which said:

LADIES AND CHILDREN NOT ADMITTED.

'There,' says he, 'if that line don't fetch them, I don't know Arkansaw!'

CHAPTER 23

Well, all day him and the king was hard at it, rigging up a stage, and a curtain, and a row of candles for footlights; and that night the house was jam full of men in no time. When the place couldn't hold no more, the duke he quit tending door and went around the back way and come onto the stage and stood up before the curtain, and made a little speech, and praised up this tragedy, and said it was the most thrill-ingest one that ever was; and so he went on a-bragging about the tragedy and about Edmund Kean the Elder, which was to play the main principal part in it; and at last when he'd got everybody's expectations up high enough, he rolled up the curtain, and the next minute the king come a-prancing out on all fours, naked; and he was painted all over, ring-streaked-and-striped, all sorts of colors, as splendid as a rainbow. And—but never mind the rest of his outfit, it was just wild, but it was awful funny. The people most killed themselves laughing; and when the king got done capering, and capered off behind the scenes, they roared and clapped and stormed and haw-hawed till he come back and done it over again; and after that, they made him do it another time. Well, it would a made a cow laugh to see the shines that old idiot cut.

Then the duke he lets the curtain down, and bows to the people, and says the great tragedy will be performed only two nights more, on accounts of pressing London engagements, where the seats is all sold aready for it in Drury Lane; and then he makes them another bow, and says if he has suc-ceeded in pleasing them and instructing them, he will be deeply obleeged if they will mention it to their friends and get them to come and see it.

Twenty people sings out:

'What, is it over? Is that *all?*'

The duke says yes. Then there was a fine time. Everybody sings out 'sold',[1] and rose up mad, and was agoing for that stage and them tragedians. But a big fine-looking man jumps up on a bench, and shouts:

'Hold on! Just a word, gentlemen.' They stopped to listen. 'We are sold—mighty badly sold. But we don't want to be the laughing-stock of this whole town, I reckon, and never hear the last of this thing as long as we live. *No.* What we want, is to go out of here quiet, and talk this show up, and sell the *rest* of the town! Then we'll all be in the same boat. Ain't that sensible?' ('You bet it is!—the jedge is right!' everybody sings out.) 'All right, then—not a word about any sell. Go along home, and advise everybody to come and see the tragedy.'

Next day you couldn't hear nothing around that town but how splendid that show was. House was jammed again, that night, and we sold this crowd the same way. When me and the king and the duke got home to the raft, we all had a supper; and by-and-by, about midnight, they made Jim and me back her out and float her down the middle of the river and fetch her in and hide her about two mile below town.

The third night the house was crammed again—and they warn't new-comers, this time, but people that was at the show the other two nights. I stood by the duke at the door, and I see that every man that went in had his pockets bulging, or something muffled up under his coat—and I see it warn't no perfumery neither, not by a long sight. I smelt sickly eggs by the barrel, and rotten cabbages, and such things; and if I know the signs of a dead cat being around, and I bet I do, there was sixty-four of them went in. I shoved in there for a minute, but it was too various for me,[2] I couldn't stand it. Well, when the place couldn't hold no more people, the duke he give a fellow a quarter and told him to tend door for him a minute, and then he started around for the stage door, I after him; but the minute we turned the corner and was in the dark, he says:

[1] *sold*: i.e., sold out; duped or betrayed.
[2] *too various for me*: too much for me.

'Walk fast, now, till you get away from the houses, and then shin for the raft like the dickens was after you!'

I done it, and he done the same. We struck the raft at the same time, and in less than two seconds we was gliding down stream, all dark and still, and edging towards the middle of the river, nobody saying a word. I reckoned the poor king was in for a gaudy time of it with the audience; but nothing of the sort; pretty soon he crawls out from under the wigwam, and says:

'Well, how'd the old thing pan out this time, Duke?'

He hadn't been up town at all.

We never showed a light till we was about ten mile below that village. Then we lit up and had a supper, and the king and the duke fairly laughed their bones loose over the way they'd served them people. The duke says:

'Greenhorns, flatheads! *I* knew the first house would keep mum and let the rest of the town get roped in; and I knew they'd lay for us the third night, and consider it was *their* turn now. Well, it *is* their turn, and I'd give something to know how much they'd take for it. I *would* just like to know how they're putting in their opportunity. They can turn it into a picnic, if they want to—they brought plenty provisions.'

Them rapscallions took in four hundred and sixty-five dollars in that three nights. I never see money hauled in by the wagon-load like that, before.

By-and-by, when they was asleep and snoring, Jim says:

'Don't it 'sprise you, de way dem kings carries on, Huck?'

'No,' I says, 'it don't.'

'Why don't it, Huck?'

'Well, it don't, because it's in the breed. I reckon they're all alike.'

'But, Huck, dese kings o' ourn is regular rapscallions; dat's jist what dey is; dey's reglar rapscallions.'

'Well, that's what I'm a-saying; all kings is mostly rapscallions, as fur as I can make out.'

'Is dat so?'

'You read about them once—you'll see. Look at Henry the Eight; this'n 's a Sunday-School Superintendent to *him*. And

look at Charles Second, and Louis Fourteen, and Louis Fifteen, and James Second, and Edward Second, and Richard
Third, and forty more; besides all them Saxon heptarchies[3]
that used to rip around so in old times and raise Cain. My,
you ought to seen old Henry the Eight when he was in bloom.[4]
He *was* a blossom. He used to marry a new wife every day,
and chop off her head next morning. And he would do it
just as indifferent as if he was ordering up eggs. "Fetch up
Nell Gwynn," he says. They fetch her up. Next morning,
"Chop off her head!" And they chop it off. "Fetch up Jane
Shore," he says; and up she comes. Next morning "Chop off
her head"—and they chop it off. "Ring up Fair Rosamun."
Fair Rosamun answers the bell. Next morning, "Chop off her
head." And he made every one of them tell him a tale every
night; and he kept that up till he had hogged a thousand and
one tales that way, and then he put them all in a book, and
called it Domesday Book[5]—which was a good name and stated
the case. You don't know kings, Jim, but I know them; and
this old rip of ourn is one of the cleanest I've struck in history. Well, Henry he takes a notion he wants to get up some
trouble with this country. How does he go at it—give notice?—
give the country a show? No. All of a sudden he heaves all
the tea in Boston Harbor overboard, and whacks out a declaration of independence, and dares them to come on. That
was *his* style—he never give anybody a chance. He had suspicions of his father, the Duke of Wellington. Well, what did
he do?—ask him to show up? No—drownded him in a butt

[3] *Saxon heptarchies*: From the sixth to the ninth centuries, England was divided
into seven kingdoms known as the Anglo-Saxon heptarchy.

[4] *My, you ought to seen old Henry the Eight ... :* The colorful history lesson
that follows concerning Henry VIII (1491–1547) confuses centuries, persons,
and events. For example, Nell Gwyn, Jane Shore, and Fair Rosamond were not
Henry's wives but rather mistresses of English kings both prior and subsequent
to Henry. In addition, Huck places the sixteenth-century Henry at the time of
the American Boston Tea Party (1773) and Declaration of Independence (1776),
and he makes the nineteenth-century Duke of Wellington Henry's father.

[5] *Domesday Book*: Huck confuses the *Arabian Nights* with the eleventh-
century *Domesday Book*, a census of land holdings in England.

of mamsey,[6] like a cat. Spose people left money laying around where he was—what did he do? He collared it. Spose he contracted to do a thing; and you paid him, and didn't set down there and see that he done it—what did he do? He always done the other thing. Spose he opened his mouth—what then? If he didn't shut it up powerful quick, he'd lose a lie,[7] every time. That's the kind of a bug Henry was; and if we'd a had him along 'stead of our kings, he'd a fooled that town a heap worse than ourn done. I don't say that ourn is lambs, because they ain't, when you come right down to the cold facts; but they ain't nothing to *that* old ram, anyway. All I say is, kings is kings, and you got to make allowances. Take them all around, they're a mighty ornery lot. It's the way they're raised.'

'But dis one do *smell* so like de nation, Huck.'

'Well, they all do, Jim. *We* can't help the way a king smells; history don't tell no way.'

'Now de duke, he's a tolerable likely man, in some ways.'

'Yes, a duke's different. But not very different. This one's a middling hard lot, for a duke. When he's drunk, there ain't no near-sighted man could tell him for a king.'

'Well, anyways, I doan' hanker for no mo' un um, Huck. Dese is all I kin stan'.'

'It's the way I feel, too, Jim. But we've got them on our hands, and we got to remember what they are, and make allowances. Sometimes I wish we could hear of a country that's out of kings.'

What was the use to tell Jim these warn't real kings and dukes? It wouldn't a done no good; and besides, it was just as I said; you couldn't tell them from the real kind.

I went to sleep, and Jim didn't call me when it was my turn. He often done that. When I waked up, just at day-break, he was setting there with his head down betwixt his knees, moaning and mourning to himself. I didn't take notice, nor let on.

---

[6] *drownded him in a butt of mamsey*: Actually, the fifteenth-century George, Duke of Clarence, not the Duke of Wellington, was said to have drowned in a butt, or cask, of malmsey, a type of wine.

[7] *lose a lie*: let a lie slip out.

I knowed what it was about. He was thinking about his wife and his children, away up yonder, and he was low and home-sick; because he hadn't ever been away from home before in his life; and I do believe he cared just as much for his people as white folks does for their'n. It don't seem natural, but I reckon it's so. He was often moaning and mourning that way, nights, when he judged I was asleep, and saying, 'Po' little 'Lizabeth! po' little Johnny! Its mighty hard; I spec' I ain't ever gwyne to see you no mo', no mo'!' He was a mighty good nigger, Jim was.

But this time I somehow got to talking to him about his wife and young ones; and by-and-by he says:

'What makes me feel so bad dis time, 'uz bekase I hear sumpn over yonger on de bank like a whack, er a slam, while ago, en it mine me er de time I treat my little 'Lizabeth so ornery. She warn't on'y 'bout fo' year ole, en she tuck de sk'yarlet-fever,[8] en had a powful rough spell; but she got well, en one day she was a-stannin' aroun', en I says to her, I says:

'Shet de do'.'[9]

'She never done it; jis' stood dah, kiner smilin' up at me. It make me mad; en I says agin, mighty loud, I says:

' "Doan' you hear me?—shet de do'!"

'She jis' stood de same way, kiner smilin' up. I was a-bilin'! I says:

' "I lay I *make* you mine!"[10]

'En wid dat I fetch' her a slap side de head dat sont her a-sprawlin'. Den I went into de yuther room, en 'uz gone 'bout ten minutes; en when I come back, dah was dat do'a s-stannin' open *yit*, en dat chile stannin' mos' right in it, a-lookin' down and mournin', en de tears runnin' down. My, but I *wuz* mad, I was agwyne for de chile, but jis' den—it was a do' dat open innerds—jis' den, 'long come de wind en slam it to, behine de chile, ker-*blam!*—en my lan', de chile never move'! My breff

---

[8] *sk'yarlet-fever*: scarlet fever, a contagious bacterial disease related to strep throat and usually contracted by children.

[9] *Shet de do*: Shut the door.

[10] *I lay I make you mine!* I swear I'll make you mind me!

mos' hop outer me; en I feel so—so—I doan' know *how* I feel. I crope out, all a-tremblin', en crope aroun' en open de do' easy en slow, en poke my head in behind de chile, sof' en still, en all uv a sudden, I says *pow*! jis' as loud as I could yell: *She never budge!* Oh, Huck, I bust out a-cryin' en grab her up in my arms, en say, "Oh, de po' little thing! de Lord God Amighty fogive po' ole Jim, kaze he never gwyne to fogive hisself as long's he live!" Oh, she was plumb deef en dumb, Huck, plumb deef en dumb—en I'd ben a-treat'n her so!'

CHAPTER 24

Next day, towards night, we laid up under a little willow tow-head out in the middle, where there was a village on each side of the river, and the duke and the king begun to lay out a plan for working them towns. Jim he spoke to the duke, and said he hoped it wouldn't take but a few hours, because it got mighty heavy and tiresome to him when he had to lay all day in the wigwam tied with the rope. You see, when we left him all alone we had to tie him, because if anybody happened on him all by himself and not tied, it wouldn't look much like he was a run-away nigger, you know. So the duke said it *was* kind of hard to have to lay roped all day, and he'd cipher out some way to get around it.

He was uncommon bright, the duke was, and he soon struck it. He dressed Jim up in King Lear's outfit—it was a long curtain-calico gown, and a white horse-hair wig and whiskers; and then he took his theatre-paint and painted Jim's face and hands and ears and neck all over a dead dull solid blue, like a man that's been drownded nine days. Blamed if he warn't the horriblest looking outrage I ever see. Then the duke took and wrote out a sign on a shingle[1] so—

Sick Arab—but harmless when not out of his head.

And he nailed that shingle to a lath, and stood the lath up four or five foot in front of the wigwam. Jim was satisfied. He said it was a sight better than laying tied a couple of years every day and trembling all over every time there was a sound. The duke told him to make himself free and easy, and if anybody ever come meddling around, he must hop out of the wigwam, and carry on a little, and fetch a howl or two like a wild beast, and he reckoned they would light out and leave him alone. Which was sound enough judgment; but you take the

[1] *shingle*: signboard.

179

average man, and he wouldn't wait for him to howl. Why, he didn't only look like he was dead, he looked considerable more than that.

These rapscallions wanted to try the Nonesuch again, because there was so much money in it, but they judged it wouldn't be safe, because maybe the news might a worked along down by this time. They couldn't hit no project that suited, exactly; so at last the duke said he reckoned he'd lay off and work his brains an hour or two and see if he couldn't put up something on the Arkansaw village; and the king he allowed he would drop over to t'other village, without any plan, but just trust in Providence to lead him the profitable way—meaning the devil, I reckon. We had all bought store clothes where we stopped last; and now the king put his'n on, and he told me to put mine on. I done it, of course. The king's duds was all black, and he did look real swell and starchy. I never knowed how clothes could change a body before. Why, before, he looked like the orneriest old rip that ever was; but now, when he'd take off his new white beaver[2] and make a bow and do a smile, he looked that grand and good and pious that you'd say he had walked right out of the ark, and maybe was old Leviticus himself.[3] Jim cleaned up the canoe, and I got paddle ready. There was a big steamboat laying at the shore away up under the point, about three mile above town—been there a couple of hours, taking on freight. Says the king:

'Seein' how I'm dressed, I reckon maybe I better arrive down from St. Louis or Cincinnati, or some other big place. Go for the steamboat, Huckleberry; we'll come down to the village on her.'

I didn't have to be ordered twice, to go and take a steamboat ride. I fetched the shore a half a mile above the village, and then went scooting along the bluff bank in the easy water. Pretty soon we come to a nice innocent-looking young

[2] *beaver*: hat made out of beaver fur.
[3] *walked right out of the ark* ... : The story of Noah's ark is told in Genesis 6–8. Leviticus is the name of a book of the Old Testament.

country jake setting on a log swabbing the sweat off his face, for it was powerful warm weather; and he had a couple of big carpet-bags by him.

'Run her nose in shore,' says the king. I done it. 'Wher' you bound for, young man?'

'For the steamboat; going to Orleans.'

'Git aboard,' says the king. 'Hold on a minute, my servant 'll he'p you with them bags. Jump out and he'p the gentleman, Adolphus'—meaning me, I see.

I done so, and then we all three started on again. The young chap was mighty thankful; said it was tough work toting his baggage such weather. He asked the king where he was going, and the king told him he'd come down the river and landed at the other village this morning, and now he was going up a few mile to see an old friend on a farm up there. The young fellow says:

'When I first see you, I says to myself, "It's Mr Wilks, sure, and he come mighty near getting here in time." But then I says again, "No, I reckon it ain't him, or else he wouldn't be paddling up the river." You *ain't* him, are you?'

'No, my name's Blodgett—Elexander Blodgett—*Reverend* Elexander Blodgett, I spose I must say, as I'm one o' the Lord's poor servants. But still I'm jist as able to be sorry for Mr Wilks for not arriving in time, all the same, if he's missed anything by it—which I hope he hasn't.'

'Well, he don't miss any property by it, because he'll get that all right; but he's missed seeing his brother Peter die—which he mayn't mind, nobody can tell as to that—but his brother would a give anything in this world to see *him* before he died; never talked about nothing else all these three weeks; hadn't seen him since they was boys together—and hadn't ever seen his brother William at all—that's the deef and dumb one—William ain't more than thirty or thirty-five. Peter and George was the only ones that come out here; George was the married brother; him and his wife both died last year. Harvey and William's the only ones that's left now; and, as I was saying, they haven't got here in time.'

'Did anybody send 'em word?'

'Oh, yes; a month or two ago, when Peter was first took;[4] because Peter said then that he sorter felt like he warn't going to get well this time. You see, he was pretty old, and George's g'yirls was too young to be much company for him, except Mary Jane the red-headed one; and so he was kinder lonesome after George and his wife died, and didn't seem to care much to live. He most desperately wanted to see Harvey— and William too, for that matter—because he was one of them kind that can't bear to make a will. He left a letter behind for Harvey, and said he'd told in it where his money was hid, and how he wanted the rest of the property divided up so George's g'yirls would be all right—for George didn't leave nothing. And that letter was all they could get him to put a pen to.'

'Why do you reckon Harvey don't come? Wher' does he live?'

'Oh, he lives in England—Sheffield—preaches there— hasn't even been in this country. He hasn't had any too much time—and besides he mightn't a got the letter at all, you know.'

'Too bad, too bad he couldn't a lived to see his brothers, poor soul. You going to Orleans, you say?'

'Yes, but that ain't only a part of it. I'm going in a ship, next Wednesday, for Ryo Janeero,[5] where my uncle lives.'

'It's a pretty long journey. But it'll be lovely; I wisht I was agoing. Is Mary Jane the oldest? How old is the others?'

'Mary Jane's nineteen, Susan's fifteen, and Joanna's about fourteen—that's the one that gives herself to good works and has a hare-lip.'

'Poor things! to be left alone in the cold world so.'

'Well, they could be worse off. Old Peter had friends, and they ain't going to let them come to no harm. There's Hobson, the Babtis' preacher; and Deacon Lot Hovey, and Ben Rucker, and Abner Shackleford, and Levi Bell, the lawyer; and

---

[4] *was first took*: was taken by sickness; fell ill.

[5] *Ryo Janeero*: Rio de Janeiro is in Brazil.

Dr Robinson, and their wives, and the widow Bartley, and—
well, there's a lot of them; but these are the ones that Peter
was thickest with, and used to write about sometimes, when
he wrote home; so Harvey'll know where to look for friends
when he gets here.'

Well, the old man he went on asking questions till he just
fairly emptied that young fellow. Blamed if he didn't inquire
about everybody and everything in that blessed town, and all
about all the Wilkses; and about Peter's business—which was
a tanner; and about George's—which was a carpenter; and about
Harvey's—which was a dissentering minister;[6] and so on, and
so on. Then he says:

'What did you want to walk all the way up to the steamboat
for?'

'Because she's a big Orleans boat, and I was afeard she
mightn't stop there. When they're deep they won't stop for a
hail.[7] A Cincinnati boat will, but this is a St. Louis one.'

'Was Peter Wilks well off?'

'Oh, yes, pretty well off. He had houses and land, and it's
reckoned he left three or four thousand in cash hid up som'ers.'

'When did you say he died?'

'I didn't say, but it was last night.'

'Funeral to-morrow, likely?'

'Yes, 'bout the middle of the day.'

'Well, it's all terrible sad; but we've all got to go, one time
or another. So what we want to do is to be prepared; then
we're all right.'

'Yes, sir, it's the best way. Ma used to always say that.'

When we struck the boat, she was about done loading, and
pretty soon she got off. The king never said nothing about
going aboard, so I lost my ride, after all. When the boat was
gone, the king made me paddle up another mile to a lonesome place, and then he got ashore, and says:

---

[6] *dissentering minister*: dissenting minister, or one who refuses to conform to
the tenets of the Anglican church.

[7] *hail*: To summon a steamboat, one would "hail" it, or wave and call out to it,
from a dock.

'Now hustle back, right off, and fetch the duke up here, and the new carpet-bags. And if he's gone over to t'other side, go over there and git him. And tell him to git himself up regardless. Shove along, now.'

I see what *he* was up to; but I never said nothing, of course. When I got back with the duke, we hid the canoe and then they set down on a log, and the king told him everything, just like the young fellow had said it—every last word of it. And all the time he was a doing it, he tried to talk like an Englishman; and he done it pretty well too, for a slouch. I can't imitate him, and so I ain't agoing to try to; but he really done it pretty good. Then he says:

'How are you on the deef and dumb, Bilgewater?'

The duke said, leave him alone for that; said he had played a deef and dumb person on the histrionic boards. So then they waited for a steamboat.

About the middle of the afternoon a couple of little boats come along, but they didn't come from high enough up the river; but at last there was a big one, and they hailed her. She sent out her yawl, and we went aboard, and she was from Cincinnati; and when they found we only wanted to go four or five mile, they was booming mad, and give us a cussing, and said they wouldn't land us. But the king was ca'm. He says:

'If gentlemen kin afford to pay a dollar a mile apiece, to be took on and put off in a yawl, a steamboat kin afford to carry 'em, can't it?'

So they softened down and said it was all right; and when we got the village, they yawled us ashore. About two dozen men flocked down, when they see the yawl a coming; and when the king says—

'Kin any of you gentlemen tell me wher' Mr Peter Wilks lives?' they give a glance at one another, and nodded their heads, as much as to say, 'What d' I tell you?' Then one of them says, kind of soft and gentle:

'I'm sorry, sir, but the best we can do is to tell you where he *did* live yesterday evening.'

Sudden as winking, the ornery old cretur went all to smash, and fell up against the man, and put his chin on his shoulder, and cried down his back, and says:

'Alas, alas, our poor brother—gone, and we never got to see him; oh, it's too, *too* hard!'

Then he turns around, blubbering, and makes a lot of idiotic signs to the duke on his hands, and blamed if *he* didn't drop a carpet-bag and bust out a-crying. If they warn't the beatenest lot, them two frauds, that ever I struck.

Well, the men gethered around, and sympathized with them, and said all sorts of kind things to them, and carried their carpet-bags up the hill for them, and let them lean on them and cry, and told the king all about his brother's last moments, and the king he told it all over again on his hands to the duke, and both of them took on about that dead tanner like they'd lost the twelve disciples. Well, if ever I struck anything like it, I'm a nigger. It was enough to make a body ashamed of the human race.

CHAPTER 25

The news was all over town in two minutes, and you could see the people tearing down on the run, from every which way, some of them putting on their coats as they come. Pretty soon we was in the middle of a crowd, and the noise of the tramping was like a soldier-march. The windows and door-yards was full; and every minute somebody would say, over a fence:

'Is it *them?*'

And somebody trotting along with the gang would answer back and say,

'You bet it is.'

When we got to the house, the street in front of it was packed, and the three girls was standing in the door. Mary Jane *was* red-headed, but that don't make no difference, she was most awful beautiful, and her face and her eyes was all lit up like glory, she was so glad her uncles was come. The king he spread his arms, and Mary Jane she jumped for them, and the hare-lip jumped for the duke, and there they *had* it! Everybody most, leastways women, cried for joy to see them meet again at last and have such good times.

Then the king he hunched the duke, private[1]—I see him do it—and then he looked around and see the coffin, over in the corner on two chairs; so then, him and the duke, with a hand across each other's shoulder, and t'other hand to their eyes, walked slow and solemn over there, everybody dropping back to give them room, and all the talk and noise stopping, people saying 'Sh!' and all the men taking their hats off and drooping their heads, so you could a heard a pin fall. And when they got there, they bent over and looked in the

---

[1] *hunched the duke, private*: huddled with the duke, or consulted with the duke privately.

coffin, and took one sight, and then they bust out a crying so you could a heard them to Orleans, most; and then they put their arms around each other's necks, and hung their chins over each other's shoulders; and then for three minutes, or maybe four, I never see two men leak the way they done. And mind you, everybody was doing the same; and the place was that damp I never see anything like it. Then one of them got on one side of the coffin, and t'other on t'other side, and they kneeled down and rested their foreheads on the coffin, and let on to pray all to theirselves. Well, when it come to that, it worked the crowd like you never see any-thing like it, and so everybody broke down and went to sob-bing right out loud—the poor girls, too; and every woman, nearly, went up to the girls, without saying a word, and kissed them, solemn, on the forehead, and then put their hand on their head, and looked up towards the sky, with the tears run-ning down, and then busted out and went off sobbing and swabbing, and give the next woman a show. I never see any-thing so disgusting.

Well, by-and-by the king he gets up and comes forward a little, and works himself up and slobbers out a speech, all full of tears and flapdoodle about its being a sore trial for him and his poor brother to lose the diseased,[2] and to miss seeing dis-eased alive, after the long journey of four thousand mile, but its a trial that's sweetened and sanctified to us by this dear sympathy and these holy tears, and so he thanks them out of his heart and out of his brother's heart, because out of their mouths they can't, words being too weak and cold, and all that kind of rot and slush, till it was just sickening; and then he blubbers out a pious goody-goody Amen, and turns himself loose and goes to crying fit to bust.

And the minute the words was out of his mouth somebody over in the crowd struck up the doxolojer,[3] and everybody

[2] *diseased*: i.e., deceased.
[3] *doxolojer*: The Doxology, a familiar hymn in many Christian congregations, begins with the line "Praise God, from Whom All Blessings Flow."

joined in with all their might, and it just warmed you up and made you feel as good as church letting out. Music *is* a good thing; and after all that soul-butter and hogwash,[4] I never see it freshen up things so, and sound so honest and bully.

Then the king begins to work his jaw again, and says how him and his nieces would be glad if a few of the main principal friends of the family would take supper here with them this evening, and help set up with the ashes of the diseased; and says if his poor brother laying yonder could speak, he knows who he would name, for they was names that was very dear to him, and mentioned often in his letters; and so he will name the same, to-wit, as follows, vizz:—Rev Mr Hobson, and Deacon Lot Hovey, and Mr Ben Rucker, and Abner Shackleford, and Levi Bell, and Dr Robinson, and their wives, and the widow Bartley.

Rev Hobson and Dr Robinson was down to the end of the town, a-hunting together; that is, I mean the doctor was shipping a sick man to t'other world, and the preacher was pinting him right. Lawyer Bell was away up to Louisville on some business. But the rest was on hand, and so they all come and shook hands with the king and thanked him and talked to him; and then they shook hands with the duke, and didn't say nothing but just kept a-smiling and bobbing their heads like a passel of sapheads whilst he made all sorts of signs with his hands and said 'Goo-goo—goo-goo-goo,' all the time, like a baby that can't talk.

So the king he blatted[5] along, and managed to inquire about pretty much everybody and dog in town, by his name, and mentioned all sorts of little things that happened one time or another in the town, or to George's family, or to Peter; and he always let on that Peter wrote him the things, but that was a lie, he got every blessed one of them out of that young flathead that we canoed up to the steamboat.

---

[4] *soul-butter and hogwash*: combination of oily sentimentality and nonsensical or worthless language.
[5] *blatted*: chattered.

Then Mary Jane she fetched the letter her father left behind, and the king he read it out loud and cried over it. It give the dwelling-house and three thousand dollars, gold, to the girls; and it give the tanyard (which was doing a good business), along with some other houses and land (worth about seven thousand), and three thousand dollars in gold to Harvey and William, and told where the six thousand cash was hid, down cellar. So these two frauds said they'd go and fetch it up, and have everything square and above-board; and told me to come with a candle. We shut the cellar door behind us, and when they found the bag they spilt it out on the floor, and it was a lovely sight, all them yaller-boys.[6] My, the way the king's eyes did shine! He slaps the duke on the shoulder, and says:

'Oh, *this* ain't bully, nor noth'n! Oh, no, I reckon not! Why, Biljy, it beats the Nonesuch, *don't* it!'

The duke allowed it did. They pawed the yaller-boys, and sifted them through their fingers and let them jingle down on the floor; and the king says:

'It ain't no use talkin'; bein' brothers to a rich dead man, and representatives of furrin[7] heirs that's got left, is the line for you and me, Bilge. Thish-yer comes of trust'n to Providence. It's the best way, in the long run. I've tried 'em all, and ther' ain't no better way.'

Most everybody would a been satisfied with the pile, and took it on trust; but no, they must count it. So they counts it, and it comes out four hundred and fifteen dollars short. Says the king:

'Dern him, I wonder what he done with that four hundred and fifteen dollars?'

They worried over that a while, and ransacked all around for it. Then the duke says:

'Well, he was a pretty sick man, and likely he made a mistake—I reckon that's the way of it. The best way's to let it go, and keep still about it. We can spare it.'

[6] *yaller-boys*: gold coins.
[7] *furrin*: foreign.

'Oh, shucks, yes, we can *spare* it. I don't k'yer noth'n 'bout that—it's the *count* I'm thinkin' about. We want to be awful square and open and above-board, here, you know. We want to lug this h-yer money up stairs and count it before everybody— then ther' ain't noth'n suspicious. But when the dead man says ther's six thous'n dollars, you know, we don't want to—'

'Hold on,' says the duke. 'Less make up the deffisit'—and he begun to haul out yaller-boys out of his pocket.

'It's a most amaz'n good idea, duke—you *have* got a rattlin' clever head on you,' says the king. 'Blest if the old Nonesuch ain't a heppin' us out agin'—and *he* begun to haul out yaller-jackets and stack them up.

It most busted them, but they made up the six thousand clean and clear.

'Say,' says the duke, 'I got another idea. Le's go up stairs and count this money, and then take and *give it to the girls*.'

'Good land, duke, lemme hug you! It's the most dazzling idea 'at ever a man struck. You have cert'nly got the most astonishin' head I ever see. Oh, this is the boss dodge,[8] ther' ain't no mistake 'bout it. Let 'em fetch along their suspicions now, if they want to—this'll lay 'em out.'

When we got up stairs, everybody gathered around the table, and the king he counted it and stacked it up, three hundred dollars in a pile—twenty elegant little piles. Everybody looked hungry at it, and licked their chops. Then they raked it into the bag again, and I see the king begin to swell himself up for another speech. He says:

'Friends all, my poor brother that lays yonder, has done generous by them that's left behind in the vale of sorrers. He has done generous by these-'yer poor little lambs that he loved and sheltered, and that's left fatherless and motherless. Yes, and we that knowed him, knows that he would a done *more* generous by 'em if he hadn't ben afeard o' woundin' his dear William and me. Now, *wouldn't* he? Ther' ain't no question 'bout it, in *my* mind. Well, then—what kind o' brothers would

---

[8] *the boss dodge*: an excellent trick to avoid suspicion.

it be, that 'd stand in his way at sech a time? And what kind o' uncles would it be that 'd rob—yes, *rob*—sech poor sweet lambs as these 'at he loved so, at sech a time? If I know William—and I *think* I do—he—well, I'll jest ask him.' He turns around and begins to make a lot of signs to the duke with his hands; and the duke he looks at him stupid and leatherheaded a while, then all of a sudden he seems to catch his meaning, and jumps for the king, goo-gooing with all his might for joy, and hugs him about fifteen times before he lets up. Then the king says, 'I knowed it; I reckon *that*'ll convince anybody the way *he* feels about it. Here, Mary Jane, Susan, Joanner, take the money—take it *all*. It's the gift of him that lays yonder, cold but joyful.'

Mary Jane she went for him, Susan and the hare-lip went for the duke, and then such another hugging and kissing I never see yet. And everybody crowded up with the tears in their eyes, and most shook the hands off of them frauds, saying all the time:

'You *dear* good souls!—how *lovely!*—how *could* you!'

Well, then, pretty soon all hands got to talking about the diseased again, and how good he was, and what a loss he was, and all that; and before long a big iron-jawed man worked himself in there from outside, and stood a listening and looking, and not saying anything; and nobody saying anything to him either, because the king was talking and they was all busy listening. The king was saying—in the middle of something he'd started in on—

'—they bein' partickler friends o' the diseased. That's why they're invited here this evenin'; but tomorrow we want *all* to come—everybody; for he respected everybody, he liked everybody, and so it's fitten that his funeral orgies sh'd be public.'

And so he went a-mooning on and on, liking to hear himself talk, and every little while he fetched in his funeral orgies again, till the duke he couldn't stand it no more; so he writes on a little scrap of paper, '*obsequies*, you old fool', and folds it up and goes to goo-gooing and reaching it over people's heads to him. The king he reads it, and puts it in his pocket, and says:

'Poor William, afflicted as he is, his *heart's* aluz right. Asks me to invite everybody to come to the funeral—wants me to make 'em all welcome. But he needn't a worried—it was just what I was at.'

Then he weaves along again, perfectly ca'm, and goes to dropping in his funeral orgies again every now and then, just like he done before. And when he done it the third time, he says:

'I say orgies, not because it's the common term, because it ain't—obsequies bein' the common term—but because orgies is the right term. Obsequies ain't used in England no more, now—it's gone out. We say orgies now, in England. Orgies is better, because it means the thing you're after, more exact. It's a word that's made up out'n the Greek *orgo*, outside, open, abroad; and the Hebrew *jeesum*, to plant, cover up; hence *inter*. So, you see, funeral orgies is an open er public funeral.'

He was the *worst* I ever struck. Well, the iron-jawed man he laughed right in his face. Everybody was shocked. Everybody says, 'Why *doctor*!' and Abner Shackleford says:

'Why, Robinson, hain't you heard the news? This is Harvey Wilks.'

The king he smiled eager, and shoved out his flapper, and says:

'*Is* it my poor brother's dear good friend and physician? I—'

'Keep your hands off of me!' says the doctor. '*You* talk like an Englishman—*don't* you? It's the worse imitation I ever heard. *You* Peter Wilks's brother. You're a fraud, that's what you are!'

Well, how they all took on! They crowded around the doctor, and tried to quiet him down, and tried to explain to him, and tell him how Harvey'd showed in forty ways that he *was* Harvey, and knowed everybody by name, and the names of the very dogs, and begged and *begged* him not to hurt Harvey's feelings and the poor girls' feelings, and all that; but it warn't no use, he stormed right along, and said any man that pretended to be an Englishman and couldn't imitate the lingo no better than what he did, was a fraud and a liar. The poor girls was hanging to the king and crying; and all of a sudden the doctor ups and turns on *them*. He says:

'I was your father's friend, and I'm your friend; and I warn you *as* a friend, and an honest one, that wants to protect you and keep you out of harm and trouble, to turn your backs on that scoundrel, and have nothing to do with him, the igno-rant tramp, with his idiotic Greek and Hebrew as he calls it. He is the thinnest kind of an impostor—has come here with a lot of empty names and facts which he has picked up some-wheres, and you take them for *proofs*, and are helped to fool yourselves by these foolish friends here, who ought to know better. Mary Jane Wilks, you know me for your friend, and for your unselfish friend, too. Now listen to me; turn this pitiful rascal out—I *beg* you to do it. Will you?'

Mary Jane straightened herself up, and my, but she was hand-some! She says:

'*Here* is my answer.' She hove up the bag of money and put it in the king's hands, and says, 'Take this six thousand dol-lars, and invest it for me and my sisters any way you want to, and don't give us no receipt for it.'

Then she put her arm around the king on one side, and Susan and the hare-lip done the same on the other. Every-body clapped their hands and stomped on the floor like a per-fect storm, whilst the king held up his head and smiled proud. The doctor says:

'All right, I wash *my* hands of the matter. But I warn you all that a time's coming when you're going to feel sick whenever you think of this day'—and away he went.

'All right, doctor,' says the king, kinder mocking him, 'we'll try and get 'em to send for you'—which made them all laugh, and they said it was a prime good hit.

CHAPTER 26

Well, when they was all gone, the king he asks Mary Jane how they was off for spare rooms, and she said she had one spare room, which would do for Uncle William, and she'd give her own room to Uncle Harvey, which was a little bigger, and she would turn into the room with her sisters and sleep on a cot; and up garret was a little cubby, with a pallet in it. The king said the cubby would do for his valley[1]—meaning me.

So Mary Jane took us up, and she showed them their rooms, which was plain but nice. She said she'd have her frocks and a lot of other traps[2] took out of her room if they was in Uncle Harvey's way, but he said they warn't. The frocks was hung along the wall, and before them was a curtain made out of calico that hung down to the floor. There was an old hair trunk in one corner, and a guitar box in another, and all sorts of little knick-knacks and jimcracks around, like girls brisken up a room with. The king said it was all the more homely and more pleasanter for these fixings, and so don't disturb them. The duke's room was pretty small, but plenty good enough, and so was my cubby.

That night they had a big supper, and all them men and women was there, and I stood behind the king and the duke's chairs and waited on them, and the niggers waited on the rest. Mary Jane she set at the head of the table, with Susan along side of her, and said how bad the biscuits was, and how mean the preserves was, and how ornery and tough the fried chickens was—and all that kind of rot, the way women always do for to force out compliments; and the people all knowed everything was tip-top, and said so—said 'How *do* you get biscuits to brown so nice?' and 'Where, for the land's sake *did* you get

[1] *valley*: valet, or personal servant.
[2] *traps*: trappings, or decorations.

these amaz'n pickles?' and all that kind of humbug talky-talk, just the way people always does at a supper, you know.

And when it was all done, me and the hare-lip had supper in the kitchen off of the leavings, whilst the others was helping the niggers clean up the things. The hare-lip she got to pumping me about England, and blest if I didn't think the ice was getting mighty thin, sometimes. She says:

'Did you ever see the king?'

'Who? William Fourth?[3] Well, I bet I have—he goes to our church.' I knowed he was dead years ago, but I never let on. So when I says he goes to our church, she says:

'What—regular?'

'Yes—regular. His pew's right over opposite ourn—on 'tother side the pulpit.'

'I thought he lived in London?'

'Well, he does. Where *would* he live?'

'But I thought *you* lived in Sheffield?'

I see I was up a stump. I had to let on to get choked with a chicken bone, so as to get time to think how to get down again. Then I says:

'I mean he goes to our church regular when he's in Sheffield. That's only in the summer-time, when he comes there to take the sea baths.'

'Why, how you talk—Sheffield ain't on the sea.'

'Well, who said it was?'

'Why, you did.'

'I *didn't*, nuther.'

'You did!'

'I didn't.'

'You did.'

'I never said nothing of the kind.'

'Well, what *did* you say, then?'

'Said he come to take the sea *baths*—that's what I said.'

'Well, then! how's he going to take the sea baths if it ain't on the sea?'

[3] *William Fourth:* William IV ruled England from 1830 to 1837.

'Looky here,' I says; 'did you ever see any Congress water?' [4]

'Yes.'

'Well, did you have to go to Congress to get it?'

'Why, no.'

'Well, neither does William Fourth have to go to the sea to get a sea bath.'

'How does he get it, then?'

'Gets it the way people down here gets Congress-water—in barrels. There in the palace at Sheffield they've got furnaces, and he wants his water hot. They can't bile that amount of water away off there at the sea. They haven't got no conveniences for it.'

'Oh, I see, now. You might a said that in the first place and saved time.'

When she said that, I see I was out of the woods again, and so I was comfortable and glad. Next, she says:

'Do you go to church, too?'

'Yes—regular.'

'Where do you set?'

'Why, in our pew.'

'*Whose* pew?'

'Why, *ourn*—your Uncle Harvey's.'

'His'n? What does *he* want with a pew?'

'Wants it to set in. What did you *reckon* he wanted with it?'

'Why, I thought he'd be in the pulpit.'

Rot him, I forgot he was a preacher. I see I was up a stump again, so I played another chicken bone and got another think. Then I says:

'Blame it, do you suppose there ain't but one preacher to a church?'

'Why, what do they want with more?'

'What!—to preach before a king? I never see such a girl as you. They don't have no less than seventeen.'

'Seventeen! My land! Why, I wouldn't set out such a string as that, not if I *never* got to glory. It must take 'em a week.'

---

[4] *Congress water*: famous mineral water from springs at Saratoga, New York.

'Shucks, they don't *all* of 'em preach the same day—only *one* of 'em.'

'Well, then, what does the rest of 'em do?'

'Oh, nothing much. Loll around, pass the plate—and one thing or another. But mainly they don't do nothing.'

'Well, then, what are they *for*?'

'Why, they're for *style*. Don't you know nothing?'

'Well, I don't *want* to know no such foolishness as that. How is servants treated in England? Do they treat 'em better 'n we treat our niggers?'

'*No!* A servant ain't nobody there. They treat them worse than dogs.'

'Don't they give 'em holidays, the way we do, Christmas and New Year's week, and Fourth of July?'

'Oh, just listen! A body could tell *you* hain't ever been to England, by that. Why, Hare-l—why, Joanna, they never see a holiday from year's end to year's end; never go to the circus, nor theatre, nor nigger shows, nor nowheres.'

'Nor church?'

'Nor church.'

'But *you* always went to church.'

Well, I was gone up again. I forgot I was the old man's servant. But next minute I whirled in on a kind of an explanation how a valley was different from a common servant, and *had* to go to church whether he wanted to or not, and set with the family, on account of it's being the law. But I didn't do it pretty good, and when I got done I see she warn't satisfied. She says:

'Honest injun, now, hain't you been telling me a lot of lies?'

'Honest injun,' says I.

'None of it at all?'

'None of it at all. Not a lie in it,' says I.

'Lay your hand on this book and say it.'

I see it warn't nothing but a dictionary, so I laid my hand on it and said it. So then she looked a little better satisfied, and says:

'Well, then, I'll believe some of it; but I hope to gracious if I'll believe the rest.'

'What is it you won't believe, Joe?' says Mary Jane, stepping in with Susan behind her. 'It ain't right nor kind for you to talk so to him, and him a stranger and so far from his people. How would you like to be treated so?'

'That's always your way, Maim—always sailing in to help somebody before they're hurt. I hain't done nothing to him. He's told some stretcher, I reckon; and I said I wouldn't swallow it all; and that's every bit and grain I *did* say. I reckon he can stand a little thing like that, can't he?'

'I don't care whether 'twas little or whether 'twas big, he's here in our house and a stranger, and it wasn't good of you to say it. If you was in his place, it would make you feel ashamed; and so you oughtn't to say a thing to another person that will make *them* feel ashamed.'

'Why, Maim, he said—'

'It don't make no difference what he *said*—that ain't the thing. The thing is for you to treat him *kind*, and not be saying things to make him remember he ain't in his own country and amongst his own folks.'

I says to myself, *this* is a girl that I'm letting that old reptle rob of her money!

Then Susan *she* waltzed in; and if you'll believe me, she did give Hare-lip hark from the tomb![5]

Says I to myself, And this is *another* one that I'm letting him rob her of her money!

Then Mary Jane she took another inning, and went in sweet and lovely again—which was her way—but when she got done there warn't hardly anything left o' poor Hare-lip. So she hollered.

'All right, then,' says the other girls, 'you just ask his pardon.'

She done it, too. And she done it beautiful. She done it so beautiful it was good to hear; and I wished I could tell her a thousand lies, so she could do it again.

I says to myself, this is *another* one that I'm letting him rob her of her money. And when she got through, they all jest

---

[5] *hark from the tomb*: a sharp reproof or scolding.

laid theirselves out to make me feel at home and know I was amongst friends. I felt so ornery and low down and mean, that I says to myself, My mind's made up; I'll hive that money for them or bust.

So then I lit out—for bed, I said, meaning some time or another. When I got by myself, I went to thinking the thing over. I says to myself, shall I go to that doctor, private, and blow on[6] these frauds? No—that won't do. He might tell who told him; then the king and the duke would make it warm for me. Shall I go, private, and tell Mary Jane? No—I dasn't do it. Her face would give them a hint, sure; they've got the money, and they'd slide right out and get away with it. If she was to fetch in help, I'd get mixed up in the business, before it was done with, I judge. No, there ain't no good way but one. I got to steal that money, somehow; and I got to steal it some way that they won't suspicion that I done it. They've got a good thing, here; and they ain't agoing to leave till they've played this family and this town for all they're worth, so I'll find a chance time enough. I'll steal it, and hide it; and by-and-by, when I'm away down the river, I'll write a letter and tell Mary Jane where it's hid. But I better hive it to-night, if I can, because the doctor maybe hasn't let up as much as he lets on he has; he might scare them out of here, yet.

So, thinks I, I'll go and search them rooms. Up stairs the hall was dark, but I found the duke's room, and started to paw around it with my hands; but I recollected it wouldn't be much like the king to let anybody else take care of that money but his own self; so then I went to his room and began to paw around there. But I see I couldn't do nothing without a candle, and I dasn't light one, of course. So I judged I'd got to do the other thing—lay for them, and eavesdrop. About that time, I hears their footsteps coming, and was going to skip under the bed; I reached for it, but it wasn't where I thought it would be; but I touched the curtain that hid Mary Jane's frocks, so I

---

[6] *blow on*: tell or report on.

jumped in behind that and snuggled in amongst the gowns, and stood there perfectly still.

They come in and shut the door; and the first thing the duke done was to get down and look under the bed. Then I was glad I hadn't found the bed when I wanted it. And yet, you know, it's kind of natural to hide under the bed when you are up to anything private. They sets down, then, and the king says:

'Well, what is it? and cut it middlin' short, because it's better for us to be down there a whoopin'-up the mournin', than up here givin' 'em a chance to talk us over.'

'Well, this is it, Capet. I ain't easy; I ain't comfortable. That doctor lays on my mind. I wanted to know your plans. I've got a notion, and I think it's a sound one.'

'What is it, duke?'

'That we better glide out of this, before three in the morning, and clip it down the river with what we've got. Specially, seeing we got it so easy—*given* back to us, flung at our heads, as you may say, when of course we allowed to have to steal it back. I'm for knocking off and lighting out.'

That made me feel pretty bad. About an hour or two ago, it would a been a little different, but now it made me feel bad and disappointed. The king rips out and says:

'What! And not sell out the rest o' the property? March off like a passel o' fools and leave eight or nine thous'n' dollars' worth o' property layin' around jest sufferin' to be scooped in?— and all good salable stuff, too.'

The duke he grumbled; said the bag of gold was enough, and he didn't want to go no deeper—didn't want to rob a lot of orphans *of everything* they had.

'Why, how you talk!' says the king. 'We shan't rob 'em of nothing at all but jest this money. The people that *buys* the property is the suff'rers; because as soon's it's found out 'at we didn't own it—which won't be long after we've slid—the sale won't be valid, and it'll all go back to the estate. These-yer orphans 'll git their house back agin, and that's enough for *them*; they're young and spry, and k'n easy earn a livin'. *They* ain't agoing to suffer. Why, jest think—there's thous'n's and thous'n's that ain't nigh so well off. Bless you, *they* ain't got noth'n to complain of.'

Well, the king he talked him blind; so at last he give in, and said all right, but said he believed it was blame foolishness to stay, and that doctor hanging over them. But the king says:

'Cuss the doctor! What do we k'yer for *him*? Hain't we got all the fools in town on our side? and ain't that a big enough majority in any town?'

So they got ready to go down stairs again. The duke says:

'I don't think we put that money in a good place.'

That cheered me up. I'd begun to think I warn't going to get a hint of no kind to help me. The king says:

'Why?'

'Because Mary Jane 'll be in mourning from this out;[7] and first you know the nigger that does up the rooms will get an order to box these duds up and put 'em away; and do you reckon a nigger can run across money and not borrow some of it?'

'Your head's level, agin, duke,' says the king; and he come a fumbling under the curtain two or three foot from where I was. I stuck tight to the wall, and kept mighty still, though quivery; and I wondered what them fellows would say to me if they catched me; and I tried to think what I'd better do if they did catch me. But the king he got the bag before I could think more than about a half a thought, and he never suspicioned I was around. They took and shoved the bag through a rip in the straw tick that was under the feather bed, and crammed it in a foot or two amongst the straw and said it was all right, now, because a nigger only makes up the feather bed, and don't turn over the straw tick only about twice a year, and so it warn't in no danger of getting stole, now.

But I knowed better. I had it out of there before they was half-way down stairs. I groped along up to my cubby, and hid it there till I could get a chance to do better. I judged I better

---

[7] *from this out*: from this time forward.

hide it outside of the house somewheres, because if they missed it they would give the house a good ransacking. I knowed that very well. Then I turned in, with my clothes all on; but I couldn't a gone to sleep, if I'd a wanted to, I was in such a sweat to get through with the business. By-and-by I heard the king and the duke come up; so I rolled off of my pallet and laid with my chin at the top of my ladder and waited to see if anything was going to happen. But nothing did.

So I held on till all the late sounds had quit and the early ones hadn't begun, yet; and then I slipped down the ladder.

CHAPTER 27

I crept to their doors and listened; they was snoring, so I tip-
toes along, and got down stairs all right. There warn't a sound
anywheres. I peeped through a crack of the dining-room door,
and see the men that was watching the corpse all sound asleep
on their chairs. The door was open into the parlor, where the
corpse was laying, and there was a candle in both rooms. I
passed along, and the parlor door was open; but I see there
warn't nobody in there but the remainders of Peter; so I shoved
on by; but the front door was locked, and the key wasn't there.
Just then I heard somebody coming down the stairs, back behind
me. I run in the parlor, and took a swift look around, and the
only place I see to hide the bag was in the coffin. The lid was
shoved along about a foot, showing the dead man's face down
in there, with a wet cloth over it, and his shroud on. I tucked
the money-bag in under the lid, just down beyond where his
hands was crossed, which made me creep, they was so cold,
and then I run back across the room and in behind the door.

The person coming was Mary Jane. She went to the coffin,
very soft, and kneeled down and looked in; then she put up
her handkerchief and I see she begun to cry, though I couldn't
hear her, and her back was to me. I slid out, and as I passed
the dining-room I thought I'd make sure them watchers hadn't
seen me; so I looked through the crack and everything was all
right. They hadn't stirred.

I slipped up to bed, feeling ruther blue, on accounts of the
thing playing out that way after I had took so much trouble
and run so much resk about it. Says I, if it could stay where it
is, all right; because when we get down the river a hundred
mile or two, I could write back to Mary Jane, and she could
dig him up again, and get it; but that ain't the thing that's
going to happen; the thing that's going to happen is, the money
'll be found when they come to screw on the lid. Then the

king 'll get it again, and it'll be a long day before he gives anybody another chance to smouch it from him. Of course I *wanted* to slide down and get it out of there, but I dasn't try it. Every minute it was getting earlier, now, and pretty soon some of them watchers would begin to stir, and I might get catched— catched with six thousand dollars in my hands that nobody hadn't hired me to take care of. I don't wish to be mixed up in no such business as that, I says to myself.

When I got down stairs in the morning, the parlor was shut up, and the watchers was gone. There warn't nobody around but the family and the widow Bartley and our tribe. I watched their faces to see if anything had been happening, but I couldn't tell.

Towards the middle of the day the undertaker come, with his man, and they set the coffin in the middle of the room on a couple of chairs, and then set all our chairs in rows, and borrowed more from the neighbors till the hall and the parlor and the dining-room was full. I see the coffin lid was the way it was before, but I dasn't go to look in under it, with folks around.

Then the people begun to flock in, and the beats[1] and the girls took seats in the front row at the head of the coffin, and for a half an hour the people filed around slow, in single rank, and looked down at the dead man's face a minute, and some dropped in a tear, and it was all very still and solemn, only the girls and the beats holding handkerchiefs to their eyes and keeping their heads bent, and sobbing a little. There warn't no other sound but the scraping of the feet on the floor, and blowing noses—because people always blows them more at a funeral than they do at other places except church.

When the place was packed full, the undertaker he slid around in his black gloves with his softy soothering ways, putting on the last touches, and getting people and things all shipshape and comfortable, and making no more sound than a cat. He never spoke; he moved people around, he squeezed

---

[1] *beats*: deadbeats or idle good-for-nothings; i.e., the king and the duke.

in late ones, he opened up passage-ways, and done it all with nods, and signs with his hands. Then he took his place over against the wall. He was the softest, glidingest, stealthiest man I ever see; and there warn't no more smile to him than there is to a ham.

They had borrowed a melodeum[2]—a sick one; and when everything was ready, a young woman set down and worked it, and it was pretty skreeky and colicky, and everybody joined in and sung, and Peter was the only one that had a good thing, according to my notion. Then the Reverend Hobson opened up, slow and solemn, and begun to talk; and straight off the most outrageous row busted out in the cellar a body ever heard; it was only one dog, but he made a most powerful racket, and he kept it up, right along; the parson he had to stand there, over the coffin, and wait—you couldn't hear yourself think. It was right down awkward, and nobody didn't seem to know what to do. But pretty soon they see that long-legged under-taker make a sign to the preacher as much as to say, 'Don't you worry—just depend on me.' Then he stooped down and begun to glide along the wall, just his shoulders showing over the people's heads. So he glided along, and the pow-wow and racket getting more and more outrageous all the time; and at last, when he had gone around two sides of the room, he dis-appears down cellar. Then, in about two seconds we heard a whack, and the dog he finished up with a most amazing howl or two, and then everything was dead still, and the parson begun his solemn talk where he left off. In a minute or two here comes this undertaker's back and shoulders gliding along the wall again; and so he glided, and glided, around three sides of the room, and then rose up, and shaded his mouth with his hands, and stretched his neck out towards the preacher, over the people's heads, and says, in a kind of a coarse whisper, '*He had a rat!*' Then he drooped down and glided along the wall again to his place. You could see it was a great satisfaction to the people, because naturally they wanted to know. A little

[2] *melodeum*: small reed organ.

thing like that don't cost nothing, and it's just the little things that makes a man to be looked up to and liked. There warn't no more popular man in town than what that undertaker was.

Well, the funeral sermon was very good, but pison[3] long and tiresome; and then the king he shoved in and got off some of his usual rubbage, and at last the job was through, and the undertaker begun to sneak up on the coffin with his screw-driver. I was in a sweat then, and watched him pretty keen. But he never meddled at all: just slid the lid along, as soft as mush, and screwed it down tight and fast. So there I was! I didn't know whether the money was in there, or not. So, says I, spose somebody has hogged that bag on the sly?—now how do *I* know whether to write to Mary Jane or not? 'Spose she dug him up and didn't find nothing—what would she think of me? Blame it, I says, I might get hunted up and jailed; I'd bet-ter lay low and keep dark, and not write at all; the thing's awful mixed, now; trying to better it, I've worsened it a hun-dred times, and I wish to goodness I'd just let it alone, dad fetch the whole business!

They buried him, and we come back home, and I went to watching faces again—I couldn't help it, and I couldn't rest easy. But nothing come of it; the faces didn't tell me nothing.

The king he visited around, in the evening, and sweetened every body up, and made himself ever so friendly; and he give out the idea that his congregation over in England would be in a sweat about him, so he must hurry and settle up the estate right away, and leave for home. He was very sorry he was so pushed, and so was everybody; they wished he could stay lon-ger, but they said they could see it couldn't be done. And he said of course him and William would take the girls home with them; and that pleased everybody too, because then the girls would be well fixed, and amongst their own relations; and it pleased the girls, too—tickled them so they clean forgot they ever had a trouble in the world; and told him to sell out as quick as he wanted to, they would be ready. Them poor things

---

[3] *pison*: poisonously.

was that glad and happy it made my heart ache to see them getting fooled and lied to so, but I didn't see no safe way for me to chip in and change the general tune.

Well, blamed if the king didn't bill the house and the niggers and all the property for auction straight off—sale two days after the funeral; but anybody could buy private beforehand if they wanted to.

So the next day after the funeral, along about noontime, the girls' joy got the first jolt; a couple of nigger traders come along, and the king sold them the niggers reasonable, for three-day drafts as they called it, and away they went, the two sons up the river to Memphis, and their mother down the river to Orleans. I thought them poor girls and them niggers would break their hearts for grief; they cried around each other, and took on so it most made me down sick to see it. The girls said they hadn't ever dreamed of seeing the family separated or sold away from the town. I can't ever get it out of my memory, the sight of them poor miserable girls and niggers hanging around each other's necks and crying; and I reckon I couldn't a stood it all but would a had to bust out and tell on our gang if I hadn't knowed the sale warn't no account and the niggers would be back home in a week or two.

The thing made a big stir in the town, too, and a good many come out flatfooted and said it was scandalous to separate the mother and the children that way. It injured the frauds some; but the old fool he bulled right along, spite of all the duke could say or do, and I tell you the duke was powerful uneasy.

Next day was auction day. About broad-day in the morning, the king and the duke come up in the garret and woke me up, and I see by their look that there was trouble. The king says:

'Was you in my room night before last?'

'No, your majesty'—which was the way I always called him when nobody but our gang warn't around.

'Was you in there yisterday er last night?'

'No, your majesty.'

'Honor bright, now—no lies.'

'Honor bright, your majesty, I'm telling you the truth. I hain't been anear your room since Miss Mary Jane took you and the duke and showed it to you.'

The duke says:

'Have you seen anybody else go in there?'

'No, your grace, not as I remember, I believe.'

'Stop and think.'

I studied a while, and see my chance, then I says:

'Well, I see the niggers go in there several times.'

Both of them give a little jump; and looked like they hadn't ever expected it, and then like they *had*. Then the duke says:

'What, *all* of them?'

'No—leastways not all at once. That is, I don't think I ever see them all come *out* at once but just one time.'

'Hello—when was that?'

'It was the day we had the funeral. In the morning. It warn't early, because I overslept. I was just starting down the ladder, and I see them.'

'Well, go on, *go* on—what did they do? How'd they act?'

'They didn't do nothing. And they didn't act anyway, much, as fur as I see. They tip-toed away; so I seen, easy enough, that they'd shoved in there to do up your majesty's room, or something, sposing you was up; and found you *warn't* up, and so they was hoping to slide out of the way of trouble without waking you up, if they hadn't already waked you up.'

'Great guns, *this* is a go!' says the king; and both of them looked pretty sick, and tolerable silly. They stood there a thinking and scratching their heads, a minute, and then the duke he bust into a kind of a little raspy chuckle, and says:

'It does beat all, how neat the niggers played their hand. They let on to be *sorry* they was going out of this region! and I believed they *was* sorry. And so did you, and so did everybody. Don't ever tell *me* any more that a nigger ain't got any histrionic talent. Why, the way they played that thing, it would fool *anybody*. In my opinion there's a fortune in 'em. If I had capital and a theatre, I wouldn't want a better lay out than that—and here we've gone and sold 'em for a song. Yes, and

ain't privileged to sing the song, yet. Say, where *is* that song?—
that draft.'

'In the bank for to be collected. Where *would* it be?'

'Well, *that's* all right then, thank goodness.'

Says I, kind of timid-like:

'Is something gone wrong?'

The king whirls on me and rips out:

'None o' your business! You keep your head shet, and mind
y'r own affairs—if you got any. Long as you're in this town,
don't you forget *that*, you hear?' Then he says to the duke, 'We
got to jest swaller it, and say noth'n: mum's the word for *us*.'

As they was starting down the ladder, the duke he chuckles
again, and says:

'Quick sales *and* small profits! It's a good business—yes.'

The king snarls around on him and says,

'I was trying to do for the best, in sellin' 'm out so quick. If
the profits has turned out to be none, lackin' considable, and
none to carry, is it my fault any more'n its yourn?'

'Well, *they'd* be in this house yet, and we *wouldn't* if I could
a got my advice listened to.'

The king sassed back, as much as was safe for him, and then
swapped around and lit into *me* again. He give me down the
banks[4] for not coming and *telling* him I see the niggers come
out of his room acting that way—said any fool would a *knowed*
something was up. And then waltzed in and cussed *himself* a
while; and said it all come of him not laying late and taking
his natural rest that morning, and he'd be blamed if he'd ever
do it again. So they went off a jawing; and I felt dreadful glad
I'd worked it all off onto the niggers and yet hadn't done the
niggers no harm by it.

[4] *give me down the banks*: scolded me.

CHAPTER 28

By-and-by it was getting-up time; so I come down the ladder and started for down stairs, but as I come to the girls' room, the door was open, and I see Mary Jane setting by her old hair trunk, which was open and she'd been packing things in it—getting ready to go to England. But she had stopped now, with a folded gown in her lap, and had her face in her hands, crying. I felt awful bad to see it; of course anybody would. I went in there, and says:

'Miss Mary Jane, you can't abear to see people in trouble, and I can't—most always. Tell me about it.'

So she done it. And it was the niggers—I just expected it. She said the beautiful trip to England was most about spoiled for her; she didn't know *how* she was ever going to be happy there, knowing the mother and the children warn't ever going to see each other no more—and then busted out bitterer than ever, and flung up her hands, and says:

'Oh, dear, dear, to think they ain't *ever* going to see each other any more!'

'But they *will*—and inside of two weeks—and I *know* it!' says I.

Laws it was out before I could think!—and before I could budge, she throws her arms around my neck, and told me to say it *again*, say it *again*, say it *again*!

I see I had spoke too sudden, and said too much, and was in a close place.[1] I asked her to let me think a minute; and she set there, very impatient and excited, and handsome, but looking kind of happy and eased-up, like a person that's had a tooth pulled out. So I went to studying it out. I says to myself, I reckon a body that ups and tells the truth when he is in a tight place, is taking considerable many resks, though I ain't

---

[1] *close place*: uncomfortable situation.

had no experience, and can't say for certain; but it looks so to me, anyway; and yet here's a case where I'm blest if it don't look to me like the truth is better, and actuly *safer*, than a lie. I must lay it by in my mind, and think it over some time or other, it's so kind of strange and unregular. I never see nothing like it. Well, I says to myself at last, I'm agoing to chance it; I'll up and tell the truth this time, though it does seem most like setting down on a kag of powder and touching it off just to see where you'll go to. Then I says:

'Miss Mary Jane, is there any place out of town a little ways, where you could go and stay three or four days?'

'Yes—Mr Lothrop's. Why?'

'Never mind why, yet. If I'll tell you how I know the niggers will see each other again—inside of two weeks—here in this house—and *prove* how I know it—will you go to Mr Lothrop's and stay four days?'

'Four days!' she says; 'I'll stay a year!'

'All right,' I says, 'I don't want nothing more out of *you* than just your word—I druther have it than another man's kiss-the-Bible.' She smiled, and reddened up very sweet, and I says, 'If you don't mind it, I'll shut the door—and bolt it.'

Then I come back and set down again, and says:

'Don't you holler. Just set still, and take it like a man. I got to tell the truth, and you want to brace up, Miss Mary, because it's a bad kind, and going to be hard to take, but there ain't no help for it. These uncles of yourn ain't no uncles at all—they're a couple of frauds—regular dead-beats. There, now we're over the worst of it—you can stand the rest middling easy.'

It jolted her up like everything, of course; but I was over the shoal water now,[2] so I went right along, her eyes a blazing higher and higher all the time, and told her every blame thing, from where we first struck that young fool going up to the steamboat, clear through to where she flung herself onto the

---

[2] *over the shoal water now*: A shoal is a sandbar in an area of shallow water, a place where a boat might go aground. Huck is over the worst part in telling Mary Ann about the true identity of the king and duke.

king's breast at the front door and he kissed her sixteen or seventeen times—and then up she jumps, with her face afire like sunset, and says:

'The brute! Come—don't waste a minute—not a *second*— we'll have them tarred and feathered, and flung in the river!' Says I:

'Cert'nly. But do you mean, *before* you go to Mr Lothrop's, or—'

'Oh,' she says, 'what am I *thinking* about!' she says, and set right down again. 'Don't mind what I said—please don't— you *won't*, now, *will* you?' Laying her silky hand on mine in that kind of a way that I said I would die first. 'I never thought, I was so stirred up,' she says; 'now go on, and I won't do so any more. You tell me what to do, and whatever you say, I'll do it.'

'Well,' I says, 'it's a rough gang, them two frauds, and I'm fixed so I got to travel with them a while longer, whether I want to or not—I druther not tell you why—and if you was to blow on them this town would get me out of their claws, and I'd be all right, but there'd be another person that you don't know about who'd be in big trouble. Well, we got to save *him*, hain't we? Of course. Well, then, we won't blow on them.'

Saying them words put a good idea in my head. I see how maybe I could get me and Jim rid of the frauds; get them jailed here, and then leave. But I didn't want to run the raft in day-time, without anybody aboard to answer questions but me; so I didn't want the plan to begin working till pretty late to-night. I says:

'Miss Mary Jane, I'll tell you what we'll do—and you won't have to stay at Mr Lothrop's so long, nuther. How fur is it?'

'A little short of four miles—right out in the country, back here.'

'Well, that'll answer. Now you go along out there, and lay low till nine or half-past, to-night, and then get them to fetch you home again—tell them you've thought of something. If you get here before eleven, put a candle in this window, and if I don't turn up, wait *till* eleven, and *then* if I don't turn up it means I'm gone, and out of the way, and safe. Then you come out and spread the news around, and get these beats jailed.'

'Good,' she says, 'I'll do it.'

'And if it just happens so that I don't get away, but get took up along with them, you must up and say I told you the whole thing beforehand, and you must stand by me all you can.'

'Stand by you, indeed I will. They sha'n't touch a hair of your head!' she says, and I see her nostrils spread and her eyes snap when she said it, too.

'If I get away, I sha'n't be here,' I says, 'to prove these rapscallions ain't your uncles, and I couldn't do it if I *was* here. I could swear they was beats and bummers, that's all; though that's worth something. Well, there's others can do that better than what I can—and they're people that ain't going to be doubted as quick as I'd be. I'll tell you how to find them. Gimme a pencil and a piece of paper. There—'*Royal Nonesuch, Bricksville.*' Put it away, and don't lose it. When the court wants to find out something about these two, let them send up to Bricksville and say they've got the men that played the Royal Nonesuch, and ask for some witnesses—why, you'll have that entire town down here before you can hardly wink, Miss Mary. And they'll come a-biling, too.'

I judged we had got everything fixed about right, now. So I says:

'Just let the auction go right along, and don't worry. Nobody don't have to pay for the things they buy till a whole day after the auction, on accounts of the short notice, and they ain't going out of this till they get that money—and the way we've fixed it the sale ain't going to count, and they ain't going to *get* no money. It's just like the way it was with the niggers—it warn't no sale, and the niggers will be back before long. Why, they can't collect the money for the *niggers*, yet—they're in the worst kind of a fix, Miss Mary.'

'Well,' she says, 'I'll run down to breakfast now, and then I'll start straight for Mr Lothrop's.'

' 'Deed, *that* ain't the ticket, Miss Mary Jane,' I says, 'by no manner of means; go *before* breakfast.'

'Why?'

'What did you reckon I wanted you to go at all for, Miss Mary?'

'Well, I never thought—and come to think, I don't know. What was it?'

'Why, it's because you ain't one of these leather-face people. I don't want no better book than what your face is. A body can set down and read it off like coarse print. Do you reckon you can go and face your uncles, when they come to kiss you good-morning, and never—'

'There, there, don't! Yes, I'll go before breakfast—I'll be glad to. And leave my sisters with them?'

'Yes—never mind about them. They've got to stand it yet a while. They might suspicion something if all of you was to go. I don't want you to see them, nor your sisters, nor nobody in this town—if a neighbor was to ask how is your uncles this morning, your face would tell something. No, you go right along, Miss Mary Jane, and I'll fix it with all of them. I'll tell Miss Susan to give your love to your uncles and say you've went away for a few hours for to get a little rest and change, or to see a friend, and you'll be back tonight or early in the morning.'

'Gone to see a friend is all right, but I won't have my love given to them.'

'Well, then, it sha'n't be.' It was well enough to tell *her* so—no harm in it. It was only a little thing to do, and no trouble; and it's the little things that smoothes people's roads the most, down here below; it would make Mary Jane comfortable, and it wouldn't cost nothing. Then I says: 'There's one more thing—that bag of money.'

'Well, they've got that; and it makes me feel pretty silly to think *how* they got it.'

'No, you're out, there. They hain't got it.'

'Why, who's got it?'

'I wish I knowed, but I don't. I *had* it, because I stole it from them: and I stole it to give to you; and I know where I hid it, but I'm afraid it ain't there no more. I'm awful sorry, Miss Mary

Jane, I'm just as sorry as I can be; but I done the best I could; I did, honest. I come nigh getting caught, and I had to shove it into the first place I come to, and run—and it warn't a good place.'

'Oh, stop blaming yourself—it's too bad to do it, and I won't allow it—you couldn't help it; it wasn't your fault. Where did you hide it?'

I didn't want to set her to thinking about her troubles again; and I couldn't seem to get my mouth to tell her what would make her see that corpse laying in the coffin with that bag of money on his stomach. So for a minute I didn't say nothing—then I says:

'I'd ruther not *tell* you where I put it, Miss Mary Jane, if you don't mind letting me off; but I'll write it for you on a piece of paper, and you can read it along the road to Mr Lothrop's, if you want to. Do you reckon that'll do?'

'Oh, yes.'

So I wrote: 'I put it in the coffin. It was in there when you was crying there, away in the night. I was behind the door, and I was mighty sorry for you, Miss Mary Jane.'

It made my eyes water a little, to remember her crying there all by herself in the night, and them devils laying there right under her own roof, shaming her and robbing her; and when I folded it up and give it to her, I see the water come into her eyes, too: and she shook me by the hand, hard, and says:

'Good-bye—I'm going to do everything just as you've told me; and if I don't ever see you again, I sha'n't ever forget you, and I'll think of you a many and a many a time, and I'll *pray* for you, too!'—and she was gone.

Pray for me! I reckoned if she knowed me she'd take a job that was more nearer her size. But I bet she done it, just the same—she was just that kind. She had the grit to pray for Judus[3] if she took the notion—there warn't no back-down to her, I judge. You may say what you want to, but in my opinion she had more sand in her than any girl I ever see; in my opinion

[3] *Judus*: Judas Iscariot was the apostle who betrayed Jesus.

she was just full of sand. It sounds like flattery, but it ain't no flattery. And when it comes to beauty—and goodness too— she lays over them all. I hain't ever seen her since that time that I see her go out of that door; no, I hain't ever seen her since, but I reckon I've thought of her a many and a many a million times, and of her saying she would pray for me; and if ever I'd a thought it would do any good for me to pray for *her*, blamed if I wouldn't a done it or bust.

Well, Mary Jane she lit out the back way, I reckon; because nobody see her go. When I struck Susan and the hare-lip, I says:

'What's the name of them people over on t'other side of the river that you all goes to see sometimes?'

They says:

'There's several; but it's the Proctors, mainly.'

'That's the name,' I says; 'I most forgot it. Well, Miss Mary Jane she told me to tell you she's gone over there in a dreadful hurry—one of them's sick.'

'Which one?'

'I don't know; leastways I kinder forget; but I think it's—'

'Sakes alive, I hope it ain't *Hanner*?'

'I'm sorry to say it,' I says, 'but Hanner's the very one.'

'My goodness—and she so well only last week! Is she took bad?'

'It ain't no name for it. They set up with her all night, Miss Mary Jane said, and they don't think she'll last many hours.'

'Only think of that, now! What's the matter with her!'

I couldn't think of anything reasonable, right off that way, so I says:

'Mumps.' [4]

'Mumps your granny! They don't set up with people that's got the mumps.'

'They don't, don't they? You better bet they do with *these* mumps. These mumps is different. It's a new kind, Miss Mary Jane said.'

---

[4] *Mumps*: a contagious viral disease.

'How's it a new kind?'

'Because it's mixed up with other things.'

'What other things?'

'Well, measles, and whooping-cough, and erysiplas, and consumption, and yaller janders,[5] and brain fever, and I don't know what all.'

'My land! And they call it the *mumps?*'

'That's what Miss Mary Jane said.'

'Well, what in the nation do they call it the *mumps* for?'

'Why, because it *is* the mumps. That's what it starts with.'

'Well, ther' ain't no sense in it. A body might stump his toe, and take pison, and fall down the well, and break his neck, and bust his brains out, and somebody come along and ask what killed him, and some numskull up and say, "Why, he stumped his *toe.*" Would ther' be any sense in that? *No.* And ther' ain't no sense in *this,* nuther. Is it ketching?'

'Is it *ketching?* Why, how you talk. Is a *harrow* catching?—in the dark? If you don't hitch onto one tooth, you're bound to on another, ain't you? And you can't get away with that tooth without fetching the whole harrow along, can you? Well, these kind of mumps is a kind of a harrow, as you may say—and it ain't no slouch of a harrow, nuther, you come to get it hitched on good.'

'Well, it's awful, *I* think,' says the hare-lip. 'I'll go to Uncle Harvey and—'

'Oh, yes,' I says, 'I *would.* Of *course* I would. I wouldn't lose no time.'

'Well, why wouldn't you?'

'Just look at it a minute, and maybe you can see. Hain't your uncles obleeged to get along home to England as fast as they can? And do you reckon they'd be mean enough to go off and leave you to go all that journey by yourselves? *You* know they'll wait for you. So fur, so good. Your uncle Harvey's a

---

[5] *erysiplas, and consumption, and yaller janders:* Erysipelas is a skin disease; consumption is another name for tuberculosis, a lung disease; and "yaller janders" is jaundice, a liver disease that often turns the skin yellow.

preacher, ain't he? Very well, then; is a *preacher* going to deceive a steamboat clerk? is he going to deceive a *ship clerk?*—so as to get them to let Miss Mary Jane go aboard? Now *you* know he ain't. What *will* he do, then? Why, he'll say, "It's a great pity, but my church matters has got to get along the best way they can; for my niece has been exposed to the dreadful pluribus-unum mumps,[6] and so it's my bounden duty to set down here and wait the three months it takes to show on her if she's got it." But never mind, if you think it's best to tell your uncle Harvey—'

'Shucks, and stay fooling around here when we could all be having good times in England whilst we was waiting to find out whether Mary Jane's got it or not? Why, you talk like a muggins.'[7]

'Well, anyway, maybe you better tell some of the neighbors.'

'Listen at that, now. You do beat all, for natural stupidness. Can't you *see* that *they'd* go and tell? Ther' ain't no way but just to not tell anybody at all.'

'Well, maybe you're right—yes, I judge you *are* right.'

'But I reckon we ought to tell Uncle Harvey she's gone out a while, anyway, so he won't be uneasy about her?'

'Yes, Miss Mary Jane she wanted you to do that. She says, "Tell them to give Uncle Harvey and William my love and a kiss, and say I've run over the river to see Mr—Mr—what *is* the name of that rich family your uncle Peter used to think so much of?—I mean the one that—'

'Why, you must mean the Apthorps, ain't it?'

'Of course; bother them kind of names, a body can't ever seem to remember them, half the time, somehow. Yes, she said, say she has run over for to ask the Apthorps to be sure and come to the auction and buy this house, because she allowed her uncle Peter would ruther they had it than anybody else; and she's going to stick to them till they say they'll come, and

[6] *pluribus-unum mumps:* The United States' motto is *e pluribus unum:* one out of many. Huck's description of the all-encompassing "new" type of mumps fulfills this motto.

[7] *muggins:* fool.

then, if she ain't too tired, she's coming home; and if she is, she'll be home in the morning anyway. She said, don't say nothing about the Proctors, but only about the Apthorps—which'll be perfectly true, because she *is* going there to speak about their buying the house; I know it, because she told me so, herself.'

'All right,' they said, and cleared out to lay for their uncles, and give them the love and the kisses, and tell them the message.

Everything was all right now. The girls wouldn't say nothing because they wanted to go to England; and the king and the duke would ruther Mary Jane was off working for the auction than around in reach of Doctor Robinson. I felt very good; I judged I had done it pretty neat—I reckoned Tom Sawyer couldn't a done it no neater himself. Of course he would a throwed more style into it, but I can't do that very handy, not being brung up to it.

Well, they held the auction in the public square, along towards the end of the afternoon, and it strung along, and strung along, and the old man he was on hand and looking his level piousest, up there longside of the auctioneer, and chipping in a little Scripture, now and then, or a little goody-goody saying, of some kind, and the duke he was around goo-gooing for sympathy all he knowed how, and just spreading himself generly.

But by-and-by the thing dragged through, and everything was sold. Everything but a little old trifling lot in the graveyard. So they'd got to work *that* off—I never see such a girafft[8] as the king was for wanting to swallow *everything*. Well, whilst they was at it, a steamboat landed, and in about two minutes up comes a crowd a whooping and yelling and laughing and carrying on, and singing out:

'*Here's* your opposition line! here's your two sets o' heirs to old Peter Wilks—and you pays your money and you takes your choice!'

---

[8] *girafft*: giraffe.

CHAPTER 29

They was fetching a very nice looking old gentleman along, and a nice looking younger one, with his right arm in a sling. And my souls, how the people yelled, and laughed, and kept it up. But I didn't see no joke about it, and I judged it would strain the duke and the king some to see any. I reckoned they'd turn pale. But no, nary a pale did *they* turn. The duke he never let on he suspicioned what was up, but just went a goo-gooing around, happy and satisfied, like a jug that's googling out butter-milk; and as for the king, he just gazed and gazed down sorrowful on them newcomers like it give him the stomach-ache in his very heart to think there could be such frauds and rascals in the world. Oh, he done it admirable. Lots of the principal people gethered around the king, to let him see they was on his side. That old gentleman that had just come looked all puzzled to death. Pretty soon he begun to speak, and I see, straight off, he pronounced *like* an Englishman, not the king's way, though the king's *was* pretty good, for an imitation. I can't give the old gent's words, nor I can't imitate him; but he turned around to the crowd, and says, about like this:

'This is a surprise to me which I wasn't looking for; and I'll acknowledge, candid and frank, I ain't very well fixed to meet it and answer it; for my brother and me has had misfortunes, he's broke his arm, and our baggage got put off at a town above here, last night in the night by a mistake. I am Peter Wilks's brother Harvey, and this is his brother William, which can't hear nor speak—and can't even make signs to amount to much, now 't he's only got one hand to work them with. We are who we say we are; and in a day or two, when I get the baggage, I can prove it. But, up till then, I won't say nothing more, but go to the hotel and wait.'

So him and the new dummy started off; and the king he laughs, and blethers out:

'Broke his arm—*very* likely *ain't* it?—and very convenient, too, for a fraud that's got to make signs, and hain't learnt how. Lost their baggage! That's *mighty* good!—and mighty ingenious—under the *circumstances*!'

So he laughed again; and so did everybody else, except three or four, or maybe half a dozen. One of these was that doctor; another one was a sharp looking gentleman, with a carpet-bag of the old-fashioned kind made out of carpet-stuff, that had just come off of the steamboat and was talking to him in a low voice, and glancing towards the king now and then and nodding their heads—it was Levi Bell, the lawyer that was gone up to Louisville; and another one was a big rough husky that come along and listened to all the old gentleman said, and was listening to the king now. And when the king got done, this husky up and says:

'Say, looky here; if you are Harvey Wilks, when'd you come to this town?'

'The day before the funeral, friend,' says the king.

'But what time o' day?'

'In the evenin—'bout an hour er two before sundown.'

'*How'd* you come?'

'I come down on the *Susan Powell*, from Cincinnati.'

'Well, then, how'd you come to be up at the Pint in the mornin'—in a canoe?'

'I warn't up at the Pint in the mornin'.'

'It's a lie.'

Several of them jumped for him and begged him not to talk that way to an old man and a preacher.

'Preacher be hanged, he's a fraud and a liar. He was up at the Pint that mornin'. I live up there, don't I? Well, I was up there, and he was up there. I *see* him there. He come in a canoe, along with Tim Collins and a boy.'

The doctor he up and says: 'Would you know the boy again if you was to see him, Hines?'

'I reckon I would, but I don't know. Why, yonder he is, now. I know him perfectly easy.'

It was me he pointed at. The doctor says:

'Neighbors, I don't know whether the new couple is frauds or not; but if *these* two ain't frauds, I am an idiot, that's all. I think it's our duty to see that they don't get away from here till we've looked into this thing. Come along, Hines; come along, the rest of you. We'll take these fellows to the tavern and affront them with t'other couple, and I reckon we'll find out *something* before we get through.'

It was nuts for the crowd, though maybe not for the king's friends; so we all started. It was about sundown. The doctor he led me along by the hand, and was plenty kind enough, but he never let *go* my hand.

We all got in a big room in the hotel, and lit up some candles, and fetched in the new couple. First, the doctor says:

'I don't wish to be too hard on these two men, but *I* think they're frauds, and they may have complices that we don't know nothing about. If they have, won't the complices get away with that bag of gold Peter Wilks left? It ain't unlikely. If these men ain't frauds, they won't object to sending for that money and letting us keep it till they prove they're all right—ain't that so?'

Everybody agreed to that. So I judged they had our gang in a pretty tight place, right at the outstart. But the king he only looked sorrowful, and says:

'Gentlemen, I wish the money was there, for I ain't got no disposition to throw anything in the way of a fair, open, out-and-out investigation o' this misable business; but alas, the money ain't there; you k'n send and see, if you want to.'

'Where is it, then?'

'Well, when my niece give it to me to keep for her, I took and hid it inside o' the straw tick o' my bed, not wishin' to bank it for the few days we'd be here, and considerin' the bed a safe place, we not bein' used to niggers, and suppos'n' 'em honest, like servants in England. The niggers stole it the very next mornin' after I had went down stairs; and when I sold 'em, I hadn't missed the money yit, so they got clean away with it. My servant here k'n tell you 'bout it gentlemen.'

The doctor and several said 'Shucks!' and I see nobody didn't altogether believe him. One man asked me if I see the niggers steal it. I said no, but I see them sneaking out of the room and hustling away, and I never thought nothing, only I reckoned they was afraid they had waked up my master and was trying to get away before he made trouble with them. That was all they asked me. Then the doctor whirls on me and says:

'Are *you* English too?'

I says yes; and him and some others laughed, and said 'Stuff!'

Well, then they sailed in on the general investigation, and there we had it, up and down, hour in, hour out, and nobody never said a word about supper, nor ever seemed to think about it—and so they kept it up, and kept it up; and it *was* the worst mixed-up thing you ever see. They made the king tell his yarn, and they made the old gentleman tell his'n; and anybody but a lot of prejudiced chuckleheads would a *seen* that the old gentleman was spinning truth and t'other one lies. And by-and-by they had me up to tell what I knowed. The king he give me a left-handed look out of the corner of his eye, and so I knowed enough to talk on the right side.[1] I begun to tell about Sheffield, and how we lived there, and all about the English Wilkses, and so on; but I didn't get pretty fur till the doctor begun to laugh; and Levi Bell, the lawyer, says:

'Set down, my boy, I wouldn't strain myself, if I was you. I reckon you ain't used to lying, it don't seem to come handy; what you want is practice. You do it pretty awkward.'

I didn't care nothing for the compliment, but I was glad to be let off, anyway.

The doctor he started to say something, and turns and says:

'If you'd been in town at first, Levi Bell—'

The king broke in and reached out his hand, and says:

'Why, is this my poor dead brother's old friend that he's wrote so often about?'

The lawyer and him shook hands, and the lawyer smiled and looked pleased, and they talked right along a while, and then got to one side and talked low; and at last the lawyer speaks up and says:

[1] *talk on the right side*: say the right thing; i.e., what the king wants to hear.

'That'll fix it. I'll take the order and send it, along with your brother's, and then they'll know it's all right.'

So they got some paper and a pen, and the king he set down and twisted his head to one side, and chawed his tongue, and scrawled off something; and then they give the pen to the duke—and then for the first time, the duke looked sick. But he took the pen and wrote. So then the lawyer turns to the new old gentleman and says:

'You and your brother please write a line or two and sign your names.'

The old gentleman wrote, but nobody couldn't read it. The lawyer looked powerful astonished, and says:

'Well, it beats *me*'—and snaked a lot of old letters out of his pocket, and examined them, and then examined the old man's writing, and then *them* again; and then says: 'These old letters is from Harvey Wilks; and here's *these* two's handwritings, and anybody can see *they* didn't write them' (the king and the duke looked sold and foolish, I tell you, to see how the lawyer had took them in), 'and here's *this* old gentleman's handwriting, and anybody can tell, easy enough, *he* didn't write them—fact is, the scratches he makes ain't properly *writing*, at all. Now here's some letters from—'

The new old gentleman says:

'If you please, let me explain. Nobody can read my hand but my brother there—so he copies for me. It's *his* hand you've got there, not mine.'

'*Well!*' says the lawyer, 'this *is* a state of things. I've got some of William's letters too; so if you'll get him to write a line or so we can com—'

'He *can't* write with his left hand,' says the old gentleman. 'If he could use his right hand, you would see that he wrote his own letters and mine too. Look at both, please—they're by the same hand.'

The lawyer done it, and says:

'I believe it's so—and if it ain't so, there's a heap stronger resemblance than I'd noticed before, anyway. Well, well, well! I thought we was right on the track of a slution, but it's gone

to grass, partly. But anyway, *one* thing is proved—*these* two
ain't either of 'em Wilkses'—and he wagged his head towards
the king and the duke.

Well, what do you think?—that muleheaded old fool wouldn't
give in *then*! Indeed he wouldn't. Said it warn't no fair test.
Said his brother William was the cussedest joker in the world,
and hadn't *tried* to write—*he* see William was going to play one
of his jokes the minute he put the pen to paper. And so he
warmed up and went warbling and warbling right along, till he
was actuly beginning to believe what he was saying, *himself*—
but pretty soon the new old gentleman broke in, and says:

'I've thought of something. Is there anybody here that helped
to lay out my br—helped to lay out the late Peter Wilks for
burying?'

'Yes,' says somebody, 'me and Ab Turner done it. We're both
here.'

Then the old man turns towards the king, and says:

'Peraps this gentleman can tell me what was tatooed on his
breast?'

Blamed if the king didn't have to brace up mighty quick, or
he'd a squshed down like a bluff bank that the river has cut
under, it took him so sudden—and mind you, it was a thing
that was calculated to make most *anybody* sqush to get fetched
such a solid one as that without any notice—because how was
he going to know what was tatooed on the man? He whitened
a little; he couldn't help it; and it was mighty still in there,
and everybody bending a little forwards and gazing at him.
Says I to myself, *Now* he'll throw up the sponge—there ain't
no more use. Well, did he? A body can't hardly believe it, but
he didn't. I reckon he thought he'd keep the thing up till he
tired them people out, so they'd thin out, and him and the
duke could break loose and get away. Anyway, he set there,
and pretty soon he begun to smile, and says:

'Mf! It's a *very* tough question, *ain't* it! *Yes*, sir, I k'n tell you
what's tatooed on his breast. It's jest a small, thin, blue arrow—
that's what it is; and if you don't look clost, you can't see it.
Now what do you say—hey?'

Well, I never see anything like that old blister for clean out-and-out cheek.[2]

The new old gentleman turns brisk towards Ab Turner and his pard,[3] and his eye lights up like he judged he'd got the king *this* time, and says:

'There—you've heard what he said! Was there any such mark on Peter Wilks's breast?'

Both of them spoke up and says:

'We didn't see no such mark.'

'Good!' says the old gentleman. 'Now, what you *did* see on his breast was a small dim P, and a B (which is an initial he dropped when he was young), and a W, with dashes between them, so: P—B—W'—and he marked them that way on a piece of paper. 'Come—ain't that what you saw?'

Both of them spoke up again, and says:

'No, we *didn't*. We never seen any marks at all.'

Well, everybody *was* in a state of mind, now; and they sings out:

'The whole *bilin'* of 'm 's frauds! Le's duck 'em! le's drown 'em! le's ride 'em on a rail!' and everybody was whooping at once, and there was a rattling pow-wow. But the lawyer he jumps on the table and yells, and says:

'Gentlemen—gentle*men*! Hear me just a word—just a *single* word—if you PLEASE! There's one way yet—let's go and dig up the corpse and look.'

That took them.

'Hooray!' they all shouted, and was starting right off; but the lawyer and the doctor sung out:

'Hold on, hold on! Collar all these four men and the boy, and fetch *them* along, too!'

'We'll do it!' they all shouted: 'and if we don't find them marks we'll lynch the whole gang!'

I *was* scared, now, I tell you. But there warn't no getting away, you know. They gripped us all, and marched us right

---

[2] *cheek*: insolent boldness.
[3] *pard*: partner.

along, straight for the graveyard, which was a mile and half down the river, and the whole town at our heels, for we made noise enough, and it was only nine in the evening.

As we went by our house I wished I hadn't sent Mary Jane out of town; because now if I could tip her the wink, she'd light out and save me, and blow on our dead-beats.

Well, we swarmed along down the river road, just carrying on like wild-cats; and to make it more scary, the sky was dark-ing up, and the lightning beginning to wink and flitter, and the wind to shiver amongst the leaves. This was the most awful trouble and most dangersome I ever was in; and I was kinder stunned; everything was going so different from what I had allowed for; stead of being fixed so I could take my own time, if I wanted to, and see all the fun, and have Mary Jane at my back to save me and set me free when the close-fit come, here was nothing in the world betwixt me and sudden death but just them tatoo-marks. If they didn't find them—

I couldn't bear to think about it; and yet, somehow, I couldn't think about nothing else. It got darker and darker, and it was a beautiful time to give the crowd the slip; but that big husky had me by the wrist—Hines—and a body might as well try to give Goliar[4] the slip. He dragged me right along, he was so excited; and I had to run to keep up.

When they got there they swarmed into the graveyard and washed over it like an overflow. And when they got to the grave, they found they had about a hundred times as many shovels as they wanted, but nobody hadn't thought to fetch a lantern. But they sailed into digging, anyway, by the flicker of the lightning, and sent a man to the nearest house a half a mile off, to borrow one.

So they dug and dug, like everything; and it got awful dark, and the rain started, and the wind swished and swushed along, and the lightning come brisker and brisker, and the thunder boomed; but them people never took no notice of it, they was so full of this business; and one minute you could see

[4] *Goliar*: The story of David and the giant Goliath is told in 1 Samuel 17.

everything and every face in that big crowd, and the shovelfuls of dirt sailing up out of the grave, and the next second the dark wiped it all out, and you couldn't see nothing at all.

At last they got out the coffin, and begun to unscrew the lid, and then such another crowding, and shouldering, and shoving as there was, to scrouge in and get a sight, you never see; and in the dark, that way, it was awful. Hines he hurt my wrist dreadful, pulling and tugging so, and I reckon he clean forgot I was in the world, he was so excited and panting.

All of a sudden the lightning let go a perfect sluice⁵ of white glare, and somebody sings out:

'By the living jingo, here's the bag of gold on his breast!'

Hines let out a whoop, like everybody else, and dropped my wrist and give a big surge to bust his way in and get a look, and the way I lit out and shinned for the road in the dark, there ain't nobody can tell.

I had the road all to myself, and fairly flew—leastways I had it all to myself except the solid dark, and the now-and-then glares, and the buzzing of the rain, and the thrashing of the wind, and the splitting of the thunder; and sure as you are born I did clip it along!

When I struck the town, I see there warn't nobody out in the storm, so I never hunted for no back streets, but humped it straight through the main one; and when I begun to get towards our house I aimed my eye and set it. No light there; the house all dark—which made me feel sorry and disappointed, I didn't know why. But at last, just as I was sailing by, *flash* comes the light in Mary Jane's window! and my heart swelled up sudden, like to bust; and the same second the house and all was behind me in the dark, and wasn't ever going to be before me no more in this world. She *was* the best girl I ever see, and had the most sand.

The minute I was far enough above the town to see I could make the towhead, I begun to look sharp for a boat to borrow;

---

⁵ *sluice*: stream of water that flows out from a floodgate. (Huck uses this word figuratively here.)

and the first time the lightning showed me one that wasn't chained, I snatched it and shoved. It was a canoe, and warn't fastened with nothing but a rope. The towhead was a rattling big distance off, away out there in the middle of the river, but I didn't lose no time; and when I struck the raft at last, I was so fagged[6] I would a just laid down to blow and gasp if I could afforded it. But I didn't. As I sprung aboard I sung out:

'Out with you Jim, and set her loose! Glory be to goodness, we're shut of them!'

Jim lit out, and was a coming for me with both arms spread, he was so full of joy; but when I glimpsed him in the lightning, my heart shot up in my mouth, and I went overboard backwards; for I forgot he was old King Lear and a drownded A-rab all in one, and it most scared the livers and lights out of me. But Jim fished me out, and was going to hug me and bless me, and so on, he was so glad I was back and we was shut of the king and the duke, but I says:

'Now now—have it for breakfast, have it for breakfast![7] Cut loose and let her slide!'

So, in two seconds, away we went, a sliding down the river, and it *did* seem so good to be free again and all by ourselves on the big river and nobody to bother us. I had to skip around a bit, and jump up and crack my heels a few times, I couldn't help it; but about the third crack, I noticed a sound that I knowed mighty well—and held my breath and listened and waited—and sure enough, when the next flash busted out over the water, here they come!—and just a laying to their oars and making their skiff hum! It was the king and the duke.

So I wilted right down onto the planks, then, and give up; and it was all I could do to keep from crying.

---

[6] *fagged*: tired out.
[7] *have it for breakfast*: leave it for tomorrow.

CHAPTER 30

When they got aboard, the king went for me, and shook me by the collar, and says:

'Tryin' to give us the slip, was ye, you pup! Tired of our company—hey?'

I says:

'No, your majesty, we warn't—*please* don't, your majesty!'

'Quick, then, and tell us what *was* your idea, or I'll shake the insides out o' you!'

'Honest, I'll tell you everything, just as it happened, your majesty. The man that had aholt of me was very good to me, and kept saying he had a boy about as big as me that died last year, and he was sorry to see a boy in such a dangerous fix; and when they was all took by surprise by finding the gold, and made a rush for the coffin, he lets go of me and whispers, 'Heel it, now, or they'll hang ye, sure!' and I lit out. It didn't seem no good for *me* to stay—I couldn't do nothing, and I didn't want to be hung if I could get away. So I never stopped running till I found the canoe; and when I got here I told Jim to hurry, or they'd catch me and hang me yet, and said I was afeard you and the duke wasn't alive, now, and I was awful sorry, and so was Jim, and was awful glad when we see you coming, you may ask Jim if I didn't.'

Jim said it was so; and the king told him to shut up, and said, 'Oh, yes, it's *mighty* likely!' and shook me up again, and said he reckoned he'd drownd me. But the duke says:

'Leggo the boy, you old idiot! Would *you* a done any different? Did you inquire around for *him*, when you got loose? *I* don't remember it.'

So the king let go of me, and begun to cuss that town and everybody in it. But the duke says:

'You better a blame sight give *yourself* a good cussing, for you're the one that's entitled to it most. You hain't done a

230

thing, from the start, that had any sense in it, except coming out so cool and cheeky with that imaginary blue-arrow mark. That *was* bright—it was right down bully; and it was the thing that saved us. For if it hadn't been for that, they'd a jailed us till them Englishmen's baggage come—and then—the penitentiary, you bet! But that trick took 'em to the graveyard, and the gold done us a still bigger kindness; for if the excited fools hadn't let go all holts and made that rush to get a look, we'd a slept in our cravats[1] tonight—cravats warranted to *wear*, too—longer than *we'd* need 'em.'

They was still a minute—thinking—then the king says, kind of absent-minded like:

'Mf! And we reckoned the *niggers* stole it!'

That made me squirm!

'Yes,' says the duke, kinder slow, and deliberate, and sarcastic, 'We did.'

After about a half a minute, the king drawls out:

'Leastways—I did.'

The duke says, the same way:

'On the contrary—I did.'

The king kind of ruffles up, and says:

'Looky here, Bilgewater, what'r you referrin' to?'

The duke says, pretty brisk:

'When it comes to that, maybe you'll let me ask, what was *you* referring to?'

'Shucks!' says the king, very sarcastic; 'but *I* don't know—maybe you was asleep, and didn't know what you was about.'

The duke bristles right up, now, and says:

'Oh, let *up* on this cussed nonsense—do you take me for a blame' fool? Don't you reckon *I* know who hid that money in that coffin?'

'*Yes*, sir! I know you *do* know—because you done it yourself!'

'It's a lie!'—and the duke went for him. The king sings out:

'Take y'r hands off!—leggo my throat!—I take it all back!'

The duke says:

---

[1] *slept in our cravats*: been hanged. A cravat is a hangman's noose.

"Well, you just own up, first, that you *did* hide that money there, intending to give me the slip one of these days, and come back and dig it up, and have it all to yourself.'

'Wait jest a minute, duke—answer me this one question, honest and fair; if you didn't put the money there, say it, and I'll b'lieve you, and take back everything I said.'

'You old scoundrel, I didn't, and you know I didn't. There, now!'

'Well, then, I b'lieve you. But answer me only jest this one more—now *don't* git mad; didn't you have it in your *mind* to hook the money and hide it?'

The duke never said nothing for a little bit; then he says:

'Well—I don't care if I *did*, I didn't *do* it, anyway. But you not only had it in mind to do it, but you *done* it.'

'I wisht I may never die if I done it, duke, and that's honest. I won't say I warn't *goin* to do it, because I *was*; but you—I mean somebody—got in ahead o' me.'

'It's a lie! You done it, and you got to *say* you done it, or—'

The king begun to gurgle, and then he gasps out:

' 'Nough!—*I own up!*'

I was very glad to hear him say that, it made me feel much more easier than what I was feeling before. So the duke took his hands off, and says:

'If you ever deny it again, I'll drown you. It's *well* for you to set there and blubber like a baby—it's fitten for you, after the way you've acted. I never see such an old ostrich for wanting to gobble everything—and I a trusting you all the time, like you was my own father. You ought to been ashamed of yourself to stand by and hear it saddled onto a lot of poor niggers and you never say a word for 'em. It makes me feel ridiculous to think I was soft enough to *believe* that rubbage. Cuss you, I can see, now, why you was so anxious to make up the deffesit—you wanted to get what money I'd got out of the Nonesuch and one thing or another, and scoop it *all!*'

The king says, timid, and still a snuffling:

'Why, duke, it was you that said make up the deffersit, it warn't me.'

'Dry up! I don't want to hear no more *out* of you!' says the duke. 'And *now* you see what you *got* by it. They've got all their own money back, and all of *ourn* but a shekel[2] or two, *besides.* G'long to bed—and don't you deffersit *me* no more deffersits, long's *you* live!'

So the king sneaked into the wigwam, and took to his bottle for comfort; and before long the duke tackled *his* bottle; and so in about a half an hour they was as thick as thieves again, and the tighter they got, the lovinger they got; and went off a snoring in each other's arms. They both got powerful mellow, but I noticed the king didn't get mellow enough to forget to remember to not deny about hiding the money-bag again. That made me feel easy and satisfied. Of course when they got to snoring, we had a long gabble, and I told Jim everything.

[2] *shekel*: coin.

CHAPTER 31

We dasn't stop again at any town, for days and days; kept right along down the river. We was down south in the warm weather, now, and a mighty long ways from home. We begun to come to trees with Spanish moss[1] on them, hanging down from the limbs like long gray beards. It was the first I ever see it growing, and it made the woods look solemn and dismal. So now the frauds reckoned they was out of danger, and they begun to work the villages again.

First they done a lecture on temperance; but they didn't make enough for them both to get drunk on. Then in another village they started a dancing school; but they didn't know no more how to dance than a kangaroo does; so the first prance they made, the general public jumped in and pranced them out of town. Another time they tried a go at yellocution;[2] but they didn't yellocute long till the audience got up and give them a solid good cussing and made them skip out. They tackled missionarying, and mesmerizering, and doctoring, and telling fortunes, and a little of everything; but they couldn't seem to have no luck. So at last they got just about dead broke, and laid around the raft, as she floated along, thinking, and thinking, and never saying nothing, by the half a day at a time, and dreadful blue and desperate.

And at last they took a change, and begun to lay their heads together in the wigwam and talk low and confidential two or three hours at a time. Jim and me got uneasy. We didn't like the look of it. We judged they was studying up some kind of worse deviltry than ever. We turned it over and over, and at last we made up our minds they was going to break into somebody's house or store, or was going into the

---

[1] *Spanish moss*: also called "long-beard", a type of tree moss found in the southern United States.

[2] *yellocution*: elocution, the art of public speaking.

counterfeit-money business, or something. So then we was pretty scared, and made up an agreement that we wouldn't have nothing in the world to do with such actions, and if we ever got the least show[3] we would give them the cold shake, and clear out and leave them behind. Well, early one morning we hid the raft in a good safe place about two mile below a little bit of a shabby village, named Pikesville,[4] and the king he went ashore, and told us all to stay hid whilst he went up to town and smelt around to see if anybody had got any wind of the Royal Nonesuch there yet. ('House to rob, you *mean*,' says I to myself; 'and when you get through robbing it you'll come back here and wonder what's become of me and Jim and the raft—and you'll have to take it out in wondering.') And he said if he warn't back by midday, the duke and me would know it was all right, and we was to come along.

So we staid where we was. The duke he fretted and sweated around, and was in a mighty sour way. He scolded us for everything, and we couldn't seem to do nothing right; he found fault with every little thing. Something was a-brewing, sure. I was good and glad when midday come and no king; we could have a change, anyway—and maybe a chance for *the* change, on top of it. So me and the duke went up to the village, and hunted around there for the king, and by-and-by we found him in the back room of a little low doggery,[5] very tight, and a lot of loafers bullyragging[6] him for sport, and he a cussing and threatening with all his might, and so tight he couldn't walk, and couldn't do nothing to them. The duke he began to abuse him for an old fool, and the king begun to sass back; and the minute they was fairly at it, I lit out, and shook the reefs[7] out of my hind legs, and spun down the river road like

---

[3] *if we ever got the least show*: if we ever got the slightest opportunity.

[4] *Pikesville*: Although the state is not identified, Pikesville and Phelps' farm (mentioned below) are probably located in southern Arkansas.

[5] *doggery*: saloon.

[6] *bullyragging*: abusing; making fun of.

[7] *reefs*: kinks or tight places.

a deer—for I see our chance; and I made up my mind that it would be a long day before they ever see me and Jim again. I got down there all out of breath but loaded up with joy, and sung out—

'Set her loose, Jim, we're all right, now!'

But there warn't no answer, and nobody come out of the wigwam. Jim was gone! I set up a shout—and then another—and then another one; and run this way and that in the woods, whooping and screeching; but it warn't no use—old Jim was gone. Then I set down and cried; I couldn't help it. But I couldn't set still long. Pretty soon I went out on the road, trying to think what I better do, and I run across a boy walking, and asked him if he'd seen a strange nigger, dressed so and so, and he says:

'Yes.'

'Whereabouts?' says I.

'Down to Silas Phelps's place, two miles below here. He's a runaway nigger, and they've got him. Was you looking for him?'

'You bet I ain't! I run across him in the woods about an hour or two ago, and he said if I hollered he'd cut my livers out—and told me to lay down and stay where I was; and I done it. Been there ever since; afeard to come out.'

'Well,' he says, 'you needn't be afeared no more, becuz they've got him. He run off 'fm down South, som'ers.'

'It's a good job they got him.'

'Well, I *reckon*! There's two hundred dollars reward on him. It's like picking up money out'n the road.'

'Yes, it is—and *I* could a had it if I'd been big enough; I see him *first*. Who nailed him?'

'It was an old fellow—a stranger—and he sold out his chance in him for forty dollars, becuz he's got to go up the river and can't wait. Think o' that, now! You bet *I'd* wait, if it was seven year.'

'That's me, every time,' says I. 'But maybe his chance ain't worth no more than that, if he'll sell it so cheap. Maybe there's something ain't straight about it.'

'But it is, though—straight as a string. I see the hand-bill myself. It tells all about him, to a dot—paints him like a picture, and tells the plantation he's frum, below Newr*leans*. No-sirree-*bob*, they ain't no trouble 'bout *that* speculation, you bet you. Say, gimme a chaw tobacker, won't ye?'

I didn't have none, so he left. I went to the raft, and set down in the wigwam to think. But I couldn't come to nothing. I thought till I wore my head sore, but I couldn't see no way out of the trouble. After all this long journey, and afer all we'd done for them scoundrels, here was it all come to nothing, everything all busted up and ruined, because they could have the heart to serve Jim such a trick as that, and make him a slave again all his life, and amongst strangers, too, for forty dirty dollars.

Once I said to myself it would be a thousand times better for Jim to be a slave at home where his family was, as long as he'd *got* to be a slave, and so I'd better write a letter to Tom Sawyer and tell him to tell Miss Watson where he was. But I soon give up that notion, for two things: she'd be mad and disgusted at his rascality and ungratefulness for leaving her, and so she'd sell him straight down the river again; and if she didn't, everybody naturally despises an ungrateful nigger, and they'd make Jim feel it all the time, and so he'd feel ornery and disgraced. And then think of *me*! It would get all around, that Huck Finn helped a nigger to get his freedom; and if I was to ever see anybody from that town again, I'd be ready to get down and lick his boots for shame. That's just the way: a person does a low-down thing, and then he don't want to take no consequences of it. Thinks as long as he can hide it, it ain't no disgrace. That was my fix exactly. The more I studied about this, the more my conscience went to grinding me, and the more wicked and low-down and ornery I got to feeling. And at last, when it hit me all of a sudden that here was the plain hand of Providence slapping me in the face and letting me know my wickedness was being watched all the time from up there in heaven, whilst I was stealing a poor old woman's nigger that hadn't ever done me no harm, and now was showing me there's One that's always on the lookout, and ain't agoing to allow no such miserable doings to go only just so fur and no further, I most dropped in my tracks I was so scared. Well, I tried the best I could to kinder soften it up somehow for myself, by saying I was brung up wicked, and so I warn't so much to blame; but something inside of me kept saying, 'There was the Sunday school, you could a gone to it; and if you'd a done it they'd a learnt you, there, that people that acts as I'd been acting about that nigger goes to everlasting fire.'

It made me shiver. And I about made up my mind to pray; and see if I couldn't try to quit being the kind of a boy I was, and be better. So I kneeled down. But the words wouldn't come. Why wouldn't they? It warn't no use to try and hide it from Him. Nor from *me*, neither. I knowed very well why they wouldn't come. It was because my heart warn't right; it was because I warn't square; it was because I was playing double. I was letting *on* to give up sin, but away inside of me I was holding on to the biggest one of all. I was trying to make my mouth *say* I would do the right thing and the clean thing, and go and write to that nigger's owner and tell where he was; but deep down in me I knowed it was a lie—and He knowed it. You can't pray a lie—I found that out.

So I was full of trouble, full as I could be; and didn't know what to do. At last I had an idea; and I says, I'll go and write the letter—and *then* see if I can pray. Why, it was astonishing, the way I felt as light as a feather, right straight off, and my troubles all gone. So I got a piece of paper and a pencil, all glad and excited, and set down and wrote:

> Miss Watson your runaway nigger Jim is down here two mile below Pikesville and Mr Phelps has got him and he will give him up for the reward if you send.   Huck Finn

I felt good and all washed clean of sin for the first time I had ever felt so in my life, and I knowed I could pray now. But I didn't do it straight off, but laid the paper down and set there thinking—thinking how good it was all this happened so, and how near I come to being lost and going to hell. And went on thinking. And got to thinking over our trip down the river; and I see Jim before me, all the time, in the day, and in the night-time, sometimes moonlight, sometimes storms, and we a floating along, talking, and singing, and laughing. But somehow I couldn't seem to strike no places to harden me against him, but only the other kind. I'd see him standing my watch on top of his'n, stead of calling me, so I could go on sleeping; and see him how glad he was when I come back out of the fog; and when I come to him again in the swamp, up there where the feud was; and such-like times; and would always call me honey, and pet me, and do everything he could think of for me, and how good he always was; and at last I struck the time I saved him by telling the men we had small-pox aboard, and he was so grateful, and said I was the best friend old Jim ever had in the world, and the *only* one he's got now; and then I happened to look around, and see that paper.

It was a close place. I took it up, and held it in my hand. I was a trembling, because I'd got to decide, forever, betwixt two things, and I knowed it. I studied a minute, sort of holding my breath, and then says to myself:

'All right, then, I'll *go* to hell'—and tore it up.

It was awful thoughts, and awful words, but they was said. And I let them stay said; and never thought no more about reforming. I shoved the whole thing out of my head; and said I would take up wickedness again, which was in my line, being brung up to it, and the other warn't. And for a starter, I would go to work and steal Jim out of slavery again; and if I could think up anything worse, I would do that, too; because as long as I was in, and in for good, I might as well go the whole hog.

Then I set to thinking over how to get at it, and turned over considerable many ways in my mind; and at last fixed up a plan that suited me. So then I took the bearings of a woody island that was down the river a piece, and as soon as it was fairly dark I crept out with my raft and went for it, and hid it there, and then turned in. I slept the night through, and got up before it was light, and had my breakfast, and put on my store clothes, and tied up some others and one thing or another in a bundle, and took the canoe and cleared for shore. I landed below where I judged was Phelps's place, and hid my bundle in the woods, and then filled up the canoe with water, and loaded rocks into her and sunk her where I could find her again when I wanted her, about a quarter of a mile below a little stream sawmill that was on the bank.

Then I struck up the road, and when I passed the mill I see a sign on it, 'Phelps's Sawmill,' and when I come to the farmhouses, two or three hundred yards further along, I kept my eyes peeled, but didn't see nobody around, though it was good daylight, now. But I didn't mind, because I didn't want to see nobody just yet—I only wanted to get the lay of the land. According to my plan, I was going to turn up there from the village, not from below. So I just took a look, and shoved along, straight for town. Well, the very first man I see, when I got there, was the duke. He was sticking up a bill for the Royal Nonesuch—three-night performance—like that other time. *They* had the cheek, them frauds! I was right on him, before I could shirk. He looked astonished, and says:

'Hel-*lo!* Where'd *you* come from?' Then he says, kind of glad and eager, 'Where's the raft?—got her in a good place?'

I says:

'Why, that's just what I was a going to ask your grace.'

Then he didn't look so joyful—and says:

'What was your idea for asking *me?*' he says.

'Well,' I says, 'when I see the king in that doggery yesterday, I says to myself, we can't get him home for hours, till he's soberer; so I went a loafing around town to put in the time, and wait. A man up and offered me ten cents to help him pull a skiff over the river and back to fetch a sheep, and so I went along; but when we was dragging him to the boat, and the man left me aholt of the rope and went behind him to shove him along, he was too strong for me, and jerked loose and run, and we after him. We didn't have no dog, and so we had to chase him all over the country till we tired him out. We never got him till dark, then we fetched him over, and I started down for the raft. When I got there and see it was gone, I says to myself, "they've got into trouble and had to leave; and they've took my nigger, which is the only nigger

I've got in the world, and now I'm in a strange country, and ain't got no property no more, nor nothing, and no way to make my living"; so I set down and cried. I slept in the woods all night. But what *did* become of the raft then?—and Jim, poor Jim!'

'Blamed if *I* know—that is, what's become of the raft. That old fool had made a trade and got forty dollars, and when we found him in the doggery the loafers had matched half dollars with him and got every cent but what he'd spent for whisky; and when I got him home late last night and found the raft gone, we said, "That little rascal has stole our raft and shook us, and run off down the river." '

'I wouldn't shake my *nigger*, would I?—the only nigger I had in the world, and the only property.'

'We never thought of that. Fact is, I reckon we'd come to consider him *our* nigger; yes, we did consider him so—goodness knows we had trouble enough for him. So when we see the raft was gone, and we flat broke, there warn't anything for it but to try the Royal Nonesuch another shake. And I've pegged along ever since, dry as a powderhorn.[8] Where's that ten cents? Give it here.'

I had considerable money, so I give him ten cents, but begged him to spend it for something to eat, and give me some, because it was all the money I had, and I hadn't had nothing to eat since yesterday. He never said nothing. The next minute he whirls on me and says:

'Do you reckon that nigger would blow on us? We'd skin him if he done that!'

'How can he blow? Hain't he run off?'

'No! That old fool sold him, and never divided with me, and the money's gone.'

'*Sold* him?' I says, and begun to cry; 'why, he was *my* nigger, and that was my money. Where is he?—I want my nigger.'

'Well, you can't *get* your nigger, that's all—so dry up your blubbering. Looky here—do you think *you'd* venture to blow

---

[8] *dry as a powderhorn*: i.e., out of money; broke.

on us? Blamed if I think I'd trust you. Why, if you *was* to blow on us—'

He stopped, but I never see the duke look so ugly out of his eyes before. I went on a-whimpering, and says:

'I don't want to blow on nobody; and I ain't got no time to blow, nohow. I got to turn out and find my nigger.'

He looked kinder bothered, and stood there with his bills fluttering on his arm, thinking, and wrinkling up his forehead. At last he says:

'I'll tell you something. We got to be here three days. If you'll promise you won't blow, and won't let the nigger blow, I'll tell you where to find him.'

So I promised, and he says:

'A farmer by the name of Silas Ph—' and then he stopped. You see he started to tell me the truth; but when he stopped, that way, and begun to study and think again, I reckoned he was changing his mind. And so he was. He wouldn't trust me; he wanted to make sure of having me out of the way the whole three days. So pretty soon he says: 'The man that bought him is named Abram Foster—Abram G. Foster—and he lives forty mile back here in the country, on the road to Lafayette.'[9]

'All right,' I says, 'I can walk it in three days. And I'll start this very afternoon.'

'No you won't, you'll start *now*; and don't you lose any time about it, neither, nor do any gabbling by the way. Just keep a tight tongue in your head and move right along, and then you won't get into trouble with *us*, d'ye hear?'

That was the order I wanted, and that was the one I played for. I wanted to be left free to work my plans.

'So clear out,' he says; 'and you can tell Mr Foster whatever you want to. Maybe you can get him to believe that Jim *is* your nigger—some idiots don't require documents—leastways I've heard there's such down South here. And when you tell him the handbill and the reward's bogus, maybe he'll believe you when you explain to him what the idea was for getting

[9] *Lafayette*: Lafayette County is in the southwest part of the state of Arkansas.

'em out. Go 'long, now, and tell him anything you want to; but mind you don't work your jaw any *between* here and there.'

So I left, and struck for the back country. I didn't look around, but I kinder felt like he was watching me. But I knowed I could tire him out at that. I went straight out in the country as much as a mile, before I stopped; then I doubled back through the woods towards Phelps's. I reckoned I better start in on my plan straight off, without fooling around, because I wanted to stop Jim's mouth till these fellows could get away. I didn't want no trouble with their kind. I'd seen all I wanted to of them, and wanted to get entirely shut of them.

CHAPTER 32

When I got there it was all still and Sunday-like, and hot and sunshiny—the hands was gone to the fields; and there was them kind of faint dronings of bugs and flies in the air that makes it seem so lonesome and like everybody's dead and gone; and if a breeze fans along and quivers the leaves, it makes you feel mournful, because you feel like it's spirits whispering—spirits that's been dead ever so many years—and you always think they're talking about *you*. As a general thing it makes a body wish *he* was dead, too, and done with it all.

Phelps's was one of these little one-horse cotton plantations; and they all look alike. A rail fence round a two-acre yard; a stile, made out of logs sawed off and up-ended, in steps, like barrels of a different length, to climb over the fence with, and for the women to stand on when they are going to jump onto a horse; some sickly grass-patches in the big yard, but mostly it was bare and smooth, like an old hat with the nap rubbed off; big double log house for the white folks— hewed logs, with the chinks stopped up with mud or mortar, and these mudstripes been whitewashed some time or another; round-log kitchen, with a big broad, open but roofed passage joining it to the house; log smoke-house back of the kitchen; three little log nigger-cabins in a row t'other side the smoke-house; one little hut all by itself away down against the back fence, and some out-buildings down a piece the other side; ash-hopper,[1] and big kettle to bile soap in, by the little hut; bench by the kitchen door, with bucket of water and a gourd; hound asleep there, in the sun; more hounds asleep, round about; about three shade-trees away off in a corner; some currant bushes and gooseberry bushes in one place by the fence; outside of the fence a garden and a water-melon

---

[1] *ash-hopper*: vat used to collect wood ash in order to make soap.

patch; then the cotton fields begins; and after the fields, the woods.

I went around and clumb over the back stile by the ash-hopper, and started for the kitchen. When I got a little ways, I heard the dim hum of a spinning-wheel wailing along up and sinking along down again; and then I knowed for certain I wished I was dead—for that *is* the lonesomest sound in the whole world.

I went right along, not fixing up any particular plan, but just trusting to Providence to put the right words in my mouth when the time come; for I'd noticed that Providence always did put the right words in my mouth, if I left it alone.

When I got half-way, first one hound and then another got up and went for me, and of course I stopped and faced them, and kept still. And such another pow-wow as they made! In a quarter of a minute I was a kind of a hub of a wheel, as you may say—spokes made out of dogs—circle of fifteen of them packed together around me, with their necks and noses stretched up towards me, a barking and howling; and more a coming; you could see them sailing over fences and around corners from everywheres.

A nigger woman come tearing out of the kitchen with a rolling-pin in her hand, singing out, 'Begone! *you* Tige! you Spot! begon, sah!' and she fetched first one and then another of them a clip and sent him howling, and then the rest followed; and the next second, half of them come back, wagging their tails around me and making friends with me. There ain't no harm in a hound, nohow.

And behind the woman comes a little nigger girl and two little nigger boys, without anything on but tow-linen shirts, and they hung onto their mother's gown, and peeped out from behind her at me, bashful, the way they always do. And here comes the white woman running from the house, about forty-five or fifty year old, bareheaded, and her spinning-stick in her hand; and behind her comes her little white children, acting the same way the little niggers was doing. She was smiling all over so she could hardly stand—and says:

'It's *you*, at last!—*ain't* it?'

I out with a 'Yes'm,' before I thought.

She grabbed me and hugged me tight; and then gripped me by both hands and shook and shook; and the tears come in her eyes, and run down over; and she couldn't seem to hug and shake enough, and kept saying, 'You don't look as much like your mother as I reckoned you would, but law sakes, I don't care for that, I'm *so* glad to see you! Dear, dear, it does seem like I could eat you up! Childern, it's your cousin Tom!—tell him howdy.'

But they ducked their heads, and put their fingers in their mouths, and hid behind her. So she run on:

'Lize, hurry up and get him a hot breakfast, right away—or did you get your breakfast on the boat?'

I said I had got it on the boat. So then she started for the house, leading me by the hand, and the children tagging after. When we got there, she set me down in a split-bottomed chair, and set herself down on a little low stool in front of me, holding both of my hands, and says:

'Now I can have a *good* look at you; and laws-a-me, I've been hungry for it a many and a many a time, all these long years, and it's come at last! We been expecting you a couple of days and more. What's kep' you?—boat get aground?'

'Yes'm—she—'

'Don't say yes'm—say Aunt Sally. Where'd she get aground?'

I didn't rightly know what to say, because I didn't know whether the boat would be coming up the river or down. But I go a good deal on instinct; and my instinct said she would be coming up—from down towards Orleans. That didn't help me much, though; for I didn't know the names of bars[2] down that way. I see I'd got to invent a bar, or forget the name of the one we got aground on—or—Now I struck an idea, and fetched it out:

'It warn't the grounding—that didn't keep us back but a little. We blowed out a cylinder-head.'

[2] *bars*: sandbars.

'Good gracious! Anybody hurt?'

'No'm. Killed a nigger.'

"Well, it's lucky; because sometimes people do get hurt. Two years ago last Christmas, your uncle Silas was coming up from Newrleans on the old *Lally Rook*,[3] and she blowed out a cylinder-head and crippled a man. And I think he died afterwards. He was a Babtist. Your uncle Silas knowed a family in Baton Rouge that knowed his people very well. Yes, I remember, now he *did* die. Mortification[4] set in, and they had to amputate him. But it didn't save him. Yes, it was mortification—that was it. He turned blue all over, and died in the hope of a glorious resurrection. They say he was a sight to look at. Your uncle's been up to the town every day to fetch you. And he's gone again, not more'n an hour ago; he'll be back any minute, now. You must a met him on the road, didn't you?—oldish man, with a—'

'No, I didn't see nobody, Aunt Sally. The boat landed just at daylight, and I left my baggage on the wharf-boat and went looking around the town and out a piece in the country, to put in the time and not get here too soon; and so I come down the back way.'

'Who'd you give the baggage to?'

'Nobody.'

'Why, child, it'll be stole!'

'Not where *I* hid it I reckon it won't,' I says.

'How'd you get your breakfast so early on the boat?'

It was kinder thin ice, but I says:

'The captain see me standing around, and told me I better have something to eat before I went ashore; so he took me in the texas to the officers' lunch, and give me all I wanted.'

I was getting so uneasy I couldn't listen good. I had my mind on the children all the time; I wanted to get them out to one side, and pump them a little, and find out who I was. But I couldn't get no show. Mrs Phelps kept it up and run on so.

[3] *Lally Rook*: like the *Walter Scott*, a steamboat named after a Romantic work. Irish writer Thomas Moore published the epic poem *Lalla Rookh* in 1817.

[4] *Mortification*: gangrene.

Pretty soon she made the cold chills streak all down my back, because she says:

'But here we're a running on this way, and you hain't told me a word about Sis, nor any of them. Now I'll rest my works a little, and you start up yourn; just tell me *everything*—tell me all about 'm all—every one of 'm; and how they are, and what they're doing, and what they told you to tell me; and every last thing you can think of.'

Well, I see I was up a stump—and up it good. Providence had stood by me this fur, all right, but I was hard and tight aground, now. I see it warn't a bit of use to try to go ahead—I'd *got* to throw up my hand. So I says to myself, here's another place where I got to resk the truth. I opened my mouth to begin; but she grabbed me and hustled me in behind the bed, and says:

'Here he comes! stick your head down lower—there, that'll do; you can't be seen, now. Don't you let on you're here. I'll play a joke on him. Childern, don't you say a word.'

I see I was in a fix now. But it warn't no use to worry; there warn't nothing to do but just hold still, and try and be ready to stand from under when the lightning struck.

I had just one little glimpse of the old gentleman when he come in, then the bed hid him. Mrs Phelps she jumps for him and says:

'Has he come?'

'No,' says her husband.

'Good-*ness* gracious!' she says, 'what in the world *can* have become of him?'

'I can't imagine,' says the old gentleman; 'and I must say, it makes me dreadful uneasy.'

'Uneasy!' she says, 'I'm ready to go distracted! He *must* a come; and you've missed him along the road. I *know* it's so—something *tells* me so.'

'Why Sally, I *couldn't* miss him along the road—*you* know that.'

'But oh, dear, dear, what *will* Sis say? He must a come! You must a missed him. He—'

'Oh, don't distress me any more'n I'm already distressed. I don't know what in the world to make of it. I'm at my wit's end, and I don't mind acknowledging 't I'm right down scared. But there's no hope that he's come; for he *couldn't* come and me miss him. Sally, it's terrible—just terrible—something's happened to the boat, sure!'

'Why, Silas! Look yonder!—up the road!—ain't that somebody coming?'

He sprung to the window at the head of the bed, and that give Mrs Phelps the chance she wanted. She stooped down quick, at the foot of the bed, and give me a pull, and out I come; and when he turned back from the window, there she stood, a-beaming and a-smiling like a house afire, and I standing pretty meek and sweaty alongside. The old gentleman stared, and says:

'Why, who's that?'

'Who do you reckon 't is?'

'I hain't no idea. Who *is* it?'

'It's *Tom Sawyer*!'

By jings, I most slumped through the floor. But there warn't no time to swap knives; the old man grabbed me by the hand and shook, and kept on shaking; and all the time, how the woman did dance around and laugh and cry; and then how they both did fire off questions about Sid, and Mary, and the rest of the tribe.

But if they was joyful, it warn't nothing to what I was; for it was like being born again, I was so glad to find out who I was. Well, they froze to me for two hours; and at last when my chin was so tired it couldn't hardly go, any more, I had told them more about my family—I mean the Sawyer family—than ever happened to any six Sawyer families. And I explained all about how we blowed out a cylinder-head at the mouth of White River and it took us three days to fix it. Which was all right, and worked first rate; because *they* didn't know but what it would take three days to fix it. If I'd a called it a bolt-head it would a done just as well.

Now I was feeling pretty comfortable all down one side, and pretty uncomfortable all up the other. Being Tom Sawyer was easy and comfortable; and it stayed easy and comfortable till by-and-by I hear a steamboat coughing along down the river—then I says to myself, spose Tom Sawyer come down on that boat?—and spose he steps in here, any minute, and sings out my name before I can throw him a wink to keep quiet? Well, I couldn't *have* it that way—it wouldn't do at all. I must go up the road and waylay him. So I told the folks I reckoned I would go up to the town and fetch down my baggage. The old gentleman was for going along with me, but I said no, I could drive the horse myself, and I druther he wouldn't take no trouble about me.

CHAPTER 33

So I started for town, in the wagon, and when I was half-way I see a wagon coming, and sure enough it was Tom Sawyer, and I stopped and waited till he come along. I says 'Hold on!' and it stopped alongside, and his mouth opened up like a trunk, and staid so; and he swallowed two or three times like a person that's got a dry throat, and then says:

'I hain't ever done you no harm. You know that. So then, what you want to come back and ha'nt *me* for?'

I says:

'I hain't come back—I hain't been *gone*.'

When he heard my voice, it righted him up some, but he warn't quite satisfied yet. He says:

'Don't you play nothing on me, because I wouldn't on you. Honest injun, now, you ain't a ghost?'

'Honest injun, I ain't,' I says.

'Well—I—I—well, that ought to settle it, of course; but I can't somehow seem to understand it, no way. Looky here, warn't you ever murdered *at all*?'

'No. I warn't ever murdered at all—I played it on them. You come in here and feel of me if you don't believe me.'

So he done it; and it satisfied him; and he was that glad to see me again, he didn't know what to do. And he wanted to know all about it right off; because it was a grand adventure, and mysterious, and so it hit him where he lived.[1] But I said, leave it alone till by-and-by; and told his driver to wait, and we drove off a little piece, and I told him the kind of a fix I was in, and what did he reckon we better do? He said, let him alone a minute, and don't disturb him. So he thought and thought, and pretty soon he says:

[1] *hit him where he lived*: was right up his alley; was just his type of thing.

251

'It's all right, I've got it. Take my trunk in your wagon, and let on it's your'n; and you turn back and fool along slow, so as to get to the house about the time you ought to; and I'll go towards town a piece, and take a fresh start, and get there a quarter or a half an hour after you; and you needn't let on to know me, at first.'

I says:

'All right; but wait a minute. There's one more thing—a thing that *nobody* don't know but me. And that is, there's a nigger here that I'm a trying to steal out of slavery—and his name is *Jim*—old Miss Watson's Jim.'

He says:

'What! Why Jim is—'

He stopped and went to studying. I says:

'I know what you'll say. You'll say it's dirty low-down business; but what if it is?—*I'm* low down; and I'm agoing to steal him, and I want you to keep mum and not let on. Will you?'

His eye lit up, and he says:

'I'll *help* you steal him!'

Well, I let go all holts then,[2] like I was shot. It was the most astonishing speech I ever heard—and I'm bound to say Tom Sawyer fell, considerable, in my estimation. Only I couldn't believe it. Tom Sawyer a *nigger stealer*!

'Oh, shucks,' I says, 'you're joking.'

'I ain't joking, either.'

'Well, then,' I says, 'joking or no joking, if you hear anything said about a runaway nigger, don't forget to remember that *you* don't know nothing about him, and *I* don't know nothing about him.'

Then we took the trunk and put it in my wagon, and he drove off his way, and I drove mine. But of course I forgot all about driving slow, on accounts of being glad and full of thinking; so I got home a heap too quick for that length of a trip. The old gentleman was at the door, and he says:

[2] *let go all holts then*: let go of all restraints. Here it means something like "went all to pieces in astonishment".

'Why, this is wonderful. Who ever would a thought it was in that mare to do it. I wish we'd a timed her. And she hain't sweated a hair—not a hair. It's wonderful. Why I wouldn't take a hunderd dollars for that horse now; I wouldn't, honest; and yet I'd a sold her for fifteen before, and thought 'twas all she was worth.'

That's all he said. He was the innocentest, best old soul I ever see. But it warn't surprising; because he warn't only just a farmer, he was a preacher, too, and had a little one-horse log church down back of the plantation, which he built it himself at his own expense, for a church and school-house, and never charged nothing for his preaching, and it was worth it, too. There was plenty other farmer-preachers like that, and done the same way, down South.

In about half an hour Tom's wagon drove up to the front stile, and Aunt Sally she see it through the window because it was only about fifty yards, and says:

'Why, there's somebody come! I wonder who 'tis? Why, I do believe it's a stranger. Jimmy' (that's one of the children), 'run and tell Lize to put on another plate for dinner.'

Everybody made a rush for the front door, because, of course, a stranger don't come *every* year, and so he lays over[3] the yaller fever, for interest, when he does come. Tom was over the stile and starting for the house; the wagon was spinning up the road for the village, and we was all bunched in the front door. Tom had his store clothes on, and an audience—and that was always nuts for Tom Sawyer. In them circumstances it warn't no trouble to him to throw in an amount of style that was suitable. He warn't a boy to meeky along[4] up that yard like a sheep; no, he come ca'm and important, like the ram. When he got afront of us, he lifts his hat ever so gracious and dainty, like it was the lid of a box that had butterflies asleep in it and he didn't want to disturb them, and says:

'Mr Archibald Nichols, I presume?'

---

[3] *lays over*: tops.
[4] *meeky along*: go meekly.

'No, my boy,' says the old gentleman, 'I'm sorry to say 't your driver has deceived you; Nichols's place is down a matter of three mile more. Come in, come in.'

Tom he took a look back over his shoulder, and says, 'Too late—he's out of sight.'

'Yes, he's gone, my son, and you must come in and eat your dinner with us; and then we'll hitch up and take you down to Nichols's.'

'Oh, I *can't* make you so much trouble; I couldn't think of it. I'll walk—I don't mind the distance.'

'But we won't *let* you walk—it wouldn't be Southern hospitality to do it. Come right in.'

'Oh, *do*,' says Aunt Sally; 'it ain't a bit of trouble to us, not a bit in the world. You *must* stay. It's a long, dusty three mile, and we *can't* let you walk. And besides, I've already told 'em to put on another plate, when I see you coming; so you mustn't disappoint us. Come right in, and make yourself at home.'

So Tom he thanked them very hearty and handsome, and let himself be persuaded, and come in; and when he was in, he said he was a stranger from Hicksville, Ohio, and his name was William Thompson—and he made another bow.

Well, he run on, and on, and on, making up stuff about Hicksville and everybody in it he could invent, and I getting a little nervous, and wondering how this was going to help me out of my scrape; and at last, still talking along, he reached over and kissed Aunt Sally right on the mouth, and then settled back again in his chair, comfortable, and was going on talking; but she jumped up and wiped it off with the back of her hand, and says:

'You owdacious puppy!'

He looked kind of hurt, and says:

'I'm surprised at you, m'am.'

'You're s'rp—Why, what do you reckon *I* am? I've a good notion to take and—say, what do you mean by kissing me?'

He looked kind of humble, and says:

'I didn't mean nothing, m'am. I didn't mean no harm. I—I— thought you'd like it.'

'Why, you born fool!' She took up the spinning-stick, and it looked like it was all she could do to keep from giving him a crack with it. 'What made you think I'd like it?'

'Well, I don't know. Only, they—they—told me you would.'

'*They* told you I would. Whoever told you's *another* lunatic. I never heard the beat of it. Who's *they?*'

'Why—everybody. They all said so, m'am.'

It was all she could do to hold in; and her eyes snapped, and her fingers worked like she wanted to scratch him; and she says:

'Who's "everybody"? Out with their names—or ther'll be an idiot short.'

He got up and looked distressed, and fumbled his hat, and says:

'I'm sorry, and I warn't expecting it. They told me to. They all told me to. They all said kiss her; and said she'll like it. They all said it—every one of them. But I'm sorry, m'am, and I won't do it no more—I won't, honest.'

'You won't, won't you? Well, I sh'd *reckon* you won't!'

'No'm, I'm honest about it; I won't ever do it again. Till you ask me.'

'Till I *ask* you! Well, I never see the beat of it in my born days! I lay you'll be the Methusalem-numskull[5] of creation before ever *I* ask you—or the likes of you.'

'Well,' he says, 'it does surprise me so. I can't make it out, somehow. They said you would, and I thought you would. But—' He stopped and looked around slow, like he wished he could run across a friendly eye, somewhere's; and fetched up on the old gentleman's, and says, 'Didn't *you* think she'd like me to kiss her, sir?'

'Why, no, I—I—well, no, I b'lieve I didn't.'

Then he looks on around, the same way, to me—and says:

'Tom, didn't *you* think Aunt Sally'd open out her arms and say, "Sid Sawyer—"'

---

[5] *I lay you'll be the Methusalem-numskull:* i.e., I swear you'll be an idiot as old as Methusaleh. Methusaleh is mentioned in Genesis 5:27 as having attained the age of 969 years.

'My land!' she says, breaking in and jumping for him, 'you impudent young rascal, to fool a body so—' and was going to hug him, but he fended her off, and says:

'No, not till you've asked me, first.'

So she didn't lose no time, but asked him; and hugged him and kissed him, over and over again, and then turned him over to the old man, and he took what was left. And after they got a little quiet again, she says.

'Why, dear me, I never see such a surprise. We warn't looking for *you*, at all, but only Tom. Sis never wrote to me about anybody coming but him.'

'It's because it warn't *intended* for any of us to come but Tom,' he says; 'but I begged and begged, and at the last minute she let me come, too; so, coming down the river, me and Tom thought it would be a first-rate surprise for him to come here to the house first, and for me to by-and-by tag along and drop in and let on to be a stranger. But it was a mistake, Aunt Sally. This ain't no healthy place for a stranger to come.'

'No—not impudent whelps, Sid. You ought to had your jaws boxed; I hain't been so put out since I don't know when. But I don't care, I don't mind the terms—I'd be willing to stand a thousand such jokes to have you here. Well, to think of that performance! I don't deny it, I was most putrified[6] with astonishment when you give me that smack.'

We had dinner out in that broad open passage betwixt the house and the kitchen; and there was things enough on that table for seven families—and all hot, too; none of your flabby tough meat that's laid in a cupboard in a damp cellar all night and tastes like a hunk of old cold cannibal in the morning. Uncle Silas he asked a pretty long blessing over it, but it was worth it; and it didn't cool it a bit, neither, the way I've seen them kind of interruptions do, lots of times.

There was a considerable good deal of talk, all the afternoon, and me and Tom was on the lookout all the time, but it warn't no use, they didn't happen to say nothing about any

---

[6] *putrified*: petrified.

runaway nigger, and we was afraid to try to work up to it. But at supper, at night, one of the little boys says:

'Pa, mayn't Tom and Sid and me go to the show?'

'No,' says the old man, 'I reckon there ain't going to be any; and you couldn't go if there was; because the runaway nigger told Burton and me all about that scandalous show, and Burton said he would tell the people; so I reckon they've drove the owdacious loafers out of town before this time.'

So there it was!—but *I* couldn't help it. Tom and me was to sleep in the same room and bed; so, being tired, we bid good-night and went up to bed, right after supper, and clumb out of the window and down the lightning-rod, and shoved for the town; for I didn't believe anybody was going to give the king and the duke a hint, and so, if I didn't hurry up and give them one they'd get into trouble sure.

On the road Tom he told me all about how it was reckoned I was murdered, and how pap disappeared, pretty soon, and didn't come back no more, and what a stir there was when Jim run away; and I told Tom all about our Royal Nonesuch rapscallions, and as much of the raft-voyage as I had time to; and as we struck into the town and up through the middle of it—it was as much as half-after eight, then—here comes a raging rush of people, with torches, and an awful whooping and yelling, and banging tin pans and blowing horns; and we jumped to one side to let them go by; and as they went by, I see they had the king and the duke astraddle of a rail—that is, I knowed it *was* the king and the duke, though they was all over tar and feathers, and didn't look like nothing in the world that was human—just looked like a couple of monstrous big soldier-plumes. Well, it made me sick to see it; and I was sorry for them poor pitiful rascals, it seemed like I couldn't ever feel any hardness against them any more in the world. It was a dreadful thing to see. Human beings *can* be awful cruel to one another.

We see we was too late—couldn't do no good. We asked some stragglers about it, and they said everybody went to the show looking very innocent; and laid low and kept dark till the poor old king was in the middle of his cavortings on the stage; then somebody give a signal, and the house rose up and went for them.

So we poked along back home, and I warn't feeling so brash as I was before, but kind of ornery, and humble, and to blame, somehow—though *I* hadn't done nothing. But that's always the way; it don't make no difference whether you do right or wrong, a person's conscience ain't got no sense, and just goes for him *anyway*. If I had a yaller dog that didn't know no more than a person's conscience does, I would pison him. It takes up more room than all the rest of a person's insides, and yet ain't no good, nohow. Tom Sawyer he says the same.

CHAPTER 34

We stopped talking, and got to thinking.

By-and-by Tom says:

'Looky here, Huck, what fools we are, to not think of it before! I bet I know where Jim is.'

'No! Where?'

'In that hut down by the ash-hopper. Why, looky here. When we was at dinner, didn't you see a nigger man go in there with some vittles?'

'Yes.'

'What did you think the vittles was for?'

'For a dog.'

'So'd I. Well, it wasn't for a dog.'

'Why?'

'Because part of it was watermelon.'

'So it was—I noticed it. Well, it does beat all, that I never thought about a dog not eating watermelon. It shows how a body can see and don't see at the same time.'

'Well, the nigger unlocked the padlock when he went in, and he locked it again when he come out. He fetched uncle a key, about the time we got up from table—same key, I bet. Watermelon shows man, lock shows prisoner; and it ain't likely there's two prisoners on such a little plantation, and where the people's all so kind and good. Jim's the prisoner. All right—I'm glad we found it out detective fashion; I wouldn't give shucks for any other way. Now you work your mind and study out a plan to steal Jim, and I will study out one, too; and we'll take the one we like best.'

What a head for just a boy to have! If I had Tom Sawyer's head, I wouldn't trade it off to be a duke, nor mate of a steamboat, nor clown in a circus, nor nothing I can think of. I went to thinking out a plan, but only just to be doing something; I knowed very well where the right plan was going to come from. Pretty soon, Tom says:

'Ready?'

'Yes,' I says.

'All right—bring it out.'

'My plan is this,' I says. 'We can easy find out if it's Jim in there. Then get up my canoe to-morrow night, and fetch my raft over from the island. Then the first dark night that comes, steal the key out of the old man's britches, after he goes to bed, and shove off down the river on the raft, with Jim, hiding daytimes and running nights, the way me and Jim used to do before. Wouldn't that plan work?'

'*Work?* Why cert'nly, it would work, like rats a fighting. But it's too blame' simple; there ain't nothing *to* it. What's the good of a plan that ain't no more trouble than that? It's as mild as goose-milk. Why, Huck, it wouldn't make no more talk than breaking into a soap factory.'

I never said nothing, because I warn't expecting nothing different; but I knowed mighty well that whenever he got *his* plan ready it wouldn't have none of them objections to it.

And it didn't. He told me what it was, and I see in a minute it was worth fifteen of mine, for style, and would make Jim just as free a man as mine would, and maybe get us all killed besides. So I was satisfied, and said we would waltz in on it. I needn't tell what it was, here, because I knowed it wouldn't stay the way it was. I knowed he would be changing it around, every which way, as we went along, and heaving in new bullinesses wherever he got a chance. And that is what he done.

Well, one thing was dead sure; and that was, that Tom Sawyer was in earnest and was actly going to help steal that nigger out of slavery. That was the thing that was too many for me. Here was a boy that was respectable, and well brung up; and had a character to lose; and folks at home that had characters; and he was bright and not leather-headed; and knowing and not ignorant; and not mean, but kind; and yet here he was, without any more pride, or rightness, or feeling, than to stoop to this business, and make himself a shame, and his family a shame, before everybody. I *couldn't* understand it, no way at all. It was outrageous, and I knowed I ought to just up and tell him so; and so be his true friend, and let him quit the thing right where he was, and save himself. And I *did* start to tell him; but he shut me up, and says:

'Don't you reckon I know what I'm about? Don't I generly know what I'm about?'

'Yes.'

'Didn't I *say* I was going to help steal the nigger?'

'Yes.'

'*Well* then.'

That's all he said, and that's all I said. It warn't no use to say any more; because when he said he'd do a thing, he always done it. But *I* couldn't make out how he was willing to go into this thing; so I just let it go, and never bothered no more about it. If he was bound to have it so, *I* couldn't help it.

When we got home, the house was all dark and still; so we went on down to the hut by the ash-hopper, for to examine it. We went through the yard, so as to see what the hounds would do. They knowed us, and didn't make no more noise than country dogs is always doing when anything comes by in the night. When we got to the cabin, we took a look at the front and the two sides; and on the side I warn't acquainted with— which was the north side—we found a square window-hole, up tolerable high, with just one stout board nailed across it. I says:

'Here's the ticket. This hole's big enough for Jim to get through, if we wrench off the board.'

Tom says:

'It's as simple as tit-tat-toe, three-in-a-row, and as easy as playing hooky. I should *hope* we can find a way that's a little more complicated than *that*, Huck Finn.'

'Well then,' I says, 'how'll it do to saw him out, the way I done before I was murdered, that time?'

'That's more *like*,' he says. 'It's real mysterious, and troublesome, and good,' he says; 'but I bet we can find a way that's twice as long. There ain't no hurry; le's keep on looking around.'

Betwixt the hut and the fence, on the back side, was a lean-to, that joined the hut at the eaves, and was made out of plank. It was as long as the hut, but narrow—only about six foot wide. The door to it was at the south end, and was padlocked. Tom he went to the soap kettle, and searched around and fetched back the iron thing they lift the lid with; so he took it and prized out one of the staples. The chain fell down, and we opened the door and went in, and shut it, and struck a match, and see the shed was only built against the cabin and hadn't no connection with it; and there warn't no floor to the shed, nor nothing in it but some old rusty played-out hoes, and spades, and picks, and a crippled plow. The match went out, and so did we and shoved in the staple again, and the door was locked as good as ever. Tom was joyful. He says:

'Now we're all right. We'll *dig* him out. It'll take about a week!'

Then we started for the house, and I went in the back door—you only have to pull a buckskin latch-string, they don't fasten the doors—but that warn't romantical enough for Tom Sawyer: no way would do him but he must climb up the lightning-rod. But after he got up half-way about three times, and missed fire and fell every time, and the last time most busted his brains out, he thought he'd got to give it up; but after he was rested, he allowed he would give her one more turn for luck, and this time he made the trip.

In the morning we was up at break of day, and down to the nigger cabins to pet the dogs and make friends with the nigger that fed Jim—if it *was* Jim that was being fed. The niggers was just getting through breakfast and starting for the fields; and Jim's nigger was piling up a tin pan with bread and meat and things; and whilst the others was leaving, the key come from the house.

This nigger had a good-natured, chuckle-headed face, and his wool was all tied up in little bunches with thread. That was to keep witches off. He said the witches was pestering him awful, these nights, and making him see all kinds of strange things, and hear all kinds of strange words and noises, and he didn't believe he was ever witched so long, before, in his life. He got so worked up, and got to running on so about his troubles, he forgot all about what he'd been agoing to do. So Tom says:

'What's the vittles for? Going to feed the dogs?'

The nigger kind of smiled around graduly over his face, like when you heave a brickbat[1] in a mud puddle, and he says:

'Yes, Mars Sid, *a* dog. Cur'us dog, too. Does you want to go en look at 'im?'

'Yes.'

I hunched Tom, and whispers:

'You going, right here in the daybreak? *That* warn't the plan.'

'No, it warn't—but it's the plan *now*.'

So, drat him, we went along, but I didn't like it much. When we got in, we couldn't hardly see anything, it was so dark; but Jim was there, sure enough, and could see us; and he sings out:

'Why, *Huck*! En good *lan*'! ain' dat Misto Tom?'

I just knowed how it would be; I just expected it. *I* didn't know nothing to do; and if I had, I couldn't a done it; because that nigger busted in and says:

'Why, de gracious sakes! do he know you genlmen?'

We could see pretty well, now. Tom he looked at the nigger, steady and kind of wondering, and says:

'Does *who* know us?'

'Why, dish-yer runaway nigger.'

'I don't reckon he does; but what put that into your head?'

"What *put* it dar? Didn' he jis' dis minute sing out like he knowed you?"

Tom says, in a puzzled-up kind of way:

'Well, that's mighty curious. *Who* sung out? *When* did he sing out? *What* did he sing out?' And turns to me, perfectly ca'm, and says, 'Did *you* hear anybody sing out?'

Of course there warn't nothing to be said but the one thing; so I says:

---

[1] *brickbat*: part of a brick or other hard material used as a missile.

'No; *I* ain't heard nobody say nothing.'

Then he turns to Jim, and looks him over like he never see him before; and says:

'Did you sing out?'

'No, sah,' says Jim; '*I* hain't said nothing, sah.'

'Not a word?'

'No, sah, I hain't said a word.'

'Did you ever see us before?'

'No, sah; not as *I* knows on.'

So Tom turns to the nigger, which was looking wild and distressed, and says, kind of severe:

'What do you reckon's the matter with you, anyway? What made you think somebody sung out?'

'Oh, it's de dad-blame' witches, sah, en I wisht I was dead, I do. Dey's awluz at it, sah, en dey do mos' kill me, dey sk'yers me so. Please to don't tell nobody 'bout it sah, er ole Mars Silas he'll scole me; 'kase he say dey *ain't* no witches. I jis' wish to goodness he was heah now—*den* what would he say! I jis' bet he couldn' fine no way to git aroun' it *dis* time. But it's awluz jis' so; people dat's *sot*, stays sot; dey won't look into nothn' en fine it out f'r deyselves, en when *you* fine it out en tell um 'bout it, dey doan' b'lieve you.'

Tom give him a dime, and said we wouldn't tell nobody; and told him to buy some more thread to tie up his wool with; and then looks at Jim, and says:

'I wonder if Uncle Silas is going to hang this nigger. If I was to catch a nigger that was ungrateful enough to run away, *I* wouldn't give him up, I'd hang him.' And whilst the nigger stepped to the door to look at the dime and bit it to see if it was good, he whispers to Jim, and says:

'Don't ever let on to know us. And if you hear any digging going on nights, it's us: we're going to set you free.'

Jim only had time to grab us by the hand and squeeze it, then the nigger come back, and we said we'd come again some time if the nigger wanted us to; and he said he would, more particular if it was dark, because the witches went for him mostly in the dark, and it was good to have folks around then.

CHAPTER 35

It would be most an hour, yet, till breakfast, so we left, and struck down into the woods; because Tom said we got to have *some* light to see how to dig by, and a lantern makes too much, and might get us into trouble; what we must have was a lot of them rotten chunks that's called fox-fire[1] and just makes a soft kind of a glow when you lay them in a dark place. We fetched an armful and hid it in the weeds, and set down to rest, and Tom says, kind of dissatisfied:

'Blame it, this whole thing is just as easy and awkward as it can be. And so it makes it so rotten difficult to get up a difficult plan. There ain't no watchman to be drugged—now there *ought* to be a watchman. There ain't even a dog to give a sleeping-mixture to. And there's Jim chained by one leg, with a ten-foot chain, to the leg of his bed: why, all you got to do is to lift up the bedstead and slip off the chain. And Uncle Silas he trusts everybody; sends the key to the punkin-headed nigger, and don't send nobody to watch the nigger. Jim could a got out of that window hole before this, only there wouldn't be no use trying to travel with a ten-foot chain on his leg. Why, drat it, Huck, it's the stupidest arrangement I ever see. You got to invent *all* the difficulties. Well, we can't help it, we got to do the best we can with the materials we've got. Anyhow, there's one thing—there's more honor in getting him out through a lot of difficulties and dangers, where there warn't one of them furnished to you by the people who it was their duty to furnish them, and you had to contrive them all out of your own head. Now look at just that one thing of the lantern. When you come down to the cold facts, we simply got to *let on* that a lantern's resky. Why, we could work with a torchlight procession if we wanted to, *I* believe. Now, whilst I

---

[1] *fox-fire*: phosphorescent light emitted from rotting wood.

think of it, we got to hunt up something to make a saw out of, the first chance we get.'

'What do we want of a saw?'

'What do we *want* of it? Hain't we got to saw the leg of Jim's bed off, so as to get the chain loose?'

'Why, you just said a body could lift up the bedstead and slip the chain off.'

'Well, if that ain't just like you, Huck Finn. You *can* get up the infant-schooliest ways of going at a thing. Why, hain't you ever read any books at all?—Baron Trenck, nor Casanova, nor Benvenuto Chelleeny, nor Henri IV, nor none of them heroes?[2] Whoever heard of getting a prisoner loose in such an old-maidy way as that? No; the way all the best authorities does, is to saw the bed-leg in two, and leave it just so, and swallow the sawdust, so it can't be found, and put some dirt and grease around the sawed place so the very keenest seneskal[3] can't see no sign of it's being sawed, and thinks the bed-leg is perfectly sound. Then, the night you're ready, fetch the leg a kick, down she goes; slip off your chain, and there you are. Nothing to do but hitch your rope-ladder to the battlements, shin down it, break your leg in the moat—because a rope-ladder is nineteen foot too short, you know—and there's your horses and your trusty vassles, and they scoop you up and fling you across a saddle and away you go, to your native Langudoc, or Navarre,[4] or wherever it is. It's gaudy, Huck. I wish there was a moat to this cabin. If we get time, the night of the escape, we'll dig one.'

---

[2] *Baron Trenck . . . none of them heroes*: Tom's heroes all attempted daring escapes, and the first three wrote their memoirs. Frederick von der Trenck (1726–1794) was a Prussian soldier and adventurer who was executed as a spy; Giacomo Casanova (1725–1798) was an Italian adventurer known especially for his love affairs; Benvenuto Cellini (1500–1571) was an Italian sculptor and goldsmith famous for his travels; and Henry IV of France (1553–1610) escaped from prison during religious conflicts between Catholics and Protestants in 1576.

[3] *seneskal*: seneschal, or a medieval lord's steward.

[4] *Langudoc, or Navarre*: Languedoc was a province in southern France during the Middle Ages; Navarre was a kingdom in the Pyrenees where Henry IV took refuge.

I says:

'What do we want of a moat, when we're going to snake him out from under the cabin?'

But he never heard me. He had forgot me and everything else. He had his chin in his hand, thinking. Pretty soon, he sighs, and shakes his head; then sighs again, and says:

'No, it wouldn't do—there ain't necessity enough for it.'

'For what?' I says.

'Why, to saw Jim's leg off,' he says.

'Good land!' I says, 'why, there ain't *no* necessity for it. And what would you want to saw his leg off for, anyway?'

'Well, some of the best authorities has done it. They couldn't get the chain off, so they just cut their hand off, and shoved. And a leg would be better still. But we got to let that go. There ain't necessity enough in this case; and besides, Jim's a nigger and wouldn't understand the reasons for it, and how it's the custom in Europe; so we'll let it go. But there's one thing—he can have a rope-ladder; we can tear up our sheets and make him a rope-ladder easy enough. And we can send it to him in a pie; it's mostly done that way. And I've et worse pies.'

'Why, Tom Sawyer, how you talk,' I says; 'Jim ain't got no use for a rope-ladder.'

'He *has* got use for it. How *you* talk, you better say; you don't know nothing about it. He's *got* to have a rope ladder; they all do.'

'What in the nation can he *do* with it?'

'*Do* with it? He can hide it in his bed, can't he? That's what they all do; and *he's* got to, too. Huck, you don't ever seem to want to do anything that's regular; you want to be starting something fresh all the time. Spose he *don't* do nothing with it? ain't it there in his bed, for a clew, after he's gone? and don't you reckon they'll want clews? Of course they will. And you wouldn't leave them any? That would be a *pretty* howdy-do, *wouldn't* it! I never heard of such a thing.'

'Well,' I says, 'if it's in the regulations, and he's got to have it, all right, let him have it; because I don't wish to go back on no regulations; but there's one thing, Tom Sawyer—if we go to tearing up our sheets to make Jim a rope-ladder, we're going to get into trouble with Aunt Sally, just as sure as you're born. Now, the way I look at it, a hickry-bark ladder don't cost nothing, and don't waste nothing, and is just as good to load up a pie with, and hide in a straw tick, as any rag ladder you can start; and as for Jim, he ain't had no experience, and so *he* don't care what kind of a—'

'Oh, shucks, Huck Finn, if I was as ignorant as you, I'd keep still—that's what *I'd* do. Who ever heard of a state prisoner escaping by a hickry-bark ladder? Why, it's perfectly ridiculous.'

'Well, all right, Tom, fix it your own way; but if you'll take my advice, you'll let me borrow a sheet off of the clothesline.'

He said that would do. And that give him another idea, and he says:

'Borrow a shirt, too.'

'What do we want of a shirt, Tom?'

'Want it for Jim to keep a journal on.'

'Journal your granny—*Jim* can't write.'[5]

'Spose he *can't* write—he can make marks on the shirt, can't he, if we make him a pen out of an old pewter spoon or a piece of an old iron barrel-hoop?'

'Why, Tom, we can pull a feather out of a goose and make him a better one; and quicker, too.'

'*Prisoners* don't have geese running around the donjon-keep[6] to pull pens out of, you muggins. They *always* make their pens out of the hardest, toughest, troublesomest piece of old brass candlestick or something like that they can get their hands on; and it takes them weeks and weeks, and months and months to file it out, too, because they've got to do it by rubbing it on the wall. *They* wouldn't use a goose-quill if they had it. It ain't regular.'

'Well, then, what'll we make him the ink out of?'

'Many makes it out of iron-rust and tears; but that's the common sort and women; the best authorities use their own blood.

---

[5] Jim *can't write*: Slaveholding states typically prohibited the teaching of slaves to read and write.

[6] *donjon-keep*: dungeon, a secure underground prison in a medieval castle.

Jim can do that; and when he wants to send any little common ordinary mysterious message to let the world know where he's captivated, he can write it on the bottom of a tin plate with a fork and throw it out of the window. The Iron Mask[7] always done that, and it's a blame' good way, too.'

'Jim ain't got no tin plates. They feed him in a pan.'

'That ain't anything; we can get him some.'

'Can't nobody *read* his plates.'

'That ain't got nothing to *do* with it, Huck Finn. All *he's* got to do is to write on the plate and throw it out. You don't *have* to be able to read it. Why, half the time you can't read anything a prisoner writes on a tin plate, or anywhere else.'

'Well, then, what's the sense in wasting the plates?'

'Why, blame it all, it ain't the *prisoner's* plates.'

'But it's *somebody's* plates, ain't it?'

'Well, spos'n it is? What does the *prisoner* care whose—'

He broke off there, because we heard the breakfast-horn blowing. So we cleared out for the house.

Along during that morning I borrowed a sheet and a white shirt off of the clothes-line; and I found an old sack and put them in it, and we went down and got the fox-fire, and put that in too. I called it borrowing, because that was what pap always called it; but Tom said it warn't borrowing, it was stealing. He said we was representing prisoners; and prisoners don't care how they get a thing so they get it, and nobody don't blame them for it either. It ain't no crime in a prisoner to steal the thing he needs to get away with, Tom said; it's his right; and so, as long as we was representing a prisoner, we had a perfect right to steal anything on this place we had the least use for, to get ourselves out of prison with. He said if we warn't prisoners it would be a very different thing, and nobody but a mean ornery person would steal when he warn't a prisoner. So we allowed we would steal everything there was that

---

[7] *Iron Mask*: A mysterious masked man was said to have been imprisoned in France from about 1669 to 1703, leading to many legends and tales. French Romantic writer Alexander Dumas popularized the story in his 1848 novel translated into English as *The Man in the Iron Mask*.

come handy. And yet he made a mighty fuss, one day, after that, when I stole a watermelon out of the nigger patch and eat it; and he made me go and give the niggers a dime, without telling them what it was for. Tom said that what he meant was, we could steal anything we *needed*. Well, I says, I needed the watermelon. But he said I didn't need it to get out of prison with, there's where the difference was. He said if I'd a wanted it to hide a knife in, and smuggle it to Jim to kill the seneskal with, it would a been all right. So I let it go at that, though I couldn't see no advantage in my representing a prisoner, if I got to set down and chaw over a lot of gold-leaf distinctions like that, every time I see a chance to hog a watermelon.

Well, as I was saying, we waited that morning till everybody was settled down to business, and nobody in sight around the yard; then Tom he carried the sack into the lean-to whilst I stood off a piece to keep watch. By-and-by he come out, and we went and set down on the wood-pile, to talk. He says:

'Everything's all right, now, except tools; and that's easy fixed.'

'Tools?' I says.

'Yes.'

'Tools for what?'

'Why, to dig with. We ain't agoing to *gnaw* him out, are we?'

'Ain't them old crippled picks and things in there good enough to dig a nigger out with?' I says.

He turns on me looking pitying enough to make a body cry, and says:

'Huck Finn, did you *ever* hear of a prisoner having picks and shovels, and all the modern conveniences in his wardrobe[8] to dig himself out with? Now I want to ask you—if you got any reasonableness in you at all—what kind of a show would *that* give him to be a hero? Why, they might as well lend him the key, and done with it. Picks and shovels—why they wouldn't furnish 'em to a king.'

---

[8] *wardrobe*: closet or piece of furniture where clothes are hung.

'Well, then,' I says, 'if we don't want the picks and shovels, what do we want?'

'A couple of case-knives.'

'To dig the foundations out from under that cabin with?'

'Yes.'

'Confound it, it's foolish, Tom.'

'It don't make no difference how foolish it is, it's the *right* way—and it's the regular way. And there ain't no *other* way, that ever *I* heard of, and I've read all the books that gives any information about these things. They always dig out with a case-knife—and not through dirt, mind you; generly it's through solid rock. And it takes them weeks and weeks and weeks, and for ever and ever. Why, look at one of them prisoners in the bottom dungeon of the Castle Deef, in the harbor of Marseilles,[9] that dug himself out that way; how long was *he* at it, you reckon?'

'I don't know.'

'Well, guess.'

'I don't know. A month and a half?'

'*Thirty-seven year*—and he come out in China. *That's* the kind. I wish the bottom of *this* fortress was solid rock.'

'*Jim* don't know nobody in China.'

'What's *that* got to do with it? Neither did that other fellow. But you're always a-wandering off on a side issue. Why can't you stick to the main point?'

'All right—I don't care where he comes out, so he *comes* out; and Jim don't, either, I reckon. But there's one thing, anyway—Jim's too old to be dug out with a case-knife. He won't last.'

'Yes he will *last*, too. You don't reckon it's going to take thirty-seven years to dig out through a *dirt* foundation, do you?'

'How long will it take, Tom?'

'Well, we can't resk being as long as we ought to, because it mayn't take very long for Uncle Silas to hear from down there

[9] *Castle Deef, in the harbor of Marseilles:* The masked prisoner (see n. 7) was supposedly held in the Château d'If near Marseilles, France. The hero of Alexander Dumas' novel *The Count of Monte Cristo* (1845) was also imprisoned in this castle.

by New Orleans. He'll hear Jim ain't from there. Then his next move will be to advertise Jim, or something like that. So we can't resk being as long digging him out as we ought to. By rights I reckon we ought to be a couple of years; but we can't. Things being so uncertain, what I recommend is this: that we really dig right in, as quick as we can; and after that, we can *let on*, to ourselves, that we was at it thirty-seven years. Then we can snatch him out and rush him away the first time there's an alarm. Yes, I reckon that'll be the best way.'

'Now, there's *sense* in that,' I says. 'Letting on don't cost nothing; letting on ain't no trouble; and if it's any object, I don't mind letting on we was at it a hundred and fifty year. It wouldn't strain me none, after I got my hand in. So I'll mosey along now, and smouch a couple of case-knives.'

'Smouch three,' he says; 'we want one to make a saw out of.'

'Tom, if it ain't unregular and irreligious to sejest it,' I says, 'there's an old rusty saw-blade around yonder sticking under the weatherboarding behind the smoke-house.'

He looked kind of weary and discouraged-like, and says:

'It ain't no use to try to learn you nothing, Huck. Run along and smouch the knives—three of them.' So I done it.

CHAPTER 36

As soon as we reckoned everybody was asleep, that night, we went down the lightning-rod, and shut ourselves up in the lean-to, and got out our pile of fox-fire, and went to work. We cleared everything out of the way, about four or five foot along the middle of the bottom log. Tom said he was right behind Jim's bed now, and we'd dig in under it, and when we got through there couldn't nobody in the cabin ever know there was any hole there, because Jim's counterpin[1] hung down most to the ground, and you'd have to raise it up and look under to see the hole. So we dug and dug, with the case-knives, till most midnight; and then we was dog-tired, and our hands was blistered, and yet you couldn't see we'd done anything, hardly. At last I says:

'This ain't no thirty-seven year job, this is a thirty-eight year job, Tom Sawyer.'

He never said nothing. But he sighed, and pretty soon he stopped digging, and then for a good little while I knowed he was thinking. Then he says:

'It ain't no use, Huck, it ain't agoing to work. If we was prisoners it would, because then we'd have as many years as we wanted, and no hurry; and we wouldn't get but a few minutes to dig, every day, while they was changing watches, and so our hands wouldn't get blistered, and we could keep it up right along, year in and year out, and do it right, and the way it ought to be done. But *we* can't fool along, we got to rush; we ain't got no time to spare. If we was to put in another night this way, we'd have to knock off for a week to let our hands get well—couldn't touch a case-knife with them sooner.'

'Well, then, what we going to do, Tom?'

---

[1] *counterpin*: counterpane, or bedspread.

'I'll tell you. It ain't right, and it ain't moral, and I wouldn't like it to get out—but there ain't only just the one way; we got to dig him out with the picks, and *let on* it's case-knives.'

'*Now* you're *talking!*' I says; 'your head gets leveler and leveler all the time, Tom Sawyer,' I says. 'Picks is the thing, moral or no moral; and as for me, I don't care shucks for the morality of it, nohow. When I start in to steal a nigger, or a watermelon, or a Sunday-school book, I ain't no ways particular how it's done so it's done. What I want is my nigger; or what I want is my watermelon; or what I want is my Sunday-school book; and if a pick's the handiest thing, that's the thing I'm agoing to dig that nigger or that watermelon or that Sunday-school book out with; and I don't give a dead rat what the authorities thinks about it nuther.'

'Well,' he says, 'there's excuse for picks and letting-on in a case like this; if it warn't so, I wouldn't approve of it, nor I wouldn't stand by and see the rules broke—because right is right, and wrong is wrong, and a body ain't got no business doing wrong when he ain't ignorant and knows better. It might answer for *you* to dig Jim out with a pick, *without* any letting-on, because you don't know no better; but it wouldn't for me, because I do know better. Gimme a case-knife.'

He had his own by him, but I handed him mine. He flung it down, and says:

'Gimme a *case-knife*.'

I didn't know just what to do—but then I thought. I scratched around amongst the old tools, and got a pick-ax and give it to him, and he took it and went to work, and never said a word.

He was always just that particular. Full of principle.

So then I got a shovel, and then we picked and shoveled, turn about, and made the fur fly. We stuck to it about a half an hour, which was as long as we could stand up; but we had a good deal of a hole to show for it. When I got up stairs, I looked out at the window and see Tom doing his level best with the lightning-rod, but he couldn't come it, his hands was so sore. At last he says:

'It ain't no use, it can't be done. What you reckon I better do? Can't you think up no way?'

'Yes,' I says, 'but I reckon it ain't regular. Come up the stairs, and let on it's a lightning-rod.'

So he done it.

Next day Tom stole a pewter spoon and a brass candlestick in the house, for to make some pens for Jim out of, and six tallow candles; and I hung around the nigger cabins, and laid for a chance, and stole three tin plates. Tom said it wasn't enough; but I said nobody wouldn't ever see the plates that Jim throwed out, because they'd fall in the dog-fennel[2] and jimpson weeds under the window-hole—then we could tote them back and he could use them over again. So Tom was satisfied. Then he says:

'Now, the thing to study out is, how to get the things to Jim.'

'Take them in through the hole,' I says, 'when we get it done.'

He only just looked scornful, and said something about nobody ever heard of such an idiotic idea, and then he went to studying. By-and-by he said he had ciphered out two or three ways, but there warn't no need to decide on any of them yet. Said we'd got to post[3] Jim first.

That night we went down the lightning-rod a little after ten, and took one of the candles along, and listened under the window-hole, and heard Jim snoring; so we pitched it in, and it didn't wake him. Then we whirled in with the pick and shovel, and in about two hours and a half the job was done. We crept in under Jim's bed and into the cabin, and pawed around and found the candle and lit it, and stood over Jim a while, and found him looking hearty and healthy, and then we woke him up gentle and gradual. He was so glad to see us he most cried; and called us honey, and all the pet names he could think of; and was for having us hunt up a cold chisel to

---

[2] *dog-fennel*: type of weed.
[3] *post*: tell; inform.

cut the chain off of his leg with, right away, and clearing out without losing any time. But Tom he showed him how unregular it would be, and set down and told him all about our plans, and how we could alter them in a minute any time there was an alarm; and not to be the least afraid, because we would see he got away, *sure*. So Jim he said it was all right, and we set there and talked over old times a while, and then Tom asked a lot of questions, and when Jim told him Uncle Silas come in every day or two to pray with him, and Aunt Sally come in to see if he was comfortable and had plenty to eat, and both of them was kind as they could be, Tom says:

'Now I know how to fix it. We'll send you some things by them.'

I said, 'Don't do nothing of the kind; it's one of the most jackass ideas I ever struck'; but he never paid no attention to me; went right on. It was his way when he'd got his plans set.

So he told Jim how we'd have to smuggle in the rope-ladder pie, and other large things, by Nat, the nigger that fed him, and he must be on the lookout, and not be surprised, and not let Nat see him open them; and we would put small things in uncle's coat pockets and he must steal them out; and we would tie things to aunt's apron strings or put them in her apron pocket, if we got a chance; and told him what they would be and what they was for. And told him how to keep a journal on the shirt with his blood, and all that. He told him everything. Jim he couldn't see no sense in the most of it, but he allowed we was white folks and knowed better than him; so he was satisfied, and said he would do it all just as Tom said.

Jim had plenty corn-cob pipes and tobacco; so we had a right down good sociable time; then we crawled out through the hole, and so home to bed, with hands that looked like they'd been chawed. Tom was in high spirits. He said it was the best fun he ever had in his life, and the most intellectural; and said if he only could see his way to it we would keep it up all the rest of our lives and leave Jim to our children to get out; for he believed Jim would come to like it better and better the more he got used to it. He said that in that way it could be strung out to as much as eighty year, and would be the best time on record. And he said it would make us all celebrated that had a hand in it.

In the morning we went out to the wood-pile and chopped up the brass candlestick into handy sizes, and Tom put them and the pewter spoon in his pocket. Then we went to the nigger cabins, and while I got Nat's notice off, Tom shoved a piece of candlestick into the middle of a corn-pone that was in Jim's pan, and we went along with Nat to see how it would work, and it just worked noble; when Jim bit into it it most mashed all his teeth out; and there warn't ever anything could a worked better. Tom said so himself. Jim he never let on but what it was only just a piece of rock or something like that that's always getting into bread, you know; but after that he never bit into nothing but what he jabbed his fork into it in three or four places, first.

And whilst we was a standing there in the dimmish light, here comes a couple of the hounds bulging in, from under Jim's bed; and they kept on piling in till there was eleven of them, and there warn't hardly room in there to get your breath. By jings, we forgot to fasten that lean-to door. The nigger Nat he only just hollered 'witches!' once, and keeled over onto the floor amongst the dogs, and begun to groan like he was dying. Tom jerked the door open and flung out a slab of Jim's meat, and the dogs went for it, and in two seconds he was out himself and back again and shut the door, and I knowed he'd fixed the other door too. Then he went to work on the nigger, coaxing him and petting him, and asking him if he'd been imagining he saw something again. He raised up, and blinked his eyes around, and says:

'Mars Sid, you'll say I's a fool, but if I didn't b'lieve I see most a million dogs, er devils, er some'n, I wisht I may die right heah in dese tracks. I did, mos' sholy. Mars Sid, I *felt* um—I *felt* um, sah; dey was all over me. Dad fetch it, I jis' wisht I could git my han's on one er dem witches jis' wunst— on'y jis' wunst—it's all I'd ast. But mos'ly I wisht dey'd lemme 'lone, I does.'

Tom says:

'Well, I tell you what *I* think. What makes them come here just at this runaway nigger's breakfast-time? It's because they're hungry; that's the reason. You make them a witch pie; that's the thing for *you* to do.'

'But my lan', Mars Sid, how's *I* gwyne to make 'm a witch pie? I doan' know how to make it. I hain't ever hearn er sich a thing b'fo'.'

'Well, then, I'll have to make it myself.'

'Will you do it, honey?—will you? I'll wusshup de groun' und' yo' foot, I will!'

'All right, I'll do it, seeing it's you, and you've been good to us and showed us the runaway nigger. But you got to be mighty careful. When we come around, you turn your back; and then whatever we've put in the pan, don't you let on you see it at all. And don't you look, when Jim unloads the pan—something might happen, I don't know what. And above all, don't you *handle* the witch-things.'

'*Hannel* 'm Mars Sid? What *is* you a talkin' 'bout? I wouldn' lay de weight er my finger on um, not f'r ten hund'd thous'n' billion dollars, I wouldn't.'

CHAPTER 37

That was all fixed. So then we went away and went to the rubbage-pile in the back yard where they keep the old boots, and rags, and pieces of bottles, and wore-out tin things, and all such truck, and scratched around and found an old tin wash-pan and stopped up the holes as well as we could, to bake the pie in, and took it down cellar and stole it full of flour, and started for breakfast and found a couple of shingle-nails that Tom said would be handy for a prisoner to scrabble his name and sorrows on the dungeon walls with, and dropped one of them in Aunt Sally's apron pocket which was hanging on a chair, and t'other we stuck in the band of Uncle Silas's hat, which was on the bureau, because we heard the children say their pa and ma was going to the runaway nigger's house this morning, and then went to breakfast, and Tom dropped the pewter spoon in Uncle Silas's coat pocket, and Aunt Sally wasn't come yet, so we had to wait a little while.

And when she come she was hot, and red, and cross, and couldn't hardly wait for the blessing; and then she went to sluicing[1] out coffee with one hand and cracking the handiest child's head with her thimble with the other, and says:

'I've hunted high, and I've hunted low, and it does beat all, what *has* become of your other shirt.'

My heart fell down amongst my lungs and livers and things, and a hard piece of corn-crust started down my throat after it and got met on the road with a cough and was shot across the table and took one of the children in the eye and curled him up like a fishing-worm, and let a cry out of him the size of a war-whoop, and Tom he turned kinder blue around the gills, and it all amounted to a considerable state of things for about a quarter of a minute or as much as that, and I would a sold

---

[1] *sluicing*: pouring in a quick and gushing manner.

out for half price if there was a bidder. But after that we was all right again—it was the sudden surprise of it that knocked us so kind of cold. Uncle Silas he says:

'It's most uncommon curious, I can't understand it. I know perfectly well I took it *off*, because—'

'Because you hain't got but one *on*. Just *listen* at the man! I know you took it off, and know it by a better way than your wool-gathering memory, too, because it was on the clo'es-line yesterday—I see it there myself. But it's gone—that's the long and the short of it, and you'll just have to change to a red flann'l one till I can get time to make a new one. And it'll be the third I've made in two years; it just keeps a body on the jump to keep you in shirts; and whatever you do manage to *do* with 'm all, is more'n I can make out. A body'd think you *would* learn to take some sort of care of 'em, at your time of life.'

'I know it, Sally, and I do try all I can. But it oughtn't to be altogether my fault, because you know I don't see them nor have nothing to do with them except when they're on me; and I don't believe I've ever lost one of them *off* of me.'

'Well, it ain't *your* fault if you haven't Silas—you'd a done it if you could, I reckon. And the shirt ain't all that's gone, nuther. Ther's a spoon gone; and *that* ain't all. There was ten, and now ther's only nine. The calf got the shirt I reckon, but the calf never took the spoon, *that's* certain.'

'Why, what else is gone, Sally?'

'Ther's six *candles* gone—that's what. The rats could a got the candles, and I reckon they did; I wonder they don't walk off with the whole place, the way you're always going to stop their holes and don't do it; and if they warn't fools they'd sleep in your hair, Silas—*you'd* never find it out; but you can't lay the *spoon* on the rats, and that I *know*.'

'Well, Sally, I'm in fault, and I acknowledge it; I've been remiss; but I won't let tomorrow go by without stopping up them holes.'

'Oh, I wouldn't hurry, next year'll do. Matilda Angelina Araminta *Phelps*!'

Whack comes the thimble, and the child snatches her claws
out of the sugar-bowl without fooling around any. Just then,
the nigger woman steps onto the passage, and says:

'Missus, dey's a sheet gone.'

'A *sheet* gone! Well, for the land's sake!'

'I'll stop up them holes *today*,' says Uncle Silas, looking
sorrowful.

'Oh, *do* shet up!—spose the rats took the *sheet? Where's* it
gone, Lize?'

'Clah to goodness I hain't no notion, Miss Sally. She wuz
on de clo's-line yistiddy, but she done gone; she ain' dah no
mo', now.'

'I reckon the world *is* coming to an end. I *never* see the beat
of it, in all my born days. A shirt, and a sheet, and a spoon,
and six can—'

'Missus,' comes a young yaller wench, 'dey's a brass cannel-
stick miss'n.'

'Cler out from here, you hussy, er I'll take a skillet to ye!'

Well, she was just a biling. I begun to lay for a chance; I
reckoned I would sneak out and go for the woods till the
weather moderated. She kept a raging right along, running her
insurrection all by herself, and everybody else mighty meek
and quiet; and at last Uncle Silas, looking kind of foolish, fishes
up that spoon out of his pocket. She stopped, with her mouth
open and her hands up; and as for me, I wished I was in Jeru-
slem or somewheres. But not long; because she says:

'It's *just* as I expected. So you had it in your pocket all the
time; and like as not you've got the other things there, too.
How'd it get there?'

'I reely don't know, Sally,' he says, kind of apologizing, 'or
you know I would tell. I was a-studying over my text in Acts
Seventeen, before breakfast, and I reckon I put it in there,
not noticing, meaning to put my Testament in, and it must be
so, because my Testament ain't in, but I'll go and see, and if
the Testament is where I had it, I'll know I didn't put it in,
and that will show that I laid the Testament down and took
up the spoon, and—'

'Oh, for the land's sake! Give a body a rest! Go 'long now, the whole kit and biling of ye; and don't come nigh me again till I've got back my peace of mind.'

I'd a heard her, if she'd a said it to herself, let alone speaking it out; and I'd a got up and obeyed her, if I'd a been dead. As we was passing through the setting-room, the old man he took up his hat, and the shingle-nail fell out on the floor, and he just merely picked it up and laid it on the mantel-shelf, and never said nothing, and went out. Tom see him do it, and remembered about the spoon, and says:

'Well, it ain't no use to send things by *him* no more, he ain't reliable.' Then he says: 'But he done us a good turn with the spoon, anyway, without knowing it, and so we'll go and do him one without *him* knowing it—stop up his rat-holes.'

There was a noble good lot of them, down cellar, and it took us a whole hour, but we done the job tight and good, and shipshape. Then we heard steps on the stairs, and blowed out our light, and hid; and here comes the old man, with a candle in one hand and a bundle of stuff in t'other, looking as absent-minded as year before last. He went a mooning around, first to one rat-hole and then another, till he'd been to them all. Then he stood about five minutes, picking tallow-drip off of his candle and thinking. Then he turns off slow and dreamy towards the stairs, saying:

'Well, for the life of me I can't remember when I done it. I could show her now that I warn't to blame on account of the rats. But never mind—let it go. I reckon it wouldn't do no good.'

And so he went on a mumbling up stairs, and then we left. He was a mighty nice old man. And always is.

Tom was a good deal bothered about what to do for a spoon, but he said we'd got to have it; so he took a think. When he had ciphered it out, he told me how we was to do; then we went and waited around the spoon-basket till we see Aunt Sally coming, and then Tom went to counting the spoons and laying them out to one side, and I slid one of them up my sleeve, and Tom says:

'Why, Aunt Sally, there ain't but nine spoons, *yet.*'

She says:

'Go 'long to your play, and don't bother me. I know better, I counted 'm myself.'

'Well, I've counted them twice, Aunty, and I can't make but nine.'

She looked out of all patience, but of course she come to count—anybody would.

'I declare to gracious ther' *ain't* but nine!' she says. 'Why, what in the world—plague *take* the things, I'll count 'm again.'

So I slipped back the one I had, and when she got done counting, she says:

'Hang the troublesome rubbage, ther's *ten* now!' and she looked huffy and bothered both. But Tom says:

'Why, Aunty, *I* don't think there's ten.'

'You numskull, didn't you see me *count* 'm?'

'I know, but—'

'Well, I'll count 'm *again.*'

So I smouched one, and they come out nine same as the other time. Well, she *was* in a tearing way—just a trembling all over, she was so mad. But she counted and counted, till she got that addled she'd start to count-in the *basket* for a spoon, sometimes; and so, three times they come out right, and three times they come out wrong. Then she grabbed up the basket and slammed it across the house and knocked the cat galley-west;[2] and she said cle'r out and let her have some peace, and if we come bothering around her again betwixt that and dinner, she'd skin us. So we had the odd spoon; and dropped it in her apron pocket whilst she was a giving us our sailing-orders, and Jim got it all right, along with her shingle-nail, before noon. We was very well satisfied with this business, and Tom allowed it was worth twice the trouble it took, because he said *now* she couldn't ever count them spoons twice alike again to save her life; and wouldn't believe she'd counted them right, if she *did*; and said that after she'd about counted her head off,

---

[2] *galley-west*: greatly askew or into confusion.

for the next three days, he judged she'd give it up and offer to kill anybody that wanted her to ever count them any more.

So we put the sheet back on the line, that night, and stole one out of her closet; and kept on putting it back and stealing it again, for a couple of days, till she didn't know how many sheets she had, any more, and said she didn't *care*, and warn't agoing to bullyrag the rest of her soul out about it, and wouldn't count them again not to save her life, she druther die first.

So we was all right now, as to the shirt and the sheet and the spoon and the candles, by the help of the calf and the rats and the mixed-up counting; and as to the candlestick, it warn't no consequence, it would blow over by-and-by.

But that pie was a job; we had no end of trouble with that pie. We fixed it up away down in the woods, and cooked it there; and we got it done at last, and very satisfactory, too; but not all in one day; and we had to use up three washpans full of flour, before we got through, and we got burnt pretty much all over, in places, and eyes put out with the smoke; because, you see, we didn't want nothing but a crust, and we couldn't prop it up right, and she would always cave in. But of course we thought of the right way at last; which was to cook the ladder, too, in the pie. So then we laid in with Jim, the second night, and tore up the sheet all in little strings, and twisted them together, and long before daylight we had a lovely rope, that you could a hung a person with. We let on it took nine months to make it.

And in the forenoon we took it down to the woods, but it wouldn't go in the pie. Being made of a whole sheet, that way, there was rope enough for forty pies, if we'd a wanted them, and plenty left over for soup, or sausage, or anything you choose. We could a had a whole dinner.

But we didn't need it. All we needed was just enough for the pie, and so we throwed the rest away. We didn't cook none of the pies in the washpan, afraid the solder would melt; but Uncle Silas he had a noble brass warming-pan[3] which he

---

[3] *warming-pan*: covered pan filled with hot coals used to warm a bed.

thought considerable of, because it belonged to one of his ances-
ters with a long wooden handle that come over from England
with William the Conqueror in the *Mayflower*[4] or one of them
early ships and was hid away up garret with a lot of other old
pots and things that was valuable, not on account of being
any account because they warn't, but on account of them being
relicts, you know, and we snaked her out, private, and took
her down there, but she failed on the first pies, because we
didn't know how, but she come up smiling on the last one.
We took and lined her with dough, and set her in the coals,
and loaded her up with rag-rope, and put on a dough roof,
and shut down the lid, and put hot embers on top, and stood
off five foot, with the long handle, cool and comfortable, and
in fifteen minutes she turned out a pie that was a satisfaction
to look at. But the person that et it would want to fetch a
couple of kags of tooth-picks along, for if that rope-ladder
wouldn't cramp him down to business, I don't know nothing
what I'm talking about, and lay him in enough stomach-ache
to last him till next time, too.

Nat didn't look, when we put the witch-pie in Jim's pan;
and we put the three tin plates in the bottom of the pan under
the vittles; and so Jim got everything all right, and as soon as
he was by himself he busted into the pie and hid the rope-
ladder inside of his straw tick, and scratched some marks on a
tin plate and throwed it out of the window-hole.

[4] *over from England with William the Conqueror in the* Mayflower: As is typical,
Huck's historical facts are confused here. William the Conquerer (c. 1027–
1087), Duke of Normandy, led the Norman Conquest of England in 1066 and
later reigned as William I of England. The *Mayflower* is the name of the ship
that brought the first group of English Separatists, or Pilgrims, to America in
1620.

CHAPTER 38

Making them pens was a distressid-tough job, and so was the saw; and Jim allowed the inscription was going to be the toughest of all. That's the one which the prisoner has to scrabble on the wall. But we had to have it; Tom said we'd *got* to; there warn't no case of a state prisoner not scrabbling his inscription to leave behind, and his coat of arms.

'Look at Lady Jane Grey,' he says; 'look at Gilford Dudley; look at old Northumberland![1] Why, Huck, spose it *is* considerble trouble?—what you going to do?—how you going to get around it? Jim's *got* to do his inscription and coat of arms. They all do.'

Jim says:

'Why, Mars Tom, I hain't got no coat o' arms; I hain't got nuffn but dish-yer ole shirt, en you knows I got to keep de journal on dat.'

'Oh, you don't understand, Jim; a coat of arms is very different.'

'Well,' I says, 'Jim's right, anyway, when he says he hain't got no coat of arms, because he hain't.'

'I reckon *I* knowed that,' Tom says, 'but you bet he'll have one before he goes out of this—because he's going out *right*, and there ain't going to be no flaws in his record.'

So whilst me and Jim filed away at the pens on a brickbat apiece, Jim a making his'n out of the brass and I making mine out of the spoon, Tom set to work to think out the coat of arms. By-and-by he said he'd struck so many good ones he

---

[1] *Lady Jane Grey . . . Gilford Dudley . . . old Northumberland!*: Lady Jane Grey (1537–1554) claimed the throne of England, held it for nine days in 1553, and was later imprisoned and executed in the Tower of London along with her husband, Guildford Dudley, and his father, the Duke of Northumberland. Tom may have read their story in a popular romance, *The Tower of London* (1840), by William Harrison Ainsworth.

didn't hardly know which to take, but there was one which he reckoned he'd decide on. He says:

'On the scutcheon[2] we'll have a bend *or* in the dexter base, a saltire *murrey* in the fess, with a dog, couchant, for common charge, and under his foot a chain embattled, for slavery, with a chevron *vert* in a chief engrailed, and three invected lines on a field *azure*, with the nombril points rampant on a dancette indented; crest, a runaway nigger, *sable*, with his bundle over his shoulder on a bar sinister: and a couple of gules for supporters, which is you and me; motto, *Maggiore fretta, minore atto*. Got it out of a book—means, the more haste, the less speed.'

'Geewhillikins,' I says, 'but what does the rest of it mean?'

'We ain't got no time to bother over that,' he says, 'we got to dig in like all git-out.'

'Well, anyway,' I says, 'what's *some* of it? What's a fess?'

'A fess—a fess is—*you* don't need to know what a fess is. I'll show him how to make it when he gets to it.'

'Shucks, Tom,' I says, 'I think you might tell a person. What's a bar sinister?'

'Oh, *I* don't know. But he's got to have it. All the nobility does.'

That was just his way. If it didn't suit him to explain a thing to you, he wouldn't do it. You might pump at him a week, it wouldn't make no difference.

He'd got all that coat of arms business fixed, so now he started in to finish up the rest of that part of the work, which was to plan out a mournful inscription—said Jim got to have one, like they all done. He made up a lot, and wrote them out on a paper, and read them off, so:

1. *Here a captive heart busted.*
2. *Here a poor prisoner, forsook by the world and friends, fretted out his sorrowful life.*

---

[2] *scutcheon*: escutcheon, or armorial shield. What follows is a confused mix of heraldic terms, resulting in a coat of arms impossibly crowded with colors, bars, and figures.

3. *Here a lonely heart broke, and a worn spirit went to its rest, after thirty-seven years of solitary captivity.*

4. *Here, homeless and friendless, after thirty-seven years of bitter captivity, perished a noble stranger, natural*[3] *son of Louis XIV.*

Tom's voice trembled, whilst he was reading them, and he most broke down. When he got done, he couldn't no way make up his mind which one for Jim to scrabble onto the wall, they was all so good; but at last he allowed he would let him scrabble them all on. Jim said it would take him a year to scrabble such a lot of truck onto the logs with a nail, and he didn't know how to make letters, besides; but Tom said he would block them out for him, and then he wouldn't have nothing to do but just follow the lines. Then pretty soon he says:

'Come to think, the logs ain't agoing to do; they don't have log walls in a dungeon: we got to dig the inscriptions into a rock. We'll fetch a rock.'

Jim said the rock was worse than the logs; he said it would take him such a pison long time to dig them into a rock, he wouldn't ever get out. But Tom said he would let me help him do it. Then he took a look to see how me and Jim was getting along with the pens. It was most pesky tedious hard work and slow, and didn't give my hands no show to get well of the sores, and we didn't seem to make no headway, hardly. So Tom says:

'I know how to fix it. We got to have a rock for the coat of arms and mournful inscriptions, and we can kill two birds with that same rock. There's a gaudy big grindstone down at the mill, and we'll smouch it, and carve the things on it, and file out the pens and the saw on it, too.'

It warn't no slouch of an idea; and it warn't no slouch of a grindstone nuther; but we allowed we'd tackle it. It warn't quite midnight, yet, so we cleared out for the mill, leaving Jim at work. We smouched the grindstone, and set out to roll her home, but it was a most nation tough job. Sometimes, do what we could, we couldn't keep her from falling over, and she come

---

[3] *natural*: illegitimate.

mighty near mashing us, every time. Tom said she was going to get one of us, sure, before we got through. We got her half-way; and then we was plumb played out, and most drownded with sweat. We see it warn't no use, we got to go and fetch Jim. So he raised up his bed and slid the chain off of the bed-leg, and wrapt it round and round his neck, and we crawled out through our hole and down there, and Jim and me laid into that grindstone and walked her along like nothing; and Tom superintended. He could out-superintend any boy I ever see. He knowed how to do everything.

Our hole was pretty big, but it warn't big enough to get the grindstone through; but Jim he took the pick and soon made it big enough. Then Tom marked out them things on it with the nail, and set Jim to work on them, with the nail for a chisel and an iron bolt from the rubbage in the lean-to for a hammer, and told him to work till the rest of his candle quit on him, and then he could go to bed, and hide the grindstone under his straw tick and sleep on it. Then we helped him fix his chain back on the bed-leg, and was ready for bed our-selves. But Tom thought of something, and says:

'You got any spiders in here, Jim?'

'No, sah, thanks to goodness I hain't, Mars Tom.'

'All right, we'll get you some.'

'But bless you, honey, I doan' *want* none. I's afeared un um. I jis' 's soon have rattlesnakes aroun'.'

Tom thought a minute or two, and says:

'It's a good idea. And I reckon it's been done. It *must* a been done; it stands to reason. Yes, it's a prime good idea. Where could you keep it?'

'Keep what, Mars Tom?'

'Why, a rattlesnake.'

'De goodness gracious alive, Mars Tom! Why, if dey was a rattlesnake to come in heah, I'd take en bust right out thoo dat log wall, I would, wid my head.'

'Why, Jim, you wouldn't be afraid of it, after a little. You could tame it.'

'*Tame* it!'

'Yes—easy enough. Every animal is grateful for kindness and petting, and they wouldn't *think* of hurting a person that pets them. Any book will tell you that. You try—that's all I ask; just try for two or three days. Why, you can get him so, in a little while, that he'll love you; and sleep with you; and won't stay away from you a minute; and will let you wrap him round your neck and put his head in your mouth.'

'*Please*, Mars Tom—*doan'* talk so! I can't *stan'* it! He'd *let* me shove his head in my mouf—fer a favor, hain't it? I lay he'd wait a pow'ful long time 'fo' I *ast* him. En mo' en dat, I doan' *want* him to sleep wid me.'

'Jim, don't act so foolish. A prisoner's *got* to have some kind of a dumb pet, and if a rattlesnake hain't ever been tried, why, there's more glory to be gained in your being the first to ever try it than any other way you could ever think of to save your life.'

'Why, Mars Tom, I doan' *want* no sich glory. Snake take 'n bite Jim's chin off, den *whah* is de glory? No, sah, I doan' want no sich doin's.'

'Blame it, can't you *try*? I only *want* you to try—you needn't keep it up if it don't work.'

'But de trouble all *done*, ef de snake bite me while I's a tryin' him. Mars Tom, I's willin' to tackle mos' anything 'at ain't onreasonable, but ef you en Huck fetches a rattlesnake in heah for me to tame, I's gwyne to *leave*, dat's *shore*.'

'Well, then, let it go, let it go, if you're so bullheaded about it. We can get you some garter-snakes and you can tie some buttons on their tails, and let on they're rattlesnakes, and I reckon that'll have to do.'

'I k'n stand' *dem*, Mars Tom, but blame' 'f I couldn' get along widout um, I tell you dat. I never knowed b'fo', 't was so much bother and trouble to be a prisoner.'

'Well, it *always* is, when it's done right. You got any rats around here?'

'No, sah, I hain't seed none.'

'Well, we'll get you some rats.'

'Why, Mars Tom, I doan' *want* no rats. Dey's de dad-blamedest creturs to sturb a body, en rustle roun' over 'im, en bite his feet, when he's trying to sleep, I ever see. No, sah, gimme g'yarter-snakes, 'f I's got to have 'm, but doan' gimme no rats, I ain' got no use f'r um, skasely.'

'But Jim, you *got* to have 'em—they all do. So don't make no more fuss about it. Prisoners ain't ever without rats. There ain't no instance of it. And they train them, and pet them, and learn them tricks, and they get to be as sociable as flies. But you got to play music to them. You got anything to play music on?'

'I ain' got nuffin but a coase comb en a piece o' paper, en a juice-harp; but I reck'n dey wouldn' take no stock in a juice-harp.'

'Yes they would. *They* don't care what kind of music 'tis. A jews-harp's plenty good enough for a rat. All animals likes music—in a prison they dote on it. Specially, painful music; and you can't get no other kind out of a jews-harp. It always interests them; they come out to see what's the matter with you. Yes, you're all right; you're fixed very well. You want to set on your bed, nights, before you go to sleep, and early in the mornings, and play your jews-harp; play The Last Link is Broken—that's the thing that'll scoop a rat, quicker'n anything else: and when you've played about two minutes, you'll see all the rats, and the snakes, and spiders, and things begin to feel worried about you, and come. And they'll just fairly swarm over you, and have a noble good time.'

'Yes, *dey* will, I reck'n, Mars Tom, but what kine er time is *Jim* havin'? Blest if I kin see de pint. But I'll do it ef I got to. I reck'n I better keep de animals satisfied, en not have no trouble in de house.'

Tom waited to think over, and see if there wasn't nothing else; and pretty soon he says;

'Oh—there's one thing I forgot. Could you raise a flower here, do you reckon?'

'I doan' know but maybe I could, Mars Tom; but it's tolable dark in heah, en I ain' got no use f'r no flower, nohow, en she'd be a pow'ful sight o' trouble.'

'Well, you try it, anyway. Some other prisoners has done it.'

'One er dem big cat-tail-lookin' mullen-stalks[4] would grow
in heah, Mars Tom, I reck'n, but she wouldn't be wuth half de
trouble she'd coss.'

'Don't you believe it. We'll fetch you a little one, and you
plant it in the corner, over there, and raise it. And don't call
it mullen, call it Pitchiola[5]—that's its right name, when it's in
a prison. And you want to water it with your tears.'

'Why, I got plenty spring water, Mars Tom.'

'You don't *want* spring water; you want to water it with your
tears. It's the way they always do.'

'Why, Mars Tom, I lay I kin raise one er dem mullen-stalks
twyste[6] wid spring water whiles another man's a *start'n* one
wid tears.'

'That ain't the idea. You *got* to do it with tears.'

'She'll die on my han's, Mars Tom, she sholy will; kase I
doan' skasely ever cry.'

So Tom was stumped. But he studied it over, and then said
Jim would have to worry along the best he could with an onion.
He promised he would go to the nigger cabins and drop one,
private, in Jim's coffee-pot, in the morning. Jim said he would
'jis' 's soon have tobacker in his coffee'; and found so much
fault with it, and with the work and bother of raising the
mullen, and jews-harping the rats, and petting and flattering
up the snakes and spiders and things, on top of all the other
work he had to do on pens, and inscriptions, and journals,
and things, which made it more trouble and worry and responsibility to be a prisoner than anything he ever undertook, that
Tom most lost all patience with him; and said he was just load-
ened down with more gaudier chances than a prisoner ever
had in the world to make a name for himself, and yet he didn't
know enough to appreciate them, and they was just about
wasted on him. So Jim he was sorry, and said he wouldn't
behave so no more, and then me and Tom shoved for bed.

---

[4] *mullen-stalks*: Mullein is a type of herb.

[5] *Pitchiola*: In the romantic novel *Picciola* (1836) by French writer Xavier Bon-
iface Saintine, a prisoner's survival is aided by his nurturing of a plant in his cell.

[6] *twyste*: twice.

CHAPTER 39

In the morning we went up to the village and bought a wire rat trap and fetched it down, and unstopped the best rat hole, and in about an hour we had fifteen of the bulliest kind of ones; and then we took it and put it in a safe place under Aunt Sally's bed. But while we was gone for spiders, little Thomas Franklin Benjamin Jefferson Elexander Phelps found it there, and opened the door of it to see if the rats would come out, and they did; and Aunt Sally she come in, and when we got back she was a standing on top of the bed raising Cain, and the rats was doing what they could to keep off the dull times for her. So she took and dusted us both with the hickry,[1] and we was as much as two hours catching another fifteen or sixteen, drat that meddlesome cub, and they warn't the likeliest, nuther, because the first haul was the pick of the flock. I never see a likelier lot of rats than what that first haul was.

We got a splendid stock of sorted spiders, and bugs, and frogs, and caterpillars, and one thing or another; and we like-to got a hornet's nest, but we didn't. The family was at home. We didn't give it right up, but staid with them as long as we could; because we allowed we'd tire them out or they'd got to tire us out, and they done it. Then we got allycumpain[2] and rubbed on the places, and was pretty near all right again, but couldn't set down convenient. And so we went for the snakes, and grabbed a couple of dozen garters and house-snakes, and put them in a bag, and put it in our room, and by that time it was supper time, and a rattling good honest day's work; and hungry?—oh, no, I reckon not! And there warn't a blessed snake up there, when we went back—we didn't half tie the sack, and they worked out, somehow, and left. But it didn't

---

[1] *dusted us both with the hickry*: beat us lightly with a stick of hickory wood.
[2] *allycumpain*: elecampane, an herb used for medicinal purposes.

293

matter much, because they was still on the premises somewheres. So we judged we could get some of them again. No,
there warn't no real scarcity of snakes about the house for a
considerble spell. You'd see them dripping from the rafters and
places, every now and then; and they generly landed in your
plate, or down the back of your neck, and most of the time
where you didn't want them. Well, they was handsome, and
striped, and there warn't no harm in a million of them; but
that never made no difference to Aunt Sally, she despised
snakes, be the breed what they might, and she couldn't stand
them no way you could fix it; and every time one of them
flopped down on her, it didn't make no difference what she
was doing, she would just lay that work down and light out. I
never see such a woman. And you could hear her whoop to
Jericho. You couldn't get her to take aholt of one of them with
the tongs. And if she turned over and found one in bed, she
would scramble out and lift a howl that you would think the
house was afire. She disturbed the old man so, that he said he
could most wish there hadn't ever been no snakes created. Why,
after every last snake had been gone clear out of the house for
as much as a week, Aunt Sally warn't over it yet; she warn't
near over it; when she was setting thinking about something,
you could touch her on the back of her neck with a feather
and she would jump right out of her stockings. It was very
curious. But Tom said all women was just so. He said they was
made that way; for some reason or other.

We got a licking every time one of our snakes come in her
way; and she allowed these lickings warn't nothing to what
she would do if we ever loaded up the place again with them.
I didn't mind the lickings, because they didn't amount to nothing; but I minded the trouble we had, to lay in another lot.
But we got them laid in, and all the other things; and you
never see a cabin as blithesome as Jim's was when they'd all
swarm out for music and go for him. Jim didn't like the spiders, and the spiders didn't like Jim; and so they'd lay for him
and make it mighty warm for him. And he said that between
the rats, and the snakes, and the grindstone, there warn't no

room in bed for him, skasely; and when there was, a body couldn't sleep, it was so lively, and it was always lively, he said, because *they* never all slept at one time, but took turn about, so when the snakes was asleep the rats was on deck, and when the rats turned in the snakes come on watch, so he always had one gang under him, in his way, and t'other gang having a circus over him, and if he got up to hunt a new place, the spiders would take a chance at him as he crossed over. He said if he ever got out, this time, he wouldn't ever be a prisoner again, not for a salary.

Well, by the end of three weeks, everything was in pretty good shape. The shirt was sent in early, in a pie, and every time a rat bit Jim he would get up and write a little in his journal whilst the ink was fresh; the pens was made, the inscrip-tions and so on was all carved on the grindstone; the bed-leg was sawed in two, and we had et up the sawdust, and it give us a most amazing stomach-ache. We reckoned we was all going to die, but didn't. It was the most undigestible sawdust I ever see; and Tom said the same. But as I was saying, we'd got all the work done, now, at last; and we was all pretty much fagged out, too, but mainly Jim. The old man had wrote a couple of times to the plantation below Orleans to come and get their runaway nigger, but hadn't got no answer, because there warn't no such plantation; so he allowed he would advertise Jim in the St. Louis and New Orleans papers; and when he men-tioned the St. Louis ones, it give me the cold shivers, and I see we hadn't no time to lose. So Tom said, now for the non-namous letters.

'What's them?' I says.

'Warnings to the people that something is up. Sometimes it's done one way, sometimes another. But there's always some-body spying around, that gives notice to the governor of the castle. When Louis XVI was going to light out of the Tool-eries,[3] a servant girl done it. It's a very good way, and so is the nonnamous letters. We'll use them both. And it's usual

---

[3] *Tooleries*: Tuileries, once a famous palace in Paris, now a park.

for the prisoner's mother to change clothes with him, and she stays in, and he slides out in her clothes. We'll do that too.'

'But looky here, Tom, what do we want to *warn* anybody for, that something's up? Let them find it out for themselves—it's their lookout.'

'Yes, I know; but you can't depend on them. It's the way they've acted from the very start—left us to do *everything*. They're so confiding and mullet-headed[4] they don't take notice of nothing at all. So if we don't *give* them notice, there won't be nobody nor nothing to interfere with us, and so after all our hard work and trouble this escape 'll go off perfectly flat: won't amount to nothing—won't be nothing *to* it.'

'Well, as for me, Tom, that's the way I'd like.'

'Shucks,' he says, and looked disgusted. So I says:

'But I ain't going to make no complaint. Anyway that suits you suits me. What you going to do about the servant-girl?'

'You'll be her. You slide in, in the middle of the night, and hook that yaller girl's frock.'

'Why, Tom, that'll make trouble next morning; because of course she prob'bly hain't got any but that one.'

'I know; but you don't want it but fifteen minutes, to carry the nonnamous letter and shove it under the front door.'

'All right, then, I'll do it; but I could carry it just as handy in my own togs.'

'You wouldn't look like a servant-girl *then*, would you?'

'No, but there won't be nobody to see what I look like, *anyway*.'

'That ain't got nothing to do with it. The thing for us to do, is just to do our *duty*, and not worry about whether anybody *sees* us do it or not. Hain't you got no principle at all?'

'All right, I ain't saying nothing; I'm the servant-girl. Who's Jim's mother?'

'I'm his mother. I'll hook a gown from Aunt Sally.'

'Well, then, you'll have to stay in the cabin when me and Jim leaves.'

---

[4] *mullet-headed*: gullible; stupid. A mullet is a type of fish known for its stupidity.

'Not much. I'll stuff Jim's clothes full of straw and lay it on his bed to represent his mother in disguise, and Jim 'll take the nigger woman's gown off of me and wear it, and we'll all evade together. When a prisoner of style escapes, it's called an evasion. It's always called so when a king escapes, f'rinstance. And the same with a king's son; it don't make no difference whether he's a natural one or an unnatural one.'

So Tom he wrote the nonnamous letter, and I smouched the yaller wench's frock, that night, and put it on, and shoved it under the front door, the way Tom told me to. It said:

> *Beware. Trouble is brewing. Keep a sharp lookout.*
> UNKNOWN FRIEND

Next day we stuck a picture which Tom drawed in blood, of a skull and crossbones, on the front door; and next night another one of a coffin, on the back door. I never see a family in such a sweat. They couldn't a been worse scared if the place had a been full of ghosts laying for them behind everything and under the beds and shivering through the air. If a door banged, Aunt Sally she jumped, and said 'ouch!' if anything fell, she jumped and said 'ouch!' if you happened to touch her, when she warn't noticing, she done the same; she couldn't face noway and be satisfied, because she allowed there was something behind her every time—so she was always a whirling around, sudden, and saying 'ouch,' and before she'd get two-thirds around, she'd whirl back again, and say it again; and she was afraid to go to bed, but she dasn't set up. So the thing was working very well, Tom said; he said he never see a thing work more satisfactory. He said it showed it was done right.

So he said, now for the grand bulge! So the very next morning at the streak of dawn we got another letter ready, and was wondering what we better do with it, because we heard them say at supper they was going to have a nigger on watch at both doors all night. Tom he went down the lightning-rod to spy around; and the nigger at the back door was asleep, and he stuck it in the back of his neck and come back. This letter said:

Don't betray me, I wish to be your friend. There is a desprate gang of cutthroats from over in the Ingean Territory[5] going to steal your runaway nigger to-night, and they have been trying to scare you so as you will stay in the house and not bother them. I am one of the gang, but have got religgion and wish to quit it and lead a honest life again, and will betray the helish design. They will sneak down from northards, along the fence, at midnight exact, with a false key, and go in the nigger's cabin to get him. I am to be off a piece and blow a tin horn if I see any danger; but stead of that, I will BA *like a sheep soon as they get in and not blow at all; then whilst they are getting his chains loose, you slip there and lock them in, and can kill them at your leasure. Don't do anything but just the way I am telling you, if you do they will suspicion something and raise whoopjamboreehoo. I do not wish any reward but to know I have done the right thing.*

U<small>NKNOWN</small> F<small>RIEND</small>

---

[5] *Ingean Territory*: Indian Territory, the land set aside by the U.S. government in the 1830s to settle forcibly displaced Indian tribes. It covered largely what is now the state of Oklahoma.

CHAPTER 40

We was feeling pretty good, after breakfast, and took my canoe and went over the river a fishing, with a lunch, and had a good time, and took a look at the raft and found her all right, and got home late to supper, and found them in such a sweat and worry they didn't know which end they was standing on, and made us go right off to bed the minute we was done supper, and wouldn't tell us what the trouble was, and never let on a word about the new letter, but didn't need to, because we knowed as much about it as anybody did, and as soon as we was half up stairs and her back was turned, we slid for the cellar cubboard and loaded up a good lunch and took it up to our room and went to bed, and got up about half-past eleven, and Tom put on Aunt Sally's dress that he stole and was going to start with the lunch, but says:

'Where's the butter?'

'I laid out a hunk of it,' I says, 'on a piece of a corn-pone.'

'Well, you *left* it laid out, then—it ain't here.'

'We can get along without it,' I says.

'We can get along *with* it, too,' he says; 'just you slide down cellar and fetch it. And then mosey right down the lightning-rod and come along. I'll go and stuff the straw into Jim's clothes to represent his mother in disguise, and be ready to *ba* like a sheep and shove soon as you get there.'

So out he went, and down cellar went I. The hunk of butter, big as a person's fist, was where I had left it, so I took up the slab of corn-pone with it on, and blowed out my light, and started up stairs, very stealthy, and got up to the main floor all right, but here comes Aunt Sally with a candle, and I clapped the truck in my hat, and clapped my hat on my head, and the next second she see me; and she says:

'You been down cellar?'

'Yes'm.'

299

'What you been doing down there?'

'Noth'n.'

'*Noth'n!*'

'No'm.'

'Well, then, what possessed you to go down there, this time of night?'

'I don't know'm.'

'You don't *know*? Don't answer me that way, Tom, I want to know what you been *doing* down there?'

'I hain't been doing a single thing, Aunt Sally, I hope to gracious if I have.'

I reckoned she'd let me go, now, and as a generl thing she would; but I spose there was so many strange things going on she was just in a sweat about every little thing that warn't yard-stick straight; so she says, very decided:

'You just march into that setting-room and stay there till I come. You been up to something you no business to, and I lay I'll find out what it is before *I'm* done with you.'

So she went away as I opened the door and walked into the setting-room. My, but there was a crowd there! Fifteen farmers, and every one of them had a gun. I was most powerful sick, and slunk to a chair and set down. They was setting around, some of them talking a little, in a low voice, and all of them fidgety and uneasy, but trying to look like they warn't; but I knowed they was, because they was always taking off their hats, and putting them on, and scratching their heads, and changing their seats, and fumbling with their buttons. I warn't easy myself, but I didn't take my hat off, all the same.

I did wish Aunt Sally would come, and get done with me, and lick me, if she wanted to, and let me get away and tell Tom how we'd overdone this thing, and what a thundering hornet's nest we'd got ourselves into, so we could stop fooling around, straight off, and clear out with Jim before these rips[1] got out of patience and come for us.

---

[1] *rips*: dissolute or immoral persons.

At last she come, and begun to ask me questions, but I *couldn't* answer them straight, I didn't know which end of me was up; because these men was in such a fidget now, that some was wanting to start right *now* and lay for them desperadoes, and saying it warn't but a few minutes to midnight; and others was trying to get them to hold on and wait for the sheep-signal; and here was aunty pegging away at the questions, and me a shaking all over and ready to sink down in my tracks I was that scared; and the place getting hotter and hotter, and the butter beginning to melt and run down my neck and behind my ears: and pretty soon, when one of them says, '*I'm* for going and getting in the cabin *first*, and right *now*, and catching them when they come,' I most dropped; and a streak of butter come a trickling down my forehead, and Aunt Sally she see it, and turns white as a sheet, and says:

'For the land's sake what *is* the matter with the child!—he's got the brain fever as shore as you're born, and they're oozing out!'

And everybody runs to see, and she snatches off my hat, and out comes the bread, and what was left of the butter, and she grabbed me, and hugged me, and says:

'Oh, what a turn you did give me! and how glad and grateful I am it ain't no worse; for luck's against us, and it never rains but it pours, and when I see that truck I thought we'd lost you, for I knowed by the color and all, it was just like your brains would be if—Dear, dear, whyd'nt you *tell* me that was what you'd been down there for, *I* wouldn't a cared. Now cler out to bed, and don't lemme see no more of you till morning!'

I was up stairs in a second, and down the lightning-rod in another one, and shinning through the dark for the lean-to. I couldn't hardly get my words out, I was so anxious; but I told Tom as quick as I could, we must jump for it, now, and not a minute to lose—the house full of men, yonder, with guns!

His eyes just blazed; and he says:

'No!—is that so? *Ain't* it bully! Why, Huck, if it was to do over again, I bet I could fetch two hundred! If we could put it off till—'

'Hurry! *hurry!*' I says. 'Where's Jim?'

'Right at your elbow; if you reach out your arm you can touch him. He's dressed, and everything's ready. Now we'll slide out and give the sheep-signal.'

But then we heard the tramp of men, coming to the door, and heard them begin to fumble with the padlock; and heard a man say:

'I *told* you we'd be too soon; they haven't come—the door is locked. Here, I'll lock some of you into the cabin and you lay for 'em in the dark and kill 'em when they come; and the rest scatter around a piece, and listen if you can hear 'em coming.'

So in they come, but couldn't see us in the dark, and most trod on us whilst we was hustling to get under the bed. But we got under all right, and out through the hole, swift but soft— Jim first, me next, and Tom last, which was according to Tom's orders. Now we was in the lean-to, and heard trampings close by outside. So we crept to the door, and Tom stopped us there and put his eye to the crack, but couldn't make out nothing, it was so dark; and whispered and said he would listen for the steps to get further, and when he nudged us Jim must glide out first, and him last. So he set his ear to the crack and listened, and listened, and listened, and the steps a scraping around, out there, all the time; and at last he nudged us, and we slid out, and stooped down, not breathing, and not making the least noise, and slipped stealthy towards the fence, in Injun file, and got to it, all right, and me and Jim over it; but Tom's britches catched fast on a splinter on the top rail, and then he hear the steps coming, so he had to pull loose, which snapped the splinter and made a noise; and as he dropped in our tracks and started, somebody sings out:

'Who's that? Answer, or I'll shoot!'

But we didn't answer; we just unfurled our heels and shoved. Then there was a rush, and a *bang, bang, bang!* and the bullets fairly whizzed around us! We heard them sing out:

'Here they are! They've broke for the river! after 'em, boys! And turn loose the dogs!'

So here they come, full tilt. We could hear them, because they wore boots, and yelled, but we didn't wear no boots, and didn't yell. We was in the path to the mill; and when they got pretty close onto us, we dodged into the bush and let them go by, and then dropped in behind them. They'd had all the dogs shut up, so they wouldn't scare off the robbers; but by this time somebody had let them loose, and here they come, making pow-wow enough for a million, but they was our dogs; so we stopped in our tracks till they catched up; and when they see it warn't nobody but us, and no excitement to offer them, they only just said howdy, and tore right ahead towards the shouting and clattering; and then we up steam again and whizzed along after them till we was nearly to the mill, and then struck up through the bush to where my canoe was tied, and hopped in and pulled for dear life towards the middle of the river, but didn't make no more noise than we was obleeged to. Then we struck out, easy and comfortable, for the island where my raft was; and we could hear them yelling and barking at each other all up and down the bank, till we was so far away the sounds got dim and died out. And when we stepped onto the raft, I says:

'Now, old Jim, you're a free man *again*, and I bet you won't ever be a slave no more.'

'En a mighty good job it wuz, too, Huck. It 'uz planned beautiful, en it 'uz *done* beautiful; en dey ain't *nobody* kin git up a plan dat's mo' mixed-up en splendid den what dat one wuz.'

We was all as glad as we could be, but Tom was the gladdest of all, because he had a bullet in the calf of his leg.

When me and Jim heard that, we didn't feel so brash as what we did before. It was hurting him considerble, and bleeding; so we laid him in the wigwam and tore up one of the duke's shirts for to bandage him, but he says:

'Gimme the rags, I can do it myself. Don't stop, now; don't fool around here, and the evasion booming along so handsome; man the sweeps, and set her loose! Boys, we done it elegant!—'deed we did. I wish *we'd* a had the handling of Louis XVI, there wouldn't a been no 'Son of Saint Louis, ascend to heaven!'[2] wrote down in *his* biography: no, sir, we'd a whooped him over the *border*—that's what we'd a done with *him*—and done it just as slick as nothing at all, too. Man the sweeps— man the sweeps!'

But me and Jim was consulting—and thinking. And after we'd thought a minute, I says:

'Say it, Jim.'

So he says:

'Well, den, dis is de way it look to me, Huck. Ef it wuz *him* dat 'uz bein' sot free, en one er de boys wuz to git shot, would he say, "Go on en save me, nemmine 'bout a doctor f'r to save dis one?" Is dat like Mars Tom Sawyer? Would he say dat? You *bet* he wouldn't! *Well*, den, is *Jim* gwyne to say it? No, sah—I doan' budge a step out'n dis place, 'dout a *doctor*; not if it's forty year!'

I knowed he was white inside, and I reckoned he'd say what he did say—so it was all right, now, and I told Tom I was ago-ing for a doctor. He raised considerble row about it, but me and Jim stuck to it and wouldn't budge; so he was for crawling out and setting the raft loose himself; but we wouldn't let him. Then he give us a piece of his mind—but it didn't do no good.

So when he see me getting the canoe ready, he says:

'Well, then, if you're bound to go, I'll tell you the way to do, when you get to the village. Shut the door, and blindfold the doctor tight and fast, and make him swear to be silent as the grave, and put a purse full of gold in his hand, and then take and lead him all around the back alleys and everywheres, in the dark, and then fetch him here in the canoe, in a round-about way amongst the islands, and search him and take his chalk away from him, and don't give it back to him till you get him back to the village, or else he will chalk this raft so he can find it again. It's the way they all do.'

So I said I would, and left, and Jim was to hide in the woods when he see the doctor coming, till he was gone again.

---

[2] *Son of Saint Louis, ascend to heaven!* The phrase comes from Scottish phi-losopher and writer Thomas Carlyle's account of the execution of Louis XVI in *The French Revolution: A History* (1837).

CHAPTER 41

The doctor was an old man; a very nice, kind-looking old man, when I got him up. I told him me and my brother was over on Spanish Island hunting, yesterday afternoon, and camped on a piece of a raft we found, and about midnight he must a kicked his gun in his dreams, for it went off and shot him in the leg, and we wanted him to go over there and fix it and not say nothing about it, nor let anybody know, because we wanted to come home this evening, and surprise the folks.

'Who is your folks?' he says.

'The Phelpses, down yonder.'

'Oh,' he says. And after a minute, he says: 'How'd you say he got shot?'

'He had a dream,' I says, 'and it shot him.'

'Singular dream,' he says.

So he lit up his lantern, and got his saddle-bags, and we started. But when he see the canoe, he didn't like the look of her—said she was big enough for one, but didn't look pretty safe for two. I says:

'Oh, you needn't be afeared, sir, she carried the three of us, easy enough.'

'What three?'

'Why, me and Sid, and—and—and *the guns*; that's what I mean.'

'Oh,' he says.

But he put his foot on the gunnel,[1] and rocked her; and shook his head, and said he reckoned he'd look around for a bigger one. But they was all locked and chained; so he took my canoe, and said for me to wait till he come back, or I could hunt around further, or maybe I better go down home and get them ready for the surprise, if I wanted to. But I said

---

[1] *gunnel*: alternative spelling of "gunwale", the top edge of a boat's side.

I didn't; so I told him just how to find the raft, and then he
started.

I struck an idea, pretty soon. I says to myself, spos'n he can't
fix that leg just in three shakes of a sheep's tail, as the saying
is? spos'n it takes him three or four days? What are we going
to do?—lay around there till he lets the cat out of the bag?
No, sir, I know what *I'll* do. I'll wait, and when he comes back,
if he says he's got to go any more, I'll get down there, too, if I
swim; and we'll take and tie him, and keep him, and shove
out down the river; and when Tom's done with him, we'll give
him what it's worth, or all we got, and then let him get shore.

So then I crept into a lumber pile to get some sleep; and
next time I waked up the sun was away up over my head! I
shot out and went for the doctor's house, but they told me
he'd gone away in the night, some time or other, and warn't
back yet. Well, thinks I, that looks powerful bad for Tom, and
I'll dig out for the island, right off. So away I shoved, and turned
the corner, and nearly rammed my head into Uncle Silas's stomach! He says:

'Why, *Tom!* Where you been, all this time, you rascal?'

'*I* hain't been nowheres,' I says, 'only just hunting for the
runaway nigger—me and Sid.'

'Why, where ever did you go?' he says. 'Your aunt's been
mighty uneasy.'

'She needn't,' I says, 'because we was all right. We followed
the men and the dogs, but they out-run us, and we lost them;
but we thought we heard them on the water, so we got a canoe
and took out after them, and crossed over but couldn't find
nothing of them; so we cruised along up-shore till we got kind
of tired and beat out; and tied up the canoe and went to sleep,
and never waked up till about an hour ago, then we paddled
over here to hear the news, and Sid's at the post-office to see
what he can hear, and I'm a branching out to get something
to eat for us, and then we're going home.'

So then we went to the post-office to get 'Sid'; but just as I
suspicioned, he warn't there; so the old man he got a letter
out of the office, and we waited a while longer but Sid didn't

come; so the old man said come along, let Sid foot it home, or canoe-it, when he got done fooling around—but we would ride. I couldn't get him to let me stay and wait for Sid; and he said there warn't no use in it, and I must come along, and let Aunt Sally see we was all right.

When we got home, Aunt Sally was that glad to see me she laughed and cried both, and hugged me, and give me one of them lickings of hern that don't amount to shucks, and said she'd serve Sid the same when he come.

And the place was plumb full of farmers and farmers' wives, to dinner; and such another clack a body never heard. Old Mrs Hotchkiss was the worst; her tongue was agoing all the time. She says:

'Well, Sister Phelps, I've ransacked that-air cabin over an' I b'lieve the nigger was crazy. I says so to Sister Damrell—didn't I, Sister Damrell?—s'I, he's crazy, s'I—them's the very words I said. You all hearn me: he's crazy, s'I; everything shows it, s'I. Look at that-air grindstone, s'I; want to tell *me* 't any cretur 'ts in his right mind 's agoin' to scrabble all them crazy things onto a grindstone, s'I? Here sich 'n' sich a person busted his heart; 'n' here so 'n' so pegged along for thirty-seven year, 'n' all that—natcherl son o' Louis somebody, 'n' sich everlast'n rubbage. He's plumb crazy, s'I; it's what I says in the fust place, it's what I says in the middle, 'n' it's what I says last 'n' all the time—the nigger's crazy—crazy 's Nebokoodneezer,[2] s'I.'

'An' look at that-air ladder made out'n rags, Sister Hotchkiss,' says old Mrs Damrell, 'what in the name o' goodness *could* he ever want of—'

'The very words I was a-sayin' no longer ago th'n this minute to Sister Utterback, 'n' she'll tell you so herself. Sh-she, look at that-air rag ladder, sh-she; 'n' s'I, yes, *look* at it, s'I—what *could* he a wanted of it, s'I. Sh-she, Sister Hotchkiss, sh-she—'

'But how in the nation'd they ever *git* that grindstone *in* there, *any*-way? 'n' who dug that-air *hole*? 'n' who—'

---

[2] *Nebokoodneezer*: In Daniel 4:25–30, King Nebuchadnezzar of Babylon goes insane as a punishment by God.

'My very *words*, Brer[3] Penrod! I was a-sayin'—pass that-air sasser o' m'lasses,[4] won't ye?—I was a-sayin' to Sister Dunlap, jist this minute, how *did* they git that grindstone in there, s'I. Without *help*, mind you—'thout *help*! *Thar's* wher' 'tis. Don't tell *me*, s'I; there *wuz* help, s'I; 'n' ther' wuz a *plenty* help, too, s'I; ther's ben a *dozen* a-helpin' that nigger, 'n' I lay I'd skin every last nigger on this place, but *I'd* find out who done it, s'I; 'n' moreover, s'I—'

'A *dozen* says you!—*forty* couldn't a done everything that's been done. Look at them case-knife saws and things, how tedious they've been made; look at that bed-leg sawed off with 'm, a week's work for six men; look at that nigger made out'n straw on the bed; and look at—'

'You may *well* say it, Brer Hightower! It's jist as I was a-sayin' to Brer Phelps, his own self. S'e, what do *you* think of it, Sister Hotchkiss, s'e? think o' what, Brer Phelps, s'I? think o' that bed-leg sawed off that a way, s'e? *think* of it, s'I? I lay it never sawed *itself* off, s'I—somebody *sawed* it, s'I; that's my opinion, take it or leave it, it mayn't be no 'count, s'I, but sich as 't is, it's my opinion, s'I, 'n' if anybody k'n start a better one, s'I, let him *do* it, s'I, that's all. I says to Sister Dunlap, s'I—'

'Why, dog my cats, they must a ben a house-full o' niggers in there every night for four weeks, to a done all that work, Sister Phelps. Look at that shirt—every last inch of it kivered over with secret African writ'n done with blood! Must a ben a raft uv 'm at it right along, all the time, amost. Why, I'd give two dollars to have it read to me; 'n' as for the niggers that wrote it, I 'low I'd take 'n' lash 'm t'll—'

'People to *help* him, Brother Marples! Well, I reckon you'd *think* so, if you'd a been in this house for a while back. Why, they've stole everything they could lay their hands on—and we a watching, all the time, mind you. They stole that shirt right off o' the line! and as for that sheet they made the rag

---

[3] *Brer*: Brother. The use of the titles "Sister" and "Brother" among the Phelps' friends is typical of certain religious congregations.

[4] *sasser o' m'lasses*: molasses sauce.

ladder out of ther' ain't no telling how many times they *didn't*
steal that; and flour, and candles, and candlesticks, and spoons,
and the old warming-pan, and most a thousand things that I
disremember, now, and my new calico dress; and me, and Silas,
and my Sid and Tom on the constant watch day *and* night, as
I was a telling you, and not a one of us could catch hide nor
hair, nor sight nor sound of them; and here at the last minute,
lo and behold you, they slides right in under our noses, and
fools us, and not only fools *us* but the Injun Territory robbers
too, and actuly gets *away* with that nigger, safe and sound,
and that with sixteen men and twenty-two dogs right on their
very heels at that very time! I tell you, it just bangs anything
I ever *heard* of. Why, *sperits* couldn't a done better, and been
no smarter. And I reckon they must a *been* sperits—because,
you know our dogs, and ther' ain't no better; well, them dogs
never even got on the *track* of 'm, once! You explain *that* to
me, if you can!—*any* of you!'

'Well, it does beat—'

'Laws alive, I never—'

'So help me, I wouldn't a be—'

'*House*-thieves as well as—'

'Goodnessgracioussakes, I'd a ben afeard to *live* in sich a—'

' 'Fraid to *live*!—why, I was that scared I dasn't hardly go to
bed, or get up, or lay down, or *set* down, Sister Ridgeway. Why,
they'd steal the very—why, goodness sakes, you can guess what
kind of a fluster *I* was in by the time midnight come, last night.
I hope to gracious if I warn't afraid they'd steal some o' the
family! I was just to that pass, I didn't have no reasoning fac-
ulties no more. It looks foolish enough, *now*, in the day-time;
but I says to myself, there's my two poor boys asleep, 'way up
stairs in that lonesome room, and I declare to goodness I was
that uneasy 't I crep' up there and locked 'em in! I *did*. And
anybody would. Because, you know, when you get scared, that
way, and it keeps running on, and getting worse and worse, all
the time, and your wits gets to addling, and you get to doing
all sorts o' wild things, and by-and-by you think to yourself,
spos'n *I* was a boy, and was away up there, and the door ain't

locked, and you—' She stopped, looking kind of wondering, and then she turned her head around slow, and when her eye lit on me—I got up and took a walk.

Says I to myself, I can explain better how we come to not be in that room this morning, if I go out to one side and study over it a little. So I done it. But I dasn't go fur, or she'd a sent for me. And when it was late in the day, the people all went, and then I come in and told her the noise and shooting waked up me and 'Sid', and the door was locked, and we wanted to see the fun, so we went down the lightning-rod, and both of us got hurt a little, and we didn't never want to try *that* no more. And then I went on and told her all what I told Uncle Silas before; and then she said she'd forgive us, and maybe it was all right enough anyway, and about what a body might expect of boys, for all boys was a pretty harum-scarum lot, as fur as she could see; and so, as long as no harm hadn't come of it, she judged she better put in her time being grateful we was alive and well and she had us still, stead of fretting over what was past and done. So then she kissed me, and patted me on the head, and dropped into a kind of a brown study; and pretty soon jumps up, and says:

'Why, lawsamercy, it's most night, and Sid not come yet! What *has* become of that boy?'

I see my chance; so I skips up and says:

'I'll run right up to town and get him,' I says.

'No you won't,' she says. 'You'll stay right wher' you are; *one's* enough to be lost at a time. If he ain't here to supper, your uncle 'll go.'

Well, he warn't there to supper; so right after supper uncle went.

He come back about ten, a little bit uneasy; hadn't run across Tom's track. Aunt Sally was a good *deal* uneasy; but Uncle Silas he said there warn't no occasion to be—boys will be boys, he said, and you'll see this one turn up in the morning, all sound and right. So she had to be satisfied. But she said she'd set up for him a while, anyway, and keep a light burning, so he could see it.

And then when I went up to bed she come up with me and fetched her candle, and tucked me in, and mothered me so good I felt mean, and like I couldn't look her in the face; and she set down on the bed and talked with me a long time, and said what a splendid boy Sid was, and didn't seem to want to ever stop talking about him; and kept asking me every now and then, if I reckoned he could a got lost, or hurt, or maybe drownded, and might be laying at this minute, somewheres, suffering or dead, and she not by him to help him, and so the tears would drip down, silent, and I would tell her that Sid was all right, and would be home in the morning, sure; and she would squeeze my hand, or maybe kiss me, and tell me to say it again, and keep on saying it, because it done her good, and she was in so much trouble. And when she was going away, she looked down in my eyes, so steady and gentle, and says:

'The door ain't going to be locked, Tom; and there's the window and the rod; but you'll be good, *won't* you? And you won't go? For *my* sake?'

Laws knows I *wanted* to go, bad enough, to see about Tom, and was all intending to go; but after that, I wouldn't a went, not for kingdoms.

But she was on my mind, and Tom was on my mind; so I slept very restless. And twice I went down the rod, away in the night, and slipped around front, and see her setting there by her candle in the window with her eyes towards the road and the tears in them; and I wished I could do something for her, but I couldn't, only to swear that I wouldn't never do nothing to grieve her any more. And the third time, I waked up at dawn, and slid down, and she was there yet, and her candle was most out, and her old gray head was resting on her hand, and she was asleep.

CHAPTER 42

The old man was up town again, before breakfast, but couldn't get no track of Tom; and both of them set at the table, thinking, and not saying nothing, and looking mournful, and their coffee getting cold, and not eating anything. And by-and-by the old man says:

'Did I give you the letter?'

'What letter?'

'The one I got yesterday out of the post-office.'

'No, you didn't give me no letter.'

'Well, I must a forgot it.'

So he rummaged his pockets, and then went off somewheres where he had laid it down, and fetched it, and give it to her. She says:

'Why, it's from St. Petersburg—it's from Sis.'

I allowed another walk would do me good; but I couldn't stir. But before she could break it open, she dropped it and run—for she see something. And so did I. It was Tom Sawyer on a mattress; and that old doctor; and Jim, in *her* calico dress, with his hands tied behind him; and a lot of people. I hid the letter behind the first thing that come handy, and rushed. She flung herself at Tom, crying, and says:

'Oh, he's dead, he's dead, I know he's dead!'

And Tom he turned his head a little, and muttered something or other, which showed he warn't in his right mind; then she flung up her hands, and says:

'He's alive, thank God! And that's enough!' and she snatched a kiss of him, and flew for the house to get the bed ready, and scattering orders right and left at the niggers and everybody else, as fast as her tongue could go, every jump of the way.

I followed the men to see what they was going to do with Jim; and the old doctor and Uncle Silas followed after Tom into the house. The men was very huffy, and some of them wanted to hang Jim, for an example to all the other niggers around there, so they wouldn't be trying to run away, like Jim done, and making such a raft of trouble, and keeping a whole family scared most to death for days and nights. But the others said, don't do it, it wouldn't answer at all, he ain't our nigger, and his owner would turn up and make us pay for him, sure. So that cooled them down a little, because the people that's always the most anxious for to hang a nigger that hain't done just right, is always the very ones that ain't the most anxious to pay for him when they've got their satisfaction out of him.

They cussed Jim considerble, though, and give him a cuff or two, side the head, once in a while, but Jim never said nothing, and he never let on to know me, and they took him to the same cabin, and put his own clothes on him, and chained him again, and not to no bed-leg, this time, but to a big staple drove into the bottom log, and chained his hands, too, and both legs, and said he warn't to have nothing but bread and water to eat, after this, till his owner come or he was sold at auction, because he didn't come in a certain length of time, and filled up our hole, and said a couple of farmers with guns must stand watch around about the cabin every night, and a bull-dog tied to the door in the day-time; and about this time they was through with the job and was tapering off with a kind of generl good-bye cussing, and then the old doctor comes and takes a look, and says:

'Don't be no rougher on him than you're obleeged to, because he ain't a bad nigger. When I got to where I found the boy, I see I couldn't cut the bullet out without some help, and he warn't in no condition for me to leave, to go and get help; and he got a little worse and a little worse, and after a long time he went out of his head, and wouldn't let me come anigh him, any more, and said if I chalked his raft he'd kill me, and no end of wild foolishness like that, and I see I couldn't do anything at all with him; so I says, I got to have *help*, somehow; and the minute I says it, out crawls this nigger

from somewheres, and says he'll help, and he done it, too,
and done it very well. Of course I judged he must be a runaway nigger, and there I *was*! and there I had to stick, right
straight along all the rest of the day, and all night. It was a
fix, I tell you! I had a couple of patients with the chills, and
of course I'd of liked to run up to town and see them, but I
dasn't, because the nigger might get away, and then I'd be to
blame; and yet never a skiff come close enough for me to
hail. So there I had to stick, plumb till daylight this morning; and I never see a nigger that was a better nuss or faith-
fuller, and yet he was resking his freedom to do it, and was
all tired out, too, and I see plain enough he'd been worked
main hard, lately. I liked the nigger for that; I tell you, gentlemen, a nigger like that is worth a thousand dollars—and
kind treatment, too. I had everything I needed, and the boy
was doing as well there as he would a done at home—better,
maybe, because it was so quiet; but there I *was*, with both
of 'm on my hands; and there I had to stick, till about
dawn this morning; then some men in a skiff come by, and as
good luck would have it, the nigger was setting by the pallet
with his head propped on his knees, sound asleep; so I
motioned them in, quiet, and they slipped up on him and
grabbed him and tied him before he knowed what he was
about, and we never had no trouble. And the boy being in a
kind of a flighty sleep, too, we muffled the oars and hitched
the raft on, and towed her over very nice and quiet, and the
nigger never made the least row nor said a word, from the
start. He ain't no bad nigger, gentlemen; that's what I think
about him.'

Somebody says:

'Well, it sounds very good, doctor, I'm obleeged to say.'

Then the others softened up a little, too, and I was mighty
thankful to that old doctor for doing Jim that good turn;
and I was glad it was according to my judgment of him,
too; because I thought he had a good heart in him and was
a good man, the first time I see him. Then they all agreed
that Jim had acted very well, and was deserving to have

some notice took of it, and reward. So every one of them promised, right out and hearty, that they wouldn't cuss him no more.

Then they come out and locked him up. I hoped they was going to say he could have one or two of the chains took off, because they was rotten heavy, or could have meat and greens with his bread and water, but they didn't think of it, and I reckoned it warn't best for me to mix in, but I judged I'd get the doctor's yarn to Aunt Sally, somehow or other, as soon as I'd got through the breakers[1] that was laying just ahead of me. Explanations, I mean, of how I forgot to mention about Sid being shot, when I was telling how him and me put in that dratted night paddling around hunting the runaway nigger.

But I had plenty time. Aunt Sally she stuck to the sickroom all day and all night; and every time I see Uncle Silas mooning around, I dodged him.

Next morning I heard Tom was a good deal better, and they said Aunt Sally was gone to get a nap. So I slips to the sickroom, and if I found him awake I reckoned we could put up a yarn for the family that would wash. But he was sleeping, and sleeping very peaceful, too; and pale, not fire-faced the way he was when he come. So I set down and laid for him to wake. In about a half an hour, Aunt Sally comes gliding in, and there I was, up a stump again! She motioned me to be still, and set down by me, and begun to whisper, and said we could all be joyful now, because all the symptoms was first rate, and he'd been sleeping like that for ever so long, and looking better and peacefuller all the time, and ten to one he'd wake up in his right mind.

So we set there watching, and by-and-by he stirs a bit, and opened his eyes very natural, and takes a look, and says:

'Hello, why I'm at *home*! How's that? Where's the raft?'

'It's all right,' I says.

'And *Jim*?'

[1] *breakers*: difficult places.

'The same,' I says, but couldn't say it pretty brash. But he never noticed, but says:

'Good! Splendid! *Now* we're all right and safe! Did you tell Aunty?'

I was going to say yes; but she chipped in and says:

'About what, Sid?'

'Why, about the way the whole thing was done.'

'What whole thing?'

'Why, *the* whole thing. There ain't but one; how we set the runaway nigger free—me and Tom.'

'Good land! Set the run—What *is* the child talking about! Dear, dear, out of his head again!'

'No, I ain't out of my HEAD; I know all what I'm talking about. We *did* set him free—me and Tom. We laid out to do it, and we *done* it. And we done it elegant, too.' He'd got a start, and she never checked him up, just set and stared and stared, and let him clip along, and I see it warn't no use for *me* to put in. 'Why, Aunty, it cost us a power of work—weeks of it—hours and hours, every night, whilst you was all asleep. And we had to steal candles, and the sheet, and the shirt, and your dress, and spoons, and tin plates, and case-knives, and the warming-pan, and the grindstone, and flour, and just no end of things, and you can't think what work it was to make the saws, and pens, and inscriptions, and one thing or another, and you can't think *half* the fun it was. And we had to make up the pictures of coffins and things, and nonnamous letters from the robbers, and get up and down the lightning-rod, and dig the hole into the cabin, and make the rope-ladder and send it in cooked up in a pie, and send in spoons and things to work with, in your apron pocket—'

'Mercy sakes!'

'—and load up the cabin with rats and snakes and so on, for company for Jim; and then you kept Tom here so long with the butter in his hat that you come near spiling the whole business, because the men come before we was out of the cabin, and we had to rush, and they heard us and let drive at us, and I got my share, and we dodged out of the path and let them go by, and when the dogs come they warn't interested in us, but went for the most noise, and we got our canoe, and made for the raft, and was all safe, and Jim was a free man, and we done it all by ourselves, and *wasn't* it bully, Aunty!'

'Well, I never heard the likes of it in all my born days! So it was *you*, you little rapscallions, that's been making all this trouble, and turned everybody's wits clean inside out and scared us all most to death. I've as good a notion as ever I had in my life, to take it out o' you this very minute. To think, here I've been, night after night, a—*you* just get well once, you young scamp, and I lay I'll tan the Old Harry out o' both o' ye!'

But Tom, he *was* so proud and joyful, he just *couldn't* hold in, and his tongue just *went* it—she a-chipping in, and spitting fire all along, and both of them going it at once, like a cat-convention; and she says:

'*Well* you get all the enjoyment you can out of it *now*, for mind I tell you if I catch you meddling with him again—'

'Meddling with *who*?' Tom says, dropping his smile and looking surprised.

'With *who*? Why, the runaway nigger, of course. Who'd you reckon?'

Tom looks at me very grave, and says:

'Tom, didn't you just tell me he was all right? Hasn't he got away?'

'*Him*?' says Aunt Sally; 'the runaway nigger? 'Deed he hasn't. They've got him back, safe and sound, and he's in that cabin again, on bread and water, and loaded down with chains, till he's claimed or sold!'

Tom rose square up in bed, with his eye hot, and his nostrils opening and shutting like gills, and sings out to me:

'They hain't no *right* to shut him up! *Shove*!—and don't you lose a minute. Turn him loose! he ain't no slave; he's as free as any cretur that walks this earth!'

'What *does* the child mean?'

'I mean every word I *say*. Aunt Sally, and if somebody don't go, *I'll* go. I've knowed him all his life, and so has Tom, there.

Old Miss Watson died two months ago, and she was ashamed she ever was going to sell him down the river, and *said* so; and she set him free in her will.'

'Then what on earth did *you* want to set him free for, seeing he was already free?'

'Well, that *is* a question, I must say; and *just* like women! Why, I wanted the *adventure* of it; and I'd a waded neck-deep in blood to—goodness alive, AUNT POLLY!'

If she warn't standing right there, just inside the door, looking as sweet and contented as an angel half-full of pie, I wish I may never!

Aunt Sally jumped for her, and most hugged the head off of her, and cried over her, and I found a good enough place for me under the bed, for it was getting pretty sultry for *us*, seemed to me. And I peeped out, and in a little while Tom's Aunt Polly shook herself loose and stood there looking across at Tom over her spectacles—kind of grinding him into the earth, you know. And then she says:

'Yes, you *better* turn y'r head away—I would if I was you, Tom.'

'Oh, deary me!' says Aunt Sally; 'is he changed so? Why, that ain't *Tom*, it's Sid; Tom's—Tom's—why, where is Tom? He was here a minute ago.'

'You mean where's Huck *Finn*—that's what you mean! I reckon I hain't raised such a scamp as my Tom all these years, not to know him when I *see* him. That *would* be a pretty howdy-do. Come out from under that bed, Huck Finn.'

So I done it. But not feeling brash.

Aunt Sally she was one of the mixed-upest looking persons I ever see; except one, and that was Uncle Silas, when he come in, and they told it all to him. It kind of made him drunk, as you may say, and he didn't know nothing at all the rest of the day, and preached a prayer-meeting sermon that night that give him a rattling ruputation, because the oldest man in the world couldn't a understood it. So Tom's Aunt Polly, she told all about who I was, and what; and I had to up and tell how I was in such a tight place that when Mrs Phelps took me for Tom

Sawyer—she chipped in and says, 'Oh, go on and call me Aunt Sally, I'm used to it, now, and 'tain't no need to change'—that when Aunt Sally took me for Tom Sawyer, I had to stand it—there warn't no other way, and I knowed he wouldn't mind, because it would be nuts for him, being a mystery, and he'd make an adventure out of it and be perfectly satisfied. And so it turned out, and he let on to be Sid, and made things as soft as he could for me.

And his Aunt Polly she said Tom was right about old Miss Watson setting Jim free in her will; and so, sure enough, Tom Sawyer had gone and took all that trouble and bother to set a free nigger free! and I couldn't ever understand, before, until that minute and that talk, how he *could* help a body set a nigger free, with his bringing-up.

Well, Aunt Polly she said that when Aunt Sally wrote to her that Tom and *Sid* had come, all right and safe, she says to herself:

'Look at that, now! I might have expected it, letting him go off that way without anybody to watch him. So now I got to go and trapse all the way down the river, eleven hundred mile, and find out what that creetur's up to, *this* time; as long as I couldn't seem to get any answer out of you about it.'

'Why, I never heard nothing from you,' says Aunt Sally.

'Well, I wonder! Why, I wrote to you twice, to ask you what you could mean by Sid being here.'

'Well, I never got 'em, Sis.'

Aunt Polly, she turns around slow and severe, and says:

'You, Tom!'

'Well—*what?*' he says, kind of pettish.

'Don't you what *me*, you impudent thing—hand out them letters.'

'What letters?'

'*Them* letters. I be bound, if I have to take aholt of you I'll—'

'They're in the trunk. There, now. And they're just the same as they was when I got them out of the office. I hain't looked into them, I hain't touched them. But I knowed they'd make trouble, and I thought if you warn't in no hurry, I'd—'

'Well, you *do* need skinning, there ain't no mistake about it. And I wrote another one to tell you I was coming; and I spose he—'

'No, it come yesterday; I hain't read it yet, but *it's* all right, I've got that one.'

I wanted to offer to bet two dollars she hadn't, but I reckoned maybe it was just as safe to not to. So I never said nothing.

CHAPTER THE LAST

The first time I catched Tom, private, I asked him what was his idea, time of the evasion?—what it was he'd planned to do if the evasion worked all right and he managed to set a nigger free that was already free before? And he said, what he had planned in his head, from the start, if we got Jim out all safe, was for us to run him down the river, on the raft, and have adventures plumb to the mouth of the river, and then tell him about his being free, and take him back up home on a steamboat, in style, and pay him for his lost time, and write word ahead and get out all the niggers around, and have them waltz him into town with a torchlight procession and a brass band, and then he would be a hero, and so would we. But I reckened it was about as well the way it was.

We had Jim out of the chains in no time, and when Aunt Polly and Uncle Silas and Aunt Sally found out how good he helped the doctor nurse Tom, they made a heap of fuss over him, and fixed him up prime, and give him all he wanted to eat, and a good time, and nothing to do. And we had him up to the sick-room; and had a high talk; and Tom give Jim forty dollars for being prisoner for us so patient, and doing it up so good, and Jim was pleased most to death, and busted out, and says:

'*Dah*, now, Huck, what I tell you?—what I tell you up dah on Jackson islan'? I *tole* you I got a hairy breas', en what's de sign un it; en I *tole* you I ben rich wunst, en gwineter to be rich *agin*; en it's come true en heah she *is*! *Dah*, now! doan' talk to *me*—signs is *signs*, mine I tell you; en I knowed jis' 's well 'at I 'uz gwineter be rich agin as I's a stannin' heah dis minute!'

And then Tom he talked along, and talked along, and says, le's all three slide out of here, one of these nights, and get an

321

outfit,[1] and go for howling adventures amongst the Injuns, over in the Territory,[2] for a couple of weeks or two; and I says, all right, that suits me, but I ain't got no money for to buy the outfit, and I reckon I couldn't get none from home, because it's likely pap's been back before now, and got it all away from Judge Thatcher and drunk it up.

'No he hain't,' Tom says; 'it's all there, yet—six thousand dollars and more; and your pap hain't ever been back since. Hadn't when I come away, anyhow.'

Jim says, kind of solemn:

'He ain't a comin' back no mo', Huck.'

I says:

'Why, Jim?'

'Nemmine why, Huck—but he ain't comin' back no mo'.'

But I kept at him; so at last he says:

'Doan' you 'member de house dat was float'n down de river, en dey wuz a man in dah, kivered up, en I went in en unkivered him and didn' let you come in? Well, den, you k'n git yo' money when you wants it; kase dat wuz him.'

Tom's most well, now, and got his bullet around his neck on a watch-guard[3] for a watch, and is always seeing what time it is, and so there ain't nothing more to write about, and I am rotten glad of it, because if I'd a knowed what a trouble it was to make a book I wouldn't a tackled it and ain't agoing to no more. But I reckon I got to light out for the Territory ahead of the rest, because Aunt Sally she's going to adopt me and sivilize me and I can't stand it. I been there before.

THE END. YOURS TRULY, HUCK FINN.

---

[1] *get an outfit*: get equipped. Tom might also be suggesting that they purchase Indian garb.

[2] *the Territory*: Indian Territory. See chapter 39, n. 5.

[3] *watch-guard*: strap or chain for a pocket watch.

Contemporary Criticism

Huckleberry Finn and American Revivalism

Anthony J. Berret, S.J.
Saint Joseph's University

In chapter 20 of *Huckleberry Finn*, Huck and the King attend a camp meeting in the woods outside Pokeville, a small town along the Mississippi. With nearly a thousand people present, the meeting includes preaching, singing, shouting, groaning, and sobbing, and the King brings the whole assembly to tears by a story about his conversion from piracy to apostleship. For his efforts, he gains eighty-seven dollars in collection money and steals a jug of whisky on the side. He calls the day one of his best "in the missionarying line".[1] This scene occurs near the center of Mark Twain's novel and represents the first fraudulent adventure of the King and the Duke, Huck's new traveling companions. The King, in fact, specializes in running temperance revivals, "workin' camp-meetin's, and missionaryin' around" (see p. 140). More of his phony religious exploits will follow. A longer version of this scene appears in Twain's original manuscript for the first half of *Huckleberry Finn*, discovered in 1990.[2] This longer version quotes an Isaac Watts hymn, "Am I a Soldier of the Cross"; adds movements and words to the preacher's exhortation; and focuses the wild activity around the mourners' bench on a black woman who tackles and smothers the white mourners, wallowing with them in the straw and "shouting glory hallelujah".[3]

---

[1] Mark Twain, *Adventures of Huckleberry Finn*, ed. Mary R. Reichardt (San Francisco: Ignatius Press, 2009), p. 153. Subsequent quotations from this edition will be cited in the text.

[2] Victor Doyno, "Forward to the Text", *Adventures of Huckleberry Finn*, by Mark Twain (New York: Random House, 1996), pp. xiii–xvii.

[3] *Adventures of Huckleberry Finn* (Random House), pp. 177–81. This edition of the book prints select passages from Twain's original manuscript, including the camp meeting scene.

Critics tend to view the camp meeting scene as a satire or parody of religious revivals and the emotionalism and hypocrisy exhibited in them. Along with other critics, Victor Doyno relates the scene to an earlier comic sketch by Johnson J. Hooper, "The Captain Attends a Camp-Meeting", which also includes a fake and very lucrative conversion story and a convulsive black woman jumping on a white man.[4] Doyno argues, however, that Twain "transformed this low comic incident" concerning the black woman by letting the woman hear the preacher's words, "one more shake and the chains are broken", as a possible liberation from slavery. Doyno also guesses that Twain may have trimmed his original description of the camp meeting in order to maintain a clear contrast between the false conversions of other characters in the novel and Huck's true growth.[5]

Huck does grow in the novel, and he also experiences a true conversion, though he may not think so or describe it as one, and conversions were the main purpose of revivals. If *Huckleberry Finn* tells the story of Huck's conversion, the camp meeting scene functions as a model or paradigm of what happens to Huck and to the reader throughout the whole novel. The scene may parody religion and revivals, as many critics have argued, but it could also mix the effects of parody and paradigm like the Shakespeare scenes that follow it. While the King bellows in the role of Juliet and stumbles practicing the swordfight from *Richard III*, the two Shakespeare scenes reflect in a distorted way the romance and tragedy between members of the feuding Grangerford and Shepherdson families in chapter 18 and the Boggs-Sherburn incident in chapter 21.[6] The

[4] Victor Doyno, "Textual Addendum", in *Adventures of Huckleberry Finn*, p. 379. For Hooper's sketch and a similar connection with Twain, see "Simon Suggs Attends a Camp-Meeting", in *The Comic Tradition in America*, ed. Kenneth S. Lynn (Garden City, N.Y.: Doubleday, 1958), pp. 105–19. Lynn sees Hooper's sketch as a satire on sexual license and unlearned preaching at camp meetings.

[5] Doyno, "Textual Addendum", in *Adventures of Huckleberry Finn*, pp. 380–81.

[6] For the mixture of parody and paradigm in these and other Shakespeare scenes, see Anthony J. Berret, "The Influence of *Hamlet* on *Huckleberry Finn*", *American Literary Realism 1870–1910* 18, nos. 1–2 (Spring and Autumn 1985):

King and the Duke even call their motley Shakespeare pro-
gram a "revival" (see p. 158).

Camp meetings represent the kind of religious revivals that
took place on the southwestern American frontier during the
first half of the nineteenth century. They constitute part of
the so-called Second Great Awakening after the first Great
Awakening that occurred in the Northeast in the mid-1700s.[7]
In his book *And They All Sang Hallelujah*, Dickson D. Bruce
describes the background, purpose, layout, personnel, and activ-
ities of these camp meetings. In the early 1800s, large numbers of Americans moved west and settled on small farms spread
over wide areas of the southwestern frontier—Kentucky, Tennessee, and western North Carolina. Since church members,
meeting houses, and full-time resident ministers were few
and far apart, itinerant or part-time preachers gathered large
numbers of people into camp meetings in order to gain new
converts and to revive and strengthen the scattered church
members and give them a sense of a broader faith community.[8] To accommodate large numbers, sometimes in the thousands, these meetings were held outdoors, usually in wooded
areas that provided material for temporary platforms, pulpits,
and benches. The people slept in tents. As the meeting pro-
ceeded with hymns, prayers, and sermons, prospective converts came forward to the "mourners' bench" or "anxious seat"
just below the pulpit, and the preacher, along with associates
both clerical and lay, mingled with the mourners and exhorted
them toward conversion. Exhortations often involved personal

197, and *Mark Twain and Shakespeare: A Cultural Legacy* (Lanham, Md.: University Press of America, 1993), pp. 170–72.

[7] For a general history of American revivals, see Bernard A. Weisberger, *They
Gathered at the River: The Story of the Great Revivalists and Their Impact upon
Religion in America* (Boston, Mass.: Little, Brown, 1958), and William G. McLough-
lin, *Revivals, Awakenings, and Reform: An Essay on Religion and Social Change in
America, 1607–1977* (Chicago: University of Chicago Press, 1978).

[8] Dickson D. Bruce Jr., *And They All Sang Hallelujah: Plain-Folk Camp-
Meeting Religion, 1800–1845* (Knoxville, Tenn.: University of Tennessee Press,
1974), pp. 38–39, 45, 50–51.

accounts or testimonials of conversions by the minister and his helpers, and the mourners told their stories too. These accounts describing progress from the world and sin to conversion included a tense and painful transition period of "conviction" when the sinner has rejected his old life but has not yet attained the peace and assurance of a new one. During this anxious mourning period, sinners and others might shout, cry, and bark, or fall and roll on the ground, jerking and twitching their bodies in spiritual turmoil. Exhorters assisted them through this ordeal toward a peaceful and assured completion.[9]

Many of these traits appear in the camp meeting described in Twain's published and manuscript versions of *Huckleberry Finn*. In a wooded setting with platforms, pulpits, and benches, dynamic singing and preaching lead people to the mourners' bench, shouting, groaning, and throwing themselves on the straw-covered ground. The King gives a testimonial of his conversion, recounting how he lost his pirate crew and all his money but landed "a changed man" and would now evangelize the pirates of the Indian Ocean (see p. 152). Of course, his whole story is false, but even that fact is consistent with revivals because preachers and exhorters had to correct and interpret such testimonials to protect people against false prophets.[10] Unfortunately, the King fools them this time. Besides frauds like the King, vendors and courting couples were also found at camp meetings, as Twain writes, along with hecklers and detached observers, so revival leaders had to fight against

[9] See ibid., chap. 3, especially pp. 61–62 (accounts), 68–69 (stages), 73–77 (personnel), and 85–87 (acts). Mark Twain could have read about Southwestern camp meetings in a book that he owned, *Autobiography of Peter Cartwright, the Backwoods Preacher*, ed. W. P. Strickland (New York: Carlton and Porter, 1857). Cartwright writes often about hostile speakers at revivals and about the topic of slavery. Twain also read travel accounts of revivals like those in Frances Trollope's *Domestic Manners of the Americans* (1832; repr., New York: Alfred A. Knopf, 1949). On Twain's owning or reading these works, see Alan Gribben, *Mark Twain's Library: A Reconstruction* (Boston: G. K. Hall, 1980), p. 131 on Cartwright and p. 713 on Trollope.

[10] Bruce, *Hallelujah*, pp. 61–62.

hostility and apathy and try constantly to discern truth from falsehood in the stories that people told.[11]

This last aspect of revivals applies most importantly to the entire story of *Huckleberry Finn*. Personal accounts like the King's fake testimonial occur throughout the novel. In a sense, they turn the whole book into a kind of camp meeting or revival. Both Huck and the reader find themselves constantly having to separate fact from fiction to determine the truth of these stories. Even Huck himself, the principal "convicted mourner" of the novel, tells tales that the reader must correct and interpret, including the overall story he is relating in his book.

To create a religious setting for these stories, and therefore to make them seem like testimonials at a revival, Twain distributes through his novel images related to the biblical Moses and the story of the Exodus. Two such images appear in his camp meeting scene: the "brazen serpent in the wilderness" in both the published and the manuscript versions (from Num 21:9), and the "rock of salvation" in the manuscript version (from Ex 17:6 and Deut 32:15). Both the serpent and the rock prove the divine power of Moses by miraculously curing snakebites and producing water in the desert. At the very beginning of *Huckleberry Finn*, the Widow Douglas, who adopts Huck and tries to "sivilize" him, reads to him about "Moses and the Bulrushers", but he loses interest when he learns that Moses is dead (see pp. 5–6). Like Moses, however, Huck too is found— not by Pharaoh's daughter but by the widow and Miss Watson— and like Moses, he is found by a river (Ex 2:1–10). Moses turns up again in a riddle told by Buck Grangerford, "Where was Moses when the candle went out?" but the literal-minded Huck does not understand (see p. 113). To get news about slave hunters during his and Jim's escape, Huck disguises himself as a girl, goes ashore, and tells Mrs. Judith Loftus that he is looking for his uncle in Goshen (see p. 72). The Jews, who lived in Goshen, were spared from the plagues inflicted on

[11] Ibid., p. 79.

other parts of Egypt (Ex 8:22; 9:26). When the King and the Duke sell the Wilks family's slaves, some go to Memphis (see p. 207), the place where the prophet Hosea predicts that the Jews will return to in slavery if they do not mend their evil ways (Hos 9:6). Besides Goshen and Memphis, the name of another Egyptian city, Cairo, appears several times in the novel. Although not in the Bible, Cairo, the one bright hope for Jim's escape, continues Twain's association of the Mississippi River with the Nile and Egypt and Huck and Jim's escape with the Exodus.

The Exodus stood out as a prominent image of the revival or camp meeting. For example, an 1859 book on revivals, *Manna in the Wilderness*, constantly relates camp meetings to the different stages of the Exodus.[12] Moreover, the thousands of people who left their farms or towns and camped in the woods easily compared themselves to the Israelites in the desert. Egypt represented the old life left behind and Canaan the new converted life or Promised Land, and both involved waterways, crossing the Red Sea from the old and the Jordan River into the new. Sacred songs from camp meetings often referred to the Jordan and Canaan: "And We'll Pass Over Jordan" and "On Jordan's Stormy Banks I Stand".[13] In Twain's novel, the Mississippi River stands for both the Red Sea and the Jordan River in offering escape from bondage as well as hope and visions of freedom. Furthermore, with its fog and storms, floating houses of sin and death, and a sinking steamboat with robbers aboard, it marks the transitional state, the middle passage of conviction, mourning, and anxiety, where souls fight a battle between the world and religion. Chapters 16 and 17 of Exodus describe a similar state in which manna falls from Heaven and water flows from a rock, but the Israelites murmur against Moses and put God to the test, still yearning for the fleshpots of Egypt.

---

[12] A. P. Mead, *Manna in the Wilderness; or, The Grove and Its Altar, Offerings, and Thrilling Incidents* (Philadelphia, Pa.: Perkinpine and Higgins, 1859).

[13] See Bruce, *Hallelujah*, pp. 90, 101, 103–4, 107, 115–17.

In this conflicted spiritual setting, various characters in *Huckleberry Finn* approach the mourners' bench to testify. First comes Pap Finn, Huck's poor, alcoholic, abusive, and racist father. When a new and naïve judge hears Pap's plea for custody of Huck and for control of Huck's recently discovered treasure, the judge pities him and takes Pap into his own home to reform him. Pap bursts into tears and resolves "to turn over a new leaf" (see p. 28). After tears, kisses, and hugs from members of the judge's family, Pap bids them shake "the hand of a man that's started in on a new life", and he even agrees to sign a temperance pledge (see p. 28). However, that very night he gets drunk, falls out the window, and breaks his arm. This typical conversion scene has emotion and dramatic change, but like the King's false pirate story, it needs interpretation and correction by a perceptive minister. Even if momentarily true, Pap's change of heart is too short-lived and financially motivated to be authentic. Since the naïve judge cannot respond to it adequately, the reader must supply the corrections.

Sometimes Huck himself can see through false testimonials. Shortly before the King delivers his pirate story at the camp meeting, both he and the Duke engage Huck and Jim with tearful accounts, if not of conversion at least of confession, about how they mishandled their lives. The Duke, for instance, blames himself for his misfortune: "I brought myself down— yes, I did it myself. It's right I should suffer" (see p. 141). He relates how he allowed the "cold world" to take everything away from him—family, property, and status. Actually, both con men admit to the falsehoods involved in their rackets, but then they concoct stories about noble birth in order to gain more sympathy. Huck soon realizes that they are humbugs but plays along with them just for comfortable living. But Huck also thinks that Jim believes the King and Duke are really royalty, and this obvious stretch may caution readers to step in and correct Huck. This need for reader correction happens many times in the novel, both to keep the readers alert and to remind them that they are experiencing their own testing and conversion as well as Huck's.

Jim too speaks at length often during the novel, and some of his speeches may be viewed as testimony. Although the races and genders were separated at the start of a camp meeting, when the time came to exhort converts around the mourners' bench, anyone could speak. Temporarily erasing the lines of age, race, gender, and office dramatized the transitional nature of the convicted state. Social orders belonged to the old world, which floated in suspension while the potential convert struggled to embrace the new. One camp meeting observer marveled at this blurring of social lines: "To see a *bold* Kentuckian (undaunted by the horrors of war) turn pale and tremble at the reproof of a weak woman, a little boy, or a poor African ... who could say the change was not supernatural?"[14] Throughout *Huckleberry Finn*, Jim speaks in various capacities—prophet, admonisher, interpreter of dreams—all with quasi-religious overtones, though not necessarily Christian. Still, some of Jim's stories come close to revival testimonies. On Jackson's Island, before giving Huck an account of his escape, Jim looks "pretty uneasy", hesitates, and wonders whether he should talk or not and whether Huck will tell on him (see p. 51). These guiltylike gestures make his story similar to a confession. Also, at the end of his escape story, Jim tells three brief stories about investing money and losing, the third of which relates his lending a dime to a man named Balaam and hoping to get it back a hundredfold. Although he loses even the dime, Jim rejoices, "I's rich now ... I owns myself" (see p. 57). To lose the world and gain himself makes Jim a kind of convert. The biblical story of Balaam and his ass occurs in the later stages of the Exodus, when the Israelites approach the towns of Canaan (Num 22–23). Balaam himself is a dreamer and diviner, something like Jim.

But Jim's most confessional story concerns an incident with his family. As he relates to Huck, when he told his daughter to shut a door and she did not obey him, he slapped her hard.

---

[14] Quoted in Bruce, *Hallelujah*, p. 87; see also pp. 73, 86, 132.

Then when the wind causes the door to slam and she does not react, he realizes she has gone deaf by smallpox and he trembles, cries, and hugs her, begging God for forgiveness. He moans and mourns as he tells the story to Huck (see pp. 177–78). This incident portrays Jim as a mourner who has done wrong and repents of it. Jim acts as an admonisher when he berates Huck for lying to him after the fog episode (see pp. 98–100). This echoes, in a way, Twain's and Hooper's accounts of the black woman jumping on the white mourner.

Women too spoke at camp meetings to testify on their own conversions or to exhort other wavering mourners.[15] Although no women in *Huckleberry Finn* give long testimonials, an important conversion of a type takes place behind the scenes. Toward the end of the novel, when Tom Sawyer learns that his complicated "evasion" plot to free Jim has failed, Tom announces that, at her death, Miss Watson set Jim free in her will because she felt ashamed about planning to sell him down the river (see p. 318). Earlier, when Jim told Huck about his escape, he mentioned that the Widow Douglas and Miss Watson had left town for the day to attend a camp meeting, and that gave him time to run off without detection for several hours (see p. 53). So the accident of a camp meeting helped Jim escape, but was there also intentionality here on Twain's part? Perhaps he suggests that Miss Watson changed her mind about slavery because of the camp meeting. Revival preachers, even in the South, often spoke against slavery and urged converts to emancipate their slaves. This policy held for the Methodist church and for many Baptist congregations as well until the southwestern frontier became more heavily populated, richer, and more organized. Only in the mid-1840s did these churches ally themselves with the South at large in supporting or ignoring slavery and breaking off from their Northern members.[16] Assuming that Twain set his novel at a time before that happened, imagine what Miss Watson's conversion story would sound like. She

---

[15] Ibid., pp. 76, 86.
[16] Ibid., pp. 57–59.

had once warned Huck about "the bad place" (see p. 7). Perhaps she worried about going there herself.

Finally, children too were permitted to speak at camp meetings.[17] Huck exercises a privilege like this in the stories he tells to other characters and in the story he tells to readers in the book as a whole, especially in the passages where he grapples with his conscience. Several times in the novel, Huck has to explain himself to others either to escape from tight situations or to protect Jim, and the stories he tells follow a set pattern. For example, when a steamboat runs over the raft and he washes ashore at the Grangerfords' plantation, he tells the Grangerfords that except for his father his family has either run off or died, lost their home and most of their money, and that finally his father died too (see p. 114). He tells almost the same story to Judith Loftus twice (see pp. 67, 72), to a ferryman (see p. 85), to slave hunters (see p. 104), and to the King and the Duke (see p. 145). All of these stories concern loss of land and loved ones, and Huck cries or "blubbers" while he tells them. Although all of the stories are false, they are true in a sense because Huck really did lose his family and he has lost Pap too, even though he does not know this through most of the novel. The crushing losses that Huck describes resemble the world or old life that converts must leave behind, and the emotions with which he recounts these losses, along with the emotions of those who hear or read about them, resemble the atmosphere around the mourners' bench.

Of course, losses make up only half of a conversion story. Spiritual gains should follow from them. Huck's moral conversion—his spiritual gain—occurs during the bouts with his conscience over Jim's freedom. In chapter 16, when he and Jim think that they are nearing Cairo and possible freedom, Huck's conscience begins to torture him for stealing a slave. He describes his feelings as "trembly", "feverish", "scorched", "mean", "low", and "miserable", and he wishes that he was dead. As he weighs the effects of turning Jim in, however, he decides

[17] Ibid., pp. 73–74, 76.

that he would feel just as bad about that and that the wages of right and wrong are, therefore, the same (see p. 106). Huck's moral dilemma reflects the ordeal of converts in the convicted state, somewhere between the old and the new. The river setting of night, fog, and a thickly wooded shore adds to the moral obscurity of the scene. No lights reveal Cairo, the way to freedom.

Huck suffers a second and more decisive battle with his conscience in chapter 31. The King and the Duke have just sold Jim, and Huck wavers between writing a letter to Miss Watson and helping Jim escape. He feels the same as he did previously—"low down", "ornery", and "wicked"—and he cannot even pray. People on the mourners' bench often complained of this inability to pray.[18] Huck tries writing the letter, but then he recalls how close he and Jim have become, how Jim stood his watch, how he lied to slave hunters for Jim, and how Jim rejoiced and petted him when Huck came out of the feud alive (see pp. 238–39). Trembling and holding his breath, Huck tears up the letter and resolves to help Jim escape, assuming that he will go to Hell for doing so. He is mistaken, of course. Converts in the convicted state often worried about damnation, even when they were making the right choices.[19] So it is left to the reader to exhort Huck to persevere through this transitional and anxious state. Since social orders and laws float in suspension during this state and therefore do not bind him, Huck rightly rejects them and the conscience that supports them. Instead, he follows what seems to be here the true criteria of conversion: personal experience and emotion, and memories of the pleasant times, sufferings, and sacrifices that he has experienced with Jim and the hugs, kisses, and tears that accompanied these incidents.[20]

[18] Ibid., p. 66.

[19] Ibid., pp. 65–66.

[20] Norris W. Yates calls Huck's conversion a "counter-conversion" because Huck sees a contradiction between official goodness (allowing slavery) and actual goodness (freeing a slave) and therefore has to choose against what he thinks is official religion. See "The 'Counter-Conversion' of Huckleberry Finn", *American Literature* 32 (March 1960): 1–10.

In the end Huck survives conviction to reach a state of assurance, though in a roundabout and comic way. When he arrives at the Phelps plantation, he does not have to make up some fictitious name or sob story, although, as usual, he is quite prepared to do so. To his surprise, the family welcomes him as their relative, Tom Sawyer. The way that Huck describes this incident has profound religious meaning. He says that "it was like being born again" (see p. 249). The symbolism is further supported when he meets the real Tom Sawyer. Tom, assuming that Huck was killed, thinks that he sees a ghost, but Huck reassures him: "You come in here and feel of me if you don't believe me" (see p. 251). These words echo what Jesus said to another Thomas who had doubts about his Resurrection (Jn 20:27). In fact, these scenes fit into a series of apparent rebirths that occur through the novel. Like Tom, Jim at first fears Huck as a ghost when he meets him on Jackson's Island just after his escape (see p. 50), he rejoices that Huck is not dead but come back again after they were separated in the fog (see p. 97), and he is glad again when he finds that Huck has survived the feud (see p. 133). These near-death experiences and escapes are more than just adventures with happy endings. They signify moral triumphs over such evils as family feuds and slavery, and they dramatize the progress, gravity, and successful outcome of Huck's conversion.

Of course, both Tom's Romantic exploits and Huck's plan fail to free Jim. Miss Watson finally sets him free. When the camp meeting ends, social order and law return. The converts, who undergo a rigorous personal change and choose the righteous path, have to return to an imperfect order. However, they are still expected to complete the good resolutions they made in the revival in a legal and acceptable way, which in Jim's case is accomplished through his emancipation. Huck made the right resolution and tried to carry it out in the only way that he could, but the owner, Miss Watson, frees Jim, and for her it may or may not be the result of a conversion. Although by her legal act of emancipation Miss Watson provides *Huckleberry Finn* with a happy ending, the dependence of enslaved persons on the wills of their owners for freedom causes Huck, perhaps, to flee an imperfect civilization and "light out for the Territory" (see p. 322).

Although largely a skeptic, Twain was interested in religion, and scholars continue to be fascinated by its influence on his writings and in his personal life. Recent studies of the topic include such titles as *Mark Twain's Religion*, *The Reverend Mark Twain*, *The Bible according to Mark Twain*, and *Mark Twain and the Spiritual Crisis of His Age*. As we have seen, the unique genre of American revivals or camp meetings provides a paradigm that shows that what initially may seem opposed to religious belief—doubt, conflict, and change—are actually integral to the faith experience. In addition, certain aspects of revivals, such as testimonies consisting of multiple points of view and unreliable narration, mirror literary techniques. As in a revival, we as readers of *Huckleberry Finn* must sift through many falsehoods in order to ascertain the truth. We respond to Huck's narrative like those who, in a revival, surround the mourners' bench: correcting, praising, and exhorting. Finally, since issues of race and slavery loom large in the novel, the revival, at least as it occurred on the southwestern frontier, provides a model of an ideal albeit unsettled period when all persons—black, white, male, female, children—are equal and boundaries removed in the light of ultimate equality before God. One should not have to oppose religion to free a slave, and Huck's "testimony" to this fact is that which endures.

Bibliography

Berret, Anthony J. "The Influence of *Hamlet* on *Huckleberry Finn*". *American Literary Realism 1870–1910* 18, nos. 1–2 (Spring and Autumn 1985): 196–207.

———. *Mark Twain and Shakespeare: A Cultural Legacy*. Lanham, Md.: University Press of America, 1993.

Bruce, Dickson D., Jr. *And They All Sang Hallelujah: Plain-Folk Camp-Meeting Religion, 1800–1845*. Knoxville, Tenn.: University of Tennessee Press, 1974.

Doyno, Victor. Foreword to *Adventures of Huckleberry Finn*, by Mark Twain. New York: Random House, 1996.

Gribben, Alan. *Mark Twain's Library: A Reconstruction*. Boston: G. K. Hall, 1980.

Lynn, Kenneth S., ed. *The Comic Tradition in America*. Garden City, N.Y.: Doubleday, 1958.

McLoughlin, William G. *Revivals, Awakenings, and Reform: An Essay on Religion and Social Change in America, 1607–1977*. Chicago: University of Chicago Press, 1978.

Mead, A. P. *Manna in the Wilderness; or, The Grove and Its Altar, Offerings, and Thrilling Incidents*. Philadelphia, Pa.: Perkinpine and Higgins, 1859.

Strickland, W. P., ed. *Autobiography of Peter Cartwright, the Backwoods Preacher*. New York: Carlton and Porter, 1857.

Trollope, Frances. *Domestic Manners of the Americans*. 1832. Reprint, New York: Alfred A. Knopf, 1949.

Weisberger, Bernard A. *They Gathered at the River: The Story of the Great Revivalists and Their Impact upon Religion in America*. Boston, Mass.: Little, Brown, 1958.

Yates, Norris W. "The 'Counter-Conversion' of Huckleberry Finn". *American Literature* 32 (March 1960): 1–10.

Huckleberry Finn as a Response to Romanticism[1]

William F. Byrne
Saint John's University

Literature, film, and other art forms serve as more than just entertainment. They are transmitters of values. That is, such works reflect their creators' understandings of reality and help to shape the views of those who experience them. One way in which they do this is by offering models from which to learn; we can become better people by imitating sound models and by rejecting bad ones. If literary works influence society and culture, then a work as enduringly popular as *Adventures of Huckleberry Finn* must be influential indeed. Much of this novel's moral, political, and literary significance is wrapped up in its relationship to Romanticism, and this is the topic that is explored in this essay.

Romanticism emerged in the eighteenth century and peaked in the nineteenth century, but is still very much with us today. Although it is commonly considered an aesthetic (or artistic) movement, its influence extends beyond literature, art, and music to politics and to one's general approach to life. It tends to emphasize strong emotion, ranging from an uplifting sense of awe to a sublime sense of mystery to gut-wrenching horror. Rejecting the humdrum and ordinary, Romantic literature and art often feature heroic figures as well as strange and exotic people and places. A fascination with the Middle Ages is some-times evident. This makes sense, since Romanticism is gener-ally seen as a reaction against modernity in general and the Enlightenment in particular.

The Enlightenment, an eighteenth-century philosophical, political, and social movement, helped to define the modern

[1] Portions of this essay were adapted, with permission, from William F. Byrne, "Realism, Romanticism, and Politics in Mark Twain", *Humanitas* 12, no. 1 (1999): 16–41, published by the National Humanities Institute.

world. It emphasized "reason", which it understood (incorrectly, some would argue) to operate in opposition to tradition, to emotion, and, for many, to religious belief. Since the Enlightenment, some people have found the resulting world to be cold, mundane, and disenchanted. Although Romanticism is usually not religious, it represents an attempt to fill a void left by a decline in piety, a loss of a sense of the sacred, and a general loss of a sense of meaning in the modern era.

Just as aspects of the modern world sparked the reaction of Romanticism, by the latter 1800s reactions to Romanticism were appearing. One reaction in the United States was the emergence of the "school" of American literary realism, centered on the author and literary critic William Dean Howells. Although Mark Twain's precise relationship to this "school" is debated, he was a friend of Howells and can be broadly classified as a fellow realist—which meant more than anything an anti-Romantic. Twain's opposition to Romanticism appears in a variety of his works, including *A Connecticut Yankee in King Arthur's Court*, which, among other things, aimed to dispel popular Romantic images of the Middle Ages. However, his most important work addressing Romanticism is *Adventures of Huckleberry Finn*.

In both *Huckleberry Finn* and *The Adventures of Tom Sawyer*, Twain uses the characters of Tom and Huck to illustrate the Romantic imagination. While Tom possesses an extraordinarily vivid boyish imagination, Huck is strangely lacking in one, as if the harsh conditions of his life have forced him to focus exclusively on mundane realities. Tom's imagination is put on display at the beginning of *Huckleberry Finn* with his "band of robbers". Tom's vision for the gang is shamelessly Romantic; at the same time, it is slavishly imitative. He has filled his head with Romantic adventure stories—the dominant literature of the time—and wants to recreate a specific vision set down "in the books". Huck, however, complains that he "couldn't see no profit in it" and that it "was only just one of Tom Sawyer's lies."[2] It is not long before all the boys resign from the "band", abandoning Tom. The shift from *Tom Sawyer* is significant. *Tom Sawyer* is primarily a children's book, and, as many have observed, children tend to be Romantics. So it would have been a very inappropriate place for a vigorous attack on Romanticism. In contrast, *Huckleberry Finn* was written primarily for adults, so here Twain does not hesitate to signal that he is at war with the Romantic imagination.

Although Twain's portrait of Tom and his imagination is unflattering, we are all familiar with such childhood fantasies and are prepared to dismiss them as harmless, even healthy. But Twain wants to convince us that Romanticism is not just silly but downright dangerous. A key example occurs in the latter part of the book after Jim has been captured and Huck is reunited with Tom. While freeing Jim could be accomplished quite easily, Tom is not about to pass up a golden opportunity to live out his fantasies. He has learned from his adventure books that the crude but efficient methods preferred by Huck and Jim are not suitable for a Romantic hero. Tom therefore concocts a "stylish" but outlandishly elaborate scheme that prolongs Jim's captivity. Following the "best authorities", Tom also wants to bring Jim rats to train as pets in his "prison cell" and wants Jim to grow a flower and water it with his tears. Tom also designs for Jim a coat of arms, displaying impressive albeit tangled knowledge of heraldic terms and devices. And, by sending Jim's captors warnings of the upcoming escape attempt, Tom greatly increases their chances of getting caught.

Tom's antics mask the fact that this is deadly serious business. Jim originally ran away from slavery in Saint Petersburg because he was to be separated from his wife and children. His only hope to be reunited is to escape to freedom and then

[2] Mark Twain, *Adventures of Huckleberry Finn*, ed. Mary R. Reichardt (San Francisco: Ignatius Press, 2009), p. 20. Subsequent quotations from this edition will be cited in the text.

buy them. Thus, although Tom professes to be helping Jim, his actual callousness is striking. He sees Jim and his plight simply as material to be exploited for the purpose of attaining his Romantic vision. Increasingly, it becomes evident that Tom has difficulty distinguishing between fantasy and reality. When he gets shot and Huck is about to go for help, Tom is still living the fantasy, telling him to "blindfold the doctor tight and fast . . . and put a purse full of gold in his hand" (see p. 304). Since Tom actually knows that the Widow Douglas has set Jim free in her will, he is prolonging Jim's captivity and risking all of their lives merely for the selfish purpose of creating a Romantic adventure for himself.

Behind the facade of boyish fun, Twain has accomplished a devastating portrayal of some of the dangers lurking in the Romantic imagination. Tom feels compelled to be a Romantic hero. However, since Jim has technically already been set free, the best Tom can do is to be a fake hero, but even this illusion of heroism is so important to Tom that he becomes a villain of a sort in order to create it, forsaking the real interests of his own friends. The need to attain a Romantic vision is allowed to overrule the demands of reality, resulting not only in foolishness but in something bordering on cruelty. This latter part of the book, full of Tom's antics, is a jarring shift from the middle of the book, dominated by Huck and Jim's trip down the river. As some commentators have maintained, the tiresome quality of the book's last section does not represent a failure by Twain but a definite purpose: "[H]e tries to separate the reader's viewpoint even further from the narrator's at the end—by making the reader sick and tired of all the boyish tricks."[3] It is important to note, however, that it is not just "boyish tricks" that we grow tired of but Tom's Romanticism, which is fueling them.

Twain sees Tom's imagination as the shaper and driver of his will. On the one hand, Tom is hindered by his Romanticism since it distances him from reality, impairing both the

---

[3] Catherine H. Zuckert, *Natural Right and the American Imagination* (Savage, Md.: Rowman and Littlefield, 1990), p. 149.

effectiveness and morality of his actions in the real world and leading him into trouble. On the other hand, Tom's imagination provides him with unusual energy, spurring him to action. Adventure novels, supplemented by a Romantic and fragmentary reading of history and geography, have become Tom's idealized models for life. He has become dissatisfied with his mundane life in Saint Petersburg and wants to lead the life of a Romantic hero. A problem exists here: the real world, at least the vast majority of the time, is not much like an adventure novel. Tom nevertheless wants to be important, special, a man with "style", and to accomplish this he needs to recreate in the real world the Romantic images that he has encountered. To do this he needs to secure the cooperation of others.

Thus, Tom's Romantic yearnings appear in part as a drive to dominate those around him. He develops a strong will. His Romanticism is also manifest in his high level of activity and creativity, which gives him a certain charisma and makes him attractive to others. Tom is a natural leader who achieves a certain success, but his plans end in disaster. This occurs because the original vision was not solidly grounded in reality; the real world ultimately cannot conform to it. In fact, in putting his plans into action, Tom downplays or ignores important real-world considerations because they conflict with the vision. Further, attempts to resolve the incompatibility between the Romantic vision and the real world prompt Tom to take actions that are at best inconsiderate and at worst downright immoral.

What is particularly troubling is Huck's response. For one thing, he does not seem to mind that Tom has deceived them. More importantly, Huck goes along with the elaborate and prolonged scheme to free Jim. Of course, Huck is unaware at this point of Tom's deception. Still, numerous opportunities exist for Jim to escape easily, but Huck encourages Jim to stick to Tom's plans instead. Why does Huck do this? After all, although he is uneducated, he is clearly not stupid, and at times he demonstrates exceptional resourcefulness and good sense for a boy. Nevertheless, he allows Tom to dominate him. Perhaps Huck has learned too well the art of meeting the world on its own

terms. His adaptability serves him well under most circumstances but makes him too accommodating in the face of a
dominating will armed with a Romantic vision. Unlike Tom,
Huck has no delusions of grandeur, and he thus has little trouble deferring to others. Even though he does not fully share in
Tom's fantasies, he is impressed by the elaborateness and drama
of Tom's plan and automatically takes it to be superior to his
own.

Lacking an active boyish imagination and anchored solely
in his immediate physical world, Huck tends to become bored
easily, as we see, for example, on Jackson's Island. This need
for excitement may make him more dependent upon Tom.
Huck wants Tom's leadership and is willing to put up with
quite a lot for it. The early twentieth-century literary scholar
Irving Babbitt, a strong critic of Romanticism, has observed
that "the poet who reduces poetry to the imaginative quest
of strange emotional adventure, and the plain citizen who
does not aspire beyond a reality that is too literal and pro-
saic, both suffer."[4] The friendship between Huck and Tom
may reflect an intuitive awareness by Twain of a close relationship between these two approaches to life and a sense
that neither approach is really correct. The friendship also
has political implications.

Energized by their need to live out Romantic visions—and
by their egos, which Romantic visions can feed—some
Romantics can become charismatic leaders. Others follow them
because they too adopt the Romantic vision, because the leader
meets other needs, or because they lack a sense of meaning
and purpose and hence desire leadership. The leader's plans,
however, often end in disaster. This occurs because they are
not grounded in a firm sense of reality, including ethical reality, and as a result they tend to be both impractical and
immoral. Twain's friend Howells had "ideas about the
connection between literary 'romanticism' and political

[4] Irving Babbitt, *Rousseau and Romanticism* (New Brunswick, N.J.: Transaction, 1991), p. 88.

tyranny."[5] Just a few decades after Twain wrote *Huckleberry Finn*, Europe would see the rise of revolutionary totalitarian mass movements with strong Romantic dimensions. Though secular and even anti-Christian, these political movements also served in part as substitutes for the traditional religiosity and sense of meaning that had eroded in Europe. Mussolini, for example, explicitly and repeatedly called Fascism a "spiritual" movement.[6] It is unlikely that Twain would have been much surprised by the rise of such movements or by how they turned out.

Twain offers a more complex and sympathetic treatment of Romanticism in the episode of the Grangerford-Shepherdson feud. In the case of Tom Sawyer, the pursuit of Romantic ideals involves hypocrisy and fraud; when considering whether to write a book about Tom's growing up, Twain concluded that "if I went on now and took him into manhood, he would just lie, like all the one-horse men in literature, and the reader would conceive a hearty contempt for him."[7] In contrast, one does not have immediate contempt for the Grangerfords who take Huck in. Their nobility is not completely phony; in some respects one could argue that they truly are embodiments of such virtues as honor, courage, duty, kindness, and generosity. They are not trying to dominate or "lord it over" anyone else. Nor do they, like Tom Sawyer, spend their time in a world of fantasy. Their fantasy has become reality. Armed with their ideals and with romanticized models such as the heroes of the American Revolution, the Grangerfords have developed high standards of behavior and generally live up to them. They certainly stand in marked contrast to the seedy and shiftless characters who tend to populate *Huckleberry Finn*. The Grangerfords have in a sense actually become Romantic heroes. They want

[5] Michael Davitt Bell, *The Problem of American Realism* (Chicago: University of Chicago Press, 1993), p. 69.

[6] See, for example, the rhetoric in Mussolini's *Doctrine of Fascism* (New York: Howard Fertig, 2006).

[7] Van Wyck Brooks, *The Ordeal of Mark Twain*, rev. ed. (New York: E. Dutton, 1933), p. 25.

to be noble, and they understand that this requires more than surface appearances; they have not tried to live out their Romantic dreams "on the cheap" as Tom has with mere illusions of heroism. The problem, of course, is the feud itself. They are killing others and deliberately perpetuating a situation that places their lives, including the lives of young boys, at great risk for no good reason. Why would otherwise good and reasonable people do something as shockingly foolish and immoral as this?

Something, it appears, has become more important to the Grangerfords than the lives of their family members. One possibility could be their hatred for the Shepherdsons, but there is no indication of this and they clearly admire their foes. Another possibility is an exaggerated and twisted sense of honor that stops them from coming to terms with their enemies. This may be closer to the mark, but Twain never brings out this point. More than anything, Twain creates the impression that the two families have made what would today be called a "lifestyle choice". In this alternative lifestyle, neighbors shoot each other. They have chosen it because it fits so well with their Romantic vision. The feud provides a perfect opportunity for them to build and demonstrate virtues like courage, duty, and honor.

Although their virtues have a degree of reality, something is rotten at the core. The feud is not a just cause, and one cannot be truly virtuous while valuing human life so cheaply. Ultimately, the Grangerfords are living a lie; imagery has won out over reality. Again, immorality and disaster result from the attempt to bridge the gap between Romantic visions and the real world. Because the model that inspires the families is not firmly anchored in reality, it has skewed their priorities and warped their perception of the world, devaluing their lives and the lives of their children. Romanticism's potential for darkness and violence, signaled here by the romantically macabre drawings popular in Twain's time, emerges once again. By decorating their home with these drawings, the Grangerfords show that they have embraced death and destruction as unavoidable components of their Romantic dreams; they are willing players in the tragedy.

Twain has again demonstrated that the Romantic imagination is a powerful shaper and driver of the will. People are inspired by Romantic ideals, and the desire to realize these ideals spurs them to action in the world. In some cases, such as that of Tom Sawyer, this spurring to action is manifest in part as a drive to dominate others; this has strong negative connotations but is also an inspiration for leadership. In the case of the Grangerfords, the spurring to action is in part directed at the self, appearing as a desire to act nobly and build character. Twain has shown us, however, that neither Tom nor the Grangerfords are sound models. If he rejects those who are possessed by Romantic dreams, what does he think of those who are not so possessed?

In general, Twain tends to depict the "common folk" with contempt. Not long after the Grangerford-Shepherdson episode, Huck finds himself in a poorly kept "lazy town". When Colonel Sherburn kills a drunk and a lynch mob forms outside his house, he dresses them down, telling them that "the average man's a coward" and "the average man don't like trouble and danger" (see p. 167). The crowd goes home; Sherburn's crime will go unpunished. One cannot help but wish that a Grangerford or Shepherdson were there. They would not hesitate to see justice served. They are not Twain's "average man". Neither is Tom Sawyer; he is, of course, just a boy, but he likes trouble and danger after a fashion. The townsfolk lack the drive not just to stand up to the colonel but to make something of themselves or to cultivate virtue. They are not just meek and passive but cruel and base. If setting fire to a dog is not beneath them, nothing is. These, we are told, are average men.

A central feature of Howells' American literary realism was "the will to be man", encompassing such traits as being a "man of action" and possessing traditional masculine virtues along with a strong sense of moral responsibility.[8] Although he conceived the idea only in masculine terms, it basically means

---

[8] Bell, *Problem of American Realism*, p. 66.

being the sort of courageous, kind, true, and strong person one can count on to do right. Is Twain putting an ironic twist on Howells and telling us that one must be a slave to the Romantic imagination if one is to be anything like a "real man"? Twain seems to believe that without the Romantic imagination spurring one on, one's "will to be a man" is too weak to accomplish much. Does this mean that our only options are to be contemptible "average men" or to be Grangerfords, whose disconnection from reality leads to fundamental moral failings and disaster? Does *Huckleberry Finn* provide any models for us to help us really become good people?

Huck and Jim represent cases of good people who are not romantically inspired. Although they do not display bravado, they generally behave morally and, on occasion, even heroically. Jim abandons his escape attempt to stay with Tom when he is shot, an action that could have cost him not just permanent separation from his family but his life. Huck protects Jim and tries to help him escape even though he believes that he may go to Hell for doing so. But they are unique characters in the novel, the exceptions that prove the rule. Huck and Jim are both portrayed as largely outside of mainstream society looking in. Since we know what Huck is thinking, we can see that his goodness is instinctive. He has not learned to be good (his father, Pap, certainly provided no model); it just comes naturally to him. We get the sense that only someone who has not been corrupted by society can really be good— although Twain never suggests that all people are born with Huck's goodness. And he seems pessimistic about the ability of people to improve themselves. His ridiculing of sentimental humanitarians or idealistic reformers in the episode with Pap and the new judge is evidence of this. If the only way to be good is to happen to be one of those born that way, then Huck does not offer us a very useful model.

It is not even clear that Twain would consider Huck a desirable model. Although he tends to do the right thing, there is also a passivity to him. For example, despite his good instincts, he never rises to the level of questioning the institution of slavery, and he accepts the conventional belief that turning Jim in would really be the right thing to do. He becomes the servant of the King and Duke, addressing them with the exalted titles they prefer even though he knows they are frauds. Of course, in reality, Huck and Jim have little power and few options, but Twain is clearly making moral and political points. Huck tells us that he goes along with the con men to "keep peace in the family" and that he has learned that the best way to get along with such people is to let them have their way (see p. 144). The King and Duke symbolize real royalty and aristocracy. We are seeing again how "the average man" responds in the face of more assertive individuals—whether they are romantically driven or, as in this case, simply opportunists. Known as a champion of democracy, Twain blamed the world's problems on tyrants and would-be aristocrats of all types. It appears that over time, he came to realize that the common folk are no better. Twain once wrote that throughout human society we find "the universal conspiracy of the silent-assertion lie".[9] The vast majority of people, he stated, will participate in all sorts of injustice and "stupidity" instead of speaking up, even if deep down they know better.

Twain would send his friends notes like this: "I have been reading the morning paper . . . well knowing that I shall find in it the usual depravities and baseness and hypocrisies and cruelties that make up civilization and cause me to put in the rest of the day pleading for the damnation of the human race."[10] Why is he so cynical and pessimistic? Babbitt noted that "realists" are often disillusioned Romantics; he also argued that realists and Romantics have something in common in that both tend to reject traditional beliefs and standards.[11] Twain seems to see two available sources of standards: hackneyed Romantic ideals, and society's cynical and corrupt conventions. Both must be rejected, but he can find nothing to offer in their place.

[9] Mark Twain, "My First Lie, and How I Got Out of It", in *Mark Twain on the Damned Human Race*, ed. Janet Smith (Clinton, Mass.: Colonial, 1962), p. 30.

[10] Quoted in Brooks, *Ordeal of Mark Twain*, p. 17.

[11] Babbitt, *Rousseau and Romanticism*, p. 105.

Twain does an excellent job illustrating the dangers of Romanticism, but this takes him to a dead end. We are left with only two options. The first is to embrace the Romantic imagination. Although for many people, Romanticism can lead to dreaminess and inaction, for others the desire to realize a Romantic vision can lead to the development of a strong will, to activity in the world, and to the exertion of leadership; it may even foster the development of some virtues. It will not, however, provide one with a sound ethical center; hence it leads to immorality and disaster. The other option is to reject Romantic visions and become, at best, meek and lifeless; at worst, corrupt, cynical, and base. One could say that the only alternative Twain offers to Romanticism is, essentially, nihilism—the belief in nothing or the sense that no truth or meaning can be found in life.

Romanticism is not a bad thing. Or it need not be. The problem is that "there is no such thing as romantic morality." [12] With its emphasis on feeling and image, Romanticism is not a sound source of moral guidance or of a sense of what the world is really like. This is compounded by the fact that Romanticism tends to be dismissive of traditional standards and of difficult self-discipline. One tends to focus on *feeling* like one is doing the right thing instead of on doing what is really right. As noted, Romanticism arose in response to a sense of flatness and loss of meaning in the modern world that was in turn largely a result of the dismissal of traditions, a decline in religious belief, and a loss of a sense that there was more to the world than surface appearances. As a response to modernity, Romanticism is superficial; it is itself very much a part of modernity and does not actually address the core problem or help one to connect with reality. Consequently, it does not offer a sound basis for right action on either a moral or practical level. Twain senses Romanticism's flaws and hence demands its rejection, but he can himself offer no source for meaning, purpose, or morality in the modern world.

[12] Ibid., p. 217.

Bibliography

Babbitt, Irving. *Rousseau and Romanticism*. New Brunswick, N.J.: Transaction, 1991.

Bell, Michael Davitt. *The Problem of American Realism*. Chicago: University of Chicago Press, 1993.

Brooks, Van Wyck. *The Ordeal of Mark Twain*. Rev. ed. New York: E. Dutton, 1933.

Mussolini, Benito. *The Doctrine of Fascism*. New York: Howard Fertig, 2006.

Twain, Mark. "My First Lie, and How I Got Out of It". In *Mark Twain on the Damned Human Race*. Edited by Janet Smith. Clinton, Mass.: Colonial, 1962.

Zuckert, Catherine H. *Natural Right and the American Imagination*. Savage, Md.: Rowman and Littlefield, 1990.

The Moral Geography of *Adventures of Huckleberry Finn*

John Francis Devanny Jr.
Saint Joseph's Catholic School

> Persons attempting to find a motive in this narrative will be
> prosecuted; persons attempting to find a moral in it will be
> banished; persons attempting to find a plot in it will be shot.[1]

Mark Twain's masterpiece, *Adventures of Huckleberry Finn*, begins
with a warning that has been ignored by generations of readers
and critics.[2] Modern critics are especially guilty, as their concern with identity has made them intent on discovering or invent-
ing a moral for the novel. At times this endeavor has yielded
brilliant insight; but more often, commentary on *Huckleberry
Finn* is laden with some of the most outlandish theories found
in American criticism. *Huckleberry Finn* has been described as a
manifestation of Twain's childhood conflicts, a homosexual awakening, and a sexist and racist harangue, among other psycho-
logical, political, and even mythological interpretations.

The moral world of the novel has also inspired keen interest among readers. Many discern a morality play of sorts in
the novel. As Huck and Jim make their way down the Mississippi River, they are exposed to external dangers of natural
and human origin. In the small towns and hamlets along the
river, they encounter an assortment of characters with glaring
moral weaknesses and a propensity for cruelty and hypocrisy.
The farther south Huck and Jim travel, the more the moral
situation deteriorates and life on shore becomes dangerous.

---

[1] Mark Twain, *Adventures of Huckleberry Finn*, ed. Mary R. Reichardt (San
Francisco: Ignatius Press, 2009), p. 4. Subsequent quotations from this edition
will be cited in the text.

[2] Richard Hill, "Overreaching: Critical Agenda and the Ending of *Adventures
of Huckleberry Finn*", in *Adventures of Huckleberry Finn*, by Mark Twain, ed. Gerald Graff and James Phelan (New York: Bedford Books of St. Martin's Press,
1995), pp. 312–13.

Huck is tormented by a terrible conflict over Jim, whom Huck is assisting in his flight from slavery. By helping Jim, Huck is violating the moral and legal code of his society. Huck finally embraces the role of the rebel; he resolves to help Jim escape from slavery, and with this act the novel seems to have reached a narrative and moral climax.

The denouement, however, leaves many modern critics and readers disappointed by what seems to be the novel's descent into coarse burlesque. Tom Sawyer, Huck's boyhood companion, reappears upon the scene and agrees to help Jim escape, only to put him through a torturous "Romantic prisoner" routine and failed escape, all inspired by Tom's desire to live out the adventures of his literary heroes. Later the reader comes to find out that Jim is already free. All's well that ends well, it seems, and Huck decides to go West to escape the evils of civilization. Huck's prior moment of moral awakening seems cheapened, or to paraphrase Ernest Hemingway, we cheat if we dare take this ending seriously.[3] Indeed, intense dissatisfaction with the ending of the novel has fueled one of the greatest controversies in American literary criticism.

But the novel's ending also has its defenders. Lionel Trilling and T. S. Eliot defended Twain's ending on the ground of form. Trilling believed Twain needed a device to allow the picaresque vagabond Huck to descend from the role of the hero. The vacuum created by Huck's abdication of the hero's role is filled by the reappearance of Tom Sawyer, who craves the attention and adulation associated with that role. Huck merges into the background and thus can begin a new journey to the West.[4] Eliot too believed in the necessity of Huck's giving way to Tom Sawyer by the end of the novel. For Eliot, the novel should end where it began, with the high jinks and escapades of Tom Sawyer. For Eliot the Mississippi River, without

---

[3] Ernest Hemingway, *The Green Hills of Africa* (New York: Scribner's, 1935), p. 22.

[4] Lionel Trilling, "The Greatness of Huckleberry Finn", in *Adventures of Huckleberry Finn*, by Samuel Langhorne Clemens (New York: W. W. Norton, 1971), pp. 318–28.

beginning or end, is the great organizing principle of the novel. The novel's circular form mirrors the river's. As Eliot states, "[I]t is impossible for Huck as for the River to have a beginning or end." Both Huck and the river remain in essence unchanged. Thus Huck, the novel's hero and the spiritual offspring of the river, must once more assume the role of the vagabond by the novel's end.[5]

The formalism of Trilling and Eliot, however, came under a powerful attack from Leo Marx. Marx found the significance of the novel in Jim's flight from slavery and Huck's identification with Jim's quest for freedom. For Marx, the journey to freedom becomes the central act of the novel. Marx viewed the tawdry and often degenerate society of the Mississippi valley with a jaundiced eye, and he is bitter in his disappointment with what he believes is Twain's surrender to the moral complacency of this society. In Marx' view, Huck and Jim's quest for freedom is reduced to light burlesque especially when the fact that Jim has already been set free by Miss Watson is revealed. Marx finds this scene intolerable. Miss Watson, in his view, is much like those Europeans during World War II who strove to live a normal moral life within earshot of the concentration camps. She is the enemy of freedom and deserves no redemption or approbation.[6]

Marx' view has not been always accepted by later critics, but it did shift the debate on *Huckleberry Finn's* ending from the ground of form to the ground of morality. The content of the moral conflict, however, underwent considerable change in the hands of some contemporary critics. For some of these critics, the novel's moral dilemma is viewed as the desire for freedom from any sort of "conscience", including the conscience or moral leanings of the reader. James Cox, for example, sees Twain championing a Rousseauean natural freedom from conscience wherein Huck can find and express his

[5] T.S. Eliot, introduction to *Adventures of Huckleberry Finn*, by Mark Twain (London: Cresset, 1950), pp. vii–xvi. The quote is from p. xvi.

[6] Leo Marx, "Mr. Eliot, Mr. Trilling, and *Huckleberry Finn*", *American Scholar* 22 (Autumn 1953): 423–40.

identity.[7] Critic Richard Hill, however, finds these debates over the novel's morality an overreaching driven by ideology.[8] Hill hoped to return criticism of the novel to the safer ground of authorial intent and historical context, yet he too was forced to respond to the moral interpretation of Marx.

Controversy still surrounds the supposed "moral" or morality of *Huckleberry Finn*. The novel's language, setting, and form have themselves become moral issues. In Twain's own time, the genteel worried about the novel's apparent coarseness and vulgarity. Today teachers and librarians worry over objections to the novel's "racist" language, its depiction of slave society, and the use of racial stereotypes. Too many contemporary readers and critics of *Huckleberry Finn*, however, are unaware of the significance of its Southern origins and influences. The novel's motifs, diction, images, institutions, and symbols are all essentially Southern. The novel's setting places the reader in the border state of Missouri and moves down the Mississippi valley into the heart of the Deep South, and the story is peopled with all types of antebellum Southerners. Twain drew from his intimate experience of the Mississippi valley to create this world, and in addition, he also had a vital and popular Southern literature tradition at hand that he made use of to lay the novel's foundations. A knowledge of this antebellum Southern literature, *Huckleberry Finn*'s kin so to speak, helps us better understand why Twain wished to "banish" those so intent on finding a moral in the story.

William Faulkner, Allen Tate, and Ernest Hemingway were correct in describing *Huckleberry Finn* as the first modern novel, but the work is also part of an older Southern literary tradition known as Southwestern humor. Authors in this tradition, such as Augustus Baldwin Longstreet, Johnson Jones Hooper, Joseph Glover Baldwin, and George Washington Harris, brought to the antebellum reader the image of a rollicking, rowdy, and often

[7] James M. Cox, "Attacks on the Ending and Twain's Attack on Conscience", in *Mark Twain: The Fate of Humor*, by James M. Cox (Princeton: Princeton University Press, 1966), pp. 172–84.

[8] Hill, "Overreaching", pp. 312–34.

uncouth backcountry South. Their stories, sketches, and tales appeared in the genteel periodicals and newspapers of the period, whose mostly male readers delighted in the escapades of the backcountry folk and appreciated the realistic narration, local-color dialect, satire, and humor the authors employed. The genre was new and fresh: there was little of the day's usual Gothic gravity or Romantic sentiment in Southwestern humor such as one might find in the work of Nathaniel Hawthorne, Edgar Allen Poe, or James Fennimore Cooper. The tales of these Southwestern authors might have magical elements, but place, dialogue, and character were realistic. Often, they were lightly fictionalized accounts of the author's real experiences in the backcountry communities of Georgia, Tennessee, Alabama, Mississippi, and Arkansas.[9]

One challenge facing the Southwestern humorist was making the earthy and often coarse and violent world of the Southern backcountry accessible to a refined audience. A typical convention used to achieve this end was to frame the story with a genteel narrator who introduced the tale and provided moral commentary upon the misdeeds of the characters. For example, Augustus Baldwin Longstreet introduced his stories in *Georgia Scenes* with a genteel educated narrator who interacts with the populace, who speak in local dialect. On occasion the narrator might offer some mild criticism on a "barbaric" custom or entertainment (fighting, gander pulling, horse swaps, and the like) of the local folk. Later Southwestern humorists, such as George Washington Harris, placed their genteel narrator further into the background, giving more prominence to the local characters. This narrative shift is prominent, for example, in Harris' famous character Sut Lovingood, who steps forward to narrate *Yarns Spun by a "Nat'ral Born Durn'd Fool"*. In Harris' work, moral commentary becomes increasingly sparse or does not exist at all.

---

[9] Before and for a time after the acquisition of Texas and the Mexican Cession of 1848, the states and territories west of the Appalachians and south of the Ohio River were considered the Southwest.

Of course, the veracity of narrators like Sut Lovingood is open to question. Sut has a realistic and even cynical view of human nature; he is not given to sentimentality. The gullibility of his fellow man, however, is too great a temptation, and Sut stands ready to spin yarns and tall tales that stretch the truth into all sorts of hilarious and dubious shapes. Twain follows Harris' lead in *Huckleberry Finn*. Here, the genteel author Mark Twain is fully in the background as Huck steps forward to perform the duty of narration after warning the reader that Mark Twain often "stretched" things (see p. 5). Much the same might be said of Huckleberry Finn, whose lies, confidence schemes, and deceits fill the novel even as they add to its suspense and humor.

If narrators such as Sut and Huck are no great friends of the truth and thus of conventional morality, we can conclude that the settings or geography of the Southwestern humor tradition and of its offspring *Huckleberry Finn* are places of moral ambivalence and ambiguity. The characters in these settings may develop moral insight, but such insight is often compromised by self-interest or self-preservation. Thus the theme of moral development is not one that concerned Southwestern humorists. Backcountry Southwest characters are, in fact, usually amoral and filled with pretense, cruelty, greed, foolishness, and hypocrisy. Gentility and sentimentality, when they do occur, are usually masks behind which the evil of the world is transacted and justified. The best characters know this truth; the worst have fooled themselves and come off as dupes or self-righteous hypocrites.

An outstanding example of this type of character occurs in Johnson Jones Hooper's story "The Captain Attends a Camp Meeting" from *Some Adventures of Captain Simon Suggs*. Simon Suggs, whose motto is "It is good to be shifty in a new country", comes upon a religious revival and takes quick stock of the situation. One of the ministers lavishes his attention upon the young women of the congregation, leading Suggs to remark, "Nater will be nater … I judge ef I was a preacher, I should save the purtiest souls fust, myself." [10] Suggs then pretends to a religious conversion and takes advantage of the religious fervor of the congregation to raise a collection for a church he plans to found. Successful in this endeavor, Suggs outwits the minister, who also desires the collection, and quickly flees the scene with the money. The camp meeting ministers are revealed as con men and hypocrites, the congregation as dupes. Suggs is no better, but at least he labors under no delusions as to the moral state of the world or his own soul. The coarse and cynical world of Simon Suggs is made palatable by Hooper only through comedic action and humor.

Twain knew and appreciated the works of the Southwestern humorists. He was familiar with Hooper's stories and the character of Captain Simon Suggs. Twain's con man the king, in fact, seems to adopt some of Suggs' tactics when he "works" a camp meeting as a reformed pirate. Early in his career, Twain also favorably reviewed Harris' Sut Lovingood stories for the newspaper the *Alta California*, although he believed that Eastern audiences would perhaps find them vulgar and low.

Twain's own bleak views on morality suggest an affinity with the hardened amorality of the Southwest hero. In a letter dated February 2, 1907, to J. Howard Moore, Twain wrote,

There is one thing that always puzzles me: as inheritors of our reptile ancestors we have improved the inheritance by a thousand grades; but in the matter of the morals which they left us we have gone backward as many grades. That evolution is strange, and to me unaccountable and unnatural. Necessarily we started equipped with their perfect blemishless morals; now we are wholly destitute; we have no real morals, but only artificial ones—morals created and preserved by the forced suppression of natural and hellish instincts. Yet we are dull enough

[10] Johnson Jones Hooper, *Some Adventures of Captain Simon Suggs* (Philadelphia: Carey and Hart, 1845), pp. 122–23.

to be vain of them. Certainly we are a sufficiently comical invention we humans.[11]

Twain's linkage of comedy to man's vanity and "artificial" morality suggests that humor is founded on man's pretenses, yet Twain does not link humor to the restoration of order, harmony, and happiness. Instead, sadness seems to be the wellspring of humor for Twain. Indeed, Twain once stated, "The secret source of humor itself is not joy, but sorrow. There is no humor in heaven."[12] For Twain, humor ameliorates somewhat the cruelties and hypocrisies of the world in which all humanity has some share, but humor does not cover the world's essential melancholy.

Twain's *Huckleberry Finn* resonates with the same verisimilitude animating Southwestern humor. Yet despite the author's view on morality and humor, Twain's Mississippi valley still possesses a share of joy, freedom, and hope. Twain is able to contrast the harsh, nearly amoral cruelty of life on the shore with the joyous freedom in nature Huck and Jim experience on the Mississippi River. Using Huckleberry Finn to narrate the story serves to soften Twain's attack on the hypocrisy, false sentimentality, and depravity of life. Huck's youth and relative innocence win over the reader's sympathy and trust while mediating the harsher aspects of life that Huck and Jim encounter. Huck is charitable to a fault and sympathizes with the misfortunes of others as only one can who has experienced great misfortune himself. When Huck sees the Duke and King tarred and feathered after the two have sold Jim to Silas Phelps, for example, he has every right to feel vindicated, but instead he feels pity for their plight: "Well, it made me sick to see it; and I was sorry for them pitiful rascals, it seemed like I couldn't ever feel any hardness against them any more in the world. It was a dreadful thing to see. Human beings *can* be awful cruel to one another" (see p. 257).

[11] Mark Twain, *Mark Twain's Letters*, ed. Albert Bigelow Paine (New York: Harper Brothers, 1917), 2:804–5.

[12] Mark Twain, *The Writings of Mark Twain*, ed. Albert Bigelow Paine, vol. 20, *Following the Equator* (New York: Harper Brothers, 1929), p. 101.

Though Huck's charm obscures his many deceptions and lies, he would probably agree with his literary kin Simon Suggs that it is good (and necessary) to be shifty in a new country. Huck has no moral problem with raiding the local farms for provisions, lying to protect Jim, or even telling "stretchers" merely for his own entertainment. An example of the latter is when Huck cruelly plays upon Jim's fears and anxiety when the two are separated by fog on the river. Huck is able to convince Jim for a time that he has dreamed the entire incident. When Jim realizes Huck has played him for a fool, he chastises Huck to the point of shame. Huck apologizes, though it takes him "fifteen minutes before I could work myself up to go and humble myself to a nigger" (see p. 100). The contrition here is, of course, backhanded; Huck may have gained great affection for Jim, but that affection is tempered by the limits of race, time, and place. Twain is too great a realist to imagine that his "hero" can rise above these conditions.

It is tempting to see in Huck's apology to Jim the beginning of a moral awakening in Huck that culminates in his decision to risk damnation in assisting Jim's flight from slavery. While the reader may rejoice when Huck chooses Hell over betraying Jim, the relationship between Jim and Huck, and even the issue of Jim's flight from slavery, is more complex. Jim's escape from Miss Watson has no ideological indignation attached to it. Jim views slavery as undesirable and a great source of sorrow, of course, but his flight is not a protest against slavery in the abstract. Miss Watson, one of the "righteous", is tempted by greed to sell Jim away from his wife and children, who reside on a nearby farm. Twain knew that slavery rested upon coercion, but he also knew as one who encountered slavery on a daily basis that it also entailed a considerable level of reciprocity between master and bondsman. In contemplating Jim's sale, Miss Watson is about to destroy that reciprocity that served to temper to a degree a fundamentally unjust institution. From Jim's perspective, Miss Watson has broken faith with him by threatening to sever him from his family.

The law and the mores of society do not support Jim's action against Miss Watson, and this creates a horrible dilemma for both Huck and Jim. Huck feels the pressure of his conscience as it was formed in a slaveholding society. And Jim knows this very well. In fact, Huck is continually a threat to Jim on a number of levels. Because of Huck's young age, the grown Jim provides some protection and guidance to Huck; he plays the role, at times, of the father figure Huck certainly did not have in Pap. Yet at any point Huck may turn Jim in to the authorities or bounty hunters. Jim needs Huck's silence as well as his talent for deception, and Jim is not above the use of manipulation to keep both. For example, Jim withholds from Huck the news of Pap's death until the end of the novel possibly to keep Huck in a state of dependency on him. Moreover, Jim often effusively appeals to Huck's friendship and affection in order to keep Huck's loyalty, praising the boy as "de *only* fren' ole Jim's got now" and "de on'y white genlman dat ever kep' his promise to ole Jim" (see p. 104). For his part, the lonely Huck enjoys Jim's companionship. Yet Jim is more than just a companion. Jim instructs Huck in the folklore of omens and talismans, lore that saves Huck from possibly drowning. It is Jim who built the wigwam shelter on the raft and who often stood watch when it was Huck's turn. Nevertheless, the reader is always aware—as is Jim—that Huck has leverage over Jim. The tensions of this complex relationship are obvious. Twain does not deny the affection Huck and Jim share, but as a realist, he recognizes the self-interest cementing their bond.

The presence of manipulation and self-interest in Huck and Jim's relationship does not keep the friendship from being an anchor of stability in the moral flux of the river's hamlets and towns. Indeed, the friendship survives murder, theft, pursuit, the Grangerford and Sheperdson feud, the deceit and greed of those despicable con artists the Duke and King, and the heartbreaking return of Jim to slavery. While Huck and Jim are not merely passive products of their time and place, their characters have been strongly shaped by their society, and both are adept at surviving in it. Neither possesses the distilled cynicism of a Captain Simon Suggs or the primitive cruelty of a Sut Lovingood, but they know and encounter people like them in their journey and can, if needed, adopt their tactics.

Twain's treatment of the villages and towns along the Great River also bears a strong resemblance to the amoral world of the Southwestern humorists. The Mississippi valley is peopled by the rough and violent, the tacky and tawdry. The absurd pretensions and mindless violence of the Grangerfords and Shepherdsons are rightly skewered. Mob violence melts into cowardice when faced with the cold and ruthless resolution of Colonel Sherburn. Many are fools of the first order, sheep for the duke and king to shear. The God-fearing elect, such as Silas and Sally Phelps and their neighbors, treat Jim with harshness when he falls into their hands. Even Tom Sawyer's elaborate "escape" plan for Jim smacks of heartlessness. Before springing Jim free from his cell in the Phelps' shack, Tom subjects Jim to snakes, spiders, and rats and insists he keep a journal of his feelings even though Jim, by society's decree, has never been taught to write. Tom's Romantic notions seem to reduce Huck and Jim to mere foils in Tom's quest for adventure.

Twain's Mississippi valley is a world full of hypocrisy, violence, cruelty, and Romantic tomfoolery. But the genius of Twain in *Huckleberry Finn* is his refusal to reduce his story only to the grimmer aspects of this society. Twain's characters show themselves also capable of friendship, hospitality, pity, and real affection. The Grangerfords are violent and vengeful, and they have a disordered sense of honor, but they are also kind and hospitable to strangers. The Phelps family treats Jim harshly before and after his abortive escape, yet they later soften in their treatment and opinion of him. Even Tom Sawyer, young Romantic though he may be, assumes the greatest risk in Jim's escape and receives a gunshot wound in the leg for his bravado. Twain is not blind to the higher motives in human nature; he does not unduly emphasize the tragedy and cruelty of life.[13]

Indeed, many characters experience what amounts to little redemptions throughout the novel, and the ending underscores these moments. Despite Leo Marx' view, Miss Watson is not the "enemy". She turns out to be human after all. True, her avarice blinds her to the duty she owes to Jim and his family, and the injustices of slavery compound this blindness. But she does repent in the end and frees Jim. Miss Watson is no paragon of moral virtue (in Twain's world, no one is), but she is capable of shame and repentance and deserves some measure of our respect. Even the thoughtless indignities Tom puts Jim through in the execution of Jim's "escape" are not done out of malice or to attain power or wealth but merely for Romantic adventure. When Huck asks Tom what he would have done if Jim's escape had been successful, Tom states that he would continue his elaborate plan. First he would travel with Jim

> plumb to the mouth of the river, and then tell [Jim] about his being free, and take him back up home on a steamboat, in style, and pay him for his lost time, and write word ahead and get out all the niggers around, and have them waltz him into town with a torchlight procession and a brass band, and then he would be a hero, and so would we. (see p. 321)

Tom is selfish and enamored of the grandiose. There is, however, no calculated evil in his actions or intentions toward Jim. In fact, as he states, he wants Jim to have the lion's share of the glory as some compensation for what Tom evidently views, at worst, as his "inconveniencing" Jim.

Twain's innovations brought the work of the Southwestern humorists to its apex, and they open vistas beyond that tradition into modern literature. He sets his tale in the heartland of the Southwestern humorist, the Mississippi valley, and he

---

[13] James E. Kibler makes a similar point about Longstreet, one that holds true for a good deal of Southern realism. See Kibler, introduction to *Georgia Scenes*, by Augustus Baldwin Longstreet (Nashville, Tenn.: J. S. Sanders, 1992), p. viii.

has his characters speak the local patois, eat the local food, travel the Great River, and know the region's places, inhabitants, and manners. Yes, this arena possesses its share of the hypocrisy, shallow sentiment, violence, and cruelty that has afflicted mankind since the Fall. Twain shows us this world, yet his genius lay in his ability to soften its rough edges and not give in completely to cynicism. He does this with his remarkable gift for humor and by his choice of the youthful narrator Huck. Freedom is possible in this world—at least for the young, like Huck and Tom—but it may also be possible at the end for the long-enslaved man Jim as well. Thus despite its dark tone in places, the novel as a whole can be said to celebrate the virtue of hope.

It is precisely this presence of freedom and hope that leads many readers to wish that they too might travel down the Mississippi River with Huck and Jim. One may have to sleep with one eye open and keep one's wits sharpened in such company, but these two make for far better traveling companions than the likes of Captain Simon Suggs or Sut Lovingood. In *Huckleberry Finn*, Twain depicts the world as it is. He criticizes hypocrisy, greed, and false Romantic sentiment, but he also does not neglect the kindness, affection, bravery, or self-sacrifice that also attend the human condition.

Bibliography

Cox, James M. "Attacks on the Ending and Twain's Attack on Conscience". In *Mark Twain: The Fate of Humor*, by James M. Cox. Princeton, N.J.: Princeton University Press, 1966.

Eliot, T. S. Introduction to *Adventures of Huckleberry Finn*, by Mark Twain. London: Cresset, 1950.

Hemingway, Ernest. *The Green Hills of Africa*. New York: Scribner's, 1935.

Hill, Richard. "Overreaching: Critical Agenda and the Ending of *Adventures of Huckleberry Finn*". In *Adventures of Huckleberry Finn*, by Mark Twain. Edited by Gerald Graff and James Phelan. New York: Bedford Books of St. Martin's Press, 1995.

Hooper, Johnson Jones. *Some Adventures of Captain Simon Suggs*. Philadelphia: Carey and Hart, 1845.

Kibler, James E. Introduction to *Georgia Scenes*, by Augustus Baldwin Longstreet. Nashville, Tenn.: J. S. Sanders, 1992.

Marx, Leo. "Mr. Eliot, Mr. Trilling, and *Huckleberry Finn*". *American Scholar* 22 (Autumn 1953): 423–40.

Trilling, Lionel. "The Greatness of Huckleberry Finn". In *Adventures of Huckleberry Finn*, by Samuel Langhorne Clemens. New York: W. W. Norton, 1971.

Twain, Mark. *Mark Twain's Letters*. Edited by Albert Bigelow Paine. 2 vols. New York: Harper Brothers, 1917.

———. *The Writings of Mark Twain*. Edited by Albert Bigelow Paine. Vol. 20, *Following the Equator*. New York: Harper Brothers, 1929.

Huck's "Sound Heart" in
Adventures of Huckleberry Finn

Thomas W. Stanford III
Christendom College

[I]n a crucial moral emergency a sound heart is a safer guide than an ill-trained conscience.

—Mark Twain, 1895[1]

Mark Twain was noted at the close of the nineteenth century for his dark cynicism toward human nature, but these words in reference to one of his most memorable characters suggest more than simply another of the author's characteristic equivocations. Indeed, Twain's trust in "a sound heart" indicates a fundamental faith in humanity that perhaps functioned as the basic motivation for his ceaseless attempts to examine human nature despite his increasing disappointment in it. While some might dismiss this faith as sentimental or unsophisticated, Twain's *Adventures of Huckleberry Finn* nevertheless examines the continual conflict within Huck between, on one hand, his intuitive, direct feelings and, on the other, his rational conscience, which has been formed and conditioned by a corrupt culture. In episode after episode, Huck's moral integrity appears to hinge upon the ability for what he *feels* to be right to win out over what he *thinks* he should feel to be right. Notably, both human emotion and human reason are fallen and appear so in the novel: for example, the dark and maudlin sentimentality identified with Emmeline Grangerford or the disturbing rational calculus by which the Grangerfords and Shepherdsons keep up their feud. Nevertheless, in

---

[1] Cited by Gregg Camfield, "Mark Twain and Amiable Humor", in *A Companion to Mark Twain*, ed. Peter B. Messent and Louis J. Budd (Malden, Mass.: Blackwell Publishing, 2005), p. 506.

situations such as his treatment of Jim, of the villains aboard the *Walter Scott*, or of the Wilks sisters, Huck's emotional response turns out to be appropriate, while his intellect, polluted by selfishness associated with the larger culture, usually fails. The key to evaluating Huck's emotional responses lies in assessing whether, in each case, they accord properly with, or are appropriate to, the motive or object that gave rise to them. As the Catholic theologian Dietrich von Hildebrand writes in his book *The Heart*, "As soon as we take enthusiasm, joy, sorrow as having their meaning in themselves, and analyze them and determine their value while prescinding from their object, we have falsified the very nature of these feelings." [2] Evaluating Huck's emotional responses in relation to their objects or motives, one finds that his misery, fear, sorrow, or joy in these situations is inevitably and inextricably bound up with charitable, selfless love, which the novel thus presents as an essential principle of good moral choices in direct contradistinction to the selfish utilitarian mindset prevailing in Huck's culture.

Significantly, Huck's heartfelt responses to many of the situations he faces may be said to accord with traditional notions of the eternal law God has written on the human heart, also known as the natural law. Sacred Scripture states that God's inviolable law has been written on the human heart: "I will put my law within them, and I will write it upon their hearts" (Ignatius Bible, Jer 31:33). In *Man and the State*, the Thomist Jacques Maritain defines the natural law as "an order or a disposition which human reason can discover and according to which the human will must act in order to attune itself to the necessary ends of the human being. The unwritten law, or natural law, is nothing more than that." [3] Ultimately, the soundness of Huck's heart depends on the fact that his heart is more properly attuned to the "necessary ends of the human being" than is his conscience, which has been formed to accord with

[2] Dietrich von Hildebrand, *The Heart: An Analysis of Human and Divine Affectivity* (Chicago: Franciscan Herald, 1977), p. 29.

[3] Jacques Maritan, *Man and the State* (Washington, D.C.: Catholic University of America Press, 1998), p. 86.

the ends and aims of a shore culture rife with selfishness, dishonesty, fraud, violence, and cruelty.

Some of the dichotomies present in *Adventures of Huckleberry Finn* have been traced by critics to Twain's reading, during his composition of *Tom Sawyer*, of W. E. H. Lecky's influential *History of European Morals* (published in 1869). Gregg Camfield proposes, "Few books had such impact on Clemens's thinking and writing as Lecky's."[4] Lecky simplifies moral history from Augustus to Charlemagne by suggesting that two "rival theories" encompass all others. The first "is generally described as the stoical, the intuitive, the independent . . . ; the other as the epicurean . . . the utilitarian, or the selfish."[5] Lecky praises the stoics because they felt duty should be the basis of morals, not a utilitarian idea of a reward or a fear of punishment. Lecky argues that one should do right for the sake of doing right and that personal advantage should not play a part in moral choice. History proves that when self-interest becomes central to moral decisions, the idea of doing right for its own sake becomes lost, and morality becomes relative to coercive power. This situation leads to what Joseph Cardinal Ratzinger, now Pope Benedict XVI, termed "a dictatorship of relativism that does not recognize anything as definitive and whose ultimate goal consists solely of one's own ego and desires."[6] The "dictatorship of relativism" is the condition in which culture, cast adrift from transcendent moral norms and an inherited knowledge of the nature and end of the human person, redefines behaviors and persons according to fallen desire and erroneous idealism. It is under such conditions that the "marriage", for example, of two men may be redefined as acceptable or that the human person may be redefined as something that exists

---

[4] Gregg Camfield, *Sentimental Twain: Samuel Clemens in the Maze of Moral Philosophy* (Philadelphia: University of Pennsylvania Press, 1994), p. 113.

[5] W. E. H. Lecky, *History of European Morals: From Augustus to Charlemagne*, 3rd ed., vol. 1 (New York: D. Appleton, 1889), pp. 2–3.

[6] Joseph Cardinal Ratzinger, Dean of the College of Cardinals, Homily, Mass for the Election of the Supreme Pontiff, St. Peter's Basilica, April 18, 2005, http://www.vatican.va/gpII/documents/homily-pro-eligendo-pontifice_20050418_en.html.

and has rights only outside the womb. In his 1987 encyclical *Sollicitudo rei socialis*, the late pontiff John Paul II describes the connection between individual sins and the gradual concretization of those sins as acceptable forms of behavior within culture: "[I]t is not out of place to speak of 'structures of sin,' which ... are rooted in personal sin and thus always linked to the concrete acts of individuals who introduce these structures, consolidate them, and make them difficult to remove. And thus they grow stronger, spread, and become the source of other sins, and so influence people's behavior."[7] These "structures of sin" pervade the culture around Huck, witnessed most clearly, perhaps, in an omnipresent and insidious utilitarian ethical system that acts to enshrine as the evaluative standard personal usefulness, or what is best for oneself, rather than objective truth, or what is best for the common good (or the "other"). The threat of this moral utilitarianism is presented most clearly in the novel's depiction of slavery, an institutionalized "structure of sin" that casts a long shadow over the culture along the river's edge. This particular "structure of sin" has developed in Huck a conscience that defines Jim as less than human and that brands aiding Jim's escape a "sin".

Huck Finn possesses a conscience formed under the influence of the self-interested, utilitarian morality of shore civilization. In Twain's novel, culture appears to have come loose from its traditional moorings and to be floundering, as "structures of sin" like greed and the objectification of others pervert it. Twain scholar Philip E. Davis notes that conscience "can mislead" because "it is too often ... a mere reflection of society's laws, customs, practices, values, and institutions."[8] In effect, Huck's conscience may be understood to have been deformed by his deformed culture, and his heart, to the degree that it is still in tune with the natural law, is often in

---

[7] John Paul II, *Sollicitudo rei socialis*, 36, http://www.vatican.va/edocs/ENG0223/_INDEX.HTM.

[8] Philip E. Davis, "Mark Twain as Moral Philosopher", *San Jose Studies* 2, no. 2 (May 1976): 90.

tension with the demands made by his culturally conditioned conscience.

In the opening chapter, when Huck describes the contrasting religious ideas of the Widow Douglas and Miss Watson, he delineates one system based on altruism and another based on self-interest; in doing so, the novel immediately identifies selflessness with intuition and free will, and selfishness with utilitarianism and determinism. The widow's loving formation of Huck's habits and prayer life uses a motivation far different from that of her sister, Miss Watson. For Miss Watson, an all-absorbing dread of going to the "bad place" drives one to be good. Miss Watson's more literal understanding of using prayer to make oneself better off contrasts to the widow's explanation that spiritual gifts, not material goods, are the reward of prayer. Huck learns that in the widow's system, "I must help other people, and do everything I could for other people, and look out for them all the time, and never think about myself." [9] The altruistic, duty-oriented system of the Widow Douglas depends upon a freewill choice to do good for its own sake. This contrasts to the coercive, fear-oriented system of Miss Watson, in which a self-interested evaluation of consequences determines moral choice. Huck discerns, in the systems of his benefactresses, "two Providences, and a poor chap would stand considerable show with the widow's Providence, but if Miss Watson's got him there warn't no help for him any more" (see p. 17). Hence, the widow's Providence allows for freedom of choice, while Miss Watson's inscrutably determines fate beforehand. Conspicuously, this dichotomy connects free will to selflessness and determinism to self-interestedness.

Huck's reaction to these systems suggests that he unconsciously *thinks* in terms of Miss Watson's deterministic, utilitarian system but somehow *feels* drawn to the widow's system. Thus, Huck's conscience is tied to Miss Watson's system, while

---

[9] Mark Twain, *Adventures of Huckleberry Finn*, ed. Mary R. Reichardt (San Francisco: Ignatius Press, 2009), p. 16. Subsequent quotations from this edition will be cited in the text.

his emotion is tied to the widow's system. He can see "no advan-
tage" in the widow's Providence, "except for other people", but he *wants* to belong to it: "I thought it all out, and reck-
oned I would belong to the widow's, if he wanted me, though I couldn't make out how he was agoing to be any better off than what he was before, seeing I was so ignorant and so kind of low-down and ornery" (see p. 17). Steeped in his father's ethics of self-interest, Huck thinks in utilitarian terms of advan-
tage, both in regarding himself and in considering how others regard him.[10] Acknowledging his base condition, he believes himself predestined and by nature unworthy. No one, he thinks, stands to gain by loving him, and he may be inclined to *think*, following the ethics of Pap, that he should love only those from whom he stands to gain, but his feelings, especially for Jim, will take him into uncharted territory and prove that an authentically fulfilling love acts not from self-interest but rather from an interest in the good of the other.

In sum, the novel presents a basic conflict between, on one hand, Huck's initial, intuitive feeling about what he should do in certain situations and, on the other hand, what his con-
science bids him do in these situations. This conflict might be understood symbolically as a conflict between the selfless ethics of the Widow Douglas and the self-interested ethics of Pap. James L. Kastely notes that Pap's ethic utilizes "the easy logic of accommodation".[11] For example, early in their voy-
age, when Huck and Jim rationalize their theft of produce, they use Pap's justification for borrowing: "Pap always said it warn't no harm to borrow things, if you was meaning to pay them back, sometime; but the widow said it warn't anything but a soft name for stealing, and no decent body would do it." Huck and Jim compromise with the feeling that they were doing wrong by deleting certain kinds of produce from their list. Huck concludes, "We warn't feeling just right, before that,

[10] For a discussion of the ethics of Huck's father, see James L. Kastely, "The Ethics of Self-Interest: Narrative Logic in *Huckleberry Finn*", *Nineteenth-Century Fiction* 40 (March 1986): 423.
   [11] Ibid, p. 421.

but it was all comfortable now" (see pp. 77–78). In this conflict, a self-interested morality wins out, but it is important that
Huck felt in his *heart*, unconsciously, that what he did was wrong.
He will have several more opportunities to act on his "sound
heart" rather than be directed by his corrupt conscience.

In the *Walter Scott* episode, Huck's intuitive morality gets
another workout, and his selfless action contrasts to the self-
interested ethics of the gang. The murderous thugs conspiring
on the wrecked steamer expose Huck to a form of Pap's utilitarian morality. One thug does some moral juggling, saying
he's "unfavorable to killin' a man as long as you can git around
it; it ain't good sense, it ain't good morals" (see p. 82). This
scoundrel suggests they let the third go down with the wreck,
since he believes they will not be liable for the third's death if
he drowns, though they have taken steps to ensure it and hence
are responsible. Prompted by appropriate feelings rather than
by his self-interested conscience, Huck acts first to save the
doomed man, then even the murderers. Huck says, "I begun
to think how dreadful it was, even for murderers, to be in such
a fix. I says to myself, there ain't no telling but I might come
to be a murderer myself, yet, and then how would *I* like it?"
(see p. 84). Though Huck ostensibly acts out of self-interest
("[H]ow would *I* like it?"), the fact that he is motivated by
sympathetic feeling ("how dreadful it was") is crucial. Though
his conscience comes in to rationalize the action, it was one
he *felt* he should do prior to the rationalization. Of course,
Huck's thoughts reveal a comical nod to the "golden rule",
Christ's injunction to do unto others as one would have others do unto oneself. This law of love pushes the human being
beyond himself by first considering another *as* oneself. That
Huck would take risks to save the gang shows a promising lack
of self-interest and indicates, as well, a freewill choice that
breaks out of Pap's ethics, which would seek to do only something only if it were to one's personal advantage.

Before Huck's efforts to save the gang prove unsuccessful
and render him "heavy-hearted", Huck enjoys a measure of
native pride in his deeds. Huck says, "I couldn't rest easy till I

could see the ferry-boat start. But take it all around, I was feeling rather comfortable on accounts of taking all this trouble for that gang, for not many would a done it. I wished the widow knowed about it. I judged she would be proud of me" (see p. 88). Though the selfish tone of these remarks might be said to mar the altruism of his work, his satisfaction occurs as an *unsought* result. Since Huck did not set out to save the gang in order to satisfy himself but rather out of empathy, his satisfaction appears not unwarranted. Certainly, the connection of such a deed with the widow's system emerges as an important recognition of Huck's potential for making a freewill choice to do selfless good, showing he need not rely on self-interest as the standard for evaluating actions. Importantly, the feeling that propels Huck in his actions aboard the *Walter Scott* contrasts to the Romantic idealism of Tom Sawyer, which is corrupted by its divorce from reality. This sentimentalism fails to recognize people and events for what they are in themselves. Though originally inspired to board the *Walter Scott* by Tom Sawyerism, or a Romantic desire for adventure, Huck quickly recognizes the seriousness of the situation and acts from selflessness. Indeed, once his life is in danger aboard the wreck, Huck deems that this "warn't no time to be sentimentering" (see p. 83).

Huck's interactions with his raft mate Jim occasion the novel's most consistently developed examination of the nature of the conflict between Huck's "sound heart" and his conscience. When Jim berates Huck for trying to fool him after the separation in the fog, Huck is made to realize that Jim has real feelings. In Huck's culturally conditioned conscience, the feelings of a slave like Jim have no importance. Yet Huck's recognition that his own actions in this episode make him "feel so mean" (see p. 100) suggests he has been affected at a deeper, more intuitive level. That it takes Huck some time to prepare to seek Jim's forgiveness indicates the degree to which Huck's conscience still holds sway. He has been raised not to care about blacks, and it is a hard habit to break. Later, Huck begins to feel guilty as his corrupted conscience kicks in to remind him that society views his actions in aiding the escape of a slave as reprehensible. Huck reflects, "It hadn't ever come home to me before, what this thing was that I was doing" (see p. 102). When at last his conscience catches up and begins to discipline his feelings toward Jim, Huck turns restless. With a chance to turn Jim in to some slave hunters and hence cleanse a nagging conscience, Huck is prevented from fulfilling his intention only by a sudden *feeling* he has—specifically a feeling of sickness, a deep remorse that arises when Jim praises Huck as a friend. Huck states, "Well, I just felt sick. But I says I *got* to do it—I can't get *out* of it" (see p. 104). These lines clearly outline the battle between what he feels and what his conscience leads him to believe must be done. Huck's inability to account for his weakening in purpose at the last moment (he does not turn in Jim) suggests that the cause of his weakness lies at a level beyond his rational conception. Huck understands why he would feel bad if he *did not* give Jim up to the men—his conscience would make him feel guilty. Huck does not understand, however, why he would feel bad if he *did* give Jim up to the men. He just intuits that he would, and his intuition in this case appears to emerge from some more profound and developing consideration for Jim rather than from a rational consideration of his own personal advantage or, more significantly, from what his culturally conditioned conscience would have him do in this situation.

After the King and the Duke join them, Huck begins to function as an observer until his feeling prompts him to act selflessly in defense of the Wilks sisters. Huck at times registers his disgust at the antics of the frauds, but perhaps fearing for himself and Jim, Huck remains inactive, although attentive enough to say that the royal pair make him "ashamed of the human race" (see p. 185). Ultimately, Huck's decision to help the Wilks sisters revolves around a conflict between what he feels is the right thing to do and his concern for his own safety. This conflict will later be recreated in Huck's famous decision to "go to Hell" by saving Jim, but in this instance, Huck's fear is for his temporal physical safety, not that of his immortal soul. Seeing the purity and kindness of the girls evokes sympathy in Huck and makes him feel so "low down" (see p. 199) that he determines he will risk himself to help them, as he explains in his note to one of the sisters about his having put the money in the coffin: "I was mighty sorry for you, Miss Mary Jane" (see p. 215). This freewill choice is thus grounded in Huck's intuitive response to the plight of the girls, which makes his "heart ache" and etches scenes like the parting between the girls and their slaves forever in his memory. Considering his options, Huck thinks, "I says to myself, I reckon a body that ups and tells the truth when he is in a tight place, is taking considerable many resks" (see p. 210). In a moral "tight place", Huck relieves his heart's discomfort at great personal risk, foreshadowing the ultimate self-sacrifice to come in his decision to save Jim.

After the frauds sell Jim, Huck's famous choice to tear up the letter to Miss Watson and to try to set Jim free acts as a culmination of the novel's examination of the conflict between Huck's culturally conformed conscience and his "sound heart". Huck's first reaction upon finding Jim missing is visceral: he cries. This flood of feeling is followed by an exasperated thought of turning the matter over to the authorities, in this case Miss Watson, and washing his hands of it; however, Huck finds he is implicated in this plot more than he would like to be. Huck's conscience produces a heavy sense of guilt, and Huck determines that this guilt "was the plain hand of Providence slapping me in the face and letting me know my wickedness was being watched all the time from up there in heaven" (see p. 237). Huck thinks this Miss Watson-style Providence now "justly" condemns his actions, but this cause-effect relationship simply shows how disabling such deterministic Providence can be. Huck's subsequent assertion that he "was brung up wicked" ironically presents the truth of the matter of his cultural conditioning. Huck knows that his connection to his culturally conditioned idea of God is threatened. He tries to pray to "be better", but he realizes he cannot be better. His feelings are what threaten his happiness here. Huck believes that his prayers will not work because he does not *mean* them: "It was because my heart warn't right; it was because I warn't square; it was because I was playing double" (see p. 238). Ultimately, the law written on Huck's heart correctly judges Jim's value as a human person, and Huck is unwilling to betray his heart.

Huck writes the letter to Miss Watson to satisfy his conscience and momentarily feels free and clean, but then memories and the feelings they inspire crowd in upon him. This sets up the dramatic scene in which a kneeling, vexed thirteen-year-old boy is unable to reconcile his feelings toward his friend with what his conscience tells him to do. Significantly, Huck's feelings are based on his actual experiences of Jim's friendship and selflessness, not on the abstract conceptions of Jim and his race that Huck has inherited from his upbringing. Huck remembers, "I see Jim before me, all the time, in the day, and in the night-time.... But somehow I couldn't seem to strike no places to harden me against him, but only the other kind" (see p. 239). These feelings of love and gratitude cannot be ignored, but Huck still respects his conscience and understands the consequences of his choice. Huck believes that God will justly condemn him for these actions, but the inference remains that Huck could not do otherwise and still live with himself.

As is evident in Huck's final intention to flee the threat of "sivilization", by the end of his adventure Huck seems to have at least attained an appreciation of the incongruity and hazards in his culture, and the reader can recognize the novel's condemnation of Huck's culturally conditioned conscience in this fear. Twain, the master ironist, dramatically pillories this corrupt culture when he has Huck, in his mind, abandon God at the very moment when, in fact, he is upholding God's law of love, even to the point of risking everything for his companion. As it is examined through Huck's intuition, the affirmation of natural law morality present in *Adventures of Huckleberry Finn* offers an important contrast to the novel's extensive cultural critique.

Bibliography

Camfield, Gregg. "Mark Twain and Amiable Humor". In *A Companion to Mark Twain*, edited by Peter B. Messent and Louis J. Budd. Malden, Mass.: Blackwell, 2005.

——. *Sentimental Twain: Samuel Clemens in the Maze of Moral Philosophy*. Philadelphia: University of Pennsylvania Press, 1994.

Davis, Philip E. "Mark Twain as Moral Philosopher". *San Jose Studies* 2, no. 2 (May 1976): 83–93.

John Paul II. *Sollicitudo rei socialis*. http://www.vatican.va/edocs/ENG0223/_INDEX.HTM.

Kastely, James L. "The Ethics of Self-Interest: Narrative Logic in *Huckleberry Finn*". *Nineteenth-Century Fiction* 40 (March 1986): 412–37.

Lecky, W. E. H. *History of European Morals: From Augustus to Charlemagne*. 3rd ed. Vol. 1. New York: D. Appleton, 1889.

Maritain, Jacques. *Man and the State*. Washington, D.C.: Catholic University of America Press, 1998.

Ratzinger, Joseph Cardinal. Homily, Mass for the Election of the Supreme Pontiff. St. Peter's Basilica, April 18, 2005. http://www.vatican.va/gpII/documents/homily-pro-eligendo-pontifice_20050418_en.html.

von Hildebrand, Dietrich. *The Heart: An Analysis of Human and Divine Affectivity*. Chicago: Franciscan Herald, 1977.

Huckleberry Finn as American Epic

Aaron Urbanczyk
Southern Catholic College

In 1835 the Frenchman Alexis de Tocqueville published the first volume of his study of American politics and culture, *Democracy in America*, which was based his visit to the United States in 1831–1832. *Democracy in America* studies the American political process, the nation's cultural practices and values, its population, its religious sensibilities, and numerous other dimensions of American civic life. In its introduction, de Tocqueville writes: "I confess that in America I saw more than America; I sought there *an image of democracy itself*, of its penchants, its character, its prejudices, its passions; I wanted to become acquainted with it if only to know at least what we ought to hope or fear from it" (italics added).[1] Mark Twain published *Adventures of Huckleberry Finn* in America in 1885. To give the reader the story's context, Twain includes the following just below the novel's title: "Scene: The Mississippi Valley. Time: Forty to Fifty Years Ago". Fifty years prior to the novel's American publication places it historically within only a few years of de Tocqueville's visit to America and coincides exactly with the initial publication of *Democracy in America* (that is, 1835).

Why is this historical coincidence relevant to understanding *Adventures of Huckleberry Finn*? Twain, like de Tocqueville, saw America as an "image of democracy", and he found this image particularly vivid during a period crucial in forming "young America's" identity. What is the American character? What are the implications of embracing democracy for culture, morality, and religion? The heart and soul of the Union were torn by the painful quest to answer such questions in the nineteenth century, particularly relating to the issues of slavery, race, the

[1] Alexis de Tocqueville, *Democracy in America*, trans. and ed. Harvey C. Mansfield and Delba Winthrop (Chicago: University of Chicago Press, 2000), p. 13.

sovereignty of individual states, and the growing cultural dif-
ferences between the North and the South. The 1830s and 1840s,
the decades in which *Huck Finn* is set, were a time of national
expansion for the United States. In this era, the concept of
"manifest destiny", the notion that America was justified in
expanding its borders west toward the Pacific and south toward
Mexico, exerted a strong influence upon the nation. America
was also facing the increasingly violent struggle between Northern and Southern states over slavery. In the decades immediately preceding the Civil War, the Union was preoccupied with
"what we ought to hope or fear" from its great experiment in
democracy. Twain locates the novel's action in a time of youthful growth and strength in America; it was an era of optimism
about the future, yet one plagued by the violence, danger, and
civil strife becoming yearly more prevalent in the Union. In a
sense, he wrote a novel of America's national adolescence. In
adolescence a young man occupies the liminal boundary between
the idyllic carefree days of boyhood and the complexities of
the adult world (which can be dangerous, violent, and frightening). Perhaps, then, it is not so strange that Twain chose
Huckleberry Finn, a boy of about thirteen or fourteen with a
questionable past and an uncertain future, as the protagonist
of his novelistic "image of democracy".

Yet this essay is not merely a reading of *Huck Finn* as a gloss
on American history. I suggest that this novel is an epic, and
because all epics have a deeply nationalistic character, a
uniquely American epic. As a novel, *Huck Finn* does not fit
the classical definition of an epic as a lengthy heroic poem,
yet the epic genre is elastic enough to find other incarnations
beyond the pattern of heroic verse established by the likes of
Homer, Virgil, and Milton. The novel can easily be considered a modern form of the classic epic genre, "a long serious
narrative poem about a hero and his heroic companions, often
set in a past that is imaged as greater than the present."[2] The

---

[2] Sylvan Barnet et al., *A Dictionary of Literary Terms* (Boston: Little, Brown,
1960), p. 36.

literary critic Louise Cowan argues that an epic is most essentially defined by its internal character rather than by external matters of literary mechanics. According to Cowan, an epic "activates a full and complete cosmos. . . . [It] displays on a panoramic scale an entire way of life—caught, it is true, at a moment of radical change and yet, viewed from an omnidimensional standpoint, in that very act transfigured and preserved."[3] To say an epic creates a cosmos is simply the observation that it embodies a particular yet totalizing world view from a certain cultural and national perspective (its perspective is "panoramic", or all-encompassing, yet all-encompassing from the point of view of a certain group of people). *Huck Finn* as an epic captures the world as seen through the eyes of a young, strong, growing, and democratic nation, one simultaneously optimistic and frightened about its future. Thus Huck Finn is an appropriate representation of American democratic culture. Huck embarks upon his adventures during the historical pressure cooker of the decades immediately preceding the Civil War, and he carries within his unique persona the complexities and tensions of his era. Twain's unlikely epic hero is an adolescent boy trying to find himself in the midst of an adolescent nation about to face its most significant test of character and cultural maturity.

In what sense can Huckleberry Finn be considered an epic hero? Several models of heroism emerge from the epic literary tradition. The martial or warrior hero is a commonly recurring trope, as exemplified in Homer's Achilles from the *Iliad*, the Aeneas of Virgil's *Aeneid* (after book 6), the titular protagonist of *Beowulf*, and, to an extent, Satan in Milton's *Paradise Lost*. Yet Huck Finn is hardly a warrior hero accomplishing great deeds on the battlefield. Yet another prominent model of epic heroism exists that is more applicable to Huckleberry Finn: the wandering hero on a moral and spiritual journey over a landscape that is both external and internal. Such journeying epic heroes

---

[3] Louise Cowan, "Introduction: Epic as Cosmopoesis", in *The Epic Cosmos*, ed. Larry Allums (Dallas, Tex.: Dallas Institute Publications, 1992), p. 3.

include Odysseus from Homer's *Odyssey*; Aeneas in the first six books of the *Aeneid*; and Dante Alighieri, who is both author and epic hero of the *Divine Comedy*. While the warrior hero faces a primarily external struggle (for example, slaying a famous opponent in battle), the epic hero on a journey faces a struggle primarily in his own soul, a moral and spiritual struggle. For instance, Odysseus struggles not only to get home to Ithaca, but he also must endure the painful realization that his arrogant exploits and lack of judgment coming home from Troy cost him the lives of all of his dear companions; Aeneas struggles to master his own desires while trying to be faithful to the gods' will in the first part of the *Aeneid*; and Dante struggles with his own sinfulness as he journeys through the afterlife in the *Divine Comedy*. Twain clearly places Huck in the tradition of the epic hero on a spiritual and moral journey. Huck accompanies Jim down the Mississippi while struggling with the moral dilemma of helping a black slave "steal" his freedom. Indeed, biographical evidence strongly suggests Twain had Homer's *Odyssey* in mind while he was completing *Adventures of Huckleberry Finn*.[4] Further, the centrality of the Mississippi River places Huck in the tradition of the epic hero on a journey that, like Odysseus', takes place over a body of water representing the powerful forces of nature. As T. S. Eliot points out, the Mississippi River (itself as primitive, potent, and capricious as a Homeric Greek god) gives form and structure to the novel because it dictates the course, direction, and even the possibility of the journey: "The River gives the book its form. But for the River, the book might be only a sequence of adventures with a happy ending. A river, a very big and powerful river, is the only natural force that can wholly determine the course of human peregrination."[5] Just as the Mediterranean Sea exposes the

[4] See, for example, Patrick J. Deneen's article "Was Huck Greek? The 'Odyssey' of Mark Twain" (*Modern Language Studies* 32, no. 2 [2002]: 35–44), in which Deneen demonstrates that Twain was composing a burlesque review of *The Odyssey* at the same time he was completing *Huck Finn*.

[5] T. S. Eliot, introduction to *Adventures of Huckleberry Finn*, by Mark Twain, ed. Thomas Cooley, 3rd ed. (New York: W. W. Norton, 1999), p. 351.

Odyssey's readers to the complexity of the Homeric Greek world, the river expands Twain's representation of America by showing the diverse peoples and communities Huck and Jim experience traveling down the Mississippi.

Huck Finn begins like all good epics, *in media res* (in the midst of things). As do other epics, Twain's novel chooses only one segment of a vast and seemingly cosmic conflict—in this case, America's struggle over slavery. Like all epics, the novel does not fully explain the origins of this conflict (which lie in the past: the war was over by the time Twain published *Huck Finn*), nor does it relate how the conflict will be resolved (the novel's action concludes well before the Civil War breaks out). Rather, it tells the story of two individuals who are caught in the midst of the conflict and are representative of it—Huck, a young white boy, and Jim, a grown man and black slave. Yet it is clear that the moral struggle facing Huck as epic hero defines and permeates the entire landscape in which the novel takes place and has a truly "cosmic" significance. The abduction of Helen by Paris completely destabilizes the ancient Greek world; Aeneas' search for a new home in Italy will fundamentally change the course of Western civilization; Satan's defiance of God has cosmic ramifications for Heaven and earth; and the moral, political, religious, and cultural fabric of America would be radically refashioned by the resolution of the debate over slavery. Thus, Huck's assisting Jim in the act of apparently "usurping" his freedom is symbolic of the seismic shift in American culture leading up to and flowing from the struggles associated with the Civil War.

While the world of Twain's novel is racially charged because of the historical context of American slavery, the heroic struggle facing Huck does not become immediately racial until he discovers Jim on Jackson's Island. After faking his own death and escaping his abusive father, Pap, Huck's future is free and undetermined; he can go wherever his boyish heart would take him—or so it seems. Jackson's Island is a metaphor for the impossibility of escaping life's difficult conflicts; one can hide there in anonymity, but not for long. The call to heroism, the call to an epic journey, comes quickly to Huck. His carefree and uncommitted state is disrupted by discovering Jim, who has just run away from Miss Watson because he heard she was planning to sell him down the river to New Orleans. Jim's own anonymous escape on Jackson's Island is as short-lived as Huck's; after Huck sneaks back to the shore to gather news, he discovers from Mrs. Judith Loftus that all of Saint Petersburg blames Jim for Huck's murder and that her husband is going that very night to search Jackson's Island for the runaway slave. Huck and Jim, like America, could not escape for long into the neutral peace of the island; the violent conflict over slavery was forced upon Huck and Jim just as it was finally forced upon the Union in 1861.

Huck Finn clearly evokes a "cosmic" world view. The tension over slavery and race permeates virtually every aspect of the novel and provides the epic dimension to Huck's journey down the Mississippi. Indeed, the dispute over slavery was merely symptomatic of the broader questions of American identity confronting the Union during Twain's lifetime (that is, in a democracy, what is the nature of freedom, citizenship, human dignity, political participation, equality between races, etc.?). Such questions are certainly epic in scope. While one can cite many examples of slavery's impact upon American culture in *Huck Finn*, two will serve to demonstrate the vast cultural and social tensions in the early nineteenth century: the attitudes of Pap and Silas Phelps regarding race and slavery. Pap's splenetic tirade in chapter 6, uttered in a drunken rage in the cabin where Pap has imprisoned Huck, captures America's divided mind in the decades preceding the Civil War. The object of Pap's contempt seems all of society itself, including the government, the free market, educational institutions, and even the right to vote, all on account of the emerging reality of black men and women becoming freed from slavery and entering civil society. He is outraged because a black man of mixed blood is more educated, wealthier, and more capable of exercising his voting rights than Pap himself.

Pap's invective is not simply the ranting of an uneducated racist. His speech artfully captures the complex levels of political, social, economic, and cultural tension regarding slavery in America, and the struggles society would endure if black men and women were to be brought into American polity as persons and citizens. Pap is outraged and confused because he finds, to his dismay, that the very cast of servants his entire civilization had long believed were subpersonal beasts of burden can now become more educated, more refined, better dressed, wealthier, and more socially prestigious than he—and virtually overnight.

Silas Phelps' views on slavery serve as a counterweight to Pap's. Huck (pretending to be Tom Sawyer) finds Uncle Silas to be a humane, gentle, and decent man in his imprisonment of Jim, who Silas believes is a runaway slave. Huck refers to Uncle Silas, a farmer and Christian preacher, as "the innocentest, best old soul I ever see",[6] and Huck relates that "Uncle Silas come in every day or two to pray with [Jim], and Aunt Sally come in to see if he was comfortable and had plenty to eat, and both of them was kind as they could be" (see p. 276). Yet Silas and Sally are not as far removed from Pap as they appear. While they are not violently hateful in their language or actions, as Pap is, their humane behavior nonetheless upholds the social, political, and economic fabric in which slavery was embedded in America. As a matter of conscience, Silas knows he cannot simply "turn free" or take for his own use another man's slave property; thus Silas and Sally maintain the status quo of slave-based society. Pap and Silas, at the beginning and ending sequences of the novel, respectively, embody the diverse reactions to the vast cultural problem of race and slavery in America. Huck will eventually choose a heroic path that rejects the essentially similar world views of Pap and Silas, one which will take him into uncharted moral and theological territory.

---

[6] Mark Twain, *Adventures of Huckleberry Finn*, ed. Mary R. Reichardt (San Francisco: Ignatius Press, 2009), p. 253. Subsequent quotations from this edition will be cited in the text.

The main characters of *Adventures of Huckleberry Finn* are complex individuals traversing an epic terrain that is both ethical and theological in significance. Even though Huck and Jim are caught within their era's cultural quandaries, they themselves are not political, social, or religious crusaders but individuals struggling to resolve their own problems. As brilliantly crafted by Twain, neither Jim's nor Huck's character is a thin symbolic representation of an abstract social, political, or moral ideal. They are not abolitionists out to change the hearts and minds of America regarding the issue of slavery. Rather, like all great epic heroes, Huck is a psychologically realistic character, and as such embarks upon an epic journey that runs along two concurrent registers: ethical and theological. His moral sensibilities and his theological bearings become radically altered as he struggles with his decision to abet a fugitive slave who willfully abandoned his master. In fact, the effect of the journey upon his own soul threatens to destabilize the moral and theological structure of the universe as he (and his nation) knows it.

If *Huck Finn* can be called an American *Odyssey*, the journey begins at the ethical level for Huck. At a superficial level, Huck exhibits the typical American pragmatism toward morality: moral ideals are nice but not always practical in the face of real-world problems. For instance, Huck, in a moment of complex moral casuistry, explains the difference between "borrowing" and "stealing" something: "Pap always said it warn't no harm to borrow things, if you was meaning to pay them back, sometime; but the widow said it warn't anything but a soft name for stealing, and no decent body would do it. Jim said he reckoned the widow was partly right and pap was partly right" (see p. 77). Huck even expresses his frustration with matters of moral principle: "[I]t don't make no difference whether you do right or wrong, a person's conscience ain't got no sense, and just goes for him *anyway*. If I had a yaller dog that didn't know no more than a person's conscience does, I would pison him. It takes up more room than all the rest of a person's insides, and yet ain't no good, nohow" (see p. 258).

Yet Huck is hardly a boy without a conscience; his frustration comes from the fact that while he may not always act in the most ethical fashion, he has a very sensitive and developed conscience. Huck is a deeply empathetic boy who keenly feels the pain of those around him. He also has a sharp intuition for justice and injustice, so much that he cannot repress his mental and emotional reactions when he observes them in his immediate surroundings. As Huck and Jim are looking for Cairo, Illinois, where they plan to take a steamboat "way up the Ohio among the free States" (see p. 94), Huck experiences a serious crisis of conscience. Twain dramatizes his sense of being morally divided through a dramatic dialogue between Huck and his conscience:

> Conscience says to me, "What had poor Miss Watson done to you, that you could see her nigger go off right under your eyes and never say one single word? What did that poor old woman do to you, that you could treat her so mean? Why, she tried to learn you your book, she tried to learn you your manners, she tried to be good to you every way she knowed how. *That's* what she done."
>
> I got to feeling so mean and so miserable I most wished I was dead. I fidgeted up and down the raft, abusing myself to myself. (see p. 102)

Huck's struggle does not simply involve the moral probity of one isolated act or set of acts (such as helping one black slave "illicitly" gain his freedom); his struggle represents a clash of two violently opposed world views and moral systems. The voice of Huck's conscience represents a particular social value code, certain dimensions of which are deeply racist and inhumane. This value code, which Huck has internalized, accepts chattel slavery as a perfectly permissible and profitable social institution. This code also dogmatically maintains the subhuman status of black men, women, and children as a natural God-given fact. In this view, they are moral creatures only when considered as property, and when viewing Jim's situation from the perspective of property rights, Huck can see only that he is maliciously defrauding a generous old widow of what belongs to her.

Yet Huck becomes aware of a competing value code that asserts the opposite of the one in which he has been raised, and the clash of these two codes within his soul is truly epic. As Huck travels with Jim, he begins to see Jim as a person in his own right, possessing the dignity Huck was used to acknowledging only in other whites. For instance, in chapter 15, Huck humbles himself to Jim after cruelly trying to trick him into thinking their separation in the fog was only a dream; in chapter 16, Huck discovers the intense loyalty and devotion Jim has to his wife and children when he hears Jim relate how, once free, he will work to purchase their freedom; and in chapter 23, Huck empathizes with Jim's identity as a loving father who had wrongfully beaten his daughter for what Jim had perceived as disrespectful behavior. Jim emerges in Huck's mind as that which the voice of his conscience cannot accept: a dignified human being and a man worthy of empathy, respect, and admiration. The violent tension between these two value codes becomes clear in Huck's problematic affirmation of Jim's nobility and dignity in chapter 40, when Jim insists on getting a doctor to save Tom Sawyer's life because Tom would have done the same thing for him. Huck effusively proclaims, "I knowed [Jim] was white inside" (see p. 304), as a matter of genuine admiration; yet this affirmation is tragically racialized. Huck can still conceive of a "true" human being only as "white", even if only on the "inside". While Huck is shedding a world view containing racist and unjust elements for something more just and virtuous, his transformation is incomplete.

Yet the most cosmic and cataclysmic dimension of Huck's epic struggle pertains to the theological foundations of creation, specifically God's Providence regarding Heaven and Hell. The novel evokes Heaven and Hell purposefully, as their significance becomes inverted for Huck as a result of his transformation in value systems. The movement in Huck's soul from viewing Jim as mere property to appreciating him as a fellow human being is not only a seismic shift in Huck's ethical world view; it is also a traumatic revaluation of the significance of Heaven and Hell. Early in the novel, Huck is instructed on the significance of Heaven and Hell as eternal reward and punishment by the Widow Douglas and Miss Watson. This education takes place in the context of the two ladies' attempt to "sivilize" Huck and is roundly comic. For example, according to Huck, Miss Watson describes Heaven as a place where one just "go[es] around all day long with a harp and sing[s], forever and ever", to which Huck responds, "I didn't think much of it" (see p. 7). The comedy is equally hilarious in Huck's reaction to her depiction of Hell: "Then she told me all about the bad place, and I said I wished I was there. She got mad, then, but I didn't mean no harm. All I wanted was to go somewheres; all I wanted was a change, I warn't particular" (see p. 7). In this early episode, Heaven and Hell are mere abstractions for Huck (and fodder for Twain's irreverent wit); they have little practical relevance for his life.

Yet the eternal dimensions of the cosmos become frighteningly real and terrifyingly inverted for Huck. Heaven and Hell will cease to be comic abstractions and will take on a deadly significance for his understanding of himself and his future. Critics rightly celebrate chapter 31 as the novel's dramatic turning point. In this chapter, Huck finally casts aside his divided mind and heart and commits himself fully to helping Jim. He does so by the noble gesture of tearing up the letter he had written to Miss Watson informing her of the location of her fugitive slave. Yet the language of Huck's conscience is no longer primarily moral; it is now startlingly theological. Huck is now speaking about Heaven and Hell, not just right and wrong, and he is going to turn the significance of Heaven and Hell on its head by his resolution to help Jim regardless of the eternal consequences. Huck's internal voice becomes theological, telling him that "people that acts as I'd been acting about that nigger goes to everlasting fire" (see p. 238). Huck is on the verge of a horrible realization for an adolescent mind: Heaven, the place he had been taught is the pinnacle of justice and right, is also the reward for those who own, buy, and sell black human beings (how could Huck think otherwise growing up in a society where "good" and "decent" Christians own slaves?). In like fashion, divine Providence consigns eternally to Hell those who choose to acknowledge the humanity of and work to free black human beings such as Jim.[7] Faced with the awful realization that to do the *right* thing, the *moral* thing, and the *humane* thing is to choose eternal separation from God, Huck has the profound internal fortitude to choose his own "damnation" rather than deny what he knows to be true about his own ethical intuitions. He knows that the manly thing to do is to accept eternal damnation in Hell if salvation in Heaven means selling out a fellow human being whom he has come to know, love, admire, and depend upon. Thus, when Huck tears up the letter, he is turning his whole universe upside down: "It was a close place. I took it up, and held it in my hand. I was a trembling, because I'd got to decide, forever, betwixt two things, and I knowed it. I studied a minute, sort of holding my breath, and then says to myself: 'All right, then, I'll *go* to hell'—and tore it up" (see p. 239). In this moment of epic heroism, Huck affirms his commitment to truth and virtue even if the cosmic forces of salvation and damnation oppose him. Heaven ceases to be attractive to him, and he would willingly take upon himself an eternity of punishment in Hell to retain his integrity. Huck's moral and theological universe now becomes a frightening, unfamiliar, and unsafe place for him, but he heroically leaps into it as a consequence of his decision. The dignity and immense significance of Huck's resolve to act heroically in committing himself to Jim's freedom can be ranked among other moments of high epic seriousness found in such characters as Homer's Achilles, Virgil's Aeneas, Dante's

---

[7] Huck's struggle to reconcile religion with a society that professes it while embracing slavery magnifies the struggle taking place in America's conscience. In his famous second inaugural address (1864), Abraham Lincoln devotes much of the speech to the issue of religion and slavery. Huck's struggle, and his rejection of Heaven and choice of Hell, resonates with Lincoln's ruminations wherein Lincoln insists that both sides, the North and the South, cannot equally receive God's favor regarding the matters of slavery.

version of himself in the *Divine Comedy*, or Milton's Satan. Indeed, the gravity and high literary significance of Huck's character has been noted by T. S. Eliot, who counts Huckleberry Finn among the greatest characters in all of Western literature.[8]

Chapter 31 marks the end of Huck's adventures on the Mississippi, which is appropriate as it dissolves the elevated and epic tone of Huck's internal struggles. But, much like Homer's *Odyssey*, the novel concludes as a comic epic: its final chapters happily and quickly resolve the external crisis and restore order to the hero and his community. Jim discovers he is a free man after all, and Huck is restored to society in that he no longer has to live the dangerous life of a vulnerable young boy on the run with a fugitive slave. The novel's concluding sequence provides comic relief that serves to heighten the nature of Huck's epic heroism. Ever since Huck departed from Jackson's Island, his life has constantly been in danger. Fear and the threat of serious injury or death are his persistent companions, and because of his commitment to helping Jim he has been forced to live a nocturnal life on the outskirts of society (which in any age is a dangerous *modus vivendi*). Once Huck reaches the Phelps' farm in Pikesville, the hilarious sequence of Huck pretending to be Tom and Tom pretending to be his half-brother Sid begins. Tom performs the absurd charade of freeing a prisoner according to the precise formulae provided by romance novels, and he compels Huck and Jim to play along solely for his own amusement. He is well aware that Jim has already been freed by the recently deceased Miss Watson. The concluding sequence of "freeing" Jim, which is purely farcical (and vapid from the point of view of character development), serves only to heighten the reader's appreciation for the epic seriousness of Huck's journey that occupies the heart of the novel.

In conclusion, *Adventures of Huckleberry Finn* is an epic "image of democracy". It shows the reader a nation in adolescence facing a struggle of cosmic proportions involving right

[8] Eliot, introduction to *Huckleberry Finn*, p. 349.

and wrong, Providence, Heaven, and Hell. Like all great epics, the novel captures a culture in flux; the America of *Huck Finn* is in the midst of a violent shift in a people's understanding of itself and its way of life. Thus the ending of the novel is quite appropriate for an epic hero emblematic of a young undetermined nation. Huck is averse to civilization and plans on leaving conventional society for the "Territory" (the great, unsettled, "wild" West) as soon as possible: "I reckon I got to light out for the Territory ahead of the rest, because Aunt Sally she's going to adopt me and sivilize me and I can't stand it. I been there before" (see p. 322). American civilization is above all an experiment in democracy, and it is one that is still incomplete—and perhaps ever will be. The concluding lines of *Adventures of Huckleberry Finn* leave the reader with a sense of the incompleteness and fluidity of American culture; Huck sets out for the unsettled West as young America expands both its geographic borders and its understanding of itself as a nation. In ducking out of civilized society and heading to the "Territory", Huck seeks what America is not yet but might become once it passes from youth to maturity. He is the epic hero gazing westward into the uncertainty of America's future and identity. Like Mark Twain himself, Huck as epic hero is looking for an "image of democracy", and he flees to the West hoping "to know at least what we ought to hope or fear" from this great experiment in democratic culture.

Bibliography

Barnet, Sylvan, et al. *A Dictionary of Literary Terms*. Boston: Little, Brown, 1960.

Cowan, Louise. "Introduction: Epic as Cosmopoesis". In *The Epic Cosmos*, edited by Larry Allums. Dallas, Tex.: Dallas Institute Publications, 1992.

Deneen, Patrick J. "Was Huck Greek? The 'Odyssey' of Mark Twain". *Modern Language Studies* 32, no. 2 (2002): 35–44.

de Tocqueville, Alexis. *Democracy in America*. Translated and edited by Harvey C. Mansfield and Delba Winthrop. Chicago: University of Chicago Press, 2000.

Eliot, T. S. Introduction to *Adventures of Huckleberry Finn*, by Mark Twain, edited by Thomas Cooley. 3rd ed., 348–54. New York: W. W. Norton, 1999.

CONTRIBUTORS

Anthony J. Berret, S.J., teaches English at Saint Joseph's University in Philadelphia. Author of *Mark Twain and Shakespeare: A Cultural Legacy*, he has produced other articles and papers on Mark Twain, Toni Morrison, and F. Scott Fitzgerald. Currently he is writing a book on the function of music in the works of Fitzgerald.

William F. Byrne is assistant professor of government and politics at Saint John's University in New York and is associate editor of the journal *Humanitas*. His articles and essays on such topics as problems of liberalism and modernity, literature and politics, and the political-philosophical thought of Edmund Burke have appeared in a variety of scholarly journals.

John Francis Devanny Jr. lectures and writes on the intellectual and cultural history of the Old South. He holds a Ph.D. in history from the University of South Carolina, where he also completed studies in Southern literature. He currently teaches history and literature at Saint Joseph's Catholic School in Greenville, South Carolina.

Mary R. Reichardt is professor of Catholic studies at the University of Saint Thomas in Saint Paul, Minnesota. She received a Ph.D. in literature from the University of Wisconsin–Madison. She has published seven books, including *Catholic Women Writers* (Greenwood, 2001), *Exploring Catholic Literature* (Sheed and Ward/Rowman and Littlefield, 2003), and the two-volume *Encyclopedia of Catholic Literature* (Greenwood, 2004).

Thomas W. Stanford III is associate professor of English language and literature at Christendom College in Front Royal, Virginia, where he also edits *Faith & Reason*, the college's academic journal.

Aaron Urbanczyk is associate professor of English at Southern Catholic College. His publications include articles and reviews primarily in the fields of American literature and literary theory.